# MERGEWORLD

## BOOK THREE

*Titles by Mason Elliott*

*The Spacer Clans Adventures, Cycle One:*

NAERO'S RUN
NAERO'S GAMBIT
NAERO'S FURY

*The Spacer Clans Adventures, Cycle Two:*

NAERO'S MASTERY
NAERO'S VALOR*

*The Citation Series, Cycle One:*

Naero's War, Book One: THE ANNEXATION WAR
Naero's War, Book Two: THE HIGH CRUSADE
Naero's War, Book Three: NAERO'S TRIAL

*The Citation Series, Cycle Two:*

Naero's War, Book Four: THE GAMMA QUADRANT

*Short Fiction in Ebook Format*

THE PERMIT

Fantasy with Author Garan R. R. Faraday
MERGEWORLD, BOOK 1
MERGEWORLD, BOOK 2
MERGEWORLD, BOOK 3
MERGEWORLD, BOOK 4*

(*Forthcoming)

# MERGEWORLD

## BOOK THREE

### Mason Elliott
### &
### Garan R. R. Faraday

# High Mark Publishing

High Mark Publishing
www.highmarkpublishing.com

Seattle & Portland, Los Angeles, Chicago, London

# Mergeworld

## Book Three
by
Mason Elliott & Garan R. R. Faraday
Trade Paperback Edition

Published by High Mark Publishing
ISBN 978-1-930451-20-9
Watch for other titles by these authors in the future.

Cover Art by
Mike Leonard
madmanmike.deviantart.com

Become a fan of my books.
Please join my Readers List:

http://bit.ly/1L2QpUL

# DAVID

Ten days after the Elkhart battle, the Allies of Michiana declared a victory celebration to be held on August first, in honor of the defeat of the Dark Khabal, the Kolugtathuloth colossus, and the Dragon Cult in Elkhart. The names of the victorious dead would be read aloud and their families honored. General Dirk Blackwood always tried to assess needs in private, make sure that the families of the fallen were taken care of, and not just left to fend for themselves.

This was yet another reason why Dirk was universally loved and respected by those who followed him. They knew that even if they went down in battle, as long as Michiana survived, those they were fighting for were going to be all right. Many of the militia leaders noticed that as well, and applied similar practices to their forces with a similar degree of success.

David and Jerriel attended the party nearest to their home, one of many such celebrations held across town in smaller groups. Most of their friends were there. Dirk and Belinda spoke briefly about the construction progress on several forts and strong points, and the massive fortresses taking shape in the center of town. Tens of thousands of people volunteered to work on constructing these safe points. The progress of so much concentrated effort by so many became staggering. Everyone wanted a fortification nearby. If the monsters overran the town again, everyone wanted a safe place to go to.

Dirk, Jerriel, and many others spoke about the rapidly expanding war with the Dark Khabal. Not just in Michiana, but most likely across both worlds of the Merge and on every continent.

David's heart always sank at the prospect of such talk. It made his efforts and the sacrifices of his friends and neighbors all seem so small and insignificant. When would such a war possibly end? How would he and Jerriel ever have a normal life together? Would they all eventually be killed?

David and Jerriel had inspected several of the new fortified safe sites. He brought up his misgivings about an endless war at the celebration.

"I hope we never need to fall back on all of those hard points," Dirk said in response. "But it's also good to be prepared. They'll be there if we need them. I won't leave us without such defenses for our civilians ever again. This could be a long war for all we know. Modern home and business structures— Pre-Merge—are now worthless for defensive purposes, against the types of foes and threats we now face. We've barely managed to survive. Now we have to think long term, into the future about so many things."

"Many other important local buildings are being hardened and fortified as well," Belinda added. "People will have any number of safe places close by to retreat to, if the town is ever cut off and attacked in the same ways."

They looked over the posted maps nearby and noted all of the coordinated locations spaced throughout town. People were assigned to hard points in their area. If that was where the people would go for protection, no wonder they worked on them with such fervor.

There were numerous artist renderings as to what the finished designs would look like. A generic, medieval castle or eighteenth century fortress look prevailed.

On a lighter, more enjoyable note, there was still sufficient food and even drink at the parties. Some of the fresh food and drink was shipped in from Elkhart and the surrounding area, so as not to waste it. Freshly slaughtered livestock of any kind: beef, pork, goats, sheep, geese, ducks, chickens was now a luxury that would need to be rationed, even at festivals. Much of it was used to feed the army and the population in general so that nothing went to waste.

Thul-Kazar and Thulkara did not complain one bit about more food to eat. They dove into the feast like the champion eaters they were. Thulls loved barbecue, all of the sauces, all of the spices and flavors.

That included the side dishes and desserts and the beer and wine that flowed freely as well. As a special thanks to their pair of valiant barbarians, Dirk made sure they had plenty to chow on, even for them.

David sat contentedly in a circle of his friends while their troops danced and made merry all around just after sunset. They utilized a hodge-podge of lawn chairs, camp chairs, and folding chairs around a bonfire in the middle of their part of camp.

Every time he glanced at Jerriel, David's heart pounded. He could barely take his eyes off her. His love and desire for her seemed only to increase with each passing second. For the time being he smiled at his own happiness and good fortune.

"What do you miss the most about the world before the Merge?" Robert Billings suddenly asked aloud.

"My smart phone, my computer," Steven Hayward blurted out almost instantly. "Video games, Wi-Fi, and the Internet, all the friends I had online. I hope they're all okay, wherever they are."

Steven was barely sixteen. He'd seen death and war up close, and still he sounded busted up more about missing his online life that he had once enjoyed so much.

The heartbreak in his voice affected everyone.

"Running water. Especially hot water," Belinda Blackwood said.

"I'm really going to miss air conditioning, after this summer," Pete Steiner added.

Lots of agreement there.

"Cell phones for sure," Carrie Daniels noted. "Talking to my mom whenever I wanted. My sister in St. Louis. Now I don't know where they are or if they're even alive."

There were a great many worries about the fate of distant relatives.

"The Tharanorians call St. Louis Kavendo. They're all probably doing the same thing there that we're trying to do here," Dirk said. "Survive and look ahead."

No one mentioned the vile Dragon Cult model for towns. Everyone hoped that atrocity was just a fluke.

"Restaurants," Tim Carroll said. "Fast Food. Junk food. Sit down places. It's funny how much of the past we took for granted, like it would always be there. Then one day, it was all gone...forever."

Several people wept.

Everyone grew quiet for a time.

Other voices spoke up from out of the shadows. "Cars. Roads. Motorcycles. Trucks. The freedom and ability go anywhere you wanted, whenever you wanted."

"It's not the same," Zack Lancaster said. "It just isn't the same."

Again, lots of agreement on that note.

"You don't see planes or jets in the sky anymore," someone else spoke up. "Except for those few hot air balloons we've been seeing, we don't fly anymore as a people."

Carrie Daniels sighed heavily and wiped her eyes, half sobbing. "I miss all of the stores and going shopping. We used to have so much fun. I remember going to the mall with my parents and my brothers and sisters. Then my friends. You just can't do that any more. All you see now is the same, tired open street markets with the same old used junk to barter and trade that they had a few months ago. Ugh!"

"Well, I still miss electricity more than anything else," Owen Sanders said. "Think about how much stuff required electricity. That's the thing we miss the most. Electricity made all of this other stuff possible."

"Movies, Blue Ray, DVD's," Jacob Meyer noted. Lots of nods and agreement there. "I was a film buff. I saw two movies a week on the big screen, usually a matinee of a new release or a dollar show. Then there were video downloads, movie rentals. None of that works anymore."

"Not without electricity," Owen persisted.

"I'm so glad to be working with the development teams," Robert Billings said. "Big things are on the way, I assure you. Just going to work is something to do each day. But doesn't anyone miss their job before the Merge, or the people they worked with?"

Several boos there.

"Hey," someone shouted. "Screw that! I hated going to work."

"Yeah, my boss was a dick!"

Lots of people laughed and chimed in.

"My friend, you gotta be kidding me," David said to Rob. "There were a lot of crummy jobs."

His friend persisted. "There still are. That doesn't change that much. Not to mention all of this survival crap. But don't we all have friends and acquaintances that we just don't see anymore? They might still be safe, or on the other side, we hope."

"You can try to find out," Jerriel said. "We're trying to reconnect people and find out which side everyone is on. And who survived, and who did not."

"Get this," Mason cut in, with a wink at Tori. "The weird thing is, some people went and started completely new lives and relationships on the other side already–within a matter of months–and now they don't want to be found by some of those people they knew before. It can be a caution."

People continued to be strange and foolish. Yet everyone had friends and family on the other side, as well as out of town. Those points kept coming up again and again.

"I miss television, TV news, World, National, local," Nick Denardi said. "I was a news junkie. Now we're cut off from everyone else. We don't know what's happening in other places, or on the other side."

"Some day we will," Belinda said, "we'll branch out and make contact with all of the other civilized areas, here in the New World, and the Old World across the pond—on both sides."

"That could take years," Ellis Newcombe said. "Maybe decades and maybe never. We could all be dead a month from now."

Someone else chipped in. "There are rumors going around that there are cities where the Urth people are at war with the people from Tharanor."

"That was bound to happen," another added. "People don't always see eye to eye, and one group often tries to dominate another. The side that has more magic than Urth people do might be tempted to remain dominant. That's the only way they know."

"We've heard those rumors as well," Belinda said. "Along with all kinds of crazy reports, everything from ghosts in many places, to bodies of giant crabs washed up on the east coast beaches."

Jerriel pointed a finger at David, her eyes wide. "I warned you about Shochi. I warned you. They do exist, and they are a major threat."

Everyone began to babble at once, going out of control until Rabbi Bergman banged on the big gong set up to call people to dinner.

"Let's try not to be so pessimistic," Bergman noted. "Or let the worst of our imaginations run away with us. We don't know the truth of any of these wild fears yet. We might be able to re-connect with other survivors more quickly if we can locate and train more travelers and other mages in general."

"We need more Champions of all kinds. Magic is the real new power. For better or worse," Dirk Blackwood said. "This is the world we live in now. The world we must fight and struggle to survive in—for the sake of each other and humanity from this point on. And we face enough threats as it is. This is our new reality. This is what matters...not what was. Not what we have lost, what is gone, either for now or forever. What we face now and what we cling to now is what matters most."

No one said anything more for a long while.

An hour later, David and Jerriel and some of their friends visited the camp of the Marrandorians.

Prince Valandin and Prince Alendel looked as if they were feeling no pain, celebrating and drinking heartily with their wizards, knights, and other troops.

They spotted Jerriel right off.

"Cousin! Noble allies. Welcome. Welcome! Join us. Please sit!

"Toast. A toast!

"A toast!" many voices took up the cry.

Thul-Kazar did not hesitate to have his massive drinking horn filled.

David took a sip from his goblet after it was topped off with golden, sweet-smelling liquid.

Mead. They drank mead, tart and delicious, tasting of honeyed blackberries. He didn't want to drink much more, his head already a bit tipsy. Getting really drunk always made him sleepy or sick and then sleepy.

David lifted his glass to the princes.

"Your Highnesses. Much honor and thanks to you and your people, especially your wizards." He saluted Pharrio, Maelen, and Urnessan again. "Without your aid, the battle in Elkhart would have been lost."

"Here here!" Thul-Kazar said. "I will drink to that. But then," he chuckled. "I will drink to most anything."

They joined him in laughter.

"The day would have been lost," Prince Valandin noted, "had you and your friends not taken out those transport gates. Not to mention your crucial alliance with the green dragon."

"Shavalkathar goes where and does what he will," David said. "I can take no credit for that. He is a force of nature. But I admit, it was a great help that he showed up and took out the red dragon for us when he did so."

"Indeed," Pharrio said, "to Shavalkathar!"

"To our ally, the green dragon!" others shouted.

Only the Thulls did not drink; they had no great love for dragons.

David wondered. 'Ally' was perhaps a bit of a stretch just yet.

Valandin took Jerriel's hand. "Dear cousin, it is so good to see you alive and well. And your radiant smile." He glanced at David and smirked. "And to see you happy, when you aren't battling demons, monsters, dragons, or otherwise fighting for your life."

"That's the truth," David said. It was good to have a break from being at war.

"I'm so glad you and dear Alendel and your people came to our aid," Jerriel said graciously. "You couldn't have arrived at a better time." She hugged them both.

Valandin looked at David for the first time and appraised him. "You have done well, Captain," he said. "Did you know that she is a princess of my royal line? Her standing is distant, yes, but a princess all the same."

"She is the queen of my stars," David said. "Jerriel is simply amazing. I could not think more highly of her than I do, or love her more. She is my world."

Jerriel looked at him and sobbed, reaching out to touch his face.

"I know your worth, my friend, on the field and as a man, from the short time that I have been with you. You have my blessing. As Prince of the Realm, I will not oppose your union with my cousin in any way."

David considered that rather odd. He had never even thought to ask for this fellow's blessing on anything, let alone his love for Jerriel. Perhaps he would have done so if Jerriel's father, had he been alive and present, but not some distant prince or cousin, ally or no.

Valandin persisted, but in his defense, he was quite tipsy. "I do so Even though you are an Urther and a commoner. And even though she was once my own betrothed, from when we were children."

David felt more than slightly uncomfortable and did not quite know what to say. "Thank you, Your Highness."

"She has told you about us, am I correct?"

"Yes?" was all that David would offer in return. This was getting rude.

Valandin breathed a sigh of relief. "Good. I did not want there to be any misunderstandings that could mar our friendship. My cousin's heart has been free for years. She has no obligation to me. I myself am betrothed, if my beloved can still make the voyage across the sea to join us here in the New World. The Merge has upset so many of our private plans."

"Congratulations," Jerriel said. "I am so happy for you, Valan."

"What does the future hold for the two of you?" Prince Alendel finally asked. "Surely two so in love must have a wedding planned?"

David took Jerriel's hand as she tried to motion him to silence. "There has scarcely been any time. If not for all of the troubles, I would marry her this instant. But we've been so busy trying to help our people survive that we've barely spoken together about our personal future."

"It has been incredibly hectic," Jerriel agreed. "The day will come when it will, when the time is right. I too would wed David this instant. So sure is my heart of him, and his place in my life."

"Well, I wouldn't put it off too much longer if I were you," Valandin warned. He took another drink which he probably shouldn't have. His speech already slurred slightly. "After all, you don't want your children to end up landless bastards."

Jerriel looked down slightly.

David tried very hard not to be angry.

He wasn't used to being around any kind of royalty, and Tharanorian royalty not at all. Perhaps princes in their world felt free to say anything they wanted, however unkind. Not surprising, since they had a more medieval mentality. Valandin was a leader from a completely different culture, age, and mindset.

7

David struggled to understand that. He tried very hard not to take offense.

He rose from where he sat and went to fill his goblet again with sweet scarlet wine this time.

Rowdy troops hooted and hollered nearby, carousing and rough housing.

A football sailed in out of nowhere and smashed David in the side of the head just as he was walking back.

As buzzed as he was, David toppled forward, crashed right into Valandin, and dumped the cold red wine all over the prince. The collision tumbled them both the ground.

Everyone gasped.

"Get off me, you drunken, bloody oaf!" Valandin roared out loud, assuming he was being attacked. He lashed out on the ground and backhanded David in the face.

David deflected further blows and tried to roll away.

"How dare you attack me!" Valandin raged, obviously drunk himself. "After I befriended you and paid you honor!"

Prince Alendel pulled his brother back.

Thul-Kazar wrapped a huge, hairy arm around David and pulled him away.

Jerriel stepped in between them all.

"Cousin, please. There must be some mistake. I'm certain that David was not trying to attack or offend you. It must have been an accident. Both of you have been celebrating far too much."

David rubbed his head and his eye. His head swirled even woozier than before.

"It's true," he said. "I meant no disrespect. I was just terribly clumsy. That was all. I admit, I've had too much."

The crown prince would not relent. "So, you were drunk and dumped your wine on me and knocked me down merely out of clumsiness? What kind of fool do you take me for?"

Jerriel looked at him confused. "David, what happened?"

"It was an accident, I swear Your Highness."

"Yes, of course it was," the prince sneered.

"It was. I went over to fill my cup, and on the way back a football came in out of the darkness and whacked me in the head! I lost my balance." He pointed at the ground in the dark, but the ball had either bounced away somewhere or been retrieved.

Valandin looked around. "And did anyone see this 'football' or whatever it was strike him?"

No one else had noticed, apparently. But they had all been talking and their heads were down. They weren't watching him.

"I was dizzy already and lost my balance when it struck me. I'm sorry!" David went down on one knee. "I truly, truly apologize my lord. The fault was entirely mine, but it was not in any way intentional."

"I must insist upon satisfaction," Valandin said proudly, wine still dripping down him and staining his clothes. "On the morrow, two hours past mid-morning."

Jerriel paled. "Cousin. Please. Do not do this."

"Not a word from you, Jerriel. You chose your man, not I. He will face me this next day and know my displeasure, or be branded a coward." He glared at David. "Your choice of weapons, bumpkin! Good night and rest well." He pulled away from Alendel violently and stalked off, his stunned guards clustered about him.

Prince Alendel looked embarrassed and turned back to them. "I guess the evening's merriment is now ended. I will speak to him. We've all had too much to drink. Things will be better in the morning."

"I hope so," Jerriel said. "David, we'd better go."

David felt at a loss for words. It was all so stupid, and yet it was still his fault. "Jerriel, I'm sorry. I didn't mean for any of this to…"

"Please. Let's just leave," she said wearily.

No one else knew what to say.

"I don't want to fight him," David said. "We're allies. We should be friends."

"If he challenges you, you must accept," Thul-Kazar said. "You are no coward. This is now a matter of honor."

"Screw that," David said. "We're allies. We can't be quarreling with each other."

"Oh, please," Jerriel said, sounding more than slightly irritated. "You were all drunk from the celebration. That makes all of you fools in this affair."

"I am not drunk, milady" Thul-Kazar said. He belched like a foghorn.

"Not yet," Alejandro said, "and not for want of trying."

"The night is still young," the big Thull said.

Jerriel shook her head. "This is ridiculous. Hopefully it will all blow over tomorrow after everyone sobers up. Alendel will talk some sense into him. Valandin usually listens to him."

"We can only hope," David said. "Any kind of duel would be a disaster. We need to inform Dirk and the Council about this incident."

"We'll send word. If a duel does take place, you cannot harm him," Jerriel said. "I mean, if he insists on fighting you."

"I'm supposed to just to stand around and let him beat on me?"

"He's the Crown Prince of Kellendra. He's family. He's an ally. You cannot harm him in any way."

"Jerriel, I have no intention of doing so. I hate this sort of thing. This is all a terrible misunderstanding!"

The next day promised to be interesting.

Prince Alendel came to them the next morning, his face somber and grim.

"You've got to be kidding me," David said, rising to his feet.

Jerriel groaned, "Oh, no."

"I'm afraid so, my friends. My brother is still angry about the incident. A bad hangover has done nothing to improve his mood, nor his judgement, I'm afraid. We must meet on the field of honor within the hour. I must take back your choice of weapons, Captain."

"Can we at least speak to him, Your Highness?" David said.

"I'm afraid that time is past. Please, your choice of weapons, my lord?"

"Boffers then," David said.

Alendel looked at a loss. "What? What in the devil are...?"

David showed him one. "Boffers. A practice weapon. Flexible plastic, covered with foam, harmless for sparring."

The prince reddened visibly. "Seriously, my lord?"

Thul-Kazar looked up from his hangover long enough to curse in disgust.

Prince Alendel frowned. "I'm afraid that will not do, Captain. They must be real weapons. No practice weapons. This is a real duel."

In that case, David came up with the best possible option. "Fists then."

Alendel raised an eyebrow.

"What, fists aren't allowed?" David asked. In most duels fisticuffs were a valid option.

"No, that is quite acceptable. Just...unusual for knights."

"I am not a knight. I'll face him open handed and settle the matter that way."

"Very well, fists it is, then. I will inform my brother. We shall await you at the appointed place."

He bowed and left them.

Thul-Kazar cheered. "Excellent. How good are you at brawling, my boy?"

David shook his head. "So-so. I'm better with swords and weapons. I had a little boxing training, and a little wrestling in High School. Three years of Karate as a kid. I earned a brown belt."

"Good, good," Thul-Kazar said. "I don't know what you are talking about, but I hope it all helps you in the brawl. I can't wait to watch."

"Thanks," David said. "I'd better stretch out. Jerriel, how good is Valandin hand-to-hand?"

"I think Alendel's a little better at it, thank goodness," she said. "I don't know. They've both had combat training since they were boys, but I never watched much of it."

"They're warriors," Jason Inada said. "You can tell just by looking at the two of them. And we've seen them on the battlefield. We know they can handle themselves. I would expect the worst."

"Excellent. A fine contest then," Thul-Kazar said.

Mason and Tori rushed in together. "We just heard," Mason said. "Is there any way to call it off?"

David shook his head. "I wish this all hadn't happened. I don't want to do this. I fight beside my friends, not against them."

"I'll be your second. What weapons did you choose?" Mason asked.

"Fists."

Tori sighed. "At least it wasn't swords, or pistols," she said, tapping one of her holsters.

"I could fight him for you," Thul-Kazar suddenly offered. "I enjoy a good brawl."

Jerriel's eyes widened in complete fear.

"No!" almost everyone said, startling even the Thull.

"No. Thank you," David told the Barbarian giant. "I appreciate your brave offer, my friend. But this is my dilemma. I will face him on my own terms."

# 

At eight in the morning, on a not so cool August morning, David and his friends met the Marrandorians on the field of honor that had been prepared nearby. A fighting circle fifty feet in diameter had been marked out in white powder, whether flour or chalk. The circle was also bisected into four quadrants by two perpendicular lines, like a mandala.

The Marrandorians lined up on one half, the Blackhawks, the Urthers, and their other allies on the other.

Valandin still looked very angry, despite a few hours rest. He took off his shirt, standing in the humid morning air and the warming sun in nothing but pants and soft boots.

Crown Prince Valandin, well-muscled and trim, had big powerful arms. He also clearly had two inches or more on David, and about twenty pounds at least, all of it muscle.

"Watch his reach," Mason warned David. "His arms and legs are longer than yours."

"Bigger men get tired faster," Alejandro said.

"That is not always true," Thul-Kazar warned.

Enough advice. David removed his hoody. Beneath it he wore a Fighting Irish tank shirt, no sleeves, with the neck cut wider by hand. Black sweat pants and black sport shoes. By comparison with the burly prince, David knew that he looked more lanky and slender than beefy.

David was all muscle in his own way, with powerful forearms, but somewhat lighter and more flexible. His fighting styles focused on speed, skill, accuracy, and endurance.

He was swordsman, not a boxer or a brawler.

One of Valandin's men blew a war horn.

The Prince strode to the centerline prepared on the ground.

David smiled at Jerriel, and entered the circle. He stepped up to the prince, bowed, and offered his hand.

"Your Highness. Please, again. The fault was completely and entirely mine. I apologize in every way. There is no need for this. We are allies and friends."

Valandin smiled and narrowed his eyes. He briefly took David's hand and tried to crush it. David resisted and squeezed back hard.

Valandin pulled away.

"Good. At least you are no coward, Captain. I give you that. But you still must prove yourself to me, Urther."

A herald, apparently acting as the official for the duel, explained the terms.

"The rules are simple. The combatants may use their hands feet, elbows and knees. No biting, gouging, or attacking the groin. There will be three passes. Three rounds marked by calls of the war horn. Any combatant unable to rise and continue or who gets knocked out of the circle during the contest will be declared the loser."

"Faugh!" Thul-Kazar fumed in disbelief. "Rules in a brawl? How very disappointing."

From the first pass, David knew he was in trouble.

Prince Valandin charged him without hesitation and unleashed a flurry of blows and combinations. David blocked most of the strikes, but suffered numerous bruising and punishing attacks. They circled each other around the combat ring, clashing and breaking. Then they clashed again.

The first round only lasted about two minutes. Already his battered arms and legs felt like lead.

While Valandin glistened, took a little water, and looked ready to continue—David already dripped with sweat.

"I'm proud of you," Jerriel said.

"Dave, it's a duel," Mason said flatly. "It's alright to hit back. Nail that princely sucker good."

"I'll do that, Mace, if I ever get the chance," he said.

And if he could find an opening. It was clear that the prince was somewhat better at boxing than he was.

The war horn summoned them to the next round.

David tried to stand his ground and give back some punishment.

He punched Valandin in the mid section, rewarded by the prince's grunt of pain. But it felt as if he were punching a tree. In return he took a glancing jab to the side of his face and a painful knee to his thigh.

He staggered away, dazed and hurt. They circled again. Valandin caught his breath and came at him.

The prince moved a shade slower, but David also felt less quick. He covered up and kept breaking away.

Then Valandin cornered him near the edge of the circle. He meant to either finish him off or force him out, winning either way. David blocked, parried and deflected as best he could. A heavy elbow strike numbed his right shoulder.

A roundhouse punch just missed his nose.

Desperate, David got in close and chopped the prince in the neck.

The prince's fist smashed into David's ribs, driving the air out of him.

He grappled suddenly and drove with his legs to force David out of the ring.

David spun, swept the leg, and they rolled to the ground, flailing at each other. The war horn sounded.

The prince got up, shook himself, and staggered to his side, sweaty, dirty, and breathing hard.

David literally crawled to his end, taking water and rubbing his aching ribs. "I think a couple of them might be broken," he said.

"You're doing well," Thul-Kazar noted. "Hit him more, lad. Hit him harder!"

"I'm trying to!" David shouted. "He's better than I am. I'm outmatched."

The big Thull laughed. "Then punish him as much as you can, even if you fall."

"I'll do that," David said. Jerriel wept. It hurt him more to see her cry than anything the prince could do to him.

His friends continued to shout encouragement to him.

The third and final round came even sooner than before.

David covered up and went on the defensive, hoping just to survive the round. At least Valandin had also slowed down more.

David never wanted to fight the prince in the first place. And he still didn't. He just wanted it to be over.

Valandin sought a very different outcome, with David senseless on his back.

David stepped too slowly and stumbled on an uneven patch of ground.

Valandin closed in quickly and saw his chance. He forced David back to the edge of the circle once more.

In desperation David unleashed a powerful side kick to the abdomen.

Valandin turned and partially deflected it with his hip and arm, but for an instant it drove him back. Whatever pain he took enraged him.

He charged in again, pummeling David's defenses.

A jab to the face raked David's mouth and nose, the pain like fire.

His own anger exploded.

He jabbed a knifehand in and clipped the prince in the throat. Then rammed the palm of his hand under the chin, snapping the head back.

He saw a roundhouse punch coming, drove with his shoulder and smashed his right fist into Valandin's face dead on.

Valandin's left crashed into Mason's side again, smashing his damaged ribs and winding him.

A heavy right clouted him on the side of the head and the sky spun.

The prince, bleeding and enraged, loomed over David, preparing to finish him off.

With the last of his strength David booted Valandin in the side of the head, even as another fist crashed into his temple.

The prince fell back.

David's vision went black.

He came to, Jerriel cradling his head in her hands.

As his vision cleared, he saw that they were both still in the battle circle. Prince Alendel and attendants tried to help Crown Prince Valandin get to his feet. They dabbed his bleeding face with cold water and towels as it swelled. Both eyes went purple black, the face mostly bruised, scraped, and cut.

There weren't any mirrors handy, but David guessed from the way he felt, that he himself didn't look much better off.

"I'm all right. Let me stand," Valandin said at last. He staggered and pushed them away. "Let our healers tend to us both."

David looked up at him and winced as he forced himself to sit up.

"The fight is yours, my lord." David said. "I concede. Are you satisfied?"

Valandin grinned and at last offered him his hand. "I am. You have faced me with honor and courage as a man should. Our disagreement has been resolved. Let us call the contest a draw, remain friends again, and speak no more of it."

David took his hand. "Thank God."

Valandin nearly toppled over, but pulled them both up to a standing position.

To steady them both, the prince embraced him.

Everyone applauded. The sense of relief in the air between the two allies was palpable.

"Quite frankly," Valandin whispered in surprise, "I've never had anyone last all three rounds. Usually they just let me knock them down and it's all over."

14

David shrugged and grinned, speaking softly, "I guess no one told me the rules, Your Highness."

The crown prince laughed. "No, I think that it is better this way."

David gaped. "For who?"

Valandin laughed. "Why, for both of us. We respect each other now in ways that we could not before."

David shook his head slightly. Too bad for that, if that's what it took.

"I'll see you again, my friend," the prince said. "After we both recover. My head was already splitting before we began all of this." He patted David on the back and limped away groaning.

Everything on David ached.

He staggered off to a nearby tent between Jerriel and Mason, Tori in tow. He rested on a cot. A medic looked him over and dressed his cuts, scrapes, and put cold compresses on his many bruises. David was a patchwork of them by the end. Valandin's personal healer, Chimuri, came by with Urth healer Stacy Keller and they treated David together.

He still took some pain medicine afterwards.

"You're going to be very sore over the next few days, Captain," Chimuri said. She was a Darshian in her early thirties, attractive, short black hair and slanted brown eyes.

"Depending on what you like," Stacey added, "you might try cool or warm baths. Not hot." She winked at Jerriel. "Gentle massages or rub downs could be soothing as well."

"Okay," he said. He raised his eyebrows at Jerriel and grinned.

Chimuri glanced around at all of them very curiously. "Just make sure he gets some rest. He's young and strong and should heal up very quickly."

Jerriel chuckled. "The problem is normally trying to keep David down."

"Sounds like fun," David joked. But when he turned over on the cot, everything erupted in blinding pain once more. He groaned.

# JERRIEL

By the third day, David felt mostly better and was up and around. Prince Valandin and his wizards came to visit him and Jerriel in their home. Together they all had a modest dinner of meat rations, instant mashed potatoes, canned veggies, and fruit that night.

Jerriel made sure that her beloved didn't drink anything stronger than fruit juice. And there was no one in the shadows to toss any wayward footballs around. No more such clumsy incidents. She cared for the humanity of both worlds, and only wished to see their peoples work together as allies.

They were fighting the enemy across two worlds now.

Senseless conflict between brothers and sisters—whatever their differences or origin—would only lead to needless discord and evil. The Dark Khabal would laugh at them for doing any of the Shadow's work for them.

Tharanor and Urth had plenty enough real enemies to deal with after the Merge. They did not need to fight with each other as well. If that was going on anywhere, which by odds it probably was, they had an obligation to put an end to such folly.

As if to prove how chaotic their worlds were, urgent messengers arrived at the house a half hour later, summoning Jerriel and David, the crown prince, his brother prince, and their wizards.

The summoners looked at each other, misread their cues, and both blurted out their messages almost at once.

"Captain Pritchard. You and the Blackhawks will assemble and report to the General Blackwood and the town council, accompanied by the wizard Jerriel."

"Prince Valandin. Dread word has reached us, my lord. Kellendra has…it has fallen, my lord!"

All present were nearly stunned senseless by the latter report. Jerriel felt her own heart shudder within her.

"Kellendra has fallen?" Valandin finally repeated. "How…how is this possible? Where are the king and queen, my parents? Our armies?"

"I'm sorry Your Highness. I have no further information to provide. They…they only sent me to summon you and your mages."

Valandin set his face as the initial shock faded. He rested one hand on his great sword. He steadied the messenger with his good right hand.

"It will be all right, lad. Our families and friends, all of us, are always in the mighty hands of the Creator. Come. Let us learn what we can."

"We're going with you," Jerriel said. "Cousin, our family, our people? How could such a disaster happen? Kellendra was—"

The prince shook his head in disbelief. "Impregnable. I know, cousin. The strongest fortress in all the west. Stronger than Tornhold, or even Vaejan!"

Jerriel weighed everything she knew about the enemy and their methods, strategy, and tactics. From what the Allies did know about the enemy and Kellendra, what was the Dark Khabal after now? They always had clear objectives, clear plans. What would she do if she were them?

She thought of the larger strategic map in her head. How would this affect the region, the two worlds?

"We're missing something, David, all of you. Our foes are after something far bigger than South Bend and Michiana in this region. They've already been exposed for who and what they are. They have no fear of that any longer. Perhaps word has even reached the Old World by now. The enemy won't let that stop them. They knew that they and their intentions were going to be exposed, eventually."

"You're right, Jerriel," David said, catching her line of thought. "They're going all out now, putting everything they have on the line. And not just here, but everywhere, just as you supposed. But for what? They strive to enslave both worlds, on the largest scale possible. This is not just about little Michiana.

"The attempt to seize control of Elkhart was a minor feint for them—a mere distraction by comparison. I'm guessing that we'll learn about many other plots and attacks to seize control of many other cities. Yet still, what could they be after in this small region? What is here for them somewhere that they could want so badly?"

"Kellendra is not prize enough?" Valandin asked.

"No, it's not," Jerriel said. "David's right. Everyone think."

"And remember," Tori told them. "Both Sides of the Merge are still very much in play, for us and for them."

They left the house and made their way to the council hall as quickly as their bikes and horses could take them. The princes and their wizards enjoyed the bicycles loaned to them immensely. In the city proper, bikes proved lighter, quicker, and more agile than their big, heavy warhorses.

The militia cleared the streets along their route to make way for them. Traffic was light as it was.

"I think I know what it might be," Pharrio said, peddling quickly. All of the wizards looked a bit comical with their robes high up to keep them away from the spinning spokes, pedals, and wheels. His thirtyish face suddenly grew very pale.

"What?" Jerriel asked him.

"I've been thinking about it a great deal my friends. I've discussed it in private with my mage brothers, Maelen and Urnessan."

"No, I still say that it's not possible," Maelen said.

Urnessan looked just as pale and shook his head. "Brother, I thought we concluded that you were mistaken."

"You concluded that, brothers. I never conceded that point. I am not wrong. I wish I was, just as much as you do."

"A pox on riddling and dissembling wizards. Simply tell us!" Valandin ordered.

"Your Highness. On Tharanor, the ley lines of power in our counterpart to this region met at an important juncture, a major nexus, days west and slightly north of Kellendra. Actually, come to think of it, it would almost be exactly near South Bend, closer and slightly northeast."

"Up in Michigan then," Tori spoke up, glancing at her own folded pocket map while they pedaled. "That would make it...somewhere around Niles or perhaps east toward Kalamazoo, in the country."

Mason added. "There's nothing there now. The monsters wiped out Niles. There's nothing left alive up around there any longer."

"Except for perhaps the enemy," Jerriel noted. "The enemy controls the monsters, remember?"

Thul-Kazar said, riding his great warhorse with Thulkara to one side on il-tempered Goliath. "I traveled through that area on my way here. I barely fought my way past the outskirts and escaped with my life. Our foes still have a heavy presence north of us. We would need more than one army to take control of that region."

"I still fail to see the significance of all of this," David said. "I'm not a wizard, or a Tharanorian, so someone please explain it to me."

"Things may function a little differently on Urth," Maelen said. "What Pharrio is getting at, is that there should, in theory, be a similar series of ley lines and nexus points on Urth as well, perhaps in the same locations."

"And?" Valandin asked.

"Oh, no," Jerriel said. "They've found and perhaps captured one or more of the Spectral Keys! Remember I told you about them, David? They were lost, unleashed by the Six High Mages in order to save both worlds when the Merge occurred."

"Yes," Urnessan said. "Each of the keys is a quasi-elemental and dimensional entity, linked and controlled by a powerful artifact. Once unleashed, the entities would be automatically drawn to places of power, such as the Cosmic nexus in this region or others."

Maelen shook his head. "In order to rule both worlds for certain, the Shadow Mages would eventually need to recover the Spectral Keys—the very artifacts used to bind the entities to a person's will once more. All six keys were set free, scattered, and dispersed when the High Wizards struggled to save both Tharanor and Urth from the cataclysm. Five of the six High Mages are now in hiding, horribly wounded, still healing from their horrendous ordeal. No one knows where the keys or their entities are or even if they can ever be located or bound once more."

"If it has been done once," Pharrio said, "a way can be found to do so again. Binding the keys and bringing the spectral powers together once more would give those who control them almost complete mastery over both worlds. Just as the Six High Mages once possessed, ruling and protecting Tharanor through their wisdom."

"But if that is true," Jerriel noted, "then both Tharanor and Urth will each have their own separate sets of Spectral or Cosmic Keys, and entities controlling their powers—in the dimensional scheme of things."

"It's much worse than that," Urnessan said. "If all that is true, then all of the entities would now be wild, possibly dangerous, confused, and even enraged. They might decide to make war against each other. They could still destroy both worlds, if enough of them came together in the same place, the wrong combination, or under the right conditions."

"Or if the Shadow Wizards forced them to do so," Jerriel said.

They drew near to the town council meeting hall. At least the weather for the early August evening looked pleasant, despite the growing bad news.

"Or," David noted out loud, "if the High Mages regained control of all of the keys on both worlds. I wonder. Could they undo the Merge and return both worlds to their original states?"

Pharrio blinked. "In theory…such a thing could be possible."

Maelen shook his head. "There would still be countless serious ramifications. Nothing on such a scale could be done lightly, and without similar dire consequences."

"That doesn't matter," Valandin said. "Just think! We could help the High Mages undo the Merge, once they have healed themselves. Then we can return both worlds to normal. But one thing at a time. Why again would one or more of the Spectral Keys be drawn to this nexus point that we speak of? This must be our destiny, I say."

Units of Blackhawks waited for them outside the council building as they pulled up and parked their bikes under guard.

"Power," Pharrio began. "The Spectral Key entities are Cosmic powers bound to this world; likewise, they are by their very nature drawn to places of great power. Both worlds generate such power naturally."

"It's the perfect time for the Dark Khabal to make its big moves," Jerriel surmised. "Think about it. Everyone is still reeling from the Merge. And because they knew when the Merge was going to occur, they still remain several steps ahead of everyone else. They've had time to plan much of what they're doing now well ahead of time, perhaps all of it."

Urnessan hung his head. "Even if they obtain just one of the keys, their powers will increase tenfold. Once they have one, they might be able to use its enhanced senses and abilities to locate and bind the others to their will."

"How do we even know what these keys are?" Mason joined in and asked. "Most of this is completely new to us Urthers. We don't know anything about these matters."

"Listen well then and take note," Pharrio said. "It may be different on Urth, but on Tharanor, the Key of Light is a perfect starstone gem the size of a fist. It controls an entity of light in the form of a great dove."

"I know it well," Jerriel said. "Raeshen Garrendil, High Wizard of Marrandor was my mother's master at one time, and she one of his brightest apprentices. I have seen the key, and the Entity of Light, and several of the other forms that it can take."

"Raeshen rests in hiding," Pharrio said. "Like the others he was gravely injured and nearly destroyed himself in the process of saving both of our worlds. Anyone who obtains control over the Key of Light might also, in theory, locate where he is concealed and attempt to destroy him. It will be the same with all of the keys and their former masters. We must consider that point as well."

"Well, we have to start somewhere with all of this," Tori said.

Officials finally ushered them into the council chamber for another important intelligence briefing. Dirk Blackwood and some of the other militia commanders sat down with them all.

"We've sent Rabbi Bergman and some of his new Astral Scouts ahead to help assess the threat around and within Toledo…er, Kellendra," Dirk said. "We should hear something more back within an hour or two. But we must be careful. Bergman reports that the enemy has some new way of detecting and even possibly capturing the Astral Scouts while their spirits are in astral form. Such methods and defenses against them are still new to us. Do you wizards from Marrandor have any advice for us?"

"Two of us are not transport mages," Urnessan admitted, deferring to Pharrio.

"To do such a thing would require great power," Pharrio explained. "That could be power similar to what they would gain if they already held mastery over one or more of the Spectral Keys."

For the next few hours they discussed the six Tharanorian keys and how they might be detected, controlled, or utilized. Conjecture on any parallel Urth keys remained limited to conjecture, by the simple fact that no one had any frame of reference.

Yet all of the mages present agreed that if such keys and their guardians existed for Tharanor, some kind of similar spectral counterparts should also exist for Urth. And they would take specific forms, but perhaps different forms from those of Tharanor.

At the end of the discussion about the Spectral Keys, Rabbi Bergman and some of his new Astral Scouts returned with news from Kellendra. He joined the council after a brief rest, appearing drained and weary. His face appeared grave but determined.

The entire town council and their new allies waited upon his report.

"The Marrandorians are fighting the enemy in the streets of the city," Rabbi Bergman said. "The King of Kellendra and his wife the queen have both been wounded somehow, perhaps by an enemy assassin. We do not know their exact conditions, but they still live.

"The enemy armies struck Toledo-Kellendra at the height of the confusion over the attack on the royals. Now the mighty Kellendran armies are hard pressed, fighting pitched battles across several wide fronts against the Khabal. They try to allow civilians time to make an ordered flight from those areas. Fortunately, it is an ongoing conflict, not a rout as we first feared. But the heavy attacks came as a surprise, and the enemy has pressed deep into their lands.

"Refugees are streaming north toward Detroit, or Tornhold, and east toward Cleveland, or Dorundia, yet initial reports say that the Thulls of Tornhold are now besieged as well. And Dorundia remains at war with itself. No place in that region is entirely safe. Yet there is one bright point to report: the Urther populations in those areas have become great allies to Marrandor, and are throwing the weight of their forces into the fray."

"The Shadows dare to attack both of the Allied cities?" Thul-Kazar asked, his eyes afire with rage and anger. A Thull champion enraged was a sight to behold.

Bergman shook his head. "My scouts and I did not make it up to Tornhold this time, but around Kellendra at night there is a massive force or perhaps several armies or hordes of torgs, ka-torgs, mor-kahls, gozogs, grun, slurgs, and even shagga. The necromancers and Shadow Mages are there in force running the show, but they spend more than half their time keeping order among their monstrous armies—keeping such fierce beings from fighting and devouring each other."

He paused and took a long drink of water. "Clearly the enemy has used transport gates to strike hard from the south and west. We weren't able to get close enough to determine just how many transport gates they have operational. We're guessing at least two.

"The Marrandorians responded bravely, holding out toward the north and east, and have sent out a call of alarm for aid. But there are a number of Ghool Lords and ghool masters allied with the foe as well from what we've seen—specialized necromancers who can control and direct large numbers of undead.

"These fiends command a vast army of undead skeletons, zombies, ghasts, and ghools, and a nasty force of greater monsters and weird creatures numbering in the hundreds and growing each day. All of these undead forces seem to be held in check to the west in reserve, away from the enemy's other forces at the front. And the enemy does this with good reason. For the undead attack anything living that comes near them, whether friend or foe."

"That all sounds very grim," Dirk noted. "The larger fight of a global conflict across two worlds begins to play out. Our foes already have Kellendra bottled up and on the defensive. They are now free to press their attack, or even use these other large concentrations of undead to sweep across Michigan and attack Tornhold or whatever they wish along the way. And we already know that the enemy has another large host spread across the middle of southern Michigan, down from the north. If they can polish off Detroit and Toledo, they'll certainly come back this way to wipe us out. And that doesn't even count the huge mercenary and other enemy forces in the south, already laying siege to Indianapolis, or Nenarra."

Bergman shook his head in despair. "Alas, the carnage is indeed taking place on a very broad scale. I agree with you, General. One can only surmise that if all of Kellendra is taken, and the Marrandorians fall, and then Detroit and the Thulls—this vast enemy will come at us. None of the other small enclaves between us and those cities have the strength to resist so great a host. Perhaps no one can defeat them. Not even Michiana."

Jerriel could scream. The two worlds descended into senseless war and madness. Would she and David ever have a chance at a happy, normal life? The problems they faced were all bigger than the needs of any two people.

"The Khabal couldn't have unleashed all of this at a worse time," Dirk said. "Here it is late summer when many of our crops still aren't ready to harvest yet. They don't even need to attack us. If they merely destroy our fields, most of us will starve this winter."

Bergman broke in again. "In fact, they are taking great pains to bypass and leave growing crops untouched, General. I think they fully mean to seize our cities, kill off or enslave any survivors, and harvest those crops themselves this fall, after we have done most of the work. They will need those foodstocks to help feed their own hosts."

Valandin looked exceptionally grim. "Indeed. They have considered every factor and planned their campaign expertly, and risked all that they have in order to succeed across the board. We must do the same. Every skill, every ally, every effort must be made to confront and defeat them, across the two worlds."

"Remember," Jerriel told them, "that the Cult of the Shadow Mages worship and ally themselves with the Dark Ghods, Devils, Demons, and the Shadow Worlds, Ghool Lords, and their many servants. I assure you, that such terrifying beings exist. They are not myths or fairy tales. The Dark Khabal serves and worships them in fanatical earnest.

"Who can forget the horror of the Kolugtathuloth that we barely defeated? We have seen first hand how these mortal servants of evil make war. They have transport magic and make regular use of it. They are clearly gating in not only conventional forces and mercenaries, but supernatural minions from the other Shadow Worlds to contest for both of our planets. If Tharanor and Urth fall, they too shall join the Shadow Worlds. All that we know will be destroyed or subjugated to the forces of slaughter, death, chaos, and destruction—becoming mere outposts and stepping stones of the Nine Hells."

"What about the Creator?" Pastor Bryan said. "We pray to God Almighty. I myself saw the might of faith work against the demon when we confronted and destroyed it."

Pharrio nodded. "The Power of Faith is indeed a mighty ally, and the powers of Light are still strong. Yet they work best through us as its agents, and the choices we make. These are our worlds, existing upon our levels, it is up to us to destroy or save them. It is our burden. We are responsible for the evils we invite or commit upon them.

"Even the dragons say that long ago, closer to the Dawn of Creation, one third of the Ancient Guardians and their allies rebelled against the Creator. They were blasted in less than an instant, and their ruinous fall flung them senseless into the very depths of the core of the Void where they crashed upon impact, reduced to mere scorched shadows.

"There in that fell place, they awakened, broken and laid waste in utter desolation. Yet the greatest of the Fallen still fed upon their own lies, for they had nothing left to them. They told themselves that even such a fall as theirs was only a mere setback. They fashioned themselves into the ruined, twisted, horrid forms they took and the leaders of the rebellion named themselves the Shadow Ghods."

"Just be careful when you speak lightly of summoning the current Celestial Guardians," Maelen said. "The Six High Wizards were forced to do so when they strove to save both Tharanor and Urth from dimensional chaos and destruction. In fact, an Avatar of *Arkalan the Defender* was sent to aid them for the space of only a few seconds. As a result, all of the High Wizards were nearly destroyed, and our two worlds brought to the brink of annihilation.

"In the end, the only way for the two worlds to be saved was through the cataclysm of the Merge and all of the destruction that it has unleashed. We will be dealing with the effects of that cataclysm for who knows how long, perhaps forever."

"Great," David said. "Not much to go on really. And what about the spectral keys and the entities of Urth? What about our nexus points, our ley lines?"

"Yours was a once a world without magic," Jerriel tried to explain to David and the Urthers "Or at least where magic was mostly dormant and unutilized. That's why Urth was so stable, and as a sister world, such a good anchor point for the Six High Wizards to link to Tharanor and thereby save both worlds. But the ley lines and nexus points—they're all here, just as they would be on any living world. And now that magic permeates Urth once more, the spectral keys and entities will most likely take their own forms, and have their own entities. Again, just as any world would."

"All of this is only theory," Pharrio added. "But who knows what the status of the keys and entities are, now that both worlds have been jumbled up together in the Merge?"

Jerriel rubbed her head with both hands. "So many variables. It is maddening just to consider it all. There's so much that could go wrong, especially if any of the keys fall into the wrong hands."

"At least now we know why the Dark Khabal risks all they have on an all out contest against the colonies and the nations," Dirk said. "With everything up for grabs, what do they have to lose? If they gain control over even some of the Spectral Keys from either world, their position will be greatly strengthened. Plus, they will have the jump on everyone in finding more of the keys. We cannot allow that to happen."

Prince Valandin sat back in his seat. "My brother and I have no choice. We must return to Kellendra this autumn, to help our people against this enemy. We will be happy to give what aid we can along the way, to any force that wishes to explore the area around this nexus up in…Michigan. But we cannot remain there long. I'm afraid I must require my wizards to return with me back to the defense of Kellendra."

"Of course," Jerriel said. "We shall miss you all when that parting comes. If we find anything around the nexus and gain control over it, our powers will be strengthened as well. We can bring that power to bear against the forces attacking Kellendra and shall rush to your aid."

"We cannot count on such good fortune," Valandin said. "But I pray that it might be so. Our need is very great, and already we stand outnumbered."

"Word is going out to Elkhart and all the other enclaves," Dirk said. "Kellendra has sent their mighty sons and daughters to bleed for us on our ground. Our council has approved an army expedition to the nexus point and beyond, to Kellendra if that becomes possible. Other areas will send what aid they can. The expedition will grow in strength as it marches. You are not alone, good princes. You have helped us more than we can ever repay you. We will send as much help as we can to aid you and your people in their time of need."

Valandin shook Dirk's hand. "Thank you, my friends. You are mighty allies. We will be glad to face any foe with you beside us."

"I wish we had more time to train our budding wizards and search for more Champions," Jerriel said. "There just isn't enough time to do everything."

"We'll train as many people as much as we can along the way," Pharrio said. "And we'll leave a few of our mages here to help further your training programs. If we can master the transport magicks we have access to, that would go a long way to giving us an important edge."

"We're trying," Jerriel said. "We're very close. We have very active plans to mass produce transport devices and share them and their secrets with any of the other cities who are willing to ally with us against the Shadows. We shall do all that we can to speed those programs up. The clever Urthers have also struggled to modify some of their ingenious machines in order to aid us, as well."

"Alas, we cannot wait for those programs to be fully completed," Dirk said. "Kellendra needs our help, and perhaps Tornhold and Nenarra next. The current expedition departs within twenty-four hours. I only wish it were sooner. Our scouts report that there are still large numbers of vulnerable survivors up in Michigan. We need to try to reach them."

"Before we talk of sweeping wars across both worlds, first let us win the battles that are at hand," David insisted. "Our vanguard and my Blackhawks can leave within hours."

He rose to his feet and rested his hand on his sword. "We will ride with the princes and their forces. The others can catch up to us along the way, once they depart. We can act as the scouts for the relief force."

"I think that would be wise," Dirk said. "Go ahead, Dave. Take whoever you need and go with the good will and blessings of all free peoples, whether from Tharanor or Urth. Whether we know it or not yet, we are all allies now, against any foes who rise up against us."

"Again, my brother and I thank you, and the council," Valandin said. "We could not ask for more."

"I am going with Captain David and the Blackhawks," Thul-Kazar said. "My people are also under attack. Our foes will regret their folly. My skills in battle are yours to command." He saluted David, and the prince.

Thulkara put her fists on her hips. "Where my prince goes to fight, I shall always be at his side."

David took their enormous hands in his own. "You two Champions are already one with us, my brother, my sister," he told them.

They left the Council Hall and prepared to depart as soon as they could make it to the assembly point.

Jerriel looked with great affection and longing at their home once they returned to it to take up the rest of their gear. They were going to war once again.

"I have found great joy here with you, my beloved," she told David, running her hands through his hair. "I fear that it will be long before we can share our nights here in peace, in our little home. How I shall miss it. We have taken on a great task. Perhaps greater than our limited powers, greater than we can guess. Yet we must try. That much is clear."

David took her into his arms. "I love this house, our house. But my home and my place are ever with you, Jerriel. At your side, wherever we must go, whatever we must face, you are my home.

"Wherever you stand and fight, there will I. Wherever you rest, I shall lie down beside you. Wherever you are, there I am happiest. And if you should fall, I will fall beside you and be content."

Jerriel felt her eyes tear up and blind her. She could not speak.

After a little more canoodling, they made their final checks and prepared to depart.

In their family room, Jerriel and some of the other mages had been studying the demon's mirror and the ruined transport mirror gate captured during the war. Despite all of their knowledge, insights, and instincts combined, they had not broken the secrets of either.

"I'll have to send these to the new Mage Council for safe keeping and further study while I'm gone," she said. "A pity we couldn't have had more time to work with them."

"Bergman and Billings and the development teams will keep going over them, when they have time. Perhaps they will make further breakthroughs. They're learning so many new things each day in the research labs."

As they left, Jerriel sighed and locked their front door behind them.

# SHAEDDOR

Shaeddor knew it was morning, but he continued to sleep in, in no hurry to rejoin the Dark Khabal's deadly intrigues and near constant tests of will.

Once he began his quest to destroy them all, that would become a long and arduous task indeed.

All of that could wait a few minutes longer.

Especially when he was having such a pleasant dream about his Jen, the simply beautiful, young Urth woman he had loved, and whom the Khabal had murdered and mutilated without a thought.

Yet in his dream, Jen was next to him, in one of those slow, lazy, golden mornings kissed by the sun. Mornings they had taken for granted. She waited for him to open his eyes, and look into hers, eyes so green that they could be concentrated sunlight blazing through verdant spring leaves.

Finally he did open his eyes, seeing her bright face, smiling at him amid her cloak of light brown hair. How he had loved her.

How he still loved her, so much so that the memory of her loss was like the stabs of hot daggers, biting through and searing his flesh. Like himself, she had been imperfect; yet they shared something deep and real.

If only he could touch her again...love her again.

They had taken her from him.

Tears scorched from his eyes as if they would melt to the very core of the planet. His tears were as fire.

The enemy would all pay–pay dearly for taking his Jen from him. He would see to that, all in good time.

Then Jen surprised him in the dream by actually speaking to him.

"I'm haunting you…" she told him. "I cannot help it, my love."

He gasped and smiled. "I want you to haunt me. Just don't ever leave me, please…"

"I have nothing left to do. I am trapped here, beloved. I fear the darkness of the underworlds, and the light shows me no way."

She stared back at him and smiled, but her body slipped off the bed, falling away from her severed head.

Shaeddor started and sat up wide awake, alone in his bedchamber.

Yet it seemed as if there was still a slender impression in the bed coverings beside him.

Damn them all. Not only was she dead, but now her lost and tormented soul wandered in Limbo, terrified, knowing no peace, unable to pass on. His sweet Jen did not deserve any of this.

She would have been better off if they had never met. That was clear.

He sighed again. Now, among so many other complex matters, he would need to do some research in the libraries and see what dangers her lost soul could still fall into. Then he could warn her ghost about what to avoid and how. That would give her more than a fighting chance.

The time came to rise up.

The time came to find the tools and weapons from which to construct his vengeance.

The first thing he needed most was information. That itself could take quite a while. He would understand them and their plots completely. Then he would become their most valued, trusted servant.

Despite being welcomed home by his master, Gorrial Lankorro, High Magus of the Dark Khabal, Shaeddor understood very well that he was still under intense scrutiny and constant suspicion.

The Khabal saw him as a traitor, and he was no longer fully trusted by the Shadow Mages, whatever he did.

He had expected all of that, and made certain that he did nothing to further such suspicions.

He might still die at any moment. They could come for him to take his life any time.

Shaeddor remained calm. He dressed as he normally would.

The time was perfect to go straight to his great master of old, and offer his services once more as an apprentice.

Gorrial and others had questioned and interrogated him on and off in the meeting and planning rooms for the first few weeks, trying to assess where his mind and his loyalties truly were.

He repeatedly needed to explain about his head injury after the Merge, his bout of amnesia, and the things he had done before he regained his true memories and who he had been. Such matters worked in his favor.

Shaeddor kept his story straight. He hadn't regained his full memories until nearer to the end, and even then he was still being watched closely by the Urthers, who never fully trusted him. He barely managed to escape as it was.

Yet in his defense, he had managed to bring a great deal of valuable information about the Urther enemy with him, and he had repeatedly argued with the other captive Dark Mages that their main responsibility was to escape and return to the Khabal for further instructions—not to pursue their own vendettas or causes. Such attitudes on the part of the other captured Dark Mages, Shaeddor insisted, was what had led to their deaths.

On the surface, it all made perfect sense. He made it sound plausible.

Shaeddor had insisted that they make good their escapes multiple times, and had been overruled and out-voted by the others. Instead of escaping when they clearly could have, the fools chose to attack a powerful enemy in the heart of their strength and were eventually wiped out.

He warned his master not to underestimate their foes. The Urthers had proven themselves time and time again to be quite stubborn, resourceful, and formidable.

Everything Shaeddor told them was logical, rational, and believeable.

Thus a month had passed, and still Shaeddor was more or less confined to his quarters, and his lab. Even as he conducted further magical research, and library research, he was given apprentices who were little more that Gorrial's handpicked informants.

Finally, his old master had agreed to a private meal and meeting, just the two of them.

"There is still one matter which I must ask you about," Gorrial said, "and let me speak plainly, Shaeddor. The others do not wish me to bother with you any longer. They simply want me to have you killed."

Shaeddor went down to one knee. "My life is yours to command, my master. It is yours to take or direct as you wish."

Gorrial kept his face impassive and continued. "Regardless of your injury and your memory loss, the fact remains. You still fought against us on the side of our enemies, and for a very long time."

Mason bowed his head. "I was not in my right mind, my master. During most of that time I did not even recall who I really was, or anything about my past. The more I began to return to myself, the more I began working toward escape. Yet I had to keep up appearances all the while. It was very difficult."

"I understand that. You were always the perfect apprentice and agent, Shaeddor, and you served me extremely well. I wish to return to a place where I can trust you, and send you forth to work for me once more. You were one of my most trusted and valuable agents. Unlike others, I do not kill needlessly if I can still find good use for a prized tool or weapon—and you are both. Talent cannot be wasted. Only fools destroy what is valuable in emotion or haste. But the question remains. Can I trust you?"

Shaeddor bowed his head again. "You can trust me, my master. Allow me to prove myself to you in any way. I am myself again. I know who I am once more and who and what I was meant to be. Allow me to serve you, Master."

"Tell me again what occurred between you and the necromancer Gultor. How did he die?"

"I slew him in single combat, my lord. He forced me to by trying to slay me. Just as we were about to make good our escape, he attacked me with spells meant to kill, not capture. He boasted openly how he had always despised me and my family, and stated clearly that he meant to supplant me in your favor, and lie and tell you that the enemy had killed me before I could escape."

Gorrial hesitated, staring at Shaeddor eye to eye. "Yes, I do think that you speak true, Shaeddor. Gultor was exactly like that. That was his way. He struck down several others from behind just that same way in order to get to his rank and position. Such behaviors are not uncommon—among ambitious Dark Mages. And from what I can read from you...you enjoyed killing him, didn't you, my boy?"

Shaeddor smiled. "I could never hide my emotions from you, Master. The man was a fool, who nearly got us all killed, when we could have easily escaped, several times over. Yet he still outranked me with the others. And yes, when he did try to kill me, I was only too happy to take that idiot down and end his petty, wretched existence."

Gorrial grinned, came forward, and clapped Shaeddor on the shoulders with both pride and glee. "I would expect no less, from my finest apprentice. But now you are back at my side, and ready to serve my will!"

"To the death, my master," Shaeddor said eagerly, "to the death." His beloved Jen's dead face flashed in his mind once more, and Shaeddor continued to grin.

"You know that the others will require that I give you some kind of test, to prove your loyalty?"

"Choose anything, my master. Command me and it shall be done."

"Very well. We still wish to reclaim your father's magickal journal. He uncovered many of our plots before his death, and was very close to discovering some of our most secret schemes, directly from our true masters, the Dark Ghods themselves."

Interesting. Shaeddor leaped ahead. "Master, the last that I knew, my sister was in possession of our father's journal when she fled from Vaejan, along with our mother's soulstone."

Gorrial nodded. "Indeed, to our knowledge your sister is still in possession of both. The stone is of no consequence, but the journal is. We must know what secrets of ours it contains, and who else has learned about them. You will retrieve the journal for us, and help us to learn its contents. And...you shall kill anyone who gets in your way. Is that clear?"

Shaeddor bowed in assent. "Yes, your will is my own, Master. It will be done. Yet she is in the very heart of our enemy's power. If I am to accomplish such a thing, I will need power to match that."

Gorrial grabbed him by both arms. "Don't worry, my boy; you shall have it, from my own hand. It's so good to have you back at my side. And don't worry about power. When the time comes, and you strike in my name and the names of the Shadow Ghods, you shall have all the power that you require. And once you return the journal and fully prove your great worth to us once more, I have even greater missions in mind for you. You shall become my right hand and my primary messenger. You shall go places where I cannot. And you shall rise high in prominence within the order."

"I will serve only as you command, my master."

"Come, my favored boy. Let us celebrate this day, your return, and the implementation of many great things in the future. Our plots go well. Our confused enemies continue to fall and give way. We have much to be grateful and thankful for. You will feast and dine at my right hand this night. Many of the Six Hundred Dark Servants are with us this evening, several of the sixty Dark Lords, and Three of the Six Dark Champions."

"I will be honored to sit at your side, my master. After this night, I shall be on my mission to serve your will."

"Good. And Shaeddor, do not hesitate to request proper assistance from me if you require such. You need not do these things all on you own."

"Thank you, master. I will come to you first when I have need of anything."

The Dark Khabal banquet that night was a mass of contradictions. It was both ordered and sedate much of the time, and yet part of it off on the fringes and sidelines was incredibly wild, depraved, and debauched–even bloody and violent.

While the High Magus feasted with and received the flow of his honored guests atop a high and broad golden dais, sumptuously appointed, at two other levels, the devoted followers made merry in their own dark ways.

Naked slaves captured from both Tharanor and Urth served the Dark Khabal in every vile capacity imaginable by the wicked. Some of both sexes and even the younger ages were drugged out of their minds to make them more pliable, docile, and obedient.

The servants of evil forced the poor slaves to dance suggestively, and get dragged down among the throngs to be violated, tortured, or even tied down upon sacrificial alters. On such alters they were mutilated, their organs and body parts burned and offered up to the Dark Ghods in a great, festering reek of foul smoke and odors. Blood ran and was splashed everywhere. There were catch pools where some of the followers bathed in it.

At any point, helpless slaves and servants could be tormented and murdered for no reason.

Shaeddor met many of the Darksworn, the Six Hundred, some of whom he had known in the past, before he had ever learned that his master was the High Magus of the Khabal in secret.

Then came more members of the Sixty Dark Lords, more revealed surprises of lords, leaders, and nobles from the Sylurrian high families, who in secret were also lords in the forbidden, Dark Khabal. Now that the Old World of Tharanor knew that the Khabal was openly at work, all of these people would have sentences of death passed on them. They could be killed on sight, without question.

Yet Shaeddor dined in honor with the High Magus, showing to all that the wayward apprentice still had Gorrial's great favor.

Shaeddor rose and bowed to three of the Six Dark Champions of the Order, each of these powerful personages only one step below the High Magus himself, and mighty in the service of the Shadow Ghods.

*Morethar the Violent* was an enormous warrior in shining, polished black steel armor, who supposedly wielded a powerful dark sword laden with evil spells and enchantments. This man, by his very nature, was contentious, quick to anger, and bloodthirsty. Even when he spoke privately with Gorrial, he seemed to barely contain his anger.

Morethar was the High General in command of all the Dark Khabal's armies, and the Knights of Darkness were his bloodguard. He barely recognized Shaeddor's presence and looked upon him with contempt and disdain. They did not shake hands.

After he finished conversing and drinking a bit with Gorrial, Morethar went down among the fighting pit arena as was his wont. There gladiators, slaves, and helpless prisoners were goaded into fighting, maiming, and killing each other, or pitted against monsters or ravenous animals. Here was blood sport for the betting pleasure of the onlookers in the stands and the catwalks above the shallow hive of the blood-drenched fighting pits.

A favorite thing in the pits was to capture an ordinary family and force them to fight each other to the death: brother or sister against brother; husband against wife; children against grandparents; mothers or fathers against their own children. Those who survived could become gladiators, and continue fighting others until they themselves fell.

The other two Dark Champions were very different.

For one thing, they were both female, although that did not make them any less vicious, bloodthirsty, or as cruel as Morethar–they were thus after their own fashions.

*Gemrienne the Vain* was on her own, and appeared young, slender, attractive, and alluring with her long, straight shining tresses of golden hair. She had blood red eyes to match her thin, painted lips. Yet behind her cloying smiles, Shaeddor could sense her seething, nearly steaming with nasty hatred and contempt for all around her.

He sensed that Gemrienne even hated herself most of all. Yet she was in charge of most of the Khabal's spies and espionage, and legend had it that she could infiltrate any place in the two known worlds and beyond. Gorrial secretly told him that Gemrienne had spies watching everyone, including herself, for matters of security and to keep her informed on how others perceived or plotted against her.

If Gemrienne grew too bored or morose, she would leave them for a time and wander around the celebration at all of its levels. She kept a large, bloodstained *korik* at her side. This weapon was little more than a steel spike nearly three feet long, with a sword handle–like a huge icepick. With it she would stalk pretty female slaves and slave children.

Without warning she would draw her korik and stab her victims with it anywhere she wished, often from behind–piercing legs, arms, feet, hands, or even through the belly or torso, or into the neck, mouth, or the eyes. She seldom killed them outright, but left them to suffer or slowly perish from their painful, bleeding wounds.

Then she would turn away and seek yet another pretty victim, or return to her place at Gorrial's high table, not bothering to wash the blood off her stained hands and garments. Then, aroused by her blood lust, she would feast and drink voraciously, or go off somewhere to have her horde of mewling body servants pleasure her in various ways.

Shaeddor noticed that many of Gemrienne's body servants had various wounds, and blatant signs of torture exposed all over them.

Very few of them also had one or both of their eyes left to them.

Gemrienne studied Shaeddor for a moment, and then scribbled something into one of the gilded notebooks she kept ever with her. After that, she completely ignored him, but seemed filled with hatred and murderous contempt reserved especially for the other female Dark Champion present at the feast.

*Cyrisella the Beautiful* was indeed all of that and more. A woman who possessed something of all that was desirable in woman, and yet she was unique in all of her charms, and unlike any other woman who drew breath. Dark, shoulder length hair draped her like soft waves of the Abyss itself–dark beyond dark–veiled her ample, sinuous body.

Her enormous dark eyes beneath the fluttering waves of her dark lashes seemed black at first to him. But no, they were dark midnight blue, as close as eyes could get to being black, and yet still gleam perceptively blue. And those eyes secretly masked the fires of lust, passion, and desire themselves.

Cyrisella's eyes had the power to seduce even strong-willed men and also women, perforce. Let alone her matchless body, the way she moved and spoke, and all else about her.

Cyrisella was the seducer of the Dark Khabal, a succubus in human form who understood every art of desire known to exist. She was also the High Witch of the Khabal's Dark Witches, the female counterparts to the male necromancers and Dark Mages. Gorrial had boasted to Shaeddor that Cyrisella, being one of the most powerful shapeshifters ever born, could take the form of anything female. Indeed, she had many powers and abilities granted solely to her by the Dark Ghods.

Yet her shapeshifting specialized in all of the varieties of the female human form. She could make herself look like any human female, of any race or age, from any culture. And she knew what it took to make others fall in love with and desire her.

Shaeddor read her mind from the very beginning. This was the whore of the Dark Ghods. She had proven that there was nothing so vile that she would not do for her masters: lie, cheat, steal, deceive, betray, and kill. She had played the roles of seducer and assassin for them many times.

Yet she had expanded her powers tenfold when she had pledged herself and all she was to the High Magus and the Dark Ghods. As her Great Offering to them to prove her bond of faithfulness, *the Gonashodul*, Cyrisella had offered up her own daughters, triplets. Triplets she had conceived with a high necromancer, one of the then Sixty Dark Lords. After which she had murdered him in their bed as well, cut his body up into chunks, and disposed of his flesh to the ghouls.

By all appearances, Cyrisella raised her three daughters: Ixijen, Ixcalphonia, and Ixxenia with all the love of any doting mother, and her children she kept shielded and pampered away from all within the Khabal.

Yet when the three girls turned six, and the time of the Great Offering was at hand, Cyrisella drugged them.

And when her babes awoke, they did so in terror, for they were chained to three of the four points of one of the blood altars in the Temple of Shadows, specially prepared for the Dark Ritual of the Gonashodul. Even as her beloved daughters shrieked and cried out to their mother to spare them, Cyrisella smiled and offered their lives, their blood, and their hearts and souls to the High Magus and the Dark Ghods. In return she gained mighty powers so great, that she would use them to make all the worlds of light tremble before her dark abilities.

One by one, the Dark Witch tortured, murdered, and mutilated her own pleading daughters before the Dark Ghods, and was filled with their vile energies. She became one of the mightiest of their servants among the Six, her powers even rivaling the High Magus himself.

And she was also forever damned by those dark acts, to know only of lust, but never of love itself of any kind from that day forth. Such was only the beginning of her personal curse, in payment for her atrocities.

Now Cyrisella appeared to be the very embodiment of Lust itself. She was a living, breathing glamour. The ribbed gown she wore seemed to be from another age entirely, and the very weave and substance must have been magickal in nature, because no normal material could be so transparent. It was as if she wore flowing glass or crystal, transformed some how into cloth.

The Beautiful One was all but naked beneath that clear material. She wore platinum, gold, and white gold caps on the nipples of her high, perfect breasts, the likes of which it appeared that they had been painted upon her succulent flesh. Cyrisella was a walking, moving, flowing statue of fluid, liquid white stone. Her dazzling flesh blazed blinding like snow reflecting the noonday sun.

She wore a similar metal cap over the cusp of her lower charms between her equally perfect legs, which also seemed painted on her luxurious body. Her delicate shoes with their tall heels seemed to be made of the same mix of platinum, gold, and white gold. She wore small waves and sprays of similar precious metals and small, brilliant flickering gemstones across her lovely neck and throat, her lythe hips, and her ankles and wrists.

An ancient sparkling crown or diadem with twin golden cobras, decorated with sacred lapis and emerald, rested on her head, placed perfectly within her dark hair, like some great pagan queen of the elder days.

Cyrisella verbally sparred with both Morethar and Gemrienne in turn, much to Gorrial's amusement. Then when she saw her chance, she slithered up onto the High Magus like a snake and pleasured him there upon his throne, for all to see. He joined with her eagerly, almost in anticipation as they decadently rutted with each other. Many stopped to watch the pair and became mesmerized and enthralled by the very sight. Some few were overcome and lost control of their loins or fainted.

And all the while, Cyrisella stared into Shaeddor's eyes and bent her power on him to make him her own, her slave, as she did with everyone she gazed upon.

She wished for all to desire her.

But to Shaeddor, the great whore was as nothing to him. He yawned and looked aside, relishing the fleeting glimpse of her shock and surprise, and feeling the blazing hate of her eyes trying to bore holes through him.

Let the vile bitch do her worst. She had no power over him.

Too late for his own sorrow, he had learned to love his sweetest, beloved Jen with all his heart and soul while she had lived. Then the mad Khabal had slain her most cruelly and stripped her away from him out of nothing more than spite, as it always did thus to others, without reason.

He knew now the fearful cost of love.

While the Khabal slew and took life indifferently, with nary a thought to the consequences.

Now they all thought him their pawn once more, but another servant. Little did they know what an enemy they had forged and fashioned.

Let them.

Let them continue to think that all was well.

Until the day came that he had each of them where he wanted them, vulnerable, helpless, and exposed—and it would be far too late.

The Black Prince would find his own ways to fulfill his vengeance upon them all, and in his own time. Of that, Shaeddor was certain. And as for himself or his own doom, he cared nothing.

# TORI

Tori and Mason skipped breakfast and rode out just before dawn to the eastern army camps. They sought out David, Jerriel, and the rest of their friends who were departing that morning for Detroit and Toledo. A dozen hand-picked militia guards went with the Pistoleros on bicycles.

The sky was clear, the light of dawn emerged like hope itself. The August air felt humid and damp, but not entirely hot just yet. They traveled calmly in easy silence, enjoying the early morning serenity of birds, bugs, and horses. The morning smelled fresh, even with the aroma of the occasional horse plops. Tori looked about them, scanning the mixed up countryside all around.

Populations on two chaotic worlds were caught up in the desperate aftermath of a terrible cataclysm, most of them working together in order to stay alive.

Within Michiana, Tori knew very well that Mace was looked upon as a local hero, and something more. Tori could see it in the eyes of others. They didn't just respect the Pistolero. Some people almost worshipped him, while others feared and even despised him for the power he wielded. But none of them knew him the way she did.

Her beloved Mason was a deep soul, and though he always did his best to put on a brave, stoic front, he felt things keenly and intensely. Tori had always known that. Everyone told her how powerfully Mason had mourned for her when he thought her dead. How his loss and grief had nearly crippled him as a person, as a man. They also explained how he fought his way back from the brink of that despair.

Yet one thing was certain to her, if not to others. Her Mace would always do his best to use his powers for the good of all. No one had to worry about him taking over or becoming some kind of corrupt warlord or evil tyrant.

Mace just wasn't that way. He'd strive to do what was right, and to help others. And she'd be right there with him, beside him all the way, no matter what.

And if anyone was stupid enough to try to harm him, they would be forced to deal with her.

As far as that went, being the new female Pistolera was weird, to put it lightly. Other than demonstrating her own shooting abilities, and some of her techniques, which were very different from some of Mace's, she had yet to prove herself, to herself and others. True, she had fought bravely at the tail end of their latest war, but she more or less followed Mace's lead and did what he did.

She was an athlete, a former gymnast and a soccer player in her earlier years. Yet that was still very different from being a Champion: an elite enchanted warrior, let alone just a soldier.

Tori knew that she wasn't that great at fighting with her hands and feet, or with various blades or spears. The combat trainers told her that all of the time. She could barely shoot a bow or a crossbow, but at least she had the basic skills down.

Yet because of her Wild Magic powers, some of the fear and respect others had for the Pistolero could not help but transfer over to her, and she strove to make positive use of that. To others, in many ways, she was just like him, and overall her powers served many of the same functions. Such powers by their very nature demanded respect.

Tori strove to be worthy of all those expectations. Even living up to that much was going to be hard enough to accomplish.

They finally joined up with the vanguard of the departing army at the assembly point, far out in front, forty minutes later.

Dirk had provided horses for David and Jerriel, two each. One was for riding, and one was for their gear and supplies. Tori spotted their friends first, readying their mounts, and waved to them. David and Jerriel waved them over. Soon they were all pitching in to help.

Both Mace and Dave loved working with horses.

Like Tori herself, Jerriel seemed fond enough of horses, but simply saw them as necessary to their purposes, and something else that had to be managed and cared for. Horses, frankly, were just more work.

Off to one side, Jerriel and David laughed and argued in jest about how much of their supplies to pack. They were always funny together.

Tori also admired Dave and Jerriel as a couple and was very fond of them. They both seemed quiet yet so deeply devoted to each other, and that was very sweet. Jerriel was stunning, but being a wizard she was also a bit odd.

But David had always been sort of an odd duck himself. To her, Mace's best friend Dave had been such a hunky medieval geek that she often wondered if he had crossed over from some other world in the same way. In that regard and many others, David and Jerriel were absolutely perfect for each other.

As for herself, Mason made Tori smile every time he looked at her. And when they were together, he seldom took his eyes off her for long. Any young woman would be lucky to have her lover look at her that way, and even before the Merge, the two of them had loved each other so tenderly.

Mason made her knees weak, her heart skip beats, and her breath catch in her throat. And all of his cowboy stuff didn't hurt either. Sometimes all that she could think about was having him touch her the way that he did. Having him touch her always seemed like something special.

The Blackhawks had loaded wagons with more supplies, and left places in each where people could rest along the way on top, if need be. Already on short sleep, many of them would be on that rotation. Overnight, many of them and an additional army of supply people had packed and made ready to set forth.

Tori and Mason joined their friends on their own horses to both see them off and ride with them a ways. They did have some last minute information to pass along.

"We've all talked it over with Dirk and the development teams," Mason said. "Just as we all hoped, Rob Billings and the rest of the enchanters worked all night, and have the first of our new transport stations ready. They've been fully tested, and they will work in conjunction with each other. Each station is linked by its own specific, magickal control and operations codes, and it disassembles into twelve pieces or interlocking plates. Each piece can be carried by one person. Our guards have brought the first set with them to be secured in the wagons."

Their guards were already unpacking the strange, wrapped up sections off their bikes and turning them over to the teamsters and officers in charge of supplies and wagons.

Tori jumped in when Mace took a breath. "We're going to send one complete station and an operations team with your army, and keep one station set up here. If, say, you get into trouble and you need more firepower–assemble your station in a secure spot and send someone through to inform us."

"There will always be someone on duty at the other end in South Bend," Mason added. "General Blackwood wants to get transport stations set up in all of the free cities ASAP. You can place yours in Kellendra, if the city can be saved. We can then send you another set to take up to Tornhold, and so on, as they are ready."

Tori took out a map and opened it up as they and their horses on point moved forward, with all of their troops on foot falling in behind them. "Dirk said that the pathfinders and road crews have been working with the eastern border forces and anyone from the other enclaves who were willing to help.

"Together they had cleared some road sections, made trails where needed, and linked trails from here to just across the Ohio line. But since the Elkhart battles, they've been pushed back, and still fall under almost constant monster attack at night."

"I've studied those maps with Jerriel, the princes, and others," David told her. "The farthest point the pathfinders and road crews reached was still a little less than a week from Toledo-Kellendra by horse or foot." David sighed. "Just think, my friends–in the past, with a car on the toll way we could have crossed the same distance in about an hour or two. Those days are long gone."

"Our mapping crews came under heavy attack just before the Elkhart business," Tori said. "They were forced to make a fighting retreat for three days, back to a fortified area where they defended themselves for another two days. Then one morning, the enemy simply melted away."

"Yeah," Pastor Bryan said, "they tend to do that after they lose."

"Have there been any other reports of enemy activities?" Jason Inada asked.

"Unfortunately, they have been too numerous to detail," Tori noted.

The local militia commander accompanying them handed David some paper reports. "There is one strange thing, sir. The scouting teams that penetrated furthest northeast up into Michigan periodically reported strange green lights in the sky at night, especially after sunset and before dawn."

"Strange lights?" Alejandro said. "How wonderful."

Jerriel laughed. "That's not exactly very much to go on."

"No matter," Prince Valandin said. "We must find our way through our foes. Fight our way through if need be."

"We'll be on guard for these silly lights," Thulkara said. "And anything else that will try to stop us on the way to Kellendra."

"Yo-ho!" Thul-Kazar bellowed. They almost broke out into a booming Thull war ballad right then and there.

David and Mason seemed to stop them from doing that at all costs.

"Guys? Guys! No singing yet. Remember we talked about this? No singing right now," David reminded them. "We've barely left South Bend and Ohio's still days of travel away. Like I was saying before, we're going to need to loop up into Michigan. Jerriel, show us on your map exactly where this Nexus point should be. You and the other mages convinced Dirk and the council that we should definitely check that location out along the way."

Jerriel pulled out one of her maps. She and the wizards had drawn strange lines and markings on it in their magical language using bright, colored marking pens. She pointed to a spot outside of Indiana, just past the known areas where the road crews left off. Actually, it wasn't far away, just north up into Michigan, mere hours across the state line.

"As long as we're already going east near that region," she said. "We should swing north to explore that area on our way. It is a place of power and could attract many things."

"Dangerous things?" David asked.

"Possibly very dangerous," Pharrio said. "The risk could be especially great if we run into a wild entity from one of the Tharanorian Spectral Keys, or one of the completely untamed Urth counterparts. They could be the most dangerous beings one might ever face—completely unpredictable."

Jerriel laughed again. "We do not know that for certain. If we encounter one, they might not be so wild or harmful at all. We might even be able to negotiate with them on some rational level."

"Or they could wipe us out without a thought," Maelen said. "That is the point. We just don't know what we will face."

"What if we do encounter one of these entities?" Jason Inada asked, suddenly looking worried. "How do we deal with it? What powers will they have? What can be done against such creatures?"

"Can we reason with it?" Pastor Bryan added. "If it is an entity, can we talk to it? As you say, Jerriel, negotiate with it?"

Jerriel shook her head. "There's just so much we still need to know. Even the High Wizards could not guide us completely here. All of our entities from both worlds are now back to being free and wild, and the Urth ones completely so. They have never been tamed our captured. We are exploring unknown territory there. Only the High Mages from long long ago on Tharanor knew what it was to first tame our entities and join with them. And they never left many notes on how exactly all of that that was done. They never thought that they would need to. The keys were simply passed down from one High Mage to the next."

David stared at her map still. "We'll need to find one of these creatures first," he noted.

Tori folded her map up and tucked it away. She glanced at Mason, and he nodded to her before he spoke. "My friends, we've most definitely come to the edge of Michiana. Tori and I will leave you here and return to town to continue our duties there. We wish you and your forces every success."

"Be safe and return to us," Tori told them. "All of you be careful and take care."

David shook hands with Mason. "Do you think Dirk will send you with those armies and the train to try to reach Indy?"

Mason smiled. "I will strongly suggest that he does. In a day or two we'll have another transport station to take down there with us. Billings and Co. want to send a few of the new balloons with us for observation purposes, and to conduct important tests for the coming dirigibles and the special steam engines to propel them."

Tori knew about all that, and did not relish the thought of them being separated again.

They all shook hands yet again, embraced, and said their final farewells. Militia commanders in the field along the way would keep David and his people informed, and a team of express riders was already with them.

"Farewell, my brother," David said. "You and Tori be well, and stay happy."

Mason grinned ear to ear. "Dave, as long as she's by my side, I'm always happy. Luck to you and Jerriel in the same way."

The two Pistoleros turned their horses around, and headed back into Michiana with their retinue of guards. Tori and Maces returned to South Bend for now, but she wasn't going to be very happy if he left shortly for Indianapolis.

# MASON

Mason and Tori had an equally nice ride back into town. They even fixed a quick breakfast at home and snuggled a bit on the couch for a brief nap afterwards.

That made up for rising before the crack of dawn.

They left word with their guards to ring their front door's mechanical bell shortly before eleven, and to make certain that the Pistoleros answered upon the hour, and made ready to attend to their duties for the remainder of that day.

It was going to be humid yet again, but there was nothing for it. Thunderstorms might roll in later in the dark toward nightfall. They would leave their horses behind and take their bikes. The carriage they were waiting for was still being built, and several other orders for that same design were still ahead of them in the queue.

Mason and Tori brushed their teeth before they went out. He smiled at his dear one. "Where are you bound for this afternoon?" he asked.

Tori spit in the sink, rinsed, washed it down, and then wiped her mouth with a hand towel. He more or less did the same thing, and when he was finished, she kissed him with great enthusiasm. "There, that will have to last you until tonight."

"Never. But we'd better go, before you kiss me like that and it's two hours more before we get out the damn door."

Tori laughed, her eyes sparking. "You're so bad."

He laughed with her. "What? Before you said I was the best. I'm hurt."

She placed her hand over his heart and met his glance with her deep brown eyes.

She would never know how lost he was in those eyes.

"You are the best, and my only, forever, Mason. Each day I pray for the sun to fall, for the joy of our nights together. If you go on that mission to Indy, I understand, but we'll still miss one another all the while." She pulled away, gathered her things together, and sighed. "I know we both have duties and responsibilities, to both sides.

Mason was already set to go. "We'll know more after today, Tori. The Astral scouts will be back and make their reports. Most of the train units are already waiting for the word to set out. I'll be with Rob Billings and the invention teams most of today. We'll be up in balloons and testing parachutes as well."

Tori shook her head. "You know I couldn't do that with my fear of heights. And mister, don't you get yourself killed skydiving, either."

Mason chuckled. "I won't be the one jumping today, just watching others do so. But some day soon I'll have to get my wings, and maybe you too!"

Her eyes got big. "Oh, no. No way in hell. Not me. I can do without my wings just fine, thank you very much."

"Honey, parachute technology was unaffected by the Merge, and we had nearly perfected that as it was. There are fast release chutes that are highly maneuverable and very reliable."

She pointed a finger straight at him and her eyes flashed. "Don't honey me. Every time you use that word it means something I'm not going to like. So you can keep your honey in a jar, and my feet flat on the ground!

"Wait until they launch the new steam powered airships, Tori. You've seen some of the designs. We'll take to the skies again. We'll have to stand in line to get on one."

"Not me. You'll be standing in that line by yourself, bucko!" She opened the front door and went out, saying good morning to the troops guarding their home.

Mason went after her and secured the door behind them.

They wore their outlaw hats to keep the sun off them, but for bike riding they kept their dusters folded up in one of their saddlebag baskets beside their rear wheels. In their roles as the Pistoleros of Michiana, each of them wore pants, boots, and a western-style, cotton bib shirts with a bandana around their necks. Mace wore all black. Tori's shirt was bright red, but her bandana was black. Her pants and all of her leathers, including her hat, were brown, and her hat band had brass accents.

They rolled their shirt sleeves up and left their bibs open somewhat when it was hot.

For ironmongery, matching their namesakes, each of them wore three pairs of loaded pistols in custom rigs. Three matching sets down each side from armpit to thigh, strapped down and secure. Naturally, Tori gravitated toward the smaller frame revolvers, but she could fire the largest hawg leg with pinpoint accuracy if she was put to it.

She and Mace practiced at the range with their reloaders every other day, usually firing their pistols dry, unless they were testing new magic ammo components.

Today was an off day.

Yet even in times of relative peace, their whereabouts were always noted by Army command, and a team of their reloaders were kept close by, ready at a moment's notice to assist them. In the recent past, things had gone sour many times, and their enemies went to great lengths to surprise them.

The Pistoleros and all of the other defenders of Michiana learned through much sorrow and hardship that they had to be ready at a moment's notice to defend what little they had left after the Merge.

"So, I'll be spending most of the day with R & D, sweetie. Where are you bound?"

Tori rolled her eyes. "First I'm doing army recruitment service at several places on the other side."

Mason chuckled. "Hey, you could tell them to join the new balloon corps there. Just suck it up. We all have to do the recruitment thing."

"Yeah, I know. I'm just not the Shooting Stars. I don't like the limelight and I'm not as perky and 'Gung Ho!' as they are about things."

"Tori, you're only six months older than both of them, and I'd say you are very perky, my beloved one."

"Thanks…" She reached out and lightly shoved him, causing him to veer slightly on the road.

"Hey!" he exclaimed.

"You know I didn't mean it *that* way, you goof. Oh. This is where I turn off. See ya tonight, loverboy!"

"Have a nice day, honey!" Their guards split off as well, half going with each of them.

Huge warehouses and factories near downtown had been converted into research and development zones, for science, engineering, magickal, and medical. And new exciting combinations of those fields of study.

There were places like this one the other side as well.

Robert Billings the Chief Enchanter had become the town's foremost magical dabbler and a major contributor and partner to a cadre of other various mages, engineers, and inventors. Both Mason and Dave had friends and acquaintances who chose to work in those fields, in one capacity or another.

In their various labs and research venues, protected by the Army and the expanding Mage Council, they did their best each day to wrangle and attempt to solve various technological and magickal problems for the survivors.

Mason was clearly recognized as the Pistolero at a set of doors, but he offered his ID up in any case to the guards, and was ushered within. He spotted his friend, working with a couple of mages and what appeared to be several engineers, gathered around something that looked like a small generator attached to a bunch of other equipment.

Rob was an unassuming guy, with his short moppish, sandy hair, shot with gray, round brass spectacles, and a bushy mustache. But since becoming an enchanter, he had a knack for perceiving magic forces and how they might be applied–a good ability to have for enchanters.

He simply wore regular Urth clothes, shirts and jeans, unlike some of the other researchers and mages who chose to wear lab coats, mage robes, or even overalls or coveralls.

The young mages took turns shooting small quantities of lightning or magical electricity into the device, which would then shudder and shake for a few seconds and then go still once more.

On one occasion, some of the wires caught fire.

The researchers were so intent on their work that none of them, including Rob, noticed Mason walking up to them.

"Hey Rob, better luck next time, eh?"

Rob turned, blinked, and smiled. "Hey, Mace. You made it." He turned to the rest of the team. "You guys continue with the tests. I know it's not very promising, but we have to test and record the full range of variables."

Rob walked away from the team and Mason followed him.

"So, Rob," he asked. "What's up with all of that?"

Rob grimaced and shook his head. "Re-harnessing electricity still eludes us. Since the Merge, gaining an understanding of it has been difficult to say the least. None of our machines or devices seem capable of doing so. It's as if electrical fields specifically work to burn them out. That's crazy.

"We can't even get simple light bulbs to work. All they do is fry or explode. Thank goodness we're having better luck in other areas. Come on. We have some time to look in on some of the other labs before the parachute tests."

Rob led him briefly outside and over to the next building with barely a nod to the guards.

As soon as they went inside they could smell various chemicals.

They walked up to Kevin Policinski and several researchers, all in lab coats and goggles. Some of them marked various plastic jugs with stickers and markers, and took them into what appeared to be a darkroom.

Kevin was working with an old mechanical 35 mm camera and even a 35 mm movie camera, taking pictures and short snippets of film. Once he was finished, the cameras were handed off to the darkroom as well.

Rob called out. "Kevin, what's up today? Any luck?"

Kevin greeted them in his normal, subdued style, his shiny dark hair swept to one side, his face further framed with a short black mustache and beard. Since the Merge he kept a rapier strapped to his side, just in case.

He flung up one hand in frustration.

"We're still trying to re-engineer photography. We can make plates and negatives with various cameras, and even magical light flashes, but the sticking point is still the developing chemicals. They don't work properly any longer. We can produce negatives and even film, but the images don't last. We can't fix them. Even the photographic paper doesn't seem to be correct. Everything is all out of whack."

Rob grimaced again. "We're even more behind with the electrical experiments, I'm afraid."

Kevin showed them the faded, blurry, almost useless pictures they were producing. "We think that we're going to have to experiment with other reagents and solutions, and more or less find completely new compounds that will do what we want them to. It's like re-inventing the wheel all over again, only worse."

"How about the magical lighting programs?" Rob said. "I haven't heard from them in days."

Kevin nodded, taking off his black rubber gloves. "They're just across the hall. And I'm pretty sure they're doing better than we are."

The three of them crossed over, into a large dark room and multitudes of glowing glass jars, tubes, and various luminous plant specimens. Mason noted three very different types of small glowing tree saplings in big wooden tubs, set upon four wheeled carts like a big version of a kid's wagon.

Kevin introduced Mason to a tall woman in her forties who came over to them, still wearing gloves and goggles. Her lab coat was splattered with glowing chemicals. "This is Trudy Oliver. She's a chemical engineer, in charge of studying the Tharanorian plants and trees with natural lighting capabilities."

Trudy smiled. "Gentlemen. I won't shake hands with you, since I have chemicals on them. So, this is the famous Pistolero. I had no idea you were so young, Captain."

Mason smiled and tipped his hat. "I get that a lot, ma'am."

"None of that. Call me Trudy, or you'll make feel even more like an old lady."

"Trudy, anything new today? Give Mason the fifty cent tour."

"Well…this is your lucky day." She walked them past their glowing plant samples, pointing out several.

"Tharanor has many luminescent plants, flowers, and trees. Luma, nistil, and siko flowers and blooms can be kept in what are basically flower boxes, watered and given good sun during the day. They will provide indoor lighting for weeks that is dim, but constant while in bloom, about that of a 25 watt bulb. Better than nothing, but free. Telepsu flowers will give off about the same light all year round in planters kept inside, safe and warm from the chill of fall and winter."

Mason looked around. "You're right. The light is dim, but it's still useful. Much preferable to total darkness."

Trudi grinned. "We're starting greenhouse programs to spread the plants throughout the populations as a back up light source, if nothing else. But we're perfecting something even better." She took them to a spot with a bunch various boxes on shelves, with clipboards and dates.

"Are these the light globes we made?" Rob asked.

Trudy nodded. "We're still testing them, but we're certain that this is going to be a breakthrough." She opened one. A brighter light flooded that area, coming from a globe in the box, shining with a blue-white liquid or energy swirling within.

"Now that's amazing," Mason said. "How fast can we make these babies?"

Trudy picked the shining globe up and held it in her hands. "We've been experimenting with various concentrations and combinations of the glowing nectar of the flowers, placed in a glass bulb or sphere, and infused with magical energy from the mages, all in a vacuum. The effect will not work in the open air.

"The resulting light is somewhere between a 40 watt, and a 60 watt bulb. More than acceptable as a potential light source, but they are difficult to make. Acres of glowing flowers must be crushed and their nectar concentrated in order to make each light globe, and then they must be infused with light magic from the enchanters like Rob."

"How long do they last?" Mason asked.

"We made this one a month ago, and it is still just as bright as when we first made it. We have different kinds, some of which naturally glow with other colors."

Mason thought about something. "I haven't seen any of this in the papers. This is amazing. When do you intend to tell the public about these new developments?"

Rob sighed. "When we're a little closer to being able to mass produce them in quantities that people can actually use. Unfortunately, this is still the testing and development phase. Otherwise, it might be too frustrating to dangle such things before the public, and then be unable to dispense them for actual use."

Trudy closed the box, and finally brought them before the glowing trees. "And here we have the famous trees of light. The first is the telepsu tree. It's leaves glow, but strangely enough, its sap does not. The leaves can be harvested and crushed and infused with magic in a light globe, but the resulting light is bright green.

"Next we have the giima tree and its glowing, mango-like fruit. Which is inedible to most humans and animals and insects, as far as we know. Only the fruit glows, and if you dry the fruit under the proper conditions, the dried fruit grows even brighter. And the seeds glow also. The fruit juice glows and can be concentrated as well."

"Wow," Mason said. "Glowing prunes."

Trudy chuckled and moved on. "Not really, but close enough. And finally, the rulka, or fire trees. That's kind of a misnomer, because rulka wood and leaves do not burn—they are completely invulnerable to fire. Which makes it highly useful as a building material in any number of ways. Just think. Wooden houses that won't burn down. Cloths made from their fibers that resist heat."

Mason took the bait. "So, why are they called—"

"Fire trees?" Rob said. "Tell him, Trudy."

"Gladly. The fire tree sap is incredibly flammable. It nearly bursts into flame on its own, and burns cleanly, slowly and efficiently. It can be tapped from the trees in great quantities. After filtration to remove impurities, it can be used as both an excellent fuel and heat source."

Kevin jumped in. "And it can be weaponized, used in various fire bombs and incendiary devices, including flamethrowers and napalm sprayers. Our enemies already know about it, and use it regularly in their fire weapons."

Mason smiled. "Impressive, guys. All of the lighting stuff alone is a huge breakthrough, and now this."

"On the magickal side," Rob told them, "some mages have learned to cast a 'light mist' spell over a large area, almost sixty feet in diameter. Depending on the wind, the mist spell can illuminate the area for almost an hour before fading. Then there are improved flash spells to temporarily blind opponents up to entire units.

"Sorcerers can even learn to reverse the process and create darkness fields that will negate and snuff out normal light sources. They can even cast darkness spells over an area in full daylight that can last for up to twenty minutes. Then there are various modification to fire spells for mages who specialize in fire magic."

"Tori and I might even be able to incorporate some of that in our gun loads," Mason said. "Rob, have samples of all of this stuff sent our reloaders and magic bullet researchers."

"I will. Kevin, Trudy, keep up the good work. We're crossing over to the steam works, and then the balloon fields."

"Will do," Trudy said.

"Hey," Kevin told them. "Let's get together at my place sometime and hang out. I can make some homemade pizza on the grill."

"You got it," Rob said.

"Sounds good," Mason added. He hadn't had a decent slice of pizza since...well, not since the Merge.

Rob led Mason out another door and they kept walking. They could hear the steam whistles and the rattle, clank, and clang of various refurbished steam engines and motors donated from museums in several of the workshops nearby. Some were still being repaired.

Mason could smell coal smoke and the steam vapor from oiled machines, and the sweat of many people laboring in the growing heat and humidity.

"The enemy screwed up in one major way," Rob noted. "When they botched up our various technologies to set us back, they apparently ignored steam power. A hundred years ago, our entire world ran on steam. Steam trains, steamships, steam machines, engines, and factories. And now we have a chance to bring that all back, but with a new twist. Now we have magic, which can be fashioned into an efficient power source. And we can incorporate that along with steam power in exciting new combinations that will be even more efficient and powerful. We call it— *Steam Magic*."

One of the refurbishing plants was near an old abandoned train depot with dilapidated locomotive repair shacks from nearly a century ago or more.

Several steam engines in various states of repair waited on separate sections of track. Those closest to being fully operational were being worked on by teams of people like ants on an anthill.

Some the locomotives were still in parts, scattered around them, marked with notes in chalk, grease pencil, or on separate boards. The notes detailed what condition they were in or what work needed to be done.

"We have trains preparing to go to Elkhart, Mishawaka, and Granger every day and back to South Bend," Rob said. "Elkhart has a number of trains from a museum there that will share the rails with ours. Antique steam tractors will work in our fields. And we have even better things on the way. That's just some of the stuff I wanted to share with you today, Mace."

They went past another area with the army train and its armored cars, and troop carriers, much of it still draped in tarps and canvas. But it was already loaded up and ready to go, simply awaiting the word to set out for Indianapolis, along with the troops and the track-laying work crews to get it there.

Even if they had to fight their way there.

The guards recognized both Rob and the Pistolero, and ushered them into just one of the steam power labs.

"We're lucky in other ways, if we can survive long enough," Rob said. "Hydraulics still function. As long as we have a stable, reliable power source, anything with compression or hydraulics will still work.

Inside the research lab, teams of engineers, scientists, designers, mages, and manufacturing experts pored over several projects designed to get factories and machines humming, and working steam technology out the door and functioning, everywhere it could be set up.

Mason saw what appeared to be combination steam and magic engines and motors of various sizes.

One massive device was an expansion of an already much smaller–yet already functioning prototype. This version was obviously meant for trains…or possibly large steamships.

Another smaller variation was being modified to propel a bus. Another, a box truck. Yet another, a semi tractor trailer. Mason didn't see a steam car, but such a version was only a matter of time.

There was even a steam engine small enough to be fitted to a motorcycle frame. And another smaller still, to propel a bicycle.

And for the army: a steam magic tank.

"A tank?" Mason said aloud. "You're kidding me!"

Rob nodded. "We'll be able to make it run, but the engine will need to be protected better. Of course the cannon and the machine guns won't work, but we could install flame throwers. Or mages could shoot spells out of the barrel or gun ports while being protected inside."

They ducked outside of that building to what appeared to be a firing range. What looked to be several kinds of cannons and guns of various sizes were connect to pressurized hoses from other numerous steam hoses or actual boilers nearby.

"These are top secret," Rob said. "Steam cannons and different steam guns, that can propel solid shot and antipersonnel rounds similar the Civil War canister and double canister cannon loads. Incendiary projectiles have also been developed, and steam propelled rounds similar to a .50 caliber machine gun. Steam rifles would be useable by onboard personnel on vehicles. Right now they're slow and fire one shot at a time. But we can work on increasing their rate of fire."

"They'll be devastating when used at fixed positions like the city walls," Mason said. "But not much good in the field. The engines and the pressure hoses leading to the steam guns will make them too vulnerable—just sever the hoses. How does the ammunition work?"

"They load shots mechanically with a simple blowback design, chambering the next slug into position. No gunpowder is needed. No cartridges. Just lock in the next projectile. There's a delay of about ten seconds between each shot fired, until sufficient pressure builds up, as measured by a simple gauge, and the weapon is ready to discharge once more."

Mace did the math easily. "Amazing. That's still six shots every minute. Yet that can be a long time with a horde of monsters charging at you. Are the rounds accurate and to what range? What kind of damage to they do upon impact?"

"With rifled barrels, the small steam guns are accurate up to two hundred meters or more. Very acceptable for the battlefield. If you look at these ballistic gelatin samples, you can see what kind of wounds they cause. Mostly just high velocity and penetration injuries, but sufficient to slay an opponent struck in a vital area, or at least riddle them with holes upon impact."

"Excellent," Mason said. "The trains and the fortresses can be armed with these along the walls, especially for stationary positions. This is a huge breakthrough."

Rob took him over to a portion of the range where they tested a semi-automatic steam rifle with its own small, steam magic backpack. Mason took off his hat, loaded one on his back, and fired away, one shot each ten seconds. He punched paper targets for spotters out to a hundred yards.

"It works!" Mason said. "Yet I still say the hoses are a big issue in the field. If they get cut, or the couplings get broken, or the engine is damaged, the entire rig is kaput! The backpack engine only weighs about twenty pounds, but it's still awkward and cumbersome."

Rob smiled. "We've considered all of that," Rob told him. "These are just prototypes. The actual working versions will be made of high strength plastic and the packs will weigh ten pounds or less. Look at this semi-auto pistol version. The steam magic power source straps right to the forearm or hip.

Mason slipped into one, the pistol looking very similar to the old broom handled Mauser machine pistols of the past century. He fired some shots at the pistol targets, making acceptable hits. "I like the tiny engine better on the arm, not the hip."

"The engine and the hoses can be protected by a light, flexible plastic housing," Rob said.

"I like the way these steam guns fire," Mason said, squeezing off a few more rounds. "And I like the mechanical clips. Because there's no gunpowder, you can carry more ammo and reload less. And there's no explosion, muzzle flash, or gun smoke to give away your position. These steam guns snap or champ with a machine sound, and very little recoil. I think you have another winner here, Rob."

His friend grinned. "And we're still developing them. We just don't have artillery s rounds that explode anymore. No HE rounds."

Mason thought on that, and about his own weapons. "You're a mage. What about explosive runes or wards enchanted on the projectiles?"

Rob sadly shook his head. "We've tried that, even with mortars. All of those tests were disasters. When you fire them, there's no delay. The explosive magic goes off, and the rounds burst in the air, if not inside the weapon itself. The principle works with arrows, bolts, catapults and trebuchets, but not with high velocity cannons and artillery pieces."

"Well," Mason said, "nothing is ever completely easy, is it?"

"No, it's not." Rob checked his old style pocket watch. "All right, we do need to get over to the air fields, now. Ready to go up in one of our observation balloons for the parachute tests?"

"I sure arm," Mason said.

"Lets check out a couple of bikes from the bike pool and pedal our butts over there."

As they did, Mason could already spot one round balloon and a larger cylindrical model with tapered ends, launching into the sunny sky ahead of them. The sky was patched with lazy white clouds and the winds were slow. A fine day for aerial tests and exercises.

If they did drive upon Indy, Mason also wanted air support to go with them.

# DAVID

In two hours time, thanks to the improved roads, David, Jerriel, and their companions reached the eastern border forts in relative fair weather. Michiana work crews, attempted to clear the way and repair some of the damage from the recent wars and near constant enemy attacks on the edge of known Michiana territory.

As soon as they passed beyond this point, they were officially off the current maps and into wild, uncharted areas that extended north, east, and south. Most of the former state of Michigan—or what the Tharanorans called *Shendor*—was now included in that.

All that David knew was that there were large enemy forces lurking out there in the unknown to their north, and human enclaves clinging to life in the former cities of Kalamazoo, Battle Creek, Jackson, Ann Arbor, and Detroit, and then back across the very southeast corner near Toledo, which they knew now was already under heavy assault by their ambitious foes.

Dead monsters and enemies stood staked out with warnings alongside them on placards. Of course the monsters could not read, but their human masters and lackeys could. The words of those warnings were boldly written, both in Urther and in Tharanorian.

The Blackhawks and the Marrandorians of the vanguard went forward with the border crews, and then the scouts, marching fearlessly into the unknown, weapons ready. The main hosts of Michiana Army Number Sixteen being sent with them stretched out half a day behind them or more, slowly meant to catch up with them over a matter of days.

By comparison, Armies Twenty-seven and Thirty-three had a full platoon of mages with them, and mirrored their progress on the other side. Their mission was similar, to reach the defender enclaves on their half with the first transport station constructed in the other dimension. They could also use the devices at preset times to remain in contact with one another.

Most of the troops in the Army on this side simply referred to themselves collectively by their army number: Sixteen.

David noticed that the border teams and militias were a mix of mostly Urthers but also some few Tharanorians who had reached them somehow. They all had hashed out their own batch of hand signs and working language as the weeks passed, and were already cooperating on a large scale. Jerriel handed out a few translation medallions to the leaders, to help further facilitate communicated between the allies.

He could not help wondering if any of these Tharanorians were spies, either for the Khabal or the Old World nations.

Yet he also found it interesting what both peoples from the very different two worlds could accomplish when their mutual survival was at stake. And when they worked together.

The Blackhawk vanguard of Sixteen turned north, following a ley line straight up into Michigan-Shendor. Jerriel had explained to him that her people considered the Upper Peninsula area to be a separate land, called Shenedar.

As they continued on, first the border teams peeled off, and then finally the border scouts grew unwilling to accompany the vanguard any further.

They would not do so without heavy reinforcements.

The bodies staked out in retaliation by the foe at that point were now Urthers—captured from the same Michiana scouts, work crews, and militias. Most of the dead were mutilated in some way, or had looks of fear and agony frozen on their faces. Many corpses were gnawed down to the bone by monsters, either before or after death.

The scout leader spat on the ground before heading back. "The enemy puts them out at night sometimes, after our people go missing. We don't see or hear anything. They just show up by dawn the next day in such places as this. We have to take the bodies back with us if we can. Otherwise, if we just bury them, the enemy sniffs out the graves and digs them right back up."

The man had a hollow look to his face. He'd clearly seen too many of his comrades and good people die.

"How much road did you lose during the retreat?" David asked, writing a quick note in his first report to send back to Dirk.

"Two day's worth; maybe three put together," the scout leader noted. "It still shifts back and forth and changes almost on a daily basis, but the attacks and raids always come from the north, now. Well, I'm sorry, but we can't guide you after this point. You have the same older maps from the few long range scout teams who made it back early on, as to where the best road segments continue north or east. You can link up with them as best you can if you need to. The road segments are the fastest way to keep traveling, if you can get to them. Some go on for miles, but many are also blocked at times by piles of old stalled cars or trucks."

"We can get around those," David said. "So, you're saying we're going to be pretty much on our own from this way forward?"

"Yep. Especially if you go north. Afraid so, Captain. Good luck to you and your people."

"We expected that at some point. Thank you, Lieutenant. Same to you." They shook hands in parting.

The vanguard continued north up the road while it lasted, reinforced teams of skirmishers front, back, and on the flanks.

The vanguard was ready to be attacked.

They fully expected to be attacked.

When the attacks did not hit them right away, they traveled a bit faster.

Close to the end of that day, they reached the farthest end of yet another stretch of broken road and David assessed the area.

Sadly, bones and old, desiccated human and animal corpses from the time of the Merge were nearly everywhere, leading down from the north.

But months later, after the summer heat and scavengers, the stench of so much death and rot had lessened. Yet the very rumor of it was still on the winds.

That region seemed haunted as the sun began to set.

Many Urthers had died in the area, trying to make it south.

Then, in some places, the signs of carnage turned from months to only weeks or even days old. Yet even these fresh kills had already been picked over by scavengers or worse, where they fell.

Most of the lesser monster spawn only came out at night, or on extremely cloudy days. They could not endure full sunlight.

Enemy mercenaries and other greater minions were another matter.

David and Jerriel and many others felt sick as they read the obvious signs on the ground.

Small bands of human survivors were clearly still out there somewhere. Hiding, desperate, most likely out of food, water, and supplies by now. Such bands struggled and traveled as best they could, trying to make it to some safer place.

These were the signs, unfortunately, that many small bands of survivors such as these reached this dead zone and were most likely cut off in the night by the monster hordes on the hunt.

They did not make it out.

David included all of their observations in his daily report, to be relayed back to Michiana by the host of special, mounted express couriers he brought with them.

David spoke with the rider he would send back.

"Send word to the road crews to reclaim this area and keep going. The main body of our army should only be ten hours behind us by now. See that these reports and messages are sped back to General Blackwood by you and the other express riders. I'm advising that our military send further reinforcements up into this hotly contested region.

"There is clear evidence that survivors from up north are still attempting to reach Michiana in significant numbers. An entire army must be sent up here to look for and retrieve them, when and where possible."

All of the express riders were young, brave beyond question, and superb riders. The teenage girl with the big brown eyes and the White Sox cap quickly saluted him. "Yes, sir. Will do, sir!"

David said a little prayer for the young girl in his heart and turned back to his business at hand. He was only a few years older than her, but now after the wars, sometimes he already felt like an old man.

Some of the army troops had horses, some of them had bikes that they pedaled slowly or walked beside. Some just walked and kept their bikes hooked on one of the wagons.

"Traveling in the wake of our army should be a huge boost for the road crews, and long range scouting patrols out this way," Jason Inada said. "It should only take another day or so for our other army to expand up this way."

Alejandro laughed. "Sure, while we do the scouting, and stumble into all of the enemy threats and traps."

"That's why we are the vanguard," Thul-Kazar said, shaking his great fist defiantly. "Just think of it, my friends. The honor of first combat is all ours!"

"How I love honor," Al muttered. Thul-Kazar laughed and lifted him off the ground in a huge bear hug.

Al protested calmly. "Please, you big scary, smelly giant of a man. Put me down this instant. This is undignified, for the Eagle of the West to be dangled in such a fashion as this."

They all had a good laugh at that. Thul-Kazar could pretty much dangle any one of them if he had a mind to. But everyone felt better with the two mighty Thulls along with them.

David turned to Jerriel to ask her something and saw that she still studied the ley line and nexus map intently.

"We'll be within range of the nexus sometime tonight, within a few more hours after dark I think," she said. The eagerness in her words were plain to hear.

"I'm not sure if that's the best idea," David told her. "Perhaps we shouldn't go there at the end of the day when all of our forces are exhausted from a long day of marching. But all of this waiting is making everyone nervous at the same time. You wizards must have ice water in your veins. You have everyone pretty spooked."

"That is not our intent, David," Jerriel said.

"I know that."

"The potential dangers are very real. We only discuss the matter openly to inform everyone as much as we can."

"I know that too," he said. "But we still have to face it all when the time comes, and I don't want a lot of our troops turning and running at the first sign of trouble, because their fears of the unknown have been hyped up."

"There might come a time when we should run," she told him.

By the height of the red sun sinking on the horizon near the end of their first day, they had less than an hour of daylight left. They had made good progress, covering many miles.

"Jerriel, I'm calling it," David said. "I don't think it's a good idea for us to keep traveling at night. We might just have to tackle this Nexus thing in the morning, when we're all fresh. Let's make camp and set up our defenses here while we have time to do so. This looks like a good place. We have a low, wooded hilltop that provides us with a full view around us for a mile or more. We can even put scouts with binoculars up in the treetops to see further out."

The vanguard kept a cold camp that evening. No fires were needed since it was still late summer. They camped concealed among the forested hilltop with pickets and defensible positions set up in rings, and plenty of scouts and listening posts established all around them.

The really scary stuff didn't start up until a few hours past midnight, beneath a clear, starlit sky and a moon that was nearly full.

The ground beneath the Vanguard rumbled. It even rippled under them at times. Trees shook violently. Some up-ended and toppled over to the ground, or rolled or slipped down the hillside.

Weird lights of green, yellow, and white flashes and bursts did in fact appear in the sky. It all took place in the distance not too far away, just beyond their range of sight.

They spotted lights to the north and slightly east nearby, right where the Nexus was.

Had they marched through the night, they would have reached it hours before, and have a front row seat for the current fireworks.

Eerie green flashes continued to arc and burst forth, tendrils of strange energy. Then scarlet lightning veined black rent the sky. Crashes of thunder split the air. Dave and everyone could make out weird cries on the rushing winds. Sudden deafening blasts and explosions split the firmament.

From their vantage points, a dark mist, a fog of shadow, or some form of weird, magickal smoke or mist swelled up from the ground and towered up into the sky in a black pillar of darkness enveloping that exact area. Only it stayed in one place like a frozen cyclone, resisting the efforts of the light breezes to disperse it. It was clearly unnatural.

The tower of dark mist grew, lit from within by continued eruptions of the strange powers that seemed to be warring against each other inside.

David and the princes looked to Jerriel and the other wizards for some kind of rational explanation. They had none to give.

Jerriel swallowed hard. "I was afraid of this. It's happening now. We have to get up there, as quickly as we can."

"We have to go in there?" Al said.

David asked her once. "Are you sure of this, Jerriel?"

She sighed and nodded.

"Strike the camp and advance with the rear guard and our skirmishers around us," David commanded "All other troops form up and move out with us. Prepare for battle. Express riders, get word to our main forces that we are engaging the enemy. They should try to join us by some time tomorrow."

"Prepare for anything," Pharrio warned them all.

Their chosen path led them rapidly across the countryside. With only a few hours of rest, they marched through shallow vales between the low hills up across fallow, unplanted farm fields now overgrown and wild.

In less than two hours they would reach the nexus and whatever was happening there.

They kept marching quickly.

An hour and a half later, just before they entered the strange dark funnel of mist a quarter mile up ahead, their scouts reported enemy monster hordes charging their way overland at top speed, through the patches of forests, fields, and grassy sloughs.

"How many?" David asked.

"We don't know for sure!" the terrified young trooper said, gasping. Someone handed him a canteen and he took a quick sip. "Three or four thousand at least. And that's just what we could see, sir!"

"What?" David said. Their vanguard was a little over a thousand troops in total, including the Marrandorians as half of that. They were already up against four to one odds at best, with the bulk of their army still camped nine hours behind them. That might as well be nine days.

"Three or four thousand at the very least, sir. What the hell do we do?"

David drew his sword and put his hand on the scout's shoulder. "We prepare to fight, soldier. We stand together and take them down. That's the only way we'll make it out of this. Together."

The trooper nodded, still petrified. "Yes, sir."

"Good man. Rejoin your unit and fight well. Protect each other. I will alert the Two Hundred. They know who they are. Two Hundred!" he called out. "Stand ready with your enchanted weapons if we need you."

There were still several minutes to pick their ground and prepare their positions. David did his best to set them up. The princes did the same thing with their people. The field of battle wasn't the greatest. It was somewhat flat and exposed, but it wasn't a deathtrap, by any means.

More reports. The enemy scattered in all directions. Torgs, ka-torgs, mor-kahls, and gozogs. The Blackhawks had fought such hordes of Darkspawn before and beaten them many times.

Strangely enough, some of the monsters weren't even carrying weapons.

Then David realized as he watched the hordes through his field glasses. These monsters weren't running to attack the vanguard.

They were panic stricken. They fled in an all out attempt to escape something behind them.

A massive explosion ripped through the area with the epicenter less than a mile away. Cries of terror and death up ahead of them were silenced moments later, as the first blast wave shattered the area with an advancing wall of thermal force.

A glowing green wall of strange transparent energy flattened everything in its path that did not get down. That included shrieking horses, wagons, and troops.

But as for the monsters, the energy wave obliterated them on contact.

Oddly enough, it spared the large standing rocks, plants, and trees somehow, washing through or over them and leaving them apparently untouched. The energy blast was selective somehow, and passed through them without crushing, snapping them off, or doing any major damage to them.

David was left breathless, flat on his back, and he had expected the entire forest around them to be flattened and laid low, or at the very least on fire.

That many trees crashing down on their forces would have killed and injured many.

With all of their wagons and horses flipped over in disarray, the damage to the vanguard appeared to be bad enough.

The dark cloud of dust scattered over the area, obscuring everything, choking man and beast.

The first thing David and his friends saw when they looked out of the vale and into the lower farm fields were deep, glowing green rents in the very earth itself, covering two or three miles of terrain. Everything within that zone of devastation had been ripped or blasted apart, including the trees, and the rocks themselves.

"By the Light itself! What are we up against?" Prince Valandin shouted against the roar of the dust winds whipped up. "What power could have done these things?"

"This is Urth Power, Urth energy. It is one of the wild Spectral Entities unleashed," Jerriel said. "It must be. Perhaps even more than one."

"Does it belong to Urth or Tharanor?" Urnessan shouted.

"We have no way to discern that, as yet," Pharrio told them.

"Jerriel," David said. "How do we fight something like this?"

Even she was staggered and at a loss. "I...I don't think we can, my love. This is a force or nature on a rampage."

More lesser blasts of power shook the ground and shuddered the very air in the distance, making them jump as the shock of them recoiled, echoed, and washed over them, even from such a distance.

"There's some kind of a major battle heating up over there," Maelen noted.

"It must be the Shadow Mages," Jerriel said. "They've gotten there ahead of us! We cannot let them seize the key and the entity for their evil purposes."

"Perhaps they've already captured one the entities and are using it to locate and ensnare another," Urnessan surmised.

"We'd better hope and pray that that is not the case," Jerriel said.

"Sir," a forward scout cried out, racing ran back to them. "Remnants of the enemy are back on their feet, coming right out of the ground where they dug in and hid themselves. There are hundreds of them and they're charging right at us."

"This is all too weird," David said. "Let's hold our position and see what happens this time."

The ground shook and trembled.

Hundreds of enemy forces streamed down the trails and fanned out, scattering into the country side as reported.

They passed on as quickly as they could, not even bothering to attack.

The terrified creatures actually bounced off of the vanguard shield wall, were put down, or otherwise streamed around the troops, seeking only to escape with their lives. They trampled and slew each other to get away.

Valandin stepped out onto the road and crossed over to David.

"Did you see their faces?" the prince asked. He himself looked stunned.

David nodded, "Yes. They weren't attacking. They were fleeing at all hazards."

"They didn't even have weapons," Valandin said. "They'd torn off their armor. They were completely terrified beyond all thought or reason!"

Then the wounded and dying monsters came upon the heels of their fellows. Horribly scorched, ripped apart–partially melted or dissolved– limping and dragging what was left of themselves, collapsing and dying as they still tried to flee.

David never thought that he could feel pity for such terrible creatures.

"What could do this to them?" Alejandro asked in awe, his face pale.

David gave the order. "Strike Force advance! Put them down. None of them will last long in this state. Put those poor creatures out of their misery!" He did feel sorry for them, as evil and destructive as they were. Any living thing reduced to such a state of suffering and despair was pitiable.

"Some of them are begging to die," Jerriel said. Even she was horrified.

"How do we keep this from happening to us?" Jason asked.

"What are you saying?" Al said.

"Do not worry," Thul-Kazar said. "As long as I draw breath, I will help any of you die if it comes to such horror as this."

"Oh, I feel so much better now," Al said. "Thank you. Is everyone ready to march forward into certain death and torment now, knowing that the big scary, hairy, smelly man will finish us all off quickly and cleanly? Well let me tell you, I certainly am."

"Al," David said. "Stop talking."

"We must go forward," Jerriel said. "That was raw, positive nature energy. It merely knocked us back and scattered us. Yet in any form it will spell death to the Darkspawn of the Shadow Worlds, or from any of the Negative Energy planes."

The other wizards agreed with her.

"We are not just going to march in blindly," David said. "We'll do so carefully, cautiously, and with discipline. Wagons to the rear. Everyone watch your backs and the people around you. Take cover or drop down if another blast like that erupts. Like the annihilator rounds of the Pistoleros, there will be a few seconds warning after the flash. It doesn't seem to damage the earth and plants much. Shield one another behind them as best you can."

They continued to move forward. They detected movement up ahead and fell voices just beyond the next ridge.

The vanguard battle mages instinctively pushed forward past the head of the column to take a first look.

David kept close to to Jerriel.

They crested the rise and emerged into yet another world. A world that neither looked like Urth, or Tharanor.

This was a realm of devastation, like one of the Nine Hells itself.

The vale within was devoid of all normal life, blasted almost completely to black and gray ash, with several enormous, arcs of exposed, glowing bedrock; deep smoldering craters decorated the landscape. Glowing pits still steamed with molten rock, or bubbling, superheated mud.

One of the pits glowed eerily with veins of red, pulsing energy, as if scarlet lighting coruscated back and forth through the rents in the ground like bloody lines of exposed force.

Trees and lifeforms had been incinerated up close near the center of the blasts, reduced to stumps and almost unrecognizable steaming or hissing lumps. The incinerated stench hanging thick in the air was beyond description. Charred wood, vegetation, and immolated corpses of animals, monsters, and people were all concentrated into a thick reek.

The strange lights shot and rocketed up into the smoke-streaked sky once more from the adjacent vale beyond their position. The thundering of feet and mounts crested the rise.

An entire Dark Khabal army, thousands strong, fought an ordered, running retreat against some as yet unseen foe. Magic from dozens of necromancers, sorcerers and other Shadow Mages ripped back at their opponent, as if tearing reality itself apart.

The various human and non-human minions of the Dark Mages shrieked in terror. The weird green glow that they spotted on the horizon now intensified, expanding and advancing rapidly with a sound like growing thunder.

Not thunder.

Enormous footsteps hammered the earth, booming like drums.

The ground trembled as if in a powerful earthquake, making it difficult to remain standing.

The enemy swept back into the vale, swirling out both ends and up the other side in an attempt to escape. They scattered everywhere.

A fantastic whirlwind of pulsating, emerald power took shape and towered up over the ridge, wrecking its way down into the vale with tremendous shocks and impacts. Its very might scattered the foe and swatted them aside, hundreds of feet away, scores at a time as it waded into them.

The lights made it difficult to see, but an enormous humanoid shape or form of some kind, moved within the vortex, guiding its might with sentience and ruinous purpose.

The Shadow Mages concentrated all of their most powerful spells on whatever lay at the heart of the emerald vortex, weakening it briefly. Yet it seemed to draw strength out of the earth itself and kept coming at them.

David stared at such a mighty force in awe and terror.

But once the entity had the Shadow Army routed, it perceived the new arrivals, lurching straight toward David's position and his forces, hurling itself directly at them or anything within range that might pose a threat.

They were about to be annihilated just as their enemies were being crushed. They had nothing among them that could withstand such a force.

He gave the command even as Jerriel, ashen faced, struggled to form words on her lips.

"Retreat!" David shouted. "Fall back to the half mile rally point. Stay together! Help one another. Do not attack this thing, whatever it is!"

"Do not draw its attention." Jerriel said. "Flee. Run!"

David's forces and those of the princes melted away with speed and precision.

He and Jerriel began to pull back with them.

She clutched at his arm and halted him. "Wait, David. Look!" she cried above the growing roar.

Dark mists and shadows swept into the area, swirling around the entity. Thirteen Shadow Wizards appeared out of that darkness.

Each of them clutched a golden staff with a sharp point on the end, which they immediately drove into the ground.

Black and scarlet energy, like lightning, like glowing blood, ripped through the earth, snaking rapidly around the entity in an attempt to ensnare it.

Topping each staff was a glowing, crystal skull, pulsating with power. Visible waves of force warped the very air and closed in around their quarry.

All of the defenders had seen the black or red skull staffs of the Dark Khabal in combat before.

The verdant vortex still blanketed the area, power crashing against power.

"They're tapping into," Jerriel said, "turning its own power against it. "They're trying to drain the entity!"

David gaped. With all of the massive, wild destruction the entity brought about, was that a bad thing?

It was if the enemy was slowly gaining control over such power.

"We can't let them capture it!" Jerriel cried. She rose up and readied her staff. "If they do, then they'll command its power. They'll be able to direct it against us!"

David nodded. Great minds. Then he looked around them.

They were the only ones left.

He had just told everyone else with them to retreat. And they had obeyed to avoid being wiped out.

Jerriel did not hesitate and charged forward alone. David sprinted to catch up with her as they raced down into the valley.

Of course, one of the Dark Wizards spotted them and pointed them out to his fellows and their guards.

Two dozen assorted slayers slipped free of their masters, and moved to intercept and fall upon them.

Jerriel unleashed a ground blast of rock and earth at their very feet, tumbling most of them to the ground.

David shot a Grun through the throat with his crossbow as they ran, circling around to try to get at the nearest Shadow Mage.

The thirteen remained focused on ensnaring the entity in their expanding dark energy trap. An armored serpent woman with four arms, a snake-like body below the waist, weapons in each hand, rushed toward Jerriel to both cut her off and slice her up.

David flung a tomahawk and buried it in the side of serpent-woman's head.

That slowed her down. She toppled over to the side and thrashed around.

In a wink, his tomahawk appeared on his belt once more, coated with green gore.

Jerriel raked a handful of the others with a violet crash of lightning.

She caught one of the wizards directly in her lightning, blasting him and his skull staff off his feet and sending him spinning away.

The energy snare around the entity visibly wavered at one place.

The Spectral Guardian sensed its chance and blasted through the weak point, drained and damaged yet still powerful.

Green tendrils and ribbons of light snapped and whipped about, crackling through the very air. The ground rumbled and rippled, then burst in a blinding green flash.

The explosion sent friend and foe flying in every direction.

A glaive stroke he hadn't even seen coming just swept past him.

The mercenary trying to attack him segmented into several neat pieces from the energy ribbons that slashed through him like giant slicer blades.

Blood sprayed in gouts.

David tried to catch Jerriel as one of the green tendrils connected with her energy shield, shattered it, and flung her and her staff away with little effort.

What felt like a giant fist punched into him, swatting him dozens of feet back toward the ridge line. He gasped, stunned and breathless in a muddy crevice that broke his fall.

Pieces of one of the Dark wizards oozed into the tortured ground around him. David tried to get up, checking to see if he himself was still in one piece.

Nothing seemed to be missing. Not yet at least.

The vortex collapsed and dissipated.

The wounded Spectral Entity stood revealed near him, a humanoid female form, thirty feet tall, with eyes of green fire and horns on her head like those of an elk. She was comprised entirely of Urth energy–raw pulsing green energy drawn from the earth itself.

She looked horribly wounded, but still unbowed, and enraged.

Her eyes narrowed and fixed upon David, the only thing left alive in that part of the vale.

She advanced on him with great strides, closing rapidly. Tendrils and ribbons of power rippled all about her and sped toward his position as if in waves.

The ground trembled and shook.

Should he draw weapons? No use.

He stood with his hands outstretched openly before him.

"We are not your enemies!" he cried. "We we're trying to help free–"

Energy tendrils like a gigantic hand ripped him off the ground and brought him face to face with those huge, glowing green eyes.

The entity studied him for the barest instant. "You are somewhat interesting, mortal."

Pain exploded in his mind and razored through his body. He screamed, trying to block it out.

"But even your gift shall not save you!" the entity boomed. "You cannot stand against me. I will not be bound. You will never make me your slave!"

Waves of energy rippled through him, each threatening to shred his mind and body.

So much pain. He couldn't speak.

He sent what thoughts he could toward the entity, struggling to ignore the pain.

*I am not with...the Dark Mages. Not with them! I am a friend...a friend!*

"Hah! All of you mortals are deceivers. The lies of the gan are many and endless. Perish with all the rest of your kind, mortal. I can still overwhelm your defenses! Did your wizards think that you could endure my power with your gift? You shall not do so for very long."

He screamed again. The pain intensified. The entity bent more of its will upon him.

"No mortal wretch shall ever enslave me!"

*I would never–*

"And you never shall!"

A mesh of black and scarlet energy ensnared the entity once more.

The Shadow Wizards, either more of them or those who survived, renewed their attacks. More skull staffs sank into the ground, hammering the entity and draining it, warping its own powers against it.

The attacks also battered David within the entity's clutches.

New agony, like burning worms of fire, felt as if they bored their way through his flesh. He tried to reason with the tormented being.

*These mages are my enemies as well!*

"You are nothing to me, mortal! I will use your negation gift as my shield and dispose of your smoking corpse when I am done with you. You shall serve *my* purposes!"

He gasped as he felt the entity pass into him, and suck itself inside of his body as if it replaced his blood with its consciousness and control. He became a puppet, his movements no longer under his control.

He was only a passive witness in his own mind. The entity's glowing green energy blazed out of his eyes like beacons as it took control of his flesh.

The entity's force of will surrounded him and plunged him underground. It moved and flowed freely through the earth with almost no resistance, sending him weaving in several directions.

He absorbed the might of the earth itself, collecting it, transferring power to the Spectral Guardian each instant.

David erupted from the ground, this time up on the ridge line.

Having escaped from the Dark Khabal's trap, the entity unleashed a flurry of energy attacks on the Dark Mages, scattering them into the dark mists and swirling shadows where they took cover. Those who did not perish struggled to reposition themselves for another combined attack with their skull staffs.

Bolts and waves of dark energy battered David and the Entity, threatening to crush or incinerate him at every instant. The entity did in fact use him as a shield, tossing him about. She deflected attacks with him and responded with intense counterstrikes of green Urth Power.

Yet the Dark Khabal continued wearing the entity down. That was clear to all.

Through the haze, as the entity weakened and fell to her knees. David saw Jerriel rush in to attack the Shadow Wizards single handed.

*That is my mate! She's trying to help us. We must work together if we are to survive!*

"Never!" She shouted.

He spoke to her mind. *Then we will die and you shall still be their slave in the end!*

"I will destroy you all!"

*Dammit. Will you just listen for once? That is my mate!* David cried. *She came back when she could have fled to safety. She's risking her life to help us! To save you and I!*

"You are all gan. Humans are evil!" the entity said, but then she hesitated, watching Jerriel hurl herself against the Khabal.

*Not all of us are evil. At least not entirely so!* David argued.

"Mortals cannot be trusted!" She used his body to deflect one of the blasts from the skull staffs that remained.

*If you use us against our will,* David said, *then you are no better than us! You're just as evil as we are. No better than the ones you despise!*

"Do not seek to bandy words with me, mortal!"

*It's the truth and you know it! Don't lie to me. Don't lie to yourself! You're doing to me exactly what you don't want these others to do to you—enslave you against your will. Admit it. There's no difference at all.*

The entity raged at the Dark Wizards again, swatting them away or chasing them back into the dark mists with a flurry of power.

David glanced down. Jerriel lay still on the ground from the fury of the battle, torn, broken, and battered, scorched by the enemy and the fierce powers unleashed all around them.

David wept. His emotions nearly overrode the entity's control.

*Help her, please! She fought for you, trying to save us both! We cannot leave her to die, please, I beg you!*

Near exhaustion, the entity dropped David to his hands and knees next to Jerriel, while it drew strength from the earth once more, re-charging.

That allowed David to touch Jerriel's face and smooth her dark hair back from her forehead with his gentle hands.

"Your feelings for you mate are incredibly strong, mortal. You begin to change my perceptions of you. But even so, you cannot control me that way either."

*Dammit! Won't you listen? I'm not trying to control you. Just help her! I'll do anything you ask. We can help each other. Please, I beg you to save her!*

"We cannot stay here," the entity said. "I will carry her with us."

David felt himself and Jerriel gathered up like small stones. Then the entity leaped fifty or sixty yards at a time out of the area.

*David,* he told her. *My name is David. Her name is Jerriel. She is a wizard. We are good people, yet we are not perfect.*

"I am not ignorant; I know many things about my world. I can easily sense who and what you are, David. That is no mystery."

*Then you know that we are the enemies of the Shadow Mages. The ones trying to harm and capture all of us.*

"They did attack us, but you are still mortal. You are the same as they. Any of you gan would enslave me to gain the use of my powers, and that, none of you shall ever do."

*I do not care about that. What about Jerriel...how is she doing?*

"She fought well, but was greatly damaged in the course of the battle. Now, she is dying. There is no need to carry her along any longer. I shall put her down and leave her to her fate."

*No! You cannot!* David shouted mentally, fighting and resisting her suddenly with all that he was, with everything he had. *I will not let you leave her behind to die alone. Not after she fought to save us both!* Jerriel spilled to the ground in any case.

David flung himself at the entity, physically and mentally, by sheer force of will, and struggled against the entity's control. He was not able to harm her, yet he sensed that he could manage to delay her.

"Stop!" the Spectral Guardian shouted. "What are you doing? Our foes are pursuing us. They will capture us and then destroy you!"

*I don't care!* He thrashed and convulsed on the ground, doing everything he could to resist the entity's control. *Help her! Save her! You must do something. I will fight you every instant!*

"She is dying. We must leave her!"

*No, I will not let you. I don't care if we are destroyed!*

They sank into the earth itself. Soil and rock closed in around them as they did. The green glow of the entity lit their way. A pocket of air formed a protective, cave-like orb around them, nestled within the power of the earth itself.

The entity placed her large hands over Jerriel, and through their connection, David felt healing energy pass through them and into his beloved.

"I control the mysteries of the Lifespark of all living things," the entity told him. "I can heal life from the very brink of death, but never after all vestiges of life's positive energies have fled."

David's mind and awareness remained joined with the entity while her energies flowed through them both. He could sense glimpses and inklings of what she said and what she was doing.

He did not need to understand. Nothing else mattered, as long as Jerriel was healed.

"Khia Llazha Eddorian," David said aloud, through his own mouth. "Your name is Khia, and like us, you are afraid."

"Do not say my true name aloud again, mortal. Our foes can use that knowledge against us! Curse the fact that I chose to join with you."

Jerriel came to, still weak and confused.

"Thank you," David said aloud He stopped resisting and probing the entity's mind.

"Thank you for saving her. Let's leave her some place safe for my friends to find her, and I will do all that I can to help you escape. I don't care what happens to me. Just make sure that she is safe. We can even leave her with some of my people if you wish. I will fight for you with everything I have. Channel your power through me and my weapons, and we will fight them together!"

"I see how you care for your mate, mortal. And I know now from your heart and soul that you speak true. We will make her safe."

He fed the entity everything that he knew about their foes, which wasn't really that much. Jerriel would probably know better how to deal with the Dark Mages than he ever could.

Khia suddenly came to that same realization.

"The link between us is still too weak, mortal. I need someone more powerful to fuse two wills together and grow stronger."

Green fire burst out of his arms, engulfing his hands. The power of the fire tormented his flesh, but did no direct harm to it. As the fire faded, gauntlets formed on each of his hands, gauntlets pulsating with energy drawn from the very ground.

One formed from segmented stone over hide, the other from living wood over leather. Both gauntlets were dexterous and flexible, forming themselves to his hands and arms as if they were a second skin.

For an instant David had a glimpse of the entity's amazing abilities and perceived the depths of its powers. Mighty indeed, yet its powers were still not infinite. Without its innate ability to regenerate energy from the ground and from the nearby Nexus, it would have already fallen.

Now fused together and linked by the gauntlets, together they could also sense the Shadow Mages charging after them, preparing to attack and attempt to ensnare them.

"Give me your might," David told Khia. "Let me fall upon them! If only my troops were within range for me to command them. They would fight for us!"

Infused with the entity's powers, David drew his swords in each gauntleted hand. Ribbons and tendrils of green light rippled out from him.

They shot up out of the ground and faced their foes.

He leaped and whirled at random. He attacked the Shadow Mages in several directions, keeping them off balance.

David's blades hewed them down, slashing into them and cutting them apart. He tore one of the Shadow Mages to pieces before it could retreat back into the mists and shadows. He sprang back and sliced through the arms of another, and cut into the golden skull staff and the crystal skull itself.

The skull staff still sucked energy in and converted it around them, even as it broke down. The skull imploded, sucking the screaming wizard into its collapsing vortex, crushing and crunching his bones and flesh.

Blood splattered everywhere.

David sprang away, resisting the power that threatened to suck him into the vortex as well. At last he pulled clear.

Arrows raked the enemy, and they withdrew once more into the shadows. Half of them remained dead on the field in the aftermath.

"They shall soon return with more numbers and hit us even harder!" Khia warned.

"Those arrows were from my archers coming to our aid," David said. "My forces will help us. Here they come. Please, do not harm them."

David and Jerriel's friends charged down into the valley toward them in the fierce battle's lull. Jerriel rose up from being healed and kept safe by the Urth entity. She appeared fully recovered and ready to fight once more, but she also looked extremely confused.

The Spectral Urth spirit Khia seemed to be waiting eagerly for the wizard's return as well.

David smiled at Jerriel, his eyes still glowing intensely green. He showed her the equally glowing green gauntlets that he wore. "These gloves are magical, but for some reason I cannot use them properly in conjunction with her. There's something wrong with me. This Spectral Entity made these artifacts to fuze her powers together with a willing human host–a partner. Her name, is Khia."

"Keys," Jerriel said in wonder. "I understand now. They are indeed Spectral Keys; I can sense their raw power from here. Entity Khia, I am a wizard," Jerriel said, turning to the energy spirit. "I offer my services to you, Khia. Not as your master in any way, but as a partner, friend…and ally!"

# JERRIEL

"A partnership with a powerful wizard would indeed work much better," Khia said.

"Yes," Jerriel said. "Take me. Fuze yourself with me. Our combined powers shall increase tenfold. I know that you will link best with a willing mage against these dire threats that we both face. Let us face them together!"

She felt certain of what she intended to do.

Khia's voice and her essence forced its way out of David's mouth. "There is wisdom in what you say, mage Jerriel. And I truly sense that a union with a wizard such as yourself would be far more powerful than with this null gan."

David shuddered. Jerriel could feel–almost see the Spectral Entity withdrawing from him.

"No," he insisted, "part of me wants to avoid putting Jerriel in further danger, another part has no wish to separate from you, Khia. Stay with me. I can still help you with my abilities!"

"Not as well as she can," Khia said, her essence pausing between them both. "Your null energy field is incredibly strong, David. But it is still not the same as fuzing with a powerful wizard. Yet, I do thank you for helping protect us all, for a time."

"My what field?" he asked.

"You possess a powerful null energy field inside and all around you, David," Jerriel tried to explain to him. "Most likely, it awakened and has grown stronger each time that you stepped into pool of Wild Magic and absorbed more of its properties. Now that anti-magic field is part of you."

"I have come in contact with a number of such pools," David said.

"Your strong null field should negate or reduce all but the most powerful magickal energies," Khia said. "Command your forces on your own, mortal. That is your gift. You will be more help to us in that capacity on your own."

David fell to his hands and knees, and watched helpless and weak, as Khia withdrew the last of her spirit essence from him and began to fuze fully with Jerriel.

Jerriel gasped and blinked, feeling Khia's essence join with her, filling her with Urth power, knowledge, and enlightenment from the earth itself. Her eyes glowed bright green. So did her staff.

Those sensations were liberating—mind expanding.

They also took time getting used to them—time they did not have.

Jerriel held her hands out urgently, instinctively reaching and yearning for the gauntlet keys. "The keys, David. Give them to me. Hurry. Khia and I will be able to make use of those much better than the two of you."

He tugged them off and handed them over.

Jerriel slipped them on, feeling more surges of power and a sense of relief. Both gloves instantly formed themselves perfectly to her hands and arms, and blazed with increased emerald might.

Jerriel gasped and turned to the northwest as the verdant aura spread over her entire body. Her senses and her awareness continued to expand on completely new levels. It was both disorienting and intoxicating to be joined with the entity.

A powerful spectral energy threat approached rapidly from the west.

"THEY ATTACK US," Khia and Jerriel spoke in unison. "AND THIS TIME—ANOTHER GREAT POWER SUCH AS WE COMES WITH THEM."

Jerriel plunged both gauntlets into the ground and fed power to herself and Khia directly from the ley line sources near the nexus. "WE MUST LINK DIRECTLY WITH THE NEXUS NEARBY IF WE ARE TO HAVE ANY HOPE TO SURVIVE THEIR GREAT ONSLAUGHT." Khia-Jerriel looked at David directly.

"DAVID. ASSEMBLE A SMALL GROUP OF YOUR FINEST WARRIORS TO TRAVEL WITH US, TO TRANSPORT DIRECTLY TO THE NEXUS. THE REST WILL NEED TO FOLLOW ON AS BEST THEY CAN. THIS BATTLE WILL BE DECIDED AT THE NEXUS ITSELF!"

It was slightly confusing. With her expanded awareness, she could hear all of the humans speaking at once in her mind, even sense some of their emotions and surface thoughts.

David turned to their friends. "Prince Valandin, we're going on ahead with a small force. Lead the rest of the vanguard in after us; I'm guessing no more than a mile or two. Strike down any foes who get in your way. Send word to the army concerning our situation."

"Captain," Prince Valandin said, "we are too few for a major battle such as this. The bulk of our forces are still many hours away from us."

"I know. That cannot be helped. This fight is going to take place now. But we must keep our side informed, even if we fall here. They must know what has happened and why."

"This battle will be long over by then," Prince Alendel said. "In hours, if not in minutes!"

"My good and valiant lords," David told them "we have no choice but to fight on and do our duty in this place at this hour. I am following Jerriel and the entity Khia to the nexus. They cannot flee, nor can they take all of us with them there. Follow on as best as possible and provide what aid and support you can. Good luck to us all!"

Khia-Jerriel watched as David turned to his troops. Even transfixed with Urth Power, her heart went out to her brave beloved. Khia was right. David was no mage; he was a leader of warriors.

"Blackhawk Strike Force One," David called out. "Assemble for battle and follow me. The rest of you, follow your unit leaders and the princes into combat. Fight hard and do your best to win the day!"

A platoon of thirty spears, swords, and archers stood with him in the strike force, all of their friends and best fighters, and with them Thul-Kazar and Thulkara.

"GATHER CLOSELY TOGETHER AROUND US," Khia-Jerriel told them.

The entity merely had to conceptualize something with her powers and abilities to bring them into being.

Green Urth Power directed through Jerriel's staff enveloped them all, lifting them off the ground a few feet, upheld upon a large, verdant energy disk. They slipped over the land, picking up speed. Terrain rushed past them.

A dark mass of gathering shadows appeared behind them, swelling and sweeping over the land, blotting out the broken clouds and the few stars that could be seen in the sky as it entered the tower of dark mist.

By then the low moon was already down.

"What is that growing menace gaining upon us?" David shouted.

Khia-Jerriel did not look back. "WE FEAR THAT ANOTHER POWER SUCH AS OURSELVES HAS COME TO CONTEST WITH US, FOR THE MASTERY OF THIS NEXUS," they said. "WHATEVER THIS FORCE IS, A MIGHTY SHADOW MAGE CONTROLS IT."

"Another Spectral Entity?" David said. "Another mage who has fuzed with one of the Spectral Keys?"

"UNCERTAIN, BUT THAT IS MOST LIKELY. IT IS EXTREMELY FORMIDABLE. PREPARE YOURSELVES. THEY'RE TRYING TO INTERCEPT US."

They lifted up over the trees and sprang through the air, clearing almost an entire half mile in one leap. David and his troops tumbled through the air and crashed into each other on the disk.

The next thing they knew, they were jumbled on the ground, trying to regain their footing. The disk had vanished.

Khia-Jerriel stood directly over the glowing nexus point. It was like a beacon, and they drew upon its power, completely encased in green flame.

But their eyes burned white-hot, fully charged with energy.

"DAVID, PROTECT US ON EITHER SIDE AND FROM BEHIND." Khia-Jerriel shouted. "GIVE US A CLEAR FIELD OF FIRE TO THE FRONT!"

David and his strike team peeled around them, taking defensive positions, readying their weapons.

A sudden gale like that of a hurricane swept in as the shadows descended upon them through the obscuring mists.

For an instant, David thought he saw the vast darkness take on the form of a gargantuan bat, with eyes black and deep as the Abyss itself.

The shadow crashed to the ground, and the blast wave and following storm of blinding dust and debris flattened and blinded them again, even as the ground shattered and broke up under their feet.

Khia-Jerriel steadied themselves, anchored to the nexus itself.

"SHALLI-HAKKAL!" they cried.

A massive storm of emerald lightning ripped through the shadow, disrupted it, and flung it back. Many dark shapes were revealed within the darkness for the barest flash of that instant.

Then the darkness and the swirling mists concealed them once more.

"They'll attack out of the shadows," David warned. "Set all weapons against a charge!"

He and his troops raised their shields and weapons and braced themselves.

A horde of enemies appeared close by out of the darkness and at a full run. They crashed into and deflected off David and his defensive lines on both flanks. The staunch defenders held firm and dealt damage.

David deflected a Grun spear and split open the goat face with his longsword.

Thul-Kazar laughed aloud, slaying and flinging foes to either side of him, his battleax spinning like a huge black saw. Thulkara fought beside him, dealing death as only a Thul could.

Khia-Jerriel nailed the enemies in front of them with blasts, tendrils, and ribbons of slicing, green Urth energy.

But a phalanx of Shadow Mages marched up directly behind the enemy shock troops, all bearing glowing skull staffs.

And behind them the even darker power lurked, veiled in shadows, but like a black hole in reality itself, its true form and nature still masked.

They could sense it more than they could see it, as it maneuvered and feinted carefully.

Khia-Jerriel valiantly stood their ground, backed by the nexus, swatting the lesser enemies away, scattering the necromancers like ten pins.

The Urth Entity unleashed a storm of magic upon the Dark Mages pressing their attack, crushing the enemy's defenses and killing some of them outright.

The hidden shadow shot up into the air, spread its vast wings, and opened its enormous maw as if meant to swallow the world itself.

A wide beam of dark power shot down and rammed into Khia-Jerriel, driving them back dozens of feet and smashing them into the ground. The earth cracked and cratered around them.

Friend and foe alike scattered from the sheer force of such an assault.

Jerriel saw David claw back up to his hands and knees, still clutching his weapons. "Jerriel!" He shouted at her.

Khia-Jerriel shot up out of the crater, barely damaged from such a massive assault as they had just endured

Rapid fire pulses of Urth force punched into the shadow, blasting holes through it and flinging it back to plummet and tumble back out of the sky from where it had blotted out the stars.

The Shadow Mages regrouped by then and charged Khia-Jerriel once more, combining and angling their attacks to drain her.

Waves of what looked like glowing dark vines suddenly whipped and whirled up out of the blackened ground, churning and lashing at the foes of the Dark Mages. Those who did not flee or deflect those attacks were ripped off their feet, slammed against the ground, and held fast.

"Face us, Dark Terror. Come on. Show thyself!" Khia-Jerriel challenged. "We do not fear you! We wield the might of the Urth and the power of the nexus. I was trained by the greatest mages of Tharanor!"

A tall shadow strode out of the darkness, and it took the form of a man with long golden hair and he spoke at her. "As was I...*sister.*"

Jerriel's focus faltered for a moment in a mix of terror and suppressed rage.

Oh no; she knew this attacker all to well.

Scores of what now were tentacles of burning shadow rippled out from the darkness, and battered and slapped Khia-Jerriel off the ground, breaking their connection with the nexus and transfixing them high up in the air, encircling her like snakes. The pair were cut off from the nexus now, losing their energies each second.

Jerriel's eyes bulged in fear, rage, and shock, as she glared at the blond young man and spat her words at him in her own voice. "Shaeddor…my dark brother!"

He curled his lip at her. "Indeed. I am the Dark Prince of our house. The merry chase is at last over, little one. I hereby claim you, this nexus, and another Spectral Key for my dread lords of the Khabal—and the Dark Ghods themselves—soon to be Masters…of *both* worlds!"

Jerriel's wrath got the best of her. "Shaeddor, how can you fight for the Dark Khabal—the fiends who murdered our parents?"

She spotted David looking on, trying to work his way in closer from behind. He had no idea how dangerous her brother was, even with David's magic negation powers, and there was no way to warn him now.

Jerriel fixed her eyes on her older brother's Spectral Key. The onyx necklace rested around Shaeddor's neck, and the bat entity of Darkness and all of its powers were his to command.

Black and Scarlet lightning emanated from him and raced up through the dark tentacles to nail Jerriel and Khia, still trying to drain and stun them. All she could do was look on and grind her teeth against the pain.

David called up his troops. "Strike Force, attack! Cut them down. Focus on taking out the enemy wizards!"

More enemy troops rushed in out of the shadows. David and his people powered into them, weapons clashing and hewing.

Thul-Kazar was the first to break through and charge full tilt at Jerriel's brother.

"Die, vile wizard!"

With barely a glance and a dismissive wave of one hand, Shaeddor encased him in a orb of mist, like a bubble of black glass. The Thul champion hurtled hundreds of feet out of the away.

"Begone, oaf! I am no wizard; I am a sorcerer. Your little friends will not save you, sister. Not this time."

He held her suspended in the air, continuing to jolt and torment her with flows of dark energy, trying to further weaken her and Khia.

Jerriel-Khia struggled to fight back, lashing out wildly with their fading powers, but they remained transfixed, their efforts to break free mostly ineffective.

Shaeddor still held them cut off, suspended in the air. They could not link with the Nexus to recharge.

The lesser enemy mages and troops formed a defensive perimeter around their leader.

David threw both of his tomahawks, wounding or disabling foes with each cast. With his swords he cut into them, trying to crash through, but the line held.

Alejandro's sword flashed on his left side, slicing and piercing enemies. Jason Inada charged in on his right, his katana whirling and spraying blood from enemy wounds. Pastor Brian led a charge on the right flank farther down that broke through.

David took up a tomahawk from his belt again and whipped it directly at Shaeddor.

The sorcerer swatted it aside and suddenly glared at him. "Mason's friend, Captain Pritchard. He told me all about you, David. The formidable warrior. Now my sister's faithful lover. Just another annoying insect. I shall deal with you shortly."

David cast his other tomahawk. Shaeddor swatted it away without even looking.

Yet on the ground, the enemy defenses continued to crumble as the vanguard attackers closed in from the flanks.

"Enough!" Shaeddor cried.

Khia dwindled to little more than a flickering green aura around Jerriel. Both of them were nearly stricken senseless. Jerriel crashed to the ground in a heap and lay still, containing and protecting the entity within herself.

Shaeddor turned at bay upon David and his forces, unleashing an energy wave attack from his countless tentacles, blasting and knocking the strike force back by the score, stunning many.

David ducked and rolled under the attack meant for him and his forces, rushed in close, and rocked the wizard's head back with a pommel strike from his longsword.

But the Shadow Mage appeared to be protected by some kind of defensive field around his body, and barely seemed to feel it. He looked more surprised and annoyed that David managed to get in so close and stood toe-to-toe with him.

Shaeddor was an inch or two taller, and seemed to swell up even larger, looming over David with the dark powers swelling within him.

"Wretch. You dare to strike me?"

David gave him another shot, such that magickal dark sparks flew. Yet he could tell it did little harm besides distracting and annoying the mage further.

"Annoying bastard. I'll take you down myself!"

"Some brother. You'd turn her over to the Dark Khabal?"

"I'm saving her life, you dolt. You have no idea what powers you are facing, Urther. With me, at least she'll be safe. Running around with you, her doom is all but certain. You're the one who's going to get her killed!" With a snarl the dark wizard raked him with lightning.

No, David. Jerriel struggled to regain enough energy to fight back, but she was so drained, she could barely lift her head.

David grunted and gnashed his teeth against her brother's lightning attack. With his enchanted sword he struggled to deflect some of the energy, but it clearly continued to course through him as he ground his teeth. It became difficult for him to keep standing, let alone push forward. The forces hammering him were just too great.

Shaeddor looked not only slightly puzzled but a bit alarmed. "Why do you not fall? At this rate you should be incinerated, fool. What is this power you possess?"

"Surprise, asshole!" David backhanded Shaeddor with a gauntleted fist.

A big spray of dark sparks erupted from the mage's energy shield.

Jerriel struggled to link with the nexus, sensing Khia's encouragement in her mind. If David's null abilities could simply keep Shaeddor distracted for another few moments.

"Are you too much of a coward to face me like a man?" David taunted.

Shaeddor sneered again and drew a curved sword from his side that looked as if it had ben forged from solid darkness itself. "I hear that you fancy yourself a swordsman, scum. Very well. Face my blade then!"

"No, brother…" Jerriel finally recovered enough to blast him full force with a power strike, flinging him back through the air.

Her dark brother tumbled, recovered, and shot back, straight at David this time.

Jerriel-Khia flung themselves before David to protect him. They launched a massive green ray of force to punch into Shaeddor and drive him off.

"David, get back. Only magic can defeat him!"

Amazingly, Shaeddor deflected some of their attacks with his weird dark energy sword. It actually seemed to absorb the Urth energy somehow.

Huge glowing green boulders tore free out of the ground, some twenty or thirty feet high, weighing many tons. They tumbled, crashed, and clashed, battering Shaeddor, smashing into him again and again.

He shattered or pulverized several of the boulders with his sword.

But in the end the massive boulders smacked him down, piled up, and buried him under tons of rock and stone.

Jerriel dropped to her hands and knees, leaning heavily on her staff with one hand. The energy of the two gauntlets she wore flickered. Their attack had nearly drained them.

Two Shadow Mages swept in and tried to attack her while she was weakened.

In desperation David cast his long sword from nearby and impaled one of the wizards. That one dropped his skull staff. The staff linked to the dying mage disrupted and exploded.

Drawing his katana, David severed the other dark wizard's arms at the wrists and then ran him through the throat.

The pile of green boulders exploded, knocking David off his feet and flinging him out of the way.

"I know not what trick you use, bumpkin." Shaeddor rose up out of the dust cloud and lashed out at David with a mighty burst.

"*This* should deal with you."

David couldn't move fast enough to dodge it.

Khia-Jerriel sped in front of him to deflect it, and took the blast full force upon themselves. It struck them with a strange effect.

Shaeddor laughed. "Hah! Even better. I serve the Dark Ghods, fools. You cannot defeat me. I will take what I wish by force. And I will not be denied!"

Khia-Jerriel was completely paralyzed, or rather frozen inside an irregular block of enchanted black ice. Now they were fairly trapped, reduced to mere spectators, her face stuck in an agonize shriek.

The sorcerous ice burned them on contact, numbing them with frigid, burning pain that they could not escape from.

Shaeddor laughed even harder at them, but turned to David. "Yes, imagine the pain they are in, oaf. The black ice of the Abyss burns with agony itself, and they are trapped within it, all around them. And they cannot even scream. But it will not slay them, at least not right away. Unless I make it so."

"Release her," David warned. He summoned his longsword back to his right hand, switching his katana to his left. "You will not take her."

"It is already done; she is already mine, fool. You cannot stand before the powers I wield, whatever your strange, null defenses are. Trust me. She will be safer in my hands."

"Let her go. Do so now!" David charged in and attacked as quickly as he could.

Shaeddor parried his blows and beat him back with punishing energy blasts and tentacle strikes. But for just an instant, he even looked slightly worried.

Jerriel marveled at David's magic negating abilities. He wasn't going down, and he certainly wasn't giving up. But the sheer weight of her brother's attacks forced him to give ground, despite severing several of the whipping tentacles.

But being made of shadow energy, the sorcerous appendages merely reformed and continued to lash at him in order to drive him off.

Shaeddor was preparing to make good his escape, and there was nothing Jerriel, David, nor anyone else could do to prevent that.

David valiantly attacked, guessing the sorcerer's intent. "Wherever you flee I will hunt you down!" he yelled.

"I dare you try," Shaeddor snarled, spinning aside. His minions cheered his name in triumph, hanging upon his every word.

"Pursue me to your doom, fool. Face facts. My sister is lost to you. She made her choice. Now another entity is ours to control and our power grows. Soon both worlds will be ours to command, and you and your pitiful allies shall be swept aside like the dust your are. We have won. You have lost!"

"Stand and face me, coward!" David challenged.

Shaeddor laughed. "Why, fool? There is no need. You matter not. I have the prizes I came for. You're nothing."

David charged in. All of his people who could still fight rushed in to assist him.

Shaeddor mocked them with laughter and withdrew into the form of the gigantic bat entity, immersing himself into it.

The huge guardian being took up the frozen block of magic ice in its clawed feet, and receded back into the tower of dark mists, effectively vanishing from sight.

Yet it stayed for a few moments, as Shaeddor observed what actions his enemies took thereafter.

From where Jerriel and Khia were trapped, they could partially sense what was going on nearby and below them.

David staggered after them in vain through the darkness. "Jerriel!" he cried in despair.

Jerriel's heart broke as she was about to be carried off. She might not see her David ever again. Jerriel had failed him and Khia both. In the end, she couldn't protect Khia or herself–especially not against the treachery and betrayal of her own old brother.

Damn it. Shaeddor had always been stronger than her, and he seemed to know and exploit all of her weaknesses at will.

It was a further waste of time and energy beating herself up about it, now. That would not help anyone. Conserve her energies. Be prepared to strike back when the time was right.

David would pursue her and anyone who threatened her to the ends of both worlds, but he would have no way to follow her now.

With the darkness she could no longer see him clearly, but she heard his voice as if from a distance. "Ready the troops," he called to his forces as the others caught up to them, by the sounds. "They have Jerriel, and the Spectral Entity Khia. We're going after them."

"We will pursue them to the death!" Thul-Kazar roared.

"Hopefully theirs," Alejandro muttered.

Prince Alendel, the quiet one, spoke up. "Jerriel is our kin, Captain. Her dark brother, a vile traitor to both our worlds. I will go with you, alone if need be. Together we shall free her and lift the siege of Kellendra—no matter what powers stand against us."

Prince Valandin sounded near to both of them.

"Come, brothers. The road lies before us and the enemy flees into the night like the cowards they are. They shall come to fear our swords!"

Jerriel took heart. For the moment, she and Khia remained captured, but they were not completely lost. In some warped way, her brother had even sounded protective of her. The most important fact was that they still lived, and she was clever, strong, and fused with the Spectral Guardian Entity Khia.

They would have their chance to break free.

Together with their valiant friends, David would find some way to locate her, face their foes down, and make their enemies pay.

Of that much she felt certain.

She heard David take to his horse as his troops brought it forward. He turned to them in the saddle, the reins in his hands.

"Blackhawks!" he shouted, drawing his sword. "Let nothing stand in our way. Send word to the army about what we face. Damn our foes and every peril. We march through Michigan to Detroit, and then south upon Kellendra!"

David's voice faded out.

Jerriel's accursed brother remained fuzed with the giant bat entity and lifted off silently, fleeing rapidly to the northeast with their prizes, virtually invisible in the night sky. The lesser foes melted away in that direction as well, and within moments, the vast tower of dark mist dispersed, dissolving into nothing.

# SHAEDDOR

Shaeddor carried his captives beyond the enemy camps massed around Huran and Bentar, further up into the region of Shendor, or what the Urthers called Michigan. He had little time to spare.

In a thick forested area, he once more located a solitary park or open lodge of some kind that was currently abandoned and unused. He had scouted out this site during one of his lengthy test flights to learn to control the Spectral Entity of the great bat.

Now he swept over that desolate place again, making certain that there were no prying eyes out that way.

When he was convinced of that fact, he landed and set down the block of magical ice. Then he absorbed the bat entity back into himself and the key, allowing it a well-deserved rest.

His master, the High Magus, had done an excellent job in teaching him how to gain full control over the entity of night through its key, and learn the full range of their combined abilities together.

All of that had served him well in his current great task.

When all was ready, Shaeddor held the green gauntlets in his left fist, the keys to the Urth Spectral Entity of nature itself. Then he dispelled the magical ice, and his little sister rolled to the soft grassy ground convulsing, still joined with the drained Spectral Entity dormant within her.

A short jolt of healing brought Jerriel around.

He had to be on guard. They might still attack him and try to get the keys back with every second that passed. Of course, that would be their hope.

He needed to play the situation carefully. For now, Jerriel and most everyone believed him to be a traitor. He could let her and everyone else continue to believe that, or he could try to let her in on his little game, if she would listen and cooperate.

Jerriel was all the family he had left, after all. Yet Shaeddor wasn't doing all that he did for reasons of sentiment or family ties. No. He was solely and simply driven by an intense, scorching, smoldering, burning lust for vengeance.

He alone knew what his former friends were up against. They had no idea what dread powers of darkness stood arrayed against them.

Shaeddor knew all of that very well. Nor did he himself care whether he himself lived or died in the end. But if his vengeance had the added bonus of weakening the enemy and helping lead to their overall and eventual defeat, then so be it. That would merely be an added bonus for all of them.

And all he had to do was continue to play the villain, and pick and choose his times to strike. Patience was extremely important.

"Brother," Jerriel spluttered, up on her hands and knees, still looking spent and desperate.

His first reaction was to go forward and help her up, but he could not take the chance of being too nice to her. He could hardly allow his little sister, of all people, to slay him.

"I am here," he told her, keeping his voice neutral.

He also chose this spot because it was relatively inert and far enough away from any major ley lines that they might feed off of. In this place it would take them days to recharge, and it was at least an hour on foot to the nearest ley line of any significant size to be of any use to them.

With the Urth Entity sufficiently drained, that would keep them both weak and easy to manage, until he was ready to let them go.

But they had to discuss a few things first, especially their father's journal.

"Why have you brought us here? What are you...going to do with us?" Jerriel said, dragging herself and Khia into a sitting position at one the wooden tables, under the open lodge's roof.

Shaeddor paced somewhat, keeping his distance.

"Why, sister, I'm merely going to question you about a few things…and then I'm going to release you in these wilds. I will tell them you got the better of me and I managed to escape before you finished me off. They will pursue you, of course, but whatever happens to you after that is your own affair, for now."

Jerriel rested her head on her hands like one extremely fatigued, and rolled her forehead from one side to the other as she groaned. "Liar!" she spat at him. "Your soul now belongs to the Dark Khabal…the Dark Ghods. You helped them kill our mother…and our father! Were they your Gonashodul? Tell me the truth, and curse you to every hell–"

The last few lines about their parents she nearly sobbed. That evoked a twinge of guilt on his part.

"I had no part or knowledge of their deaths, not directly at least, sister. And I have not become a necromancer nor made any Great Offering. You know my feelings about any religion, let alone one so stifling and idiotic. I'm afraid that I am less than half the devil that you wish to take me for. Again, I was not a member of the Dark Khabal at times of our parent's deaths, nor was I aware that my master, Gorrial Lankorro was the High Magus of that cult.

"He was one of the Six High Wizards of Tharanor, and I was his most loyal apprentice to him and our nation. Of course I served him without question. Yet I do not do so now."

She lifted her head and glared at him. "Deceiver! No one can trust the words that slip so easily out of your mouth like that of a viper. You always manipulated and played everyone against one another, even in our family. You are an expert such things."

Shaeddor knitted his hands together. "It matters not what you choose to believe about me, now. I do have my own secret agenda, and you might just be surprised at what it is."

She pointed her finger at him directly. "You knew about the Merge, and you helped Gorrial cause it! You are responsible, at least in part, for the deaths of millions, perhaps hundreds of millions of people on both Tharanor and Urth!"

He made a face and waggled his hands in the air. "Yes, yes. Damn me to each of the Nine Hells in turn and all that rot. Let me save us all the time. Yet it does not help either of us very much right now, does it? Listen to me, sister. It is imperative that I study our father's journal, and I need to know what you and others have learned of its secrets?"

Jerriel laughed weakly. "I bet you do."

Shaeddor lifted his trump cards in his fist, the Spectral Keys. "Little one, if you indeed know me as you claim, you will also understand what I can do to you and the entity Khia with these, while you are joined together. Do not force my hand. I can sense that our father's journal is magically concealed upon your person somehow, a simple conceal and carry spell, no doubt.

"Let us save both of us the wasted time and energy it would take me to torment you both, and in the end, force you to produce the journal in any case. The legacy of that journal belongs to us both. And I shall not use it in the ways you might think I will. I am not as much your enemy as you see me to be, Jerriel. Come now. Let us have a look at father's journal."

She seemed to believe him for once, and spoke the spell commands to unlock the location of the journal in its hiding place in her robes, and produce it between them on the table.

"Good girl," Shaeddor told her. "You were always such a sweet, obedient, reasonable, and practical child. That's what makes you so predictable."

First he took up the journal, stepped away, and sealed his sister and the entity within a shield dome of opaque air energy. That way, they could not bother or attack him if he became self-absorbed.

Shaeddor perceived and bypassed the journal's basic wards and defenses. His father never knew it, but as a magical prodigy, his savant son had peeked into his father's secret journal many times since the age of ten.

The real trick to the journal was getting time with it alone, and—unlocking their father's ingenious, shifting magical code. The enchanted code which he almost always wrote in, out of habit, in a world of intrigue.

As a clever boy, it had taken Shaeddor nearly three years to figure that shifting code out. The magical keys to the enchanted code we're, in the end, mostly mathematical. One was even a song, and could be briefly spelled silently, whistled, or sung.

At last the journal opened its secrets to him, and Shaeddor skimmed through all of its newer sections.

Toward the end of their father's notations, it was clear that both of their parents feared the worst—that the Sixth High Mage of Tharanor, the High Sorcerer of mighty Sylurria—was in fact leading them all to some kind of destruction.

Gorrial was most likely the High Magus of the Dark Khabal, which over the course of thousands of years, had grown great once more and infiltrated every land. Great enough now to challenge all of the nations of Tharanor, and wrest control of their world from them via some terrible curse or cataclysm, and offer them all up to the Shadow Ghods.

Little did anyone else know that yet another sister world to their own, in another dimension adjacent to theirs, would also be horribly maimed and involved directly. And so Urth was ensnared in their plots as well. The Khabal sought to create not one, but two new Shadow Worlds for their Dark Masters.

Toward the end of the last winter, their parents took steps to send word in secret, and raise the alarm in the colonies and in to the Old World. They did so at great peril to themselves and their children. The Dark Khabal suspected something amiss. Their father's worst fears were confirmed, when their mother's ship from Kellendra to Tornhold was suddenly wrecked at night in a strange, violent storm with all hands lost.

Their father could do nothing, not with the lives of his two children at stake. He attempted to send them both away in secret, yet after Shaeddor innocently divulged this to his master, his father had been found dead after another fierce battle upon the walls of Vaejan within the week.

The Merge was triggered only days after that, with Jerriel already on the run in wilds near Urthara.

The rest Shaeddor knew from his own experiences on the side of the Merge with Mason and the others there, and his amnesia.

One more thing their father had made note of, among the Dark Khabal's many schemes. There was something called 'the Great Plot' and involved two names written down that Shaeddor had not heard before: *Lyssiel* and some other being with two names, Naerel and Zhoggoroth.

The latter was apparently some kind of infernal plan of the Dark Ghods against the Celestial Guardians themselves. That was all that the sketchy notations recorded.

Was this the matter that Gorrial was so concerned about?

Shaeddor took the time to make a quick, magickal copy of the journal for his own purposes, and magickally tucked it away for safe keeping in his own robes.

Then he cast an enchantment of his own on the journal. After that, he tore out the few pages of notes regarding the Khabal's plans, destroying all knowledge of them. It wasn't really that much in any case. Their parents had not been given time to divulge very much at all about their foe's machinations.

Within days of those sketchy notes, both of their parents had been eliminated.

Shaeddor negated the air shield around his sister and the entity. Jerriel lifted her pretty head up from where she had been resting it on her slender arms.

"Quickly, sister. I need to know how much of this journal you have deciphered, what you have read, and who you have told these things to?" He brandished the gauntlet keys once more, just for good measure.

She lifted one hand briefly, and licked her lips. "I've gone through it a page at a time, and made my own notes along the way. I was only through part of it. There's been so much heavy fighting up until now this year, that I didn't have time to do much more."

"Where did you leave off?"

"What does it matter?" she said.

"It could mean your death, Jerriel."

"After..." her voice caught in her throat. "A-after mother died, and father was certain that the Khabal was involved and that Gorrial must be their High Magus. The Khabal was plotting many evil things, like capturing cities around the world after some great calamity that was coming. I didn't get any further than that. But there really wasn't much more left to decipher."

Shaeddor studied her. She was telling the truth. There really wasn't much left to decode after that point, and apparently she hadn't even made it through the rest.

He tossed the journal back in front of her with a slight thump.

"Sister, who have you told these things to?"

Jerriel sat up straight and defiant. "To everyone I could, to expose you and your murdering master, and all of your foul kind."

Shaeddor smiled. "How self-righteous. Know that I was not, am not now, or never will be a sworn member of the Dark Khabal, even if they kill me. I shall never make the vow, offer them my soul, or make the Gonashodul–although, if put to it, I might need to flirt with that somewhat, if they force me too. I know that you may not understand or believe me, after what all has passed.

"But for many reasons, some of them my own, your enemies are secretly my enemies, Jerriel. When all has come to pass, no matter what happens to me, I shall seek my vengeance upon them from within, as only I can pursue it and see it done, in my own time. I ask for no one's pity. Believe what you will."

Jerriel laughed. "You viper, you loathsome snake. You expect me–your sister–to believe this madness that you spew out? After all that you have done? Just more of your dissembling to confuse everyone, throw them off, and keep them guessing."

He smiled what he felt to be a sad smile at his little sister. "Then what if I tell you that the Khabal has unleashed a plan across both worlds to seize them, city by city, and claim them for the Shadows?"

Jerriel laughed again. "Anyone might guess that. That is simply what the Khabal always does. That is nothing new. Such is always their goal. You'll have to do much better than that, Shae, if you ever expect to gain my trust again."

"Everything I tell you is true. Be careful who you divulge these things to, in case they are traced back to me."

"Oh, I'm sure," she mocked. "Perhaps I'll go right before the High Magus and expose you as the great traitor in his midst?"

Shaeddor sighed. "I certainly hope not. Sister, I would dearly, dearly regret being forced to kill you!"

"Liar! You can't wait to murder me, just like you killed mother and father. For all I know, Gorrial commanded you to do so—with your own two hands!"

"I did not. I swear I did not. I would never—!"

"Who else could have snuck up on father and murdered him up close, his chest blown out from the back, by magic? I went to the crypt in secret and saw father's body and mourned and wept over him in secret. I did that for him. Not you! He was not riddled with arrows and spears of the enemy, as Gorrial claimed."

Shaeddor could not help wiping his eyes.

"Oh, good," Jerriel mocked. "Spare me your dragon's tears. I know what a superb actor you are, brother."

He flung the shield up once more and turned his back on her for awhile to be left with his conflicted thoughts.

Then, when he had composed himself once again, he brought the barrier down and glared at her.

Jerriel stiffened a bit. "So what now? Do you simply kill me here, or turn me over to the Khabal for further torture and questioning?"

"There's more for me to tell you, and then, as promised, I'm letting you go, whether you believe me or not. Yet you might have to flee north up into Shendor and survive for a day or two. The Khabal will not give up their pursuit of you very easily. Don't try to go south for a time, or in your weakened state they will detect and capture you for certain."

Jerriel raised both eyebrows in mock astonishment. "Oh, very well. So, we're still playing out this façade, this fantasy? Right. You're just going to let me go. How stupid do you think I am?"

"Right now, pretty stupid, sis. I have to say it. Of course, I'll have to injure myself in some way, something close enough to lethal so that the Khabal is convinced that you nearly killed me. Then I barely managed to escape with the help of my entity. And as I said, they will still pursue you for many days after I am gone, so head north, as far as you can for a time to shake them off of your trail."

"Yes, of course, we'll be certain to do just that," she said."

"Believe me or not, Jerriel, that's your best chance at escape. Right now, all of the Khabal's Shendor forces are down south here, except for some kind of weird, solo military mission heading up across the straights, near the broken old Urth bridge into Shenedar.

"Now, as for the attacks across southern Shendor. The Khabal will take victories where they can, of course, but all of these attacks and others are all feints, mere distractions to keep everyone on both sides busy and confused."

"Oh, I'm sure they are. So tell me, is the real target Michiana once again?"

"No, not at all. The real objectives are Nenarra, Kavendo, and Jashakal. From their key anchor point at Kavendo, if they can capture those three cities to the south, they can split the continent in half and easily take control of the eastern half and all of the inner seas. Once they have consolidated those gains, they will move in earnest upon the western half."

"Got it."

"Oh, and did I mention that the Khabal has an undead army that is sweeping east from Vaejan, at least ten million strong? They intend to use the undead as shock troops against the entire region."

"How wonderful."

"They also have millions of more undead at their command, from all of the other overpopulated Urth cities that became deathtraps after the Merge, all across both worlds. Undead will swell their ranks even more in their bid for conquest across the two worlds."

Jerriel smiled and gritted her teeth. "Well good for them. At least they aren't all gathered together in one place, I suppose. Well then, I guess you'd better get going older brother. Is that about it? Are we done here?"

Shaeddor nodded. "I suppose so. Oh, and as you might guess, they're still on the look out to capture any of the Spectral Entities from either world, and to capture and kill any of the other recovering High Mages from Tharanor. I'll leave the keys to Khia with you, at a safe distance, right before I depart."

"Uh huh. Sure you will."

He sensed something was wrong; something was different.

Suddenly Jerriel sped straight at him with a lightning dagger raised high in both hands, already plunging down toward his heart.

Her face was a mask of hate.

Too late, he realized his mistake. The Urth entity had separated from Khia.

Jerriel had recovered part of her own formidable strength.

She wasn't weak any longer.

His speed only eluded death for an instant, as the lightning dagger pierced his right breast and tore through his lung, paralyzing him as he staggered and gasped.

He was paralyzed, transfixed on the lightning blade.

"Now I've got you, brother dear. Drop the gauntlets!"

She didn't notice that he had already done so.

If he broke free before she could kill him, he could heal himself, even from near death, with the powers of his own entity.

Yet he could not do so once he was already dead.

"Now you're our prisoner, brother. Try to resist, and I'll kill you."

91

He clearly could not let himself be captured, and suffer his own Spectral Key and Entity to be stripped from him.

Jerriel was already reaching for his onyxian crystal necklace in triumph.

He had to surprise her, no matter the cost.

Shaeddor spun to the right and dragged the lightning dagger easily through the rest of his chest, severing his right arm just below the armpit.

The agony was beyond belief. He nearly blacked out, but the razor-thin lightning blade cauterized the grim wounds instantly.

He almost missed grabbing his falling arm with his left hand, and summoned the power of his own entity, even as Jerriel sought to finish the job.

Lightning seared his back just as the entity's defenses snapped up with the barest thought.

Instantly he raced through the sky toward Vaejan, struggling to stay conscious, trying to heal himself and re-attach his own arm. He discovered that he could not achieve the latter on his own, without assistance, but somehow he sustained his life.

Jen's ghost suddenly took shape beside him. He could almost feel her wrapped around himself. A wide, red velvet choker seemed to hold her head on.

"I can almost feel your touch," he told her.

She smiled. "The closer you are to death, the closer you are to me, my heart. I am drawn to you. I cannot help it. I have nowhere else to go."

Only the great speed of the Entity of Night could save him now, and he lingered on in pain and horror for what seemed hours, but was probably mere minutes.

Jen's shade faded away. He nearly cried out.

Somehow he reached the Khabal fortresses in Vaejan and dropped down before the feet of his master, more than half dead.

# TORI

Tori went through one of the portals and met up with the Shooting Stars at their own practice range on the other side, an expansive area cleared from the wreckage of the last war. Their custom shooting area was much like a baseball field, with range bands and targets noted by bright colored blocks and placards spread out before them.

As for the stars themselves, Minnie Patterson and Hannah Masters were less than a year younger than herself, both of them bright and beautiful. Both of them were cheerful, despite being veterans from the Michiana Wars against the enemy. They wore suits of white leather and shining, polished metal plate armor, designed to protect them as much as possible, and yet not get in the way of their efforts as elite archers.

Because they were not currently at war, they did not wear their battle helmets. Their long hair flowed free, pulled back only by thin, braided leather headbands tied in the back. With the summer sun they wore sunscreen to avoid sunburn, but they also had slight tans.

As far as Tori understood it, Minnie and Hannah were Wild Magic infusion sorcerers, similar to herself and Mason. Instead of enchanted black powder weapons, they focused their abilities and powers through their chosen weapons—bows and arrows. Minnie preferred a compound or wheelbow, and Hannah preferred an older-style recurve. By this time, after so much training, both of them were expert archers.

Minnie was five feet nothing with stunning blond hair and dazzling blue eyes. Hannah was about Tori's height, only a a few inches taller, with curly brown hair and brown eyes. They worked in tandem, supporting each other.

"During the Merge," Minnie explained, "Hannah and I were hurled into a pond of Wild Magic, just like Mace was. When we came out of the small lake, we were infused with a similar kind of Wild Magic."

"Yet our situation is a slightly different version," Hannah said. "We can actively infuse our arrows with various magical abilities and powers."

"At first we did it with rocks and stones and slingshots," Minnie added.

"But then, when we were given bows and arrows, we found them to be much more accurate and effective," Hannah said.

Tori grinned, readying her own pistols. "Before I show you my stuff, this is the first time we've had a chance to have a little fun together. Show me what you two can do."

The Shooting Stars giggled. "Luckily, we can infuse our arrows ahead of time, even in large quantities," Minnie said. "They seem to last indefinitely, and do not degrade in any way."

"But we have to fire them to get them to work, "Hannah noted, "from a bow that we use. Like your and Mason's firearms, no one else can fire our arrows and get them to work. Our powers are unique and specifically attuned to us."

Minnie was the first to take aim at a target. "We have four types of arrows, each of them clearly marked, and with different colored fletchings. Each type causes a specific blast of powerful, destructive Wild Magic that affects an area about thirty to forty feet in diameter. For example, this is a standard explosive arrow."

She loosed. Her shaft struck a standing target set within the center of a stand of two score wooden stick dummies, representing a platoon of enemy troops or creatures.

The explosive blast shredded almost every dummy target.

"This is lightning arrow," Hannah said. Her arrow blasted another target zone of cardboard boxes with lightning and electricity.

"Fire arrow," Minnie said, firing and immolating the area around a huge metal monster target.

"And last but not least," Hannah said, "an ice arrow."

The ice blast covered a series of posts with thick ice, freezing them together within a similar area.

Tori studied each of the four blasts areas. "Hmmm…you are correct. Just like you said, between thirty and forty feet. That's about the same area of effect as a mage's spell."

"Ahh," Minnie noted. "Yet mages use up their energies quickly, and then they are exhausted, if they don't have a focus like a staff or a wand or such. While we can fire our arrows one after the other, and infuse them ahead of time, or in an instant, in all four modes."

"You Pistoleros can fire even faster that we can," Hannah said, "and out to farther ranges, doing even greater damage, with your devastator and annihilator rounds. Do they really incorporate uranium, Tori"

"The sure do. We're even trying to figure out how to weaponize very small quantities of cobalt and plutonium, but we don't want to wipe ourselves out at the same time. The blast effects might encompass us as well."

Minnie put her wheelbow down and leaned on the fence. "All right, that's almost all of our tricks. We hear that you can produce effects that Mace can't. Can you show us what they are?"

Tori stepped forward and readied all of her rigs. "Well, both of us can fire our weapons dry–without them actually being loaded with powder and shot–and still produce an effect. Mason fires destructive blasts that are orange, and can still be lethal. But what we discovered, is that my dry blasts are blue, and they do not kill. They merely stun anything living that they hit."

"That's something new," Hannah said. "We don't have a non-lethal attack."

She showed them her blue stun blasts, which only seemed to lightly shake or jar the targets, without doing much damage. "I have an ice blast as well, very similar to yours," Tori said, switching pistols and zapping another set of targets with ice.

"Mace can't do that. But like him, I can negate other magic attacks attacks if I time my shots right. And I have the standard explosive and flame rounds, and other specialized rounds that the loaders can produce with unique components. But neither of us have an electrical or a lightning round, the way that you two have lightning arrows."

Hannah looked knowingly at Minnie. "Let's show her what we've been working on."

Minnie nodded and stepped up to the line.

She did not draw an arrow.

Instead she simply drew her empty bowstring back.

But a glowing form of a bright blazing arrow took shape all the same, out of nothing.

Hannah grinned. "We call it...the spirit arrow. We can form it out of pure energy."

"Omigosh!" Tori said. "That's amaz—"

Minnie let fly.

There was a blinding eruption.

When they could see again, the entire target field was wiped out, and the grass was scorched down to the smoking dirt. The dirt was baked hard, and the core of the impact crater was fused to a disk of clear, crystal glass.

Hannah moved, caught Minnie, and held her up, when her friend nearly fainted. "Steady, steady. Wow, Min. That one was the strongest yet!"

Minnie shook her head, looking paler than normal. "Uh-huh...but every one of those spirit arrows takes a lot out of you."

Tori warned them. "You must be creating those spirit arrows out of your own energies. Check with the mages and the healers before you use them any more. If you drain your own life forces too much, you could kill yourselves. So be careful."

The targeting area would have to be repaired and re-set. They were done practicing for that day. Tori still found it amazing that a select few of them had these amazing abilities. People called them The Champions.

For her part, Tori found it humbling. Minnie and Hannah seemed to just go with it all and take it in stride. For them, all of this was normal now.

"So," Tori asked, "what do you girls do for fun when you're not blasting monsters to smithereens?"

Hannah grinned sadly and shook her head. "The army keeps us busy with a lot of promotional stuff all around the area."

"Yeah, we're sort of their cover girls. Sometimes it's fun. Other times, not so much."

Hannah looked very serious all of the sudden. "Our families are still missing. We spend a lot of time on our own searching for them still, on both sides."

"A lot of refugees were pushed south of town during the first months and battles after the Merge," Minnie noted. "Our families might have been caught up in all of that."

"They might have been captured by the enemy mercenaries, or they might have made it to Indianapolis," Hannah said. "We keep wanting to go there, but the Army wants to keep us here, just in case they need us."

Minnie gathered up her gear. "That's why we can't wait for Mace to lead that train expedition to try to reach Indy. If travel between the two cities can be established, eventually, one or both of us might be able to go down there and search for our missing families."

Hannah grinned. "So, Tori, what's it like dating Mace?"

Now that they saw an opening, they didn't waste any time.

"We know he's taken," Minnie said. "But we've always thought he was dreamy. What a cowboy."

Tori smiled. "I think so too. I'm really lucky. And whatever anyone says about him, I want you know what a good guy he is. He has a big heart, and he's a man, not some boy. He's not perfect. None of us are, but I love him in every way possible."

"We know he really loves you," Hannah noted.

"Yeah," Minnie said. "Anyone can see that."

She sighed. "I just hope that I can live up to this reputation he's given me. And I know that some still see the Pistolera as Pistolero-Light."

Hannah laughed. "Yeah, we kinda went through that, too. Just be yourself and you'll be fine."

Minnie added, "That's all that you can do any way. Shake off anything else. It doesn't matter what people who don't know you think."

"Hey, Tori said. "We now have some time on our hands. Why don't we go back across and visit him with the balloonists?"

Minnie's eyes almost popped. "Heck yeah! We might be able to catch a ride."

Tori opened her mouth, but realized her foot was in it.

"I'll go with you guys," Hannah said, "but I'm afraid of heights."

"I was just kidding myself," Tori told them. "I'm probably more scared of heights than you are."

Hannah's eyes got pretty big out of fear. "I doubt that."

"But come on, it could still be fun watching from the ground or up in one of the observation towers. I'm glad some people have the nerve to go up in those contraptions."

"I can't wait to go up in one," Minnie said. She was always fearless it seemed. "You guys ready?"

# MASON

Mason finished securing his parachute pack around him, opened the side hatch, and climbed into the basket of the observation balloon. He secured the hatch behind him. Anyone going up was required to wear a parachute. Eventually, Mason would need to get checked out on them and earn his wings.

The balloon he and Rob were in was one of the first working models, more or less a standard round, hydrogen-filled balloon. The basket and its frame and floor were made of high strength, light weight materials. It normally had a crew of four, who were training as aerial spotters and observers.

Normal hot air balloons had been tried at first, but they were fickle and not very maneuverable, more or less carried about on the prevailing winds.

Rob beamed and showed Mason the new lightweight, steam magic engine they had installed, complete with an extended propeller that wasn't in use at the moment. As tethered observers, they would simply go up and down on a rope over the practice fields, no more than a few hundred feet.

"The engine only has a top speed of twenty miles an hour, give or take the wind. But its cruising speed is abut ten or eleven, and it can run for up to a week without much maintenance."

"But aren't you worried about the hydrogen problem?" Mason said, looking up at the big bag of flammable gas. That did make him a little nervous.

"Future versions will use helium instead," Rob noted. "But we're rapidly expanding beyond this basic form." He pointed at one of the slightly larger, cylinder-shaped dirigibles, tapered on both ends, as they rose up to about a hundred feet. The aerial grounds shrank in scale beneath them both.

"The Buteo class blimps like *The Vulturo* there are twice as fast, much more maneuverable, and can carry a crew of a dozen. We are also using it to test some of the new steam cannons, steam guns, and incendiary bombs—even flechette rounds like they used from WWI through Vietnam. That makes these airships our first practical gunships and bombing platforms. Flame throwers would simply be too impractical."

"Right," Mason noted, "an airship would have to get down too low and make itself vulnerable to direct attack in order to use flamethrowers."

"Exactly. We want to rule the skies and rain destruction down upon our foes from safely up above. We're testing various shapes, designs, and scale models for aerodynamics and maneuverability in makeshift wind tunnels, powered by steam engines. With planks and flameproof fibers from the fire trees, we can even armor them to some degree. They won't burn at least."

They were now up to almost two hundred feet above the ground and still going. Even that seemed incredibly high to Mason when he looked down. "Dragons could be a major threat," Mason noted.

"Indeed," Rob said with a customary grimace. "Dragons or other flying menaces could be serious threats to anyone, on the ground, or up in the sky in one of our balloons. And Jerriel and the other mages have warned us that there are even some mages who can levitate and fly. So that could be a problem as well. Nothing is ever completely safe or invulnerable in warfare. Ahh…they've signaled us. They're ready to start the tests. Let's watch for a bit, and then I'll have a nice surprise for us today."

They leveled off finally. Mason did not bother to look down. The light wind tugged them up tight against the tether, causing the basket to sway slightly. He didn't expect that. "How high are we up now?" he asked.

Rob lowered his field glasses. "About three hundred feet. Don't worry. The rapid deployment chutes we have on us should still save us even if deployed as low as two hundred feet—if you're well-trained.

"If something did go wrong, you'd jump free of the balloon, pull one or both rip cords, and hang onto the maneuvering handles to guide yourself down, usually in circles, aiming for a clear spot to land on. Grass being preferable to concrete, trees, buildings, or water. If you can't stay up, tuck and roll, protecting your head. Keep your wits and get out of your chute as fast as you can so that it won't drag you."

Mason felt the blood drain from his own face as he processed all of that. "So, you've done all of this before?"

"Nope," Rob said. "Only in simulation. But we're all scheduled to have our day. General Dirk Blackwood got his wings with us eight days ago. We are so lucky that we have that guy leading us."

Mason chuckled. "That figures. That fearless, crazy old bastard. He wasn't a Special Forces colonel for nothing, back in his day. This stuff must be child's play for guys like him. Well, I'll do my duty, but not today."

"Yeah," Rob said, "me too."

"So, what are we supposed to observe?" Mason asked.

"Oh, we don't have to do much," Rob told him. He jammed a thumb at the other two crew, working diligently with binoculars, stopwatches, pens and clipboards. "Joshua and Sam are studying how each parachute design performs. All of these are fast release chutes, like the ones used by base jumpers. They usually like to jump from at least five hundred to a thousand feet up. Base jumpers enjoy the thrill of freefall before they open."

"They can have mine," Mace said. "How high up are the test jumpers?"

"Yeah, we don't give a damn about freefall. *The Vulturo* is going to hover at various altitudes from seven hundred, down to as little as three hundred feet. Some of the jumpers will use static lines that deploy their chutes as soon as they jump out of the dirigible. Others will free jump and open their chutes manually. If something goes wrong, they have reserve chutes, but they will need to deploy them very quickly at short fall distances such as these."

"How high to skydivers normally jump from?"

"Oh, usually about two thousand feet up."

"Wow, so these are short fall jumps. I'm glad as hell that those chutes are designed to open fast."

Rob chuckled. "So are our test jumpers. But all them are experienced base jumpers and or ex-military paratroopers. They're all experts. We're conducting these tests to find the safest, most reliable parachute designs to mass produce for our future air force and paratroopers."

"Gosh, that will be something to see."

"I still have one question," Mason said. "I hate to ask it, but these are all tests, like you say. What happens if both chutes don't open?"

Rob sighed. "That has happened, once out of many thousands of test jumps. One test jumper was killed. Since then we've done our best, installing big nets and a huge air mattress, four stories high, under the test zone. But these tests are dangerous by their very nature. Look at it from where we are, only three hundred feet up. That mattress would still be hard to hit, while tumbling and falling, or spinning down on a tangled chute. One test jumper bounced off the edge of the air mattress, fell, and still broke both legs in multiple places. They all understand the risks."

The airship *The Vulturo* had a skeleton crew of two people, the captain and the engineer steering the ship. They more or less rose up and down, ferrying the test jumpers up to specific low altitudes to conduct their jumps, one batch after another. The various chutes seemed to be of many different styles, shapes, and designs.

Drama did occur that day. One jumper was forced to open his reserve chute, after his main chute did not open properly. The young woman made it down safely. The defective main chute would be gone over very carefully to see what had gone wrong and how it could be corrected.

The tests ended that day, shortly after four p.m. The winches below them began to bring them down. "And now for our little surprise," Rob said.

A large hangar opened up, and a sleek new blimp design rolled out among teams of horses and people. The shape was unlike any blimp or dirigible Mason had ever seen before. In fact, it looked more like a flying wing, or some kind of flying devilfish, or manta ray.

It was four the times the size of *The Vulturo*, still circling around up above. It's steam magic engines and propellers were big, and there were three engines spread out on each side, under the wing and to the rear of the airship. It had six of the big new engines in total, and that was impressive.

The network of gondola cabins beneath the vessel were all equally aerodynamic, and self-contained.

"Are those cabins pressurized?" Mason asked.

"If they need to be. Good eye, Mace. The cowling on the motors will also help prevent icing. This is the prototype for the Sky Falcon class of airships. She was christened, *The Gray Falcon*, and she's heading out today on her maiden test flight. We can join her and her crew, if you like."

"Mercy," Mason said aloud. "just get us over there before she takes off!"

As soon as they disembarked from the observation balloon, Mason heard familiar voices calling to them.

"Mace, Rob!"

They looked back and saw Tori and the Shooting Stars hopping off their bikes, dropping them to the ground. The trio of pretty ladies ran up to them.

"Excellent timing if you want a ride!" Rob told them.

Mason could not contain his own excitement. "Hey, how would you ladies like to take a trip up into the sky in Michiana's newest airship, *The Gray Falcon?*"

"Let's go!" Minnie Patterson blurted out. She ran straight for the craft, not waiting for any of them.

Tori and Hannah hung back a bit. They even looked a little sick.

"Oh, come on," Mason told them. "I know the two of you don't like heights, but it's perfectly safe."

Rob handed them their parachutes. " Here you go. Just put these on."

Tori's eyes grew even bigger than Hannah's. "If it's so safe, why do we have to wear parachutes?"

"Just a precaution, I assure you," Rob told them. "It is a test flight, so everyone on board has to go along with certain protocols."

"It's going to be fine," Mason told them. "Let's go. This will be great!"

"Don't forget to take the bag with your gloves, goggles, and crash helmet," Rob reminded them.

Mason glared at him for an instant. "Saying anything with 'crash' in it right now isn't helping, Rob."

"Oh, sorry."

Tori and Hannah went with them, but they did not appear to be enjoying themselves very much.

As soon as they were all loaded up inside, buckled into their lightweight, ergo dynamic flight seats, the airship cleared its moorings, and prepared to take off on its first voyage.

Then at the last instant, warning bells awoke throughout South Bend, erupting all over the city. Something big was up, and right before *The Gray Falcon* lifted off, a military messenger just barely leaped on board.

Tori and Hannah looked petrified, and glared straight at Mason.

"So what's that all about?" Tori demanded.

Mason smiled. "A military courier just joined us. I'm sure we'll find out soon enough."

"I bet we will," Tori said. She reached over and clutched Hannah's trembling hand. Hannah clutched back, both of them in the literal grips of white-knuckled fear.

Neither of the ladies stopped glaring at Mason and Rob.

The buildings outside the windows suddenly receded as the airship floated straight up. Then the mighty engines hummed louder, increasing their power and driving *The Gray Falcon* forward.

"Eureka!" Rob cried aloud. "Success. We are aloft. Hooray!"

Almost everyone clapped and cheered. Minnie unbuckled herself without permission and ran over to one of the observations windows. "Wow, we're gaining altitude fast. This is so great. Look how high up we are already!"

Tori and Hannah closed their eyes tight and actually clung to each other, praying hard and fast. "Oh, god in heaven, will that girl shut up," Tori finally exclaimed.

Mason laughed. "See, guys? It's perfectly fine."

Tori glared over at him. "You know, I do have loaded guns. I could shoot your dumb ass right now for talking us into this madness!"

Relax," Mason told them.

One of the airship's officers made his way toward them, followed by the Army messenger.

It was another of their friends, Pete Steiner, now a lieutenant in the Airship Corps, of all things. But he looked pretty grim at the moment.

"Pete," Mason said, rising up out of his seat. "Great to see you, buddy. You look good in that monkey suit. How are you doing?"

"Thanks, not too bad." Pete nodded; the two of them shook hands. "Good to see you folks, too," Pete said. "But if you pardon me, we'll need to dispense with the pleasantries for now. Just as we launched, this messenger came to us directly from General Blackwood and the High Command of Michiana.

"By orders I am to summon the Pistoleros, the Shooting Stars, and Robert Billings, the chief enchanter before my captain, Captain Llewellyn McKay, for further orders and instructions. If you would please follow me."

The five of them gathered together and went with Pete.

"Tell us what it is, Pete," Tori said. "What are we up against this time?"

"According to what we know, we're about to be under heavy attack by the enemy once more."

"Damnation," Mason exclaimed, resting his hands on his pistols. "What the hell is it this time?"

Pete stopped at the door he was about to open for them, leading forward to the bridge. "From what we've been told, it's zombies. Millions and millions of zombies from Chicago, flooding this way, and spilling out north and south."

"Screw that," Minnie said. "I hate zombies. They freak me out!"

Tori laughed and then sighed. "Well, at least we'll be able to fight them on the ground."

# DAVID

The vanguard for Army 16 kept marching for another hour, traveling due east toward Kalamazoo-Bentar. They had no further sign of the enemy after they left the nexus behind them.

It was still mid-morning.

Jerriel and Khia were gone, captured by Jerriel's insane brother, working for the Dark Khabal.

David shuddered.

But exhausting the vanguard and his friends wasn't going to help Jerriel and the Spectral Entity, or solve much of anything.

They found a good, defensible spot to make camp. Let the vanguard rest up. Let the full might of Army 16 catch up to them the next day. After a half day of travel together, they would finally be in sync, and ready to pursue the enemy full on. Then they could attempt to locate and win the captives back.

He could only guess that the captives would travel with their captors, with Jerriel's brother, and the leaders of the enemy forces in Shendor. Find them, and find the captives.

But what if he was wrong? The enemy could use their own transport devices to send the captives anywhere: back near Michiana, or to Vaejan, or

Kellendra, or some other enemy stronghold they didn't even know about—on either side.

What then? What could they do?

He couldn't lose her. What would the enemy do to her and Khia?

David struggled with his fears, frustrations, and other wild thoughts and emotions. He had to keep it together. He had an army to help lead. Think. Think like a leader. Defeat the enemy in the field. That was the only thing that could make anything better.

Focus on their operations. Stay strong. That's what Jerriel would do. She would never give up. He needed to be the same way.

Something would break for them.

Even as they made camp, he thought of the Khabal's next moves in the region. Keep his scouts and patrols collecting information and move quickly on anything they found. Stay prepared for further enemy attacks; they knew that more attacks were coming. The enemy would continue to hammer them and hit them hard at every opportunity, degrade them and wipe them out, if possible.

Their mission had to continue. Try to help Kalamazoo and Battle Creek along the way to Detroit. Then march down to Toledo and break the siege of Kellendra. Get the transport station set up there. If Kellendra was lost, take the station back up to Detroit. Get word to Cleveland, somehow.

And all the while, try to locate Jerriel and Khia and safely win them back.

He made camp. He went into his tent to try to rest after checking with the princes and his other friends.

Al, Jason, Pastor Brian, and Stacy Keller, his private healer came to his tent to check on him.

"My friend," Jason said. "We're all worried about Jerriel, and we can only imagine how upset you must be. We've come to offer you some help, if we can."

David sat with his head in his hands, exhausted but unable to sleep. He raked his hands through his hair. "I appreciate the support, guys. But there's just not much that anyone can do."

"We can give you some rest, David," Pastor Brian said, placing a big armored hand on his shoulder softly. "That will help you keep up your strength and your wits. Exhausting yourself and going sleepless won't do you or anyone any good."

David chuckled sadly. "Well, unless you intend to wrestle me down and knock me out, I don't see how you can force me to go to sleep."

The other three turned to Stacy. She came closer and took David's right hand in hers. "As part of my new healing abilities, if you don't resist my efforts, I can give several hours of decent sleep. Better than you might have on your own, under the circumstances. It will just be like normal sleep. If something goes wrong, you'll wake up. But you're safe right now and under close guard. All of your friends are close at hand. We'll be trying to rest as well. Are you willing to give it a try?"

David nodded. "Thanks guys."

Stacy had him lie down on his cot and make himself as comfortable as possible. To help sooth him, she told him to close his eyes and breathe normally, and she hummed a tune softly.

As Stacy put forth her her healing energies, he slowly drifted off, in spite of his troubled thoughts.

Naturally, he had dreams of Jerriel up against various dangers and threats, always just out of his reach where he could not help her.

He tossed and turned a bit, but he did sleep.

When he snapped awake at the bright sunlight the next day, the time on his watch read almost eleven.

At least he felt somewhat rested and energized. He sat up on his cot.

Stacy, Al, Jason, and Brian had all pulled their cots into his tent and were sleeping in a protective circle around him. He was lucky to have them as his family now.

He snuck out to hit the latrine. Let his friends sleep a bit more.

Army 16 should be catching up to them very soon, and then the vanguard would give the new arrivals a short rest. They they all would travel together for another half a day.

The day after that, they should reach Kalamazoo and see what they would see.

David gathered his things and dressed in back of his pavilion, putting on his armor and weapons with the help of some of his Blackhawk guards.

The instant he finished, he heard the marching sounds of Army 16 rejoining them on their extreme left flank. Drums rumbled. Battle horns called out, and were answered by similar horn calls from the vanguard.

He heard groans from inside his tent. At least he didn't have to worry about waking his friends up.

The vanguard mess unit had been given orders to start lunch that day, and the Army 16 mess teams simply joined in as they arrived.

They had a quick lunch for ten thousand plus troops completed by one o'clock. That was a major feat of discipline and efficiency within itself.

Then the Army people rested for one hour while the fresh vanguard forces spent the time double-checking the mounts, wagons, and equipment.

David and the princes went over their situation with the Army 16 one star general, positioned their units for travel and defensive operations, and sent a fresh report back toward Michiana via express rider.

General Deacon Culpepper was about forty-four and couldn't have been tougher if he had been forged out of pig iron. He was five foot ten, with a rough, short flat top so stiff, it looked like one might use it to file steel. He was a little thicker around the waist, but he still had the muscled look of a football running back.

His skin was the dark brown, shiny color of chocolate syrup, and his dark brown eyes were as quick to laugh, as they were to ignite when he dressed some idiot down who damn well needed it.

Culpepper was the real deal. Everything about him shouted toughness and intelligent, calculated mean. He had been a decorated captain in what he called the 'U.S. of A Army' before the Merge, rose through the ranks, and was battle-tested many times over–a natural born leader.

During the defense of downtown South Bend, Culpepper as a captain and one of the few surviving officers, had protected half of that area with a dwindling force of militia for three crucial days and nights against heavy odds.

Half of them perished in that desperate ordeal, but the other half were forged into an elite fighting unit that would never give in until death claimed them. Each trooper, male or female, counted themselves equal to a full score of the enemy.

They were the foundation of Army 16, and they prided themselves on their toughness, smarts, and their fearless fighting spirit. They were a combat unit, pure and simple, and they made in known that anyone who joined up with them had better be ready to live up to that creed.

They'd follow Damnation Deke Culpepper and their officers and non-coms into the fires of Hell itself and back.

David and his elite Blackhawks could not have asked to be the vanguard for a tougher, more capable army unit.

From what their L.R.R.P. scouts told them, they were in for it. Even the balloon unit spotters had gone up in the sky, tethered to their winch wagon, and saw masses of enemy troops and mercenaries ignoring them, for the time being, and swarming around Kalamazoo and Battle Creek like vast, dark plagues.

"Gentlemen and ladies," Deke said calmly, as they made their final plans on the maps. "We estimate the enemy strength at minimal to be fifty thousand strong. And that's just on this side. With their monster hordes at night and these rumors of countless undead we keep hearing about, those numbers could quickly become twice that, against our ten thousand or so. The odds didn't really make any difference to Sixteen. Yet on a practical level, that was still either five to one, or ten to one at best."

David nodded. "No, those numbers don't lie, and that doesn't even include what the enemy is using to bottle up Detroit and attack Toledo.

The enemy has been preparing for this for a long while. Those forces must be just as large, if not larger."

Thulkara spoke up bravely, as any Thul might. "A mass of cowards and slaves mean nothing, however great. All of you faced far great odds in defense of your Urthara cities."

"Quite true," Deke agreed. "Yet we are on the move across open and varied terrain, to say the least. We no longer have the home field advantage of defending in built up areas where we can bleed the foe every inch that they advance. As we have already discussed at length, we need to stay foxy and be careful. I have been in touch, briefly, with Generals Lloyd and Ridley on the other other side, commanding Armies 27 and 33.

"They are reporting very light resistance and no major masses of enemy troops yet. So it appears that the enemy will try to take us out first on this side. If they succeed, naturally they will shift over to the other side and try to do the same to our armies there."

"The point is well-taken," Prince Valandin said. "Clearly, we all see what no one has yet put into words. If the enemy knows where we are, and they have all of these superior numbers at their ready command, why don't they simply fall upon us, surround us and cut us off, and then wipe us out?"

"Because that's not their plan," David said. "Now that they have Jerriel and the Spectral Entity, they could care less about us and what we do. By all reports, they're barely scouting us. We're not part of their big picture for right now, and with the Marrandorians with us, they're most likely expecting us to race straight to Kellendra."

Prince Alendel raised one eyebrow, his armored arms crossed in front of him. "Might I ask, why we are not doing just that?"

Prince Valandin cut David off with a raised hand. "Captain, I want to rescue our cousin Jerriel from the enemy as badly as you do, and we certainly can't allow our foes to gain another Spectral Entity to use as a weapon against. We've seen first hand what such beings are capable of.

"But let us face facts. We don't even know where they are or if they're still alive. Meanwhile, my brother is right. There are countless lives at stake in Kellendra, your Toledo, which we know is under siege this very moment–Tharanorians, and Urthers–waiting for us to get there and help lift the siege."

"While we roam around exploring the Hand of Shendor," Alendel said.

David held his ground. "Your Highnesses, your points are well taken, apart from the concerns you mention, we must study what the enemy is doing. We may not be able to defeat the foe in the open field, but we could certainly upset their plans along the way in this vital area, on the doorstep of their main colonial stronghold of Vaejan.

"From all that Jerriel said, the enemy is fighting a big picture strategy, across both sides, on both worlds, and they are attacking on all fronts with everything they have. They are totally committed. Even before we left, this was the path that we agreed to take, and along the way, we all agreed to investigate the situation and hit the enemy where we could do the most good."

"Your Highnesses," Deke joined in. "Captain Pritchard is more than correct. We can only guess that Kalamazoo-Bentar and Battle Creek-Huran are under just as much threat, if not more, than Kellendra-Toledo. And the populations holding out there are smaller and much more vulnerable. We cannot bypass them and leave them to their fates, without at least checking with them and offering them some assistance. That would be inhumane, even criminal. Both sides of those cities, post Merge, are probably defending whatever they have left with populations of about twenty to thirty thousand in total, with only a third to a half of them of fighting age."

David shuffled through their latest scouting reports. "And there can be no doubt now. The foe is bending all of their forces on crushing these two smaller cities, first on this side. They have them surrounded now and are laying siege to them with catapults, mass attacks, magic, and everything that they brought to bear against us in Michiana. But the difference was— we had enough numbers to fight them off."

"Unless we bring them some relief, and at least give their civilians a chance to escape, both cities will fall in a blood bath that is going to make Niles look like a goddam cotillion! I say we stay together, hit the enemy hard, and try to relieve first one city, and then the next. I'm just sorry that we can't do both at the same time."

"We can set up the transport station again and funnel civilians through it, back to Michiana if we have to," David said. "We just can't march by and leave all of those people to their doom."

Alendel looked to his brother, and then nodded. Valandin turned back to them. "Then it is agreed. We will attack, harry, and weaken the enemy along the way, helping these cities as we can. But then, when that is done, we march to Tornhold as we agreed before, and then south to Kellendra. We cannot delay any more than that."

Both Deke and David nodded. "Agreed," they said in unison.

General Culpepper added. "I will only call the other armies in as a last resort. Remember, if we pull them over to our side, the enemy could easily switch sides and destroy our civilians over there."

The action grew hot that night just after dark.

Kalamazoo-Bentar was so close that they decided to keep going after a quick respite and another bite to eat. The troops were still in good shape, and by now, they were eager for a fight.

They found one ready made.

The siege of Kalamazoo-Bentar was as hot a contest as any they had ever witnessed.

The Urther defenders clearly fought for their very lives. Everyone who could wield a weapon fought to hold the enemy back. Sadly, that included not just men and women of fighting age, but old people and older children as well. They fought with anything that could be used as a weapon, from baseball bats and lengths of closet poles made into spears, to kitchen knives and hand tools.

Some of them wore what helmets and protective gear they had been able to piece together. David spotted a lot of football helmets put into service for lack of anything better. He shuddered and for a moment relived several similar grim moments from the early days of the South Bend Militia.

Other defenders only fought with the clothes they had on, and no protective gear at all. The tally of dead and wounded on the lines was grim to behold. Their defensive lines were little more than rings of vehicles pushed up end to end and barricades of furniture and wreckage and rubble patched together in what appeared to be broke rings.

The Urthers were clearly in a bad way, and had very few arrows or missile weapons left, other than hurling heavy objects, and bricks, or other debris.

The enemy didn't even need to risk their battle mages and probably didn't even have them on the line. They sent their monster hordes up front as shock troops to press the attack, while the Dark Khabal troops and mercenary units fired arrows and crossbows from massed flights, and even catapults and ballistae from behind their lines.

Even without a military mind, it was clear to anyone that this end of the city was going to fall by morning, if not within the next hour or so.

David and the Blackhawks planned to hit the enemy as hard as possible from behind, the near flanks, and try to overrun the artillery positions. Then the Sixteen infantry would march in with pike and sword at the fore, fall upon the massed enemy archers and crossbowmain to reduce them. Archers from 16 would help clean up and slaughter anything that was left in the wake of the main assault.

Together, they would shatter the enemy position at that point. Then the army would drive their foes to either side, rolling them up as far as they could along the flanks, where they least expected to be attacked.

The vanguard would proceed to link up with the defenders, assess the situation, and go from there. Archers throughout all units were held back and kept ready to riddle any enemy battle mages they or others spotted with arrows.

David led the initial charge through the enemy rear defenses and among the artillery.

The first thing the enemy knew, they were being put down with Blackhawk spears and pikes, rank after rank, followed on hard by lines of sword and shield.

The situation quickly turned to a rout of the foe, as David and the Vanguard penetrated all the way through the enemy lines, causing great destruction and confusion.

After the up front assault was finished, the archers who brought up their rear with a thin line of spear and shield finished off the enemy fallen with their hand axes and short swords.

Why waste arrows?

As Deke's army rolled up the flanks, David and the princes hailed the defenders. All appeared to be going well to plan, but they knew that the advantage of surprise would not last long.

The Khabal still had waves of attackers that it could hurl at them.

"Hail to the defenders of Kalamazoo!" David shouted once more. "We've brought help from South Bend, Michiana. We are friends and allies. May we speak with your militia commanders?"

"Hold on," a voice called out. "Give us a chance to see who's still alive! We don't doubt you, but we can't just let you walk in with the numbers you have, either. We saw you mow those bastards down. Thanks for that. We're in a pretty bad way, here."

Seconds later, another voice called out. "I'm Captain Neal Harding of the Kalamazoo militia. Am I correct in assuming that you are from the vanguard of Army 16 out of Indiana? We've had some limited contact with one of your scouts who joined us to avoid being killed or captured. He told us very quickly about you folks. Unfortunately, he offered to fight beside us on the front lines, and died bravely about an hour ago."

"Thank you for the information," David said. "I'm David Pritchard."

"Captain of the Blackhawks? We heard a few stories that have reached us. Do you have your wizard girl with you?"

David frowned. "I don't like shouting at each other in the darkness. Can a small party of us approach to parlay in private? We'll even lay our weapons down and leave them behind if you prefer that."

"No, you'd better hang onto those. You might need them any minute around here. Come ahead, with no more than a dozen of your people, and we can talk. There's a lot going on. We need to be quick about things."

David went in beyond the defender front line with Prince Alendel and ten of his friends and bodyguards. They left Valandin and the Thulls with the vanguard to keep watch.

Captain Neal Harding took off his Kevlar army helmet with the cracked riot face shield. He wield a glaive polearm and had a double-bitted axe at his side, along with several hunting knives. Metal and plastic protective plates had been glued to his fatigue jacket and pants, even over his hockey gloves to deflect blows.

He shook David's hand, but his eyes looked weary, horror-stricken, and desperate. "Captain Pritchard, our defenses are collapsing as we speak. We can fight it out for a few more hours, but Kalamazoo is in the process of being overwhelmed. There's just too many of them for us to fight off, and we're too few, too worn out, and too disorganized. The enemy's already carving us up. We need to hold them off so that the bulk of our civilians and as many of us as we can spare can lead them toward Battle Creek. That's the next safe haven."

"I hate to inform you, Captain Harding, but Battle Creek is surrounded and under siege as well. They're probably just as bad off as you are here."

The man let out a breath and turned very pale. His eyes watered. When he spoke, it was like something between a sob and a groan. "Then we're going to see an awful lot of death tonight. What about South Bend and Michiana? It's days away, but that might be our only choice. They could try to make it there. Your forces could keep them ahead of you, and fight the enemy off from the rear, while the militia holds the enemy back for as long as we can."

David shook his head. "It's too far for refugees without supplies to make it, Captain. They'd be too spread out and the enemy is too numerous. The foe could easily cut us off and then fall upon the civilians out in the open."

"We have no choice," Harding erupted. "We've got to try something or we're all dead!"

"We have something else. Our mages—"

Harding stared at him wide-eyed. "We only had a few who could do magic. Most of them are dead by now."

David continued. "Do you have a safe place set up nearby where your civilians are hiding?"

"Safe enough for now, but not for long. And our civies are hiding in numerous places toward our center, but most of them are the very old, the sick, and little kids."

David called out to Prince Valandin. "Your Highness, send the wagons with the transport station plates and your mages with the assembly and operations team. We're going to need it up and running, and fast!"

"What are you talking about?" Captain Harding said.

"Captain, we're going to transport as many of your civies back to Michiana as we can. They'll be safe there. We'll have to hold off the enemy while your people pour through the gateway to safety. Spread the word. Pull your forces in and get your civilians on the way here ASAP! If they can't run or walk, pile them into wagons, or have them carried on litters. Just get them here, pronto. Otherwise, they'll have to be left behind. This is their last chance. Got me?"

Harding nodded frantically, tears in his eyes. "Affirmative. Let them through!" Harding shouted at his militia forces. "These people are our saviors. Do whatever they say. Work with them."

He turned back to David. "Yes, yes, I'll spread the word. The civilians will be brought to the school area by the thousands. Sergeant Glass, take these new allies of ours to the safe point at the school nearby. The rest of you, help them hold this area at all costs, and let them set up whatever they wish. Follow their orders and we might just save some of our civilians out of this mess." The man ran away frantically calling out to all of the defenders he saw.

David looked at the militia people, ragged and exhausted, while he waited for the transport station to be wheeled in.

"Kalamazoo militia," David commanded, "there are hundreds if not thousands of enemy dead out here with proper weapons, bows, arrows, and armor that they can no longer make use of. Assemble foraging teams to proceed to strip the enemy dead and properly arm yourselves. Spread the booty around to anyone who can use them. The enemy might even hesitate to attack you if they think you are some of them for an instant, and you can use that confusion to your advantage. Hurry!"

The militia did not wait to be told a second time. Hundreds poured out to strip the fallen of their gear. The few vanguard wounded had already been carried out and tended to.

The wagons came up seconds later, with the teams and wizards.

David led them toward the school in question, with the assistance of Sargent Glass, an older soldier in his early sixties.

There was a clear, paved area in front of the school, most likely used for buses to line up in before the Merge. Lot's of people could converge upon that spot and pour in from the streets nearby.

David point outed where he wanted the transport station set up, and let the team go to work. He set up the troops to help operate and defend the station.

The school still flew the American flag and the Michigan state flag proudly from their tall flagpoles, whipping in the night air. That made him smile.

Sargent Glass had gone in to speak with the troops protecting the civies inside the school. Other militia troops went around to start spreading the word house to house.

As miraculous as it sounded, there was an escape route for civilians, and the evacuation was about to begin.

David had a quick note scribbled down to send to Dirk and the High Command of Michiana. Without Jerriel and the Spectral Entity, he requested that either one of the Pistoleros or one of the Shooting Stars join them. If Jerriel's brother and that bat thing came back to attack them, they were going to need more magickal firepower.

The assembly team had the plates setup within a few minutes, on both sides, and activated them. A wide, dark oval tunnel hummed ominously, like the maw of a cave.

The wizards checked it over, the gateway was declared stable, and the messenger was sent through to test it. David waited for a confirmation reply.

By the time word came back, civilians from the school and the surrounding neighborhoods were filtering in to line up.

Dirk informed Dave that Michiana and Indy were about to be attacked by tens of thousands of enemy zombies from Vaejan. But he would still send Tori, her three reloading teams, and a full company of troops to guard the Pistolero as soon as possible. The gate operators would signal through the gateway when the unit was ready to cross over, and they could then halt the flow of civilians on their side for a few minutes to accomplish that.

Some of the civilians were hesitant to step through the transport portal. "You're city is falling," David explained. "This magic portal will transport you to South Bend, Indiana. I know it sounds weird, but it works. My messenger just came back with an answer for me from our people there. Our troops here are fighting the enemy, holding them off to give all of you time to get to safety. We have no time to waste.

"Go through, keep moving, and make way for the people behind you. Rush the children through first, and then the elderly. Please, file through in an orderly manner. Anyone who causes trouble or delays the evacuation will be pulled aside and go last, if at all. When Kalamazoo finally falls into enemy hands, you do not want to be here."

At last, people started to pour through the gateway. Teachers led small children through in groups, the kids holding hands. They looked so helpless and tiny, their eyes big and huge.

But even as the civilians went through in steady, flowing lines, conflicts and commotions broke out. Gangs of thugs, mostly males from their late teens to their fifties, tried to force their way up front to get through.

David expected some of that, but not quite so soon. "Pikes, swords, archers. Form a shield wall around the transport station. Cut down anyone who tries to use violence. Al, Jason, Brian. Take your units and form security details on the streets leading in to the station. You have permission to use lethal force against thugs and rioters. No arguments. Kids and the elderly go through first. If these people want to fight, send them to the front lines where they should be. Maintain order, and we'll save more people."

Other people were simply too infirm. They hobbled on crutches, with walkers, and canes, with oxygen tanks. Mason felt sorry for them, but they couldn't be allowed to hold up others behind them who could get through faster.

He sent more troops to collect the slower people in wheelchairs, carts, and wagons to haul them through the gateway in batches. It might be a little uncomfortable and humiliating, but at least they'd get through and survive. Wheelchairs were all right, as long as there was someone to help push them and keep them moving. David wished for a fleet of them.

When bigger kids and young teens came in, some of them were drafted and paired with a person in a wheelchair to see them through to the other side. Everyone was afraid, but at least now they had hope that they might get out alive.

Then the signal crystals on the transport station flashed red.

People gasped, not knowing what that meant.

"Relax everyone," David said. "Let the current batch continue going through, and hold up the next. They're signaling us from South Bend that some reinforcements are ready to come through. We'll signal them when we're ready on this side, and the gateway is clear."

They waited a few more moments, and then sent a runner through. He returned seconds latter.

Battle horns rang out in warning nearby.

Messengers rode up. "Captain Pritchard. General Culpepper needs all defenders to the front lines immediately. The enemy is making a massive counterattack, and they're throwing their Dark Mages and even some of those necromancers with those skull staffs against our forces, causing great damage."

The other messenger from the other flank added. "The massive force of the enemy's superior numbers are driving our forces and the defenders back. The enemy is slaughtering everyone left behind. There's a general panic among the civilians, and a massive number of refugees flooding toward the transport gate all at once."

David gave his final orders to protect the transport station to the last sword. That had to be protected at all costs and kept out of the hands of the enemy.

Even if that meant dismantling it, taking it away, and leaving civilians behind to face their fate at enemy hands. Even if it meant having the wizards destroy one or all of the plates.

No one liked that last possibility, but they could not allow the station to be captured by their foes.

They would save as many people as they could, but they could not always save everyone.

"When Tori the Pistolero comes through," David said, "have her help protect the transport station until the last moment. Try to get as many civilians through as possible, without risk to the station."

He led the vanguard through the center of Kalamazoo to help bolster the defenders.

Directly in front of them, a mass of monsters and foes piled up at the front lines, waiting for their chance to attack.

"Bolster the shield wall!" David shouted. "Archers, pour it at them. We must hold for as long as we can.

This did not look good. The enemy had already crushed and set fire to about one fifth of the city by the looks of things. That much of Kalamazoo was a total loss. David didn't see how anyone in those parts of town could still be left alive.

He rotated their fighting units in, including his own.

They were like a buzz saw of steel, ripping the enemy apart as they clashed. David's own weapons were quickly drenched in enemy blood.

But at the rate they were being forced back, even with the help of Army 16, the entire city would still be overtaken in a matter of hours.

There was no stopping that. They could only slow it down.

And they still had thousands of helpless people to evacuate.

After that, once the transport station was packed up, their only hope would be to retreat east toward Battle Creek, and link up with the defenders there.

# JERRIEL

Jerriel had fully meant to slay her own brother, she was so angry. It had taken her by surprise that he was willing to injure himself so severely, in his attempt to make good his escape.

But from being joined with the Spectral Entity, she herself had already been healed from the brink of death. Once Shaeddor escaped, his entity would eventually be able to heal and restore his physical body in the same manner.

She felt certain that after he was healed, her wicked brother would someday come after both her and Khia once again, perhaps sooner than she expected. The Dark Khabal would not let one of the Spectral Entities escape them for very long.

Thus, for the time being, she and Khia were free. But they were also alone in the middle of nowhere with nothing but her staff, a small pack, and few supplies. Khia was so drained and so weak that she could barely maintain a wisp of her former self. Clearly she was in no condition to either fight or travel, and the nearest ley line was at least an hour away in a place that could be crawling with enemies.

And what was all of that crap about Shaeddor pretending to be secretly on her side? Right. He always did things like that to keep people guessing about him. She didn't buy any of that for a minute.

She should have killed him.

Jerriel slipped the gauntlets back on, giving Khia what energy she could, to allow her to sustain her physical form, instead of going dormant.

Khia passed into the keys. Jerriel could feel her trying to heal and regenerate herself.

It was up to Jerriel, for the time being, to get them to somewhere safe.

Her evil brother had warned her to go north instead of south.

South it was then.

Yet Jerriel had no idea where they were. Who knew where he had taken them? She guessed that it had been within a couple of hours of the nexus—somewhere east. Perhaps past Bentar and somewhere near Huran. She smiled, at what David and the Urthers would call Kalamazoo and Battle Creek. What odd names.

It was night by then. Slightly behind her, to the southwest, there was light in the distance.

She took them toward the light. But first she cast a shadowmist spell on herself to hide them within the folds of the night.

As she drew closer to the lights, she caught foul smoke upon the light winds. Clouds began to gather and darken. There would be rain the next day for certain, if not later that night.

Then she spotted around two thousand mercenaries, leading a large horde of Urther captives away, many in chains. Some of the adults had shreds of makeshift armor on them still.

These were prisoners, from a battle.

Not a battle. More than that.

An enemy victory.

Jerriel kept going, taking great care.

She spotted hordes of monsters, cooking dead corpses and near dead corpses in the gloom, or simply gnawing and working their raw meat in the shadows.

Then she came to a stretch of Urther worked stone roads.

She saw a rusty green and white way sign that had been torn down.

Battle Creek.

She crested another low rise. Most of the city, for as far as she could see, was on fire and being razed to ground. Bodies and skeletons were silhouetted in the burning trees.

And surrounding the dead city, the armies of the Dark Khabal celebrated their grim triumph. Jerriel could hear them cheering, laughing, singing, roaring, and getting drunk.

Perhaps she could find the Khabal's main camp.

Maybe she could find her brother where he was resting and healing more.

Perhaps she could finish the job.

Her brother had helped kill an entire city, whether he participated in the battle or not. He was a part of whatever the Dark Khabal did now. The blood they spilled was on his hands.

The shadowmist spell helped her slip past the guards in the darkness.

She searched the camp. Why was it so empty? Inside one of tents, on a map table, she found a stack of what looked to be secret enemy reports from several areas. No time to read them all now, but they might prove vital later. Jerriel stuffed them neatly into her bag.

Why did the camp look nearly abandoned? Were the enemy still out fighting? She saw nothing more than drowsy and drunk camp guards and a number of recovering wounded that the Dark Mages left behind, and in quite a hurry by the looks of things.

Oh, no, she suddenly realized.

After a victory such as this, with tens of thousands of new captives, the Dark Khabal would curse the earth itself, and perform a Grand, Dark Ritual.

That's where they were. And her insane brother might even take part.

The necromancers would carefully select a spot, and prepare six hundred and sixty-six captives for sacrifice, and dedicate their lives, their souls, and their blood and burnt flesh to the Dark Ghods in an orgy of horrid, cannibalistic death.

And Jerriel couldn't do anything to stop them, even if it had not taken place yet. She was merely one against so many.

She turned away to find a place in the wilds to hug her knees and weep at what was taking place.

Then some slight signal from Khia tingled in both of her hands through the gauntlet keys.

An alert of some kind? A warning? Jerriel studied the area around her with all of her senses. Suddenly she thought she heard strange crying, somewhere nearby.

Strange in that the resonance of the crying did not sound human.

The sounds led her to a dark, secluded part of the forest, encircled by rings of drunken and sleeping guards.

In the center she spotted a huge cage, covered with a magic shroud of air to defeat prying eyes. The inhuman crying sounds came from within. And around the cage, within what must be just beyond a long span of reach from whatever the cage contained, the Dark Khabal had drawn a red circle, a blood ring around that cage.

Whatever was in that cage must be incredibly dangerous. Any who stepped within the red circle could be attacked or slain by whatever was in that massive cage. From the sand and dirt thrown over dark red patches of blood, the signs only confirmed that.

As Jerriel slipped in closer, the shadowmist spell protecting her, she noted how impossibly thick the bars were.

That cage was constructed to hold a gigantic mountain bear, or even a behemoth, or some other fabled monster of legend.

Whatever it was, it could not touch her in her shadowmist form until she willed herself to become solid once again.

In for a closer peek.

Something within the cage sprang at her faster than thought, it's long hairy arms thrashing through the bars as the body of the thing slammed into them with amazing force.

This creature was magical in nature. It could touch her. Too late, Jerriel felt one enormous hand close around her head and neck. The other hand wrapped around her lower legs, and it hoisted her in the air as if it meant to tear or twist her in half.

She gasped and smelled something rank and stifling. She saw two narrowed, glowing red eyes within the darkness of the cage.

Jerriel instinctively reached up and pushed against the huge hairy hand covering her face with her own gauntleted hands.

The Spectral Keys flashed green and jolted the creature with Urth Power.

Then, even stranger, the creature gasped and dropped her in the dirty grass outside the cage.

Even as she fell, Jerriel thought she saw the creature vanish.

Jerriel hit the ground and grunted, then she rose up on her hands and knees, nearly breathless. She looked into the cage, but it appeared empty.

Yet she could smell the same reek.

The next instant, the creature in the cage was back in view, crouched against the far side of the cage. And this time it spoke to her. As it did, Jerriel felt the entity Khia stir herself, and suddenly the animalistic words became coherent. Jerriel understood them, and she could converse with this strange creature.

"We are both of the earth," Jerriel-Khia said. "Why did you attack me?"

"I'm sorry, mother. I have been kept trapped in this bad thing in pain and I cannot get out. I lash out at anything that comes near. I am thirsty and hungry."

Jerriel sensed Khia put forth her powers slightly. She produced food for this creature. A bough filled with numerous apples, a dozen wild squash, and a crude, deep wooden bowl filled with fresh water.

*This is a child of earth from our sister world,* Khia explained in their minds.

From Tharanor, my world? Jerriel said.

*Yes, from the northlands of the New World.*

The large hairy creature took up the bowl with both hands and slurped down all of the water. Then it ate the squash whole and cleaned all of the apples off the bough with its lips, mashing them with its omnivorous teeth.

The bowl and the bough melted back into the ground from whence Khia had formed them, once they were set down.

"Ahh…" the creature sighed. "Thank you, mother."

"Why do you call me mother?" Jerriel asked.

"I am a lowly earth spirit, yet you are an earth mother, far greater than I. As soon as you touched me with your power, I could tell."

Jerriel laughed. "An earth sister, perhaps."

"I hope I did not harm you, earth sister. At first I thought you were one of the Dark Ones who captured, tormented me, and brought me to this vile place, far away from my home. I try to kill them if they are careless and come close enough. I have slain four of them. They are defilers. They run with Darkspawn. Have you come to free me?"

Jerriel came closer. "If I can. What is your name? What are you? How were you captured?"

The Urth creature rose up, nearly seven feet tall and very broad and powerful. Bigger than even the Thulls, as amazing as that was. And she was covered with long fur or hair. "I am Luin of the Hoonga, at your service, earth sister. I am still a youngling. There was a big landslide up in the mountains. I was nearly crushed by big rocks and washed down into the inner seas. Injured, I clung to a piece of a floating tree, and washed up on the shore of the south. There I was found on the beach, almost dead, and taken. After days I came to this place."

"Well met, Luin of the Hoonga. I am the wizard and enchantress Jerriel, joined with the Spectral Guardian, Khia of Urth, our sister world. Now, let us see if there is a way to free you. You must remain quiet and still. If we can get you out of this cage, we can all slip away."

"I understand, sister," Luin said. She curled up on the iron floor of the cage, covered with a thin layer of straw, and pretended to rest.

Jerriel examine the iron bars, thicker than her legs. How can we get past these bars, Khia?

*Iron is from the Urth, and will return to it with the pressure of heat, cold, salt, water, and air. I shall speed all of those effects up at the top and bottom of several bars. Then the Hoonga child's might can twist the soft rust free. But warn her to be quiet. Let us begin.*

Through the gauntlets, Jerriel-Khia quickly corroded the iron bars at the top and down at the base, causing them to rust through.

Jerriel said to Khia in their shared mind: This Hoonga is a girl, not an adult? But she's so huge!

*Luin is still an adolescent, as your mind would call her. The Hoonga are the mighty guardians of the north in the New World. The adults can be up to twelve feet in height, and with their magicks, none but the most powerful can enter their lands and return alive. That is why there are no monster hordes north up in Khanada.*

I didn't know that. What happened to the monster hordes there?

*Long ago, when the Darkspawn were fashioned by evil and loosed upon Tharanor, they spread north in the New World, just as they tried to spread everywhere across Tharanor, killing and destroying. But when they crossed over into Khanada, they met with the Hoonga earth guardians in great numbers. A terrible war was fought, and with their enormous strength and their earth powers and magicks, the normally gentle Hoonga were roused to anger and became terrifying opponents, who taught the spawn the meaning of fear, to the few who escaped. That is why, even to this day, the monster hordes will not dare to cross over into the north, and even the powers of the Dark Ghods themselves cannot compel them to do so. For the wroth of the mighty Hoonga awaits them there still.*

They were finished. Jerriel spoke to Luin softly. "Try these bars, one at a time, Luin. Pull them out quietly and lay them down just as quietly, off to the side."

Luin nodded and rose up, towering over Jerriel-Khia, and grasped the first bar that was pointed to, She wrenched and twisted it free in seconds as the thick rust powdered and crumbled. She placed it off to the side, between bars that were not affected by the rust. Luin was extremely quiet and stealthy, going quickly from one bar to the next.

Finally she had enough room to squeeze her bulk out.

Jerriel stepped back, reminded of where the stink came from. Luin stunk like a cave bear, but she was a natural creature. That was just her way.

As soon as she was free of the cage, Luin vanished, and that startled Jerriel.

Khia, the Hoonga can turn invisible?

*Yes, and immaterial, at will. That is their great magic. That is why their bodies are never found when they die. Their bodies dissolve permanently and return their energies to the earth itself. Yet even magickal creatures cannot pass through cold iron; its properties disrupt their powers.*

Can you teach me this unclad ability?

Khia laughed. *You wish to walk unclad? You are not Hoonga. This is their magic, not yours. With enough energy, I can duplicate it while we are joined, but I cannot do so now while I am weak. The Hoonga can work their magic naturally, at will, as long as they are still strong and unhurt. The Dark Ones must have indeed found Luin injured or near death in order to capture her as they did and trap her within an iron cage. They must consider her a great prize.*

Well, not anymore, she isn't.

Both of them took great pleasure at that.

*I will adjust our abilities so that we can sense her magical energies.*

You have such power?

*She is of the Urth. That ability I can teach you, to use like one of your spells. With it you can see magical energies and spirit forms, yet not when she walks unclad.*

Jerriel wondered. There was probably some similar way that the Dark Khabal could see the Urth spies in astral form. They must have a similar spell, artifact, or ability.

A fuzzy, hazy general sense of Luin's presence was all that they could detect, at best. But when she only made herself invisible, her large body came into focus, but in this form, she glowed with faint green Urth energy.

"Luin," Jerriel called to her softly. The Hoonga-girl's senses were exceptionally keen. She turned her broad, smiling face to Jerriel-Khia.

"Sister, you can still see me when I am invisible?" Luin sounded impressed once more.

"Yes. Come this way with us, Luin. We'll try to escape to the southeast."

Luin nodded and began to follow, but then she halted and sniffed the air. She shook her head. "The way you go is very bad. Many Dark Ones. Much blood and death. They kill the gan their kin, and make slaves of many others. We must not go that foul way."

"Who are the gan?" Jerriel asked.

*Humans,* Khia said.

"Where should we go, Luin?"

The Hoonga continued to sniff the air, leading them north. "Most of the bad ones have come south to this bad place. Right now, most of the north is free and clear. We should go there. When we reach the inner seas, I can find a way across and make it back to my home and my kin, in Khanada. You can come with me, sisters. We will be safe from the bad ones among my kind."

Even as they spoke together, and walked north, a commotion arose in the camp.

Luin's escape had been discovered, all too soon.

Two necromancers led the Dark Mages, and put together a hurried search party of about three hundred troops. They seemed to be using their glowing skull staffs or some other ability to track Luin somehow, perhaps by tracing her magic or her general scent. But in any case, Jerriel and her friends were now being tracked and pursued.

There had to be a way to elude that pursuit, but for now, they simply needed to put some distance between them and the Dark Khabal.

"Luin, we must—"

The Hoonga girl sniffed the air and snatched up Jerriel, taking off at high speed, flashing across the countryside. "Some of the bad ones are after us. We must flee from them. They are too many."

Amazing. Obviously, the Hoonga were fantastic runners as well.

*They can run at great speed for hours without rest.*

Good thing we fed her.

But going north took them further away from David and the army.

*Once we reach a ley line, I can assume my avian form, and we can fly to wherever we wish.*

Jerriel nodded. All right. For now, that's our plan.

# SHAEDDOR

Jen's ghost floated above him to his right, crying. She kept trying to kiss him and could not, adding to her torment. She faded away, still reaching out to him in despair.

Shaeddor blinked and then glanced over at his right arm, not even seeing a scar. It felt perfectly healed and re-attached by the Spectral Entity's restorative powers, enough to properly re-attach the limb, with some assistance. It no longer burned or ached, and he had the full range of motion. He could even summon his sorcerous spell glow, just as he always did.

Seeing one's arm separated from the body was never a good thing for anyone, and quite memorable. But he had been forced to do so in order to escape.

And, without anyone noticing, he had also managed to insert two special Istyxian energy crystals into his body on the way to Vaejan.

One crystal into the deep wounds of his right breast and lung, and the other into his good right arm between the shoulder and the elbow.

After the magical restoration, the power crystals were now a part of him. He could feel them, waiting to be charged with either magickal,

Cosmic, Celestial, or Spectral energy. He would now be able to store and make use of such powers at will, once he gained access to a direct source, such as a ley line or nexus, or even a Celestial or Cosmic being or plane.

That learning to do so was going to be agonizing at first made no difference. If he was going to declare his secret war upon the Dark Khabal and his masters, he needed power. As much as he could get his hands on.

He felt grateful that his mother secretly had a small chest of the priceless energy storage crystals that he had appropriated at the time of her loss.

Her son had the foresight to know that they would come in handy at some point in the future. And now he would put them to good use, no matter what pain the crystals caused him.

Yet they had to be precisely fused with the body in some supernatural way in order for them to be of any practical use. Otherwise they only drained the users and shortened their life by half, not unlike a form of cancer.

What could be better than the restorative energies of one of the Six Spectral Entities? Now he understood the procedure, and he had more crystals yet. If he took great harm again, he could make use of those services once more.

He had to get stronger by any means possible.

Shaeddor turned over smiling.

His blood went cold.

He stared in to the dark eyes of Cyrisella the Beautiful, naked in his bed beside him, a sheen of glistening, crystal sweat dripping over her body as her one sculpted hand teased her own peaked, perfumed breasts, and her other hand worked between her silken thighs.

He tasted her warm, sweet breath as it slipped out from her red lips on the air like syrup—lips pouting, partying, and panting slightly, mere inches from his own.

"I grew impatient for you to awake from your healing, my little Black Prince. I decided to make myself ready for you." She licked those perfect lips. Then raised her lower, sculpted hand and licked her own two glistening fingers with their dripping, painted nails.

"Do you wish me to make you ready for me now as well?" she asked softly with a wicked, eager smile.

Her tongue flashed over her upper teeth like the head of a small serpent.

Rage filled Shaeddor to the brim and he resisted the very strong urge to strike or blast her. How he despised being played and trifled with.

Yet she was one of the Six Dark Champions of the Khabal.

To do so would be extremely unwise.

He did the worst thing he could get away with.

He turned his back on her and rose up from his bed, sensing her surprise and anger once again. "Away with you. Get out of my chambers. Most do not know your secret, witch. You're a disease of the mind, not just of the flesh. I have no wish to fall under your power, Cyrisella. Get you gone."

The Avatar of Lust laughed at him in sweet mockery, stretching and writhing on his bed before him like an entire nest of snakes within a feminine skin.

She pouted. "You don't like me this way? Very well then. I have many more."

And with each twist of her serpentine body, she flashed and transformed into the form of another alluring female from all the known lands.

A lythe, tall skinny blond Thul girl in her early teens with long braids, green eyes, giggling and blushing.

Next, a dark Sylurrian temptress in her mid-twenties with blazing blue cobalt eyes. Flesh so pale and transparent it nearly had a blue tint and glow to it. He could see her blue veins pulsing.

An acrobatic, dark-skinned Maurn Amazon warrior from Khairun, who painted their bodies and only fought naked at night in their deserts with their spears, javelins, and strangely shaped throwing weapons. Yet legends had it, that they were among the most accomplished, dedicated, and attentive lovers in all the known world. Her mantle of hair was as white as the mountain snows, her ample lips were purple, and her eyes were as amber as those of the lioness.

Shaeddor did his best to ignore and magically dress himself as she continued.

"I savor a test of wills," she told him. "Delaying our pleasure only makes it more delicious when the release finally…comes. I'll keep trying. I shall eventually find something you like, Shaeddor. Now, how about this one?"

A petite, ivory-skinned Jattaran courtesan, late twenties, complete with the intricate hair style and face painting. The veiled, angular black eyes that twinkled, skilled in all the ninety-nine arts of love, and every sexual position possible.

"I find it strange that no one is able to read your mind, Shaeddor. A very convenient talent, that. A gift from the head injury that you suffered? Did you by chance have some hurt down below that ruined you for women?"

He burst out laughing at that. "We have but one thing in common, you inhuman whore. Know this, for by your tricks, and for all your arts and powers, you shall never know me, either in flesh or mind. I have a male lust to match your own and better, but I have known real love–something which you can perceive. Think on that and despair."

She turned into a a buxom, lusty maid of Marrandor, delicious curves, full bodied, high-breasted, and eager to make love at nineteen or twenty, flowing, golden brown tresses, and deep brown eyes.

She laughed back at him. "Brave words. The stoutest male cannot outlast the least of women. All men are fools and braggarts who always fall short...in the end."

Cyrisella transformed into a young, red haired Darshian bride, with her sleek, almond eyes veiled and alluring, her bronze skin on her soft, slender shoulders, and her traditional *aishina* wedding gown with the hoop skirt and lace veil.

Darshian brides were instructed by the women in their family or village how to best please their mates, and wore no undergarments under all of that other stuff. It was tradition for their mates to unwrap them like a wedding present and for the couple to stay inside and make love for three straight nights and days, as meals of fine food and drink were brought to them, and left at their door.

Shaeddor sighed. "You can stay here if you wish. I care not. I'm going out."

Cyrisella shook her head with a frown. "I don't do it often, and it taxes me, but if it's what you really like, I can turn into an attractive young man or boy for you—if that's what does it for you?"

Shaeddor halted and sighed. "Do as you please, witch. But whatever you try, it is not going to happen between you and I. I prefer beautiful women, and unlike you, they must be human and real. Now, good day to you!"

"My, how touchy. You are a indeed a strange one. What a challenge indeed. So prickly. You know...I did happen to see those sad little sketches you keep hidden in the bottom of your one drawer, of that auburn haired, Urther slut you dallied with in the backwoods. The little bitch that Gultor beheaded?"

Shaeddor froze in the doorway but did not turn back.

"Gultor probably did you a favor. But some still say that you actually, somehow cared for the little calf. Come now, that cannot be. The Black Prince himself, in love with a common Urth slattern?"

He clenched his fists.

"If...you let me see a vision of her from your mind, I could make myself look just like her, if that is what will stiffen your—"

Blazing scarlet magefire raced up both of his arms.

Shaeddor blasted the bed, blew out the walls of his own chamber, and nearly brought down the high tower they were in itself. He laid waste to practically everything in the room with spell, lightning, and blasts of power.

The attacks that flashed out of his right arm with the crystal in it were ten times as explosive and devastating.

Khabal guards rushed into his shattered chambers, expecting a major battle. The guards were astonished at the destruction. Others in the upper levels above him were already screaming and evacuating.

"My lord," the sergeant of the guards said. "What took place here?"

Shaeddor snapped to a quick lie. "Forgive me. I had an unstable, magic artifact that I was tinkering with and attempting to repair. It went out of control and exploded. I did my best to contain the damage. Have word sent to my master that I am well, and ready to speak with him at his pleasure. I await his word."

He quickly performed earth and stone spells to reinforce the structure enough before it toppled. Others could finish the mundane repairs after that.

The guards bowed and left to do his bidding and summon the workers. Shaeddor looked around.

Cyrisella had vanished and fled somehow, even as the attack began. Her speed and her own powerful defenses had been bestowed upon her by the Dark Ghods themselves. She and the other Six Dark Champions were still more than a match for him.

A shadowy wisp shot in through a shattered window, hovered before him, and blinked at about eye level. Cyrisella's voice emanated from it.

"My, my, what powers you possess. Had I remained, you might have even caused me pain and made you my enemy. But we can't have that. As it is, our little game continues, and you have my full interest now—you pretty, pretty, boy. So few have been able to resist me for so long. I find that...so tantalizing. You are indeed a fitting challenge; one that I cannot resist!"

"Stop wasting our time, Cyrisella. I'm not interested, and I serve Gorrial, the High Magus—not you. And if you ever dare try to take anything even close to the form of my dead beloved again, from that day on, I shall seek to destroy you in any way that I possibly can."

"Ahh...a rare thing, a dark heart that is still capable of love. Now I simply must have you for my own!"

Shaeddor rolled his eyes in frustration. "Oh, please. You only want that which you cannot have, and then you murder it." He stretched out one finger and blasted the dark message wisp to dust, silencing it.

As soon as he continued to make it known, through his servants, that he was hale and well, his master summoned him to sit again with him, to the right of the Dark Throne of the High Magus.

It was early for dinner, but they dined together, just the two of them and a small clamor of servants and entertainers.

A young Urther girl sang sad songs of her world very well, without accompaniment, as she sat and stood in little but her slave chains and wept.

"You should keep that one safe," Shaeddor said. "She has a fine voice. Many of your guests will enjoy it."

Gorrial grinned. "I'll see how she sings to me in my bed tonight, after my women bathe, oil, and bring her to me, before I decide whether or not to let her live. Why, I've already had dozens of these wretched Urthers put to death. The tiresome cows are as bad as the bulls. They don't seem to understand what it is to be a pleasure servant, or a slave of any kind.

"I swear, what blockheads. I have a different bed slave each night, but these Urther females of any age, despite being very pretty, either break down and cry and scream all night, or they try to find something to try to attack or stab me with. I just don't get them. It's like they want me to kill them all off.

"Shaeddor, I swear to the Dark Ghods, one young Urth woman actually tried to bash my brains in with a damn candlestick. I was forced to melt her head off her pretty neck. Yet I must say, even her cold dead body was so delightful, I had it washed, scented, and kept handy for days thereafter for me to enjoy."

Shaeddor smiled. "Urthers are known to be rather thick and stubborn, my master. Who can understand such peasants?"

*You I'm going to try to kill last, you murderous, loathsome, rutting hog. You think you are so clever. For you it must be something special. I will have to think long and hard upon a fitting demise for the Great High Magus.*

"Shaeddor, we must speak together. I know you always do things that vex me. That is your nature, and I endure it because I love you like a son and you are so worth it.

"Take the recent madness in your room, and don't bother lying to me. I know that Cyrisella is doing all that she can to bed you. But I can't let the two of you become enemies and be at each others' throats all of the time. She screws like a thousand mink in heat, trapped within a glass cage. Why not just give into her and have done with it? I won't let her slay you afterwards, the way she usually deals with her past conquests. She will move on. She always does. You're both far too valuable to me. She's one of my best weapons, and I know that you are going to be yet another."

Shaeddor bowed his head. "I thank you, master."

"Now as for your latest mission. You did well, but I still have several reservations."

"Wait, master. Before you pick everything apart and find fault with practically everything as you normally do, let me just say a few things in my defense."

The High Magus had a sense of humor. He knitted his fingers together behind his head and leaned back with a big belch. "Go right ahead."

"I did everything you asked of me, and more. You sent me after my father's secret journal, and I obtained it. I even made a copy of it to bring back for you and others to study, and destroyed all of the pertinent parts of the original, that the enemy had not even deciphered yet."

"Why did you not bring back the original?" he asked.

"Look at it this way. I can now track both it and her. But we don't need it from what I saw. And now our foes will waste months, if not years, trying to decipher and hunt through pages and pages of meaningless dreck that won't do them any good!"

Gorrial hesitated, staring at him.

"Brilliant, Shaeddor. Genius. Even I would not have thought ahead in such a devious manner. Excellent work, my boy. But how much did your sister know, and who had she told it to?"

Shaeddor shook his head. "I had her sealed in agonizing black ice. In the pain and terror that she was in, she begged to tell me everything I wanted to know, and as turned out–it wasn't much. She herself said that there hadn't been that much time, with all of the fighting, to actually work on decoding the journal.

"Master, the idiot was going at it page by page. She hadn't skimmed ahead yet. I saw the notes of her progress. She'd barely gotten through the section where my father suspected that the Dark Khabal was at work in the New World, Vaejan, and were planning something big. She didn't know anything of consequence. And the Urthers she told it to were so stupid, they could not have cared less. They already knew that the Dark Khabal was at work, so she wasn't telling them anything new."

"Good. More good news. And you deciphered the rest?"

Shaeddor shrugged. "There wasn't much more. My father didn't know that much either, not in any specific detail. His last two lines only briefly mentioned something about a secret plot involving the Celestial Guardians. And then there were simply two or three names–"

Gorrial raised his hands, waving them wildly. "Do not even speak them, my boy. Or I might be forced by my masters to have you put to death."

"What? Who are–"

"Trust me. Forget about them. It is better that you know anything further. Yet it only proves your loyalty and veracity to me. So, now tell me how your younger sister broke free and nearly slew you?"

"It was that damned Urth Spectral Entity, the nature entity!"

"Stop right there." Gorrial called up a recorder. "Now, describe everything you can remember. You say the Spectral Keys were a pair of gauntlets. What did they look like?"

Shaeddor rattled off everything he recalled about the entity. That took a span of time to do so.

"And your sister had already joined with said Urth Entity?" Gorrial said. "How unfortunate."

"Yes, they were quite formidable and extremely difficult to capture. I assumed that the entity was also trapped and immobilized by the properties of the magical black ice."

"I too would assume such. You mean they actually broke free out of the magic ice and attacked you? That's incredible!"

"I know, imagine my surprise. One minute I'm tormenting them and getting the answers I need, the next moment they burst free, attack me, and then when I try to escape, they nearly kill me!"

Gorrial shook his head. "You were in terrible shape when the bat entity brought you to us. Mere seconds away from dying, really. You had me worried when I saw you in pieces like that, my boy. But we quickly saved you from the brink."

"Thank you, master. I'm just sorry they escaped from us. I wanted to present another Spectral Key to you. Perhaps I was too overconfident and attempted too much."

"At least you strove in the attempt, Shaeddor. I have few among my servants who would have challenged such a powerful foe head on. Not to worry. We have large forces in that area. And you weakened them considerably. I've send teams of determined hunters after them. We'll bring them to in."

"Now that I am healed, I would be glad to go after them again, master."

"No, Shaeddor. I have another mighty task for you. And to be up front, some who do not like or trust you, whisper that you allowed your sister and the Spectral Entity escape. And that you still have friends among the Urthers who cause conflict with your loyalties to me and the Khabal."

"My enemies have always spread lies and rumors against me, master."

"I know that as well. But for now, in order to squash those rumors, I'm sending you on a vital mission far away, out toward the west coast of the colonies and back, to establish our new transport gate network. I trust you to get these things done. We must stay ahead of our foes. Yet I also want you to be my eyes and ears, and report back to me on the loyalty and disposition of my servants in all of the cities we hope to take over."

Shaeddor eagerly clenched his fists and his teeth. "Yes, we'll be able to rush forces into one city after another, and continually tip the scales in our favor. The cities on both sides will fall to our dominion, one after the other, as we target them and our foes for destruction and enslavement! I shall be happy to fulfill this mission for you, my master."

"Good, because we cannot wait, and this mission will also take you far away from many of your enemies here and return you in glory. You and your new forces will depart upon the morrow. Look over the plans I will send to your new personal chambers. They will detail your new mission in full."

"I will not fail you, master. I will see these things done, with speed and efficiency. And I will report back to you alone in secret, as to my impressions about your other servants, and the quality of work they are doing for you and our great ones."

"Good. Shaeddor, I wish you would reconsider committing your devotion fully to our Dark Masters. That would go a long way to putting an end to these lies about you, once and for all. Consider it. And know that one day, the Dark Ghods themselves might require such an oath from you, and the great ritual of faithfulness."

Shaeddor shook his head. "Master, you know my mind, and my force of will. No one forces me to do anything. I do what I do because I choose to do it. I would choose death over being forced to do anything against my will. Such is my pride. I am a devout atheist. I despise any religion, dark or light. I have declared openly that I do not believe the Dark Ghods to be actual gods. I do not believe in any ghods.

"There might very well be powerful beings or entities, worthy of being respected, followed, and obeyed, yet I will never lie to myself and bend to worship them as nothing but an ignorant slave. I will not blindly call any entities ghods. I contend that if I choose to follow you and them of free will, that I am not limited in any way. If I follow and serve you and them willingly, of my own free will by choice, that I am much stronger than others, more valuable to our cause, and I shall prove it so!"

Gorrial sighed. "Part of me sides with you, my boy. I do believe you, and I think that for yourself, you are right in your opinions. But these dangerous things are not always in my hands to decide. The Great Ones might very well call upon you to answer to them alone, and in person, one day. You may be forced to stand before their naked might, and make your arguments to them. It is they who shall judge you and decide your fate. But go now, serve my will in the crucial weeks and months to come, and do well my bidding. Perform all of these things and I shall heap reward upon you, and make you great among our servants. Serve me faithfully and well, and beware of those on both sides who will seek your life!"

Shaeddor bowed with deep respect. "As always, my lord and master," he said with a knowing smile. "As always."

# TORI

Tori still felt somewhat airsick being on the dirigible, *The Gray Falcon*. Her insides did flip-flops at first, like a bass landed on the shore.

But at least she had something else to occupy her mind now. If the enemy was attacking Michiana with zombies, that meant that there would be work for everyone to do.

And that included the Pistoleros, both Mason and herself.

She would prove to herself and everyone that she could cut it, in her own way.

Champions, gifted people such as them, the Shooting Stars, and the various mages had to serve the people as weapons, as specialized artillery, to help combat whatever the enemy threw at them. The obligation and responsibility were simply too great.

Their efforts could save so many lives.

She didn't know Mason's friend Pete Steiner as much as Mace and Dave did, but he seemed all right. They said that he was now dating Vicky Powell, one of the new healers. Pete had been wounded during one of the last battles, struck from behind by a grun. Vicky had helped save his life, and they got together shortly after that.

Tori had no idea how someone like Pete, with his impaired vision, ended up a trooper in the first place, or later as an officer with the balloonists of the budding Air Force of Michiana. But she remembered Mason saying something about Pete having a keen mind, and always had hopes of becoming some kind of technical inventor or engineer. And up in the sky, binoculars made up for much of his vision problem.

As much as anyone, Pete wanted to serve and fight.

Thus it was probably natural that he would gravitate toward the invention and re-invention teams, working on trains, blimps, and combining steam power with with magical energies and enchantments. Pete knew Rob and Kevin and they all understood that there was clearly plenty of important work to be done to help save humanity.

She shook herself when Pete led them through the hatch onto the bridge gondola.

Captain McKay was there—tall in high boots, impossibly blond, with a mane of golden hair hanging down over her impeccable light and dark blue captain's uniform. The crowd of people on the bridge parted, and McKay's dark black eyes focused on the new guests that her lieutenant brought in. She wore a crossbow pistol on one hip, and a long, curved sabre or cutlass on the other, just like most of the airship officers.

"Ahh...welcome. The Pistoleros, the Shooting Stars, and Master Enchanter Billings. Let me speak plainly. I have last minute orders from General Blackwood to proceed at once to perform a recon sweep from the air, circling north, west, and south of South Bend, to assess the approaching threat.

"As you may or may not have heard, countless hordes of zombies and other undead are marching straight toward Michiana from the west, from what we assume to be Chicago-Vaejan. They cannot be allowed to enter our towns, or infest our fields. They will trample our crops and make harvesting our food for the winter impossible. Many of us will starve."

"How do we stop that many of them?" Tori asked.

Captain McKay frowned. "That is what we are meant to help ascertain. You four can test your various powers and weapons, and assess what they can do against such numbers. Enchanter Billings can help oversee the testing of his various new weapon systems. Then we can present our findings and recommendations to the general and th High Command of Michiana."

Mason spoke up. "How fast can we build more of these airships? If we could get enough firebombs, we could eradicate large numbers of these creatures from the air. They're all out in the open."

Rob shook his head and frowned. "We can't produce any of those things fast enough to deal with a threat this big. But we will do our best.

The falcon class airships like this one are just the beginning. The next generation, the hawk class, will be four times the size of the falcons. But it takes time to construct each one."

"Time is always our enemy it seems," Tori said.

They had a few hours to make their assessment run before nightfall. They made a wide sweeping arc coming down from the north, passing over areas that were more or less a dead wasteland. From up above, the results of the Merge could be plainly discerned. Patches of Urth were mixed up with patches of Tharanor in a crazy quilt of wild madness.

Then they saw them, or at least the first signs of the insanity that was yet to come.

Urth animals, birds, and even Tharanorian monsters fled out in front of the advancing threat.

The main bulk of the zombies and undead were still a day or two out. Corpses and rotting skeletons, shuffling and shambling to the east, and spreading out to go both north and south.

The smell alone was horrible, even high above them.

As Tori recalled, undead were bodies possessed and animated by evil spirits, sent forth to kill anything that lived.

Supernatural energies held them together.

The sheer numbers made everyone gape and gasp. A million zombies or more were simply impossible to imagine, seeing them stretch out for mile after mile into the distance, even from the air.

"Prepare weapons tests," Captain McKay said. "Pistoleros, Shooting stars; go to the gun ports or one of the bomb bay doors and prepare to join the firing lines when they open."

They tried everything: firebombs, steam cannons, and steam guns, devastator rounds, annihilator rounds, and magic blasting arrows.

Hannah masters ever tried a spirit arrow, which actually proved to be the most effective weapon of all, wiping out a large swath of the monsters. But she had to lie down after doing so, and was completely drained. Minnie sat with her and held her hand.

Yet overall, the results were more or less the same.

They barely put a dent in the sea of the monsters heading toward Michiana, and other places. They fired weapons into a sea of millions swarming and sweeping their way until their ammunition was mostly depleted.

Captain McKay continued studying the flow of undead with her field glasses. "That's strange. Over two thirds of them are now heading southeast."

Mason picked up some binoculars and studied the movement patterns.

Tori looked down. Anyone could see the proof from the air.

"Mace, why are so many of them heading south?"

He pulled his field glasses down and shouted back at the captain. "Captain McKay, we've seen enough, don't you think?"

McKay nodded. "I quite agree. It will be an hour past dark when we return to our moorings in South Bend. Lieutenant Steiner, get us back as fast as we are able."

"Aye-aye, sir. Helm. Come about and take us home. Full speed."

Mason turned to Tori. "The enemy is clearly sending their largest forces south. These other forces are just to keep us busy and bottled up in the north here. The key to the enemy's plans appears to be Indianapolis. They obviously mean to wipe it out."

High winds delayed them, despite the crew squeezing every ounce of airspeed from the new steam magic engines.

Rob Billings and Pete quickly said their farewells shortly after they landed. They all wished each other good luck in the battles to come.

The four of them reported their findings directly to General Blackwood, who sent news on to General Avery on the other side. None of the news appeared to be good.

Word reached them that there seemed to be just as many zombies massed and approaching on the other side. Everyone was going to be in big trouble.

Mason came right out and insisted that they send forth the train and the additional ten armies to help save Indy. "We can lay the tracks all the way there, and defend them. Once we link up with Indy, they can help. Rob has another transport station ready."

Dirk nodded, "Yes, I know. The station meant for Tornhold."

"We need to send it to Indy first, as a life line. Another station will be ready within a week. Send that one to Tornhold."

Dirk looked at them. "And what if Army 16 gets into trouble and needs backup? If you go to Indy, who do I send to assist Dave and Jerriel?"

Tori stepped forward, hands on hips. "Send me."

"That leaves the Shooting Stars to help defend Michiana."

Minnie and Hannah nodded. "We can do that," Minnie said.

"Yeah," Hannah added. "Our families might still be around Indianapolis. We can't let it be wiped out."

Dirk weighed it all in his mind for a minute longer. "Our defenses are now much stronger than what they were. We've doubled the numbers of our armies. We have more mages. All right. Mace, take the train, the ten armies, and three of the six dirigibles we have operational. We need to get that transport station to Indy, and keep the train running if possible. If we can do that by winter, we just might break the enemy's back."

"We'll leave tonight," Mason said.

Tori felt her own heart sink like a lump of lead. They had only been together for a few days. Now they were being parted once again, and heading off into deadly battles.

But it was either fight for all that mattered these days, or just lie down and die somewhere in some nasty way.

Or worse, become a slave.

So fight it was.

They weren't going to wait for the enemy. They were going to fight these battles on their terms, in the places they chose.

Like him, Tori didn't argue. Both of them knew that would only waste more of their time.

They found a room with a big soft bed and left orders not to be bothered. They said their goodbyes as only true lovers could. They peeled off their leather and steel and made the most of what was left.

Everything after that was mere duty and obligation.

They would see each other again, when all was done. That much they promised each other.

Tori waved bravely to Mason when they parted. She prayed earnestly for his safety, as she seldom did. But when she did so, she meant it.

Then she went through one of the gateways to cross over to the other side with some of Dirk's military aides. They conferred with General Avery and together, they helped coordinate the military efforts of both sides against the coming zombie threat.

Tori slept alone, trying not to think where her Mace was.

When she went back over to the other side to confirm still more operations and preparations with General Blackwood, she learned from Dirk that they had word from Army 16.

More bad news.

"In an intense battle with the Dark Khabal, the wizard Jerriel had been captured by the enemy, and whisked away. David and his forces are in pursuit and searching for her, but at last report, her whereabouts are still unknown."

Tori closed her eyes and said another little prayer for her friend. Jerriel was a sweet person, and Dave doted on her. She couldn't imagine the pain and uncertainty he must be going through.

"Tori," General Blackwood said, "I need you to prepare a rapid deployment strike force. Three or four platoons should do it."

"Very well, sir. What's the mission?"

"They're going to be your body guards, Tory, if I have to send you to help Dave and Army 16. You all need to stay ready. With Jerriel out of the picture at present, Dave might not have enough magickal firepower to get the job done. I want to be sure that he and the princes get through to Detroit and Toledo. That is vital to our plans."

Tori didn't quite know how to demonstrate her willingness, so she saluted. "Understood, sir. If the time comes, I'll see it done."

Dirk grinned. "God I'm glad we have two of you now."

The strike force was assembled by nightfall.

The call woke her up that night while she was still tossing and turning.

As expected, Dave needed them bad. It was time to cowgirl up.

Tori had her guns, her horse Pepper, three faithful reloading teams their wagons, and three platoons of hand-picked fighters.

When all was assembled and ready, they passed through the transport gateway, and from one battle zone to the next.

When they emerged near what they were told was the fall of Kalamazoo-Bentar, the situation was beyond insane. Most of the city seemed to be on fire. Screams, and chaos, and panicked civilians was the order of the night.

The Blackhawks helping guard the transport station hustled her and her people to one side, and started up the evacuation once more in high gear.

"Sergeant, where's Captain Pritchard?" she shouted above the madness.

"Sir, everyone that could be spared is needed on the front lines. The enemy is pressing us hard. We'll have to dismantle the transport station and bug out soon, in order to prevent it from falling into enemy hands."

She still wasn't used to being called 'sir,' but both Pistoleros now held the rank of first lieutenant in the army.

The screaming around them exploded. Tori wheeled about, pistols ready.

Monsters had somehow squeezed through the crumbling front lines to attack anyone they could reach.

Tori screamed at the station guards. "Get these people through. We'll hold them off!" She rallied all of the available fighters. "Everyone else with me. Let's cut them down!"

Fiery red and orange blasts from her pistols swept the foes away up close, in swaths and waves, hurling them back. Tori charged right in through the paths she cleared, and slipped and stumbled over the black, bloody ground.

She'd forgotten just how bad pureed quantities of Darkspawn smelled.

Hands helped her stand upright. She kept blazing away, firing into the packed ranks of the growing enemy advance.

Look out, sir! An exploding ray blew up the guard right next to her on the left, who bravely took the hit meant for her.

Tori shot the Dark Mage that had killed the trooper right through the face and kept advancing. She switched pistols. Runners for the reloaders took the empty guns from her hands back to the wagons. Others waited steps behind, crouched down but still risking their lives, ready to hand her more loaded guns, or even to slip them into her holsters, if she stood still long enough.

After fifteen minutes of heavy fighting, the breach was closed and the line held once more, less that two hundred yards from the transport station.

Tori looked at the mass of refugees still trying to pour through the gateway, running all the way back toward the front lines.

At best, the station team had fifteen or twenty minutes more before they would need to shut down and make a run for it.

Most of these civilians were about to be stranded and left behind, facing almost certain death.

The Pistolera needed to buy them some more time.

Fifty yards away, an observation balloon team was being hoisted down as fast as they could crank. They had to bug out as well.

Tori called to her reloaders. "Bring up every one of my rifles. Make it quick!"

The she raced over toward the balloon wagon, just as the basket was coming down to be secured. The four person spotting team was already climbing down.

"Captain," she called out to the balloonist commander. "Please. Take a few minutes to send me up about a hundred feet. I only need a few minutes." She regretted she didn't know the man's name.

He gaped with his mouth open and his face grew both alarmed and stern. "I'm sorry Lieutenant, but our position is about to be overrun. We have to get the hell out of here or die."

"Please, sir. I'm trying to buy us some time with my guns. It could save thousands of lives." They stared at each other. Finally the captain blinked.

"Very well. Get up there, damn it."

Tori climbed like a chimp into the basket.

She heard one of the troopers nearby lament, "Dammit to hell. They sent the girl Pistolero. I wish they would have sent us the real one."

"Be happy they sent her," a female trooper snapped at him.

Her runners and the troops present quickly formed a bucket brigade to hand her long guns up to her. Ten of them in total, all of them loaded with annihilator rounds.

"Take her up to one hundred feet," the captain shouted. "Pistolera, I'm giving you ten damn minutes at most. Not a second more!"

They got her up that high in no time.

The devastation was something awful, like out of a hellish nightmare.

She took aim on the left with one of her long guns. Thousands of monsters and rows of mercenary army troops were bunched up and putting Kalamazoo to fire and sword–man, woman, and children of any age.

"You murdering bastards!" Tori screamed. "Eat this!"

The first round rocketed out almost a mile before it arced down, like a white star falling from heaven itself.

By then, Tori aimed her second long rifle and fired once more. She was reaching for her third when the first round detonated, and she shielded her eyes, counting the seconds.

The magic uranium round ignited and even with her arm covering her eyes, everything went white, and the fireball incinerated everything within a radius of half a mile.

She cocked and fired number three just before the second round exploded. She covered her eyes and fumbled for rifle number four as the night sky went blinding white again.

When it cleared, there were two glowing orange craters, and soon to be a third. Tori hurried to take aim on the far right this time and pull the trigger.

Another blinding flash, even with her eyes clenched tight.

She ducked down as the blast waves began to hit, hot and blistering, setting things on fire. When she could see again, in the distance, the enemy had turned and was fleeing in great haste.

That would take some of the pressure off.

She might be able to get two more shots off before the largest masses of them were out of range.

She aimed one and kept the other to hand.

"Flee, you sons of bitches!" Tori pulled the trigger. Then quickly she aimed and shut her eyes tight at the last moment, aiming at the last packed enemy center dispersing.

She pulled the trigger just as the fourth round on the far right cooked off."

Then rounds five and six detonated. Tori covered her eyes with blankets in the balloon. Then she stayed down, waiting for the blast waves to sweep past.

"Fire. Fire!" voices cried. She felt the balloon lurch and then come down quickly.

When she looked up, out, and down, many of the balloon lines were on fire, including the main tether. She scrambled to put out what flames she could reach with water and sand and smothered them with damp blankets.

The basket was actually on fire in places. She tried to put those flames out, even with the water from her own two canteens.

She was up in the air, she didn't have a parachute on, and it was too low for her to use one and jump any way.

A sudden terrible thought struck her. Mason had told her that these old round balloons had still been using hydrogen at some point.

If true, the burning balloon could go up like a bomb any second.

And it might even ignite the uranium rounds in her other four rifles.

That would kill her and everyone within a mile.

In a panic, she flung her rifles over the side without thinking.

Voices cried out in pain below from being struck by them.

And just her luck, the wind whipped up, fanned the flames, and tugged the balloon upward, making it harder to bring her in.

"Get me down!" she said. "Take those rifles to my reloading wagons and have them get the hell away from this place."

The ballooning captain yelled back up. "Well damn it to hell. If you stop throwing rifles down on our heads, maybe we can crank you down and put out the flames with our hoses!"

A crew stood by with a tank pumper ready. They had all of the flames out about forty feet around, but she was still too high up.

"I hope this balloon isn't filled with hydrogen!" she yelled.

"No!" the captain shouted back. "We switched to helium when we went in to combat."

Tori could only wait the bare seconds it would take to crank her down with the winch. She stepped away from the part of the gondola basket that was still on fire.

When she looked out over Kalamazoo, there were still masses of enemies pressing toward the transport station once more. If she took them down, she would have killed herself and everyone else at the same time.

They would still have to fight their way out.

The only logical place to flee would be Battle Creek-Huran to the east. Even performing a fighting retreat, they could probably march there within a day or so.

She certainly kept them from being completely overwhelmed, but that did not save them from what was shaping up to be one hellacious, running battle all night long.

Tori was still thinking on all of these matters when the fireteam drenched her with the hose, putting out the fires, making her gasp, cold and wet.

They got the balloon down and she jumped out, and ran to catch her last reloading team. "Wait, wait! I need to you to stay with me as part of the retreat!"

They barely heard her and stopped, turning around.

One of the flabbergasted loaders said, "But you said for us to–"

"I know what I said. Now I'm changing that. I'm not in a burning, flying bomb with micro-atomic weapons set to go off anymore!"

"What?"

"Never mind. Guards and reloaders, follow me!"

"You're welcome!" the flustered ballooning captain shouted, from off to the side.

There was no time for politeness and pleasantries just yet.

She jumped on Pepper where someone held her horse for her. Then she raced back to the front, which was only about seventy yards away by that time.

After ten minutes more of steady fighting, they were about fifty yards away, and all of Tori's pistols, except the ones she had on her, were being reloaded by then.

She raced back to the transport team, who were already pushing the remaining civilians back by force and dismantling the station to bug out. But the several hundred people left realized what was going on.

Word spread fast and they were about to riot and trample the army people who had been helping them.

Tori dry fired two of her pistols in the air to get their attention, riding in between the refugees and the army people.

"Stay back! There isn't any time. All of you people need to start marching in an orderly fashion, keeping the army between you and the enemy. You have to keep up, or you'll die. Put anyone who can't move into a wagon or cart."

"Where are we going?" people demanded.

"East toward Battle Creek, the only place we can go. The monster attacks will stop after dawn."

"Battle Creek's as bad off as we are!" others said.

"We can't help that. Get moving, folks. Hurry now. Stay ahead of the army. In fifteen minutes or less, the only people left in this spot will be our enemies and the dead."

"Just shoot us, Pistolera!"

Others took up the cry. "Yeah. Just blow us and our kids away with your guns. At least then our ends will be quick. A lot better than getting ripped apart, cooked, and eaten alive by the enemy!"

Tori rose up in her stirrups. "Now I am sure as hell not doing any of that. You people get your asses running, and keep moving. Do it now, or we shall have no choice but to leaving you behind!"

Faced with that prospect, the civilians picked up what they could carry and headed east at top speed, which unfortunately was not very fast.

Tori helped hold the line, as Army 16 fell back, repulsing the enemy again and again.

Where was David and the bulk of the Blackhawks? Were the princes still with him?

Tori was rejoined by all three of her reloading wagons. For the rest of that night, they all fought off attack after attack, pressing them hard from the rear in an attempt to get at the civilians just beyond the defenders.

The Pistolera held firm, with the army on her left and right flanks, standing tall, and the vanguard to the north on their extreme right, keeping them from being cut off.

But it was a grim march, and the ditches on either side were filled with people who had heart attacks, or entire families who couldn't bear up against the strain, and cut their children's throats and then their own.

Such desperate acts were devastating to witness.

The fear of falling into the hands of the enemy was that strong.

Tori lost track of time and kept fighting. They shouted at the exhausted civilians, "Keep going, keep moving if you want to live! We'll make it to Battle Creek and you can rest there."

By the time dawn rose, and the monsters withdrew, she could barely lift her arms and almost rolled out of the saddle.

He guards tied her to the neck of her horse, and put a pillow under her head and torso.

The enemy continued to harry them at every opportunity, but the attacks still lessened greatly after sunrise, and they could finally slow down a bit.

Army 16 maneuvered properly to give the stumbling civilians some breathing room.

General Culpepper specifically ordered Tori to get, as he put it, some goddam rest. They were going to need her fit and ready again that night if not sooner. That much was certain.

At least she didn't hear any more nutjobs complaining about having the 'girl' Pistolero with them.

They tied Pepper to one of the reloading wagons, and she curled up inside with one of her reloading teams as they all slept, huddled together.

# MASON

Old steam train Number 15 headed out of South Bend and got up to top speed as fast as it could. She was known as the Fireball Fifteen, and in her day she had been one of the fastest steam trains in that part of the country for two decades running.

Now she was refitted and loaded up as little more than an Army train, and a track layer, but with a vital mission for the survival of humanity.

The Pistolero departed on board at night with scout teams going out ahead of them, and army units already posted along the way. Their job was to inspect and keep watch on the tracks that were already laid, south of Michiana.

Not only did they make use of some of the new magical light sources, amplified by reflectors, but they even had two developing light mages. These wizards specialized in various types of light magic, and nothing more.

They took turns keeping the area around the speeding train well lit, and one of them even rode up in *The Vulturo* to shine light down around them.

Number 15 had its own round observation balloon that was deployable from a special train car with a big, slide-back hatch on the roof.

The three Buteo class dirigibles escorted the train as well.

They went forth fully intending to go to war. Ten armies from Michiana would stretch out along the rails in an effort to protect them. All proof of how vital the mission was to relieve Indianapolis-Nenarra, establish a rail line, and a transport station there to link up with another surviving Urth city and its people.

Mason took his eyes off his maps and suddenly recognized young Steven Hayward, attached to the scouts, with his wheelbow, arrows, and twin samurai swords. Dave said that Steven was a superb swordsman and archer, even at his age. And Dave knew his stuff.

Mason knew Steven's parents and walked over to the young warrior. "Glad to have you with us, Steven. Enjoying the evening air this night?"

The youth smiled and nodded. "I am, sir." Then he seemed to remember himself and snapped to attention, saluting. "Sorry, sir."

Mason chuckled and waved his hands. "At ease. I'm not big on the officer thing. Just watch it with the regulars. And call me Mace, Mason, or Pistolero if you prefer. I'll answer to any of those three."

"Okay, Mace."

"Do you prefer Steve, now?"

"Nope. I actually like Steven. So what are we in for, sir? I mean, Mace?"

Mason blew out a breath. "I'm thinking it's going to be holy hell on a stick. There's plenty of foes encircling Indy already, and more on the way. You heard about the zombies on their way, right?"

Steven frowned. "Yep. Zombies as far as the eye can see, nothing but shambling freaks, shuffling about ten miles each day without stopping."

"We shouldn't forget," Mason added, "that most of those zombies were Urthers—human beings just like I us, living their lives and minding their own business before the Merge.

"None of them deserved this. After they were killed or starved to death, or perished from disease, the enemy took their bodies and imbued them with evil spirits to hold them together and use them to kill more people."

"That's bad," Steven said. "We need to kill those bastards that did all of that and wipe out this scourge. Hell, I thought zombie wars were just for the movies and novels. I never thought I'd be up to my ears right in the middle of one!"

"Me either," Mason said.

They had left as early as they could in an attempt to bypass the zombies on their way south, get to the end of the line, and start laying tracks to reach Indy.

That was going to be a race indeed. The track-laying teams had practiced in earnest, but they still could only lay so much track each day.

Just before dawn, a few hours later, they met with the track laying team that had worked all night, and relieved them with a fresh crew.

They now had three teams total, and decided to switch them off in four hour shifts, around the clock.

The military and construction units had spent two weeks since the war ended, having the armies and teamsters haul out large quantities of supplies to set up and guard along the way, but they were still less than half way to Indianapolis-Nenarra.

And they were still vulnerable to enemy attacks.

Several supply depots, those closest to Indy, had been raided and burned to the ground. The army reinforcements were hoping to minimize that, and already marched ahead of the train. Reports said that all of the forward units had suffered attacks by monster hordes and skirmishers, but they continued to advance in the face of any threat.

Number 15's observation balloon went up in the air, now that the train stopped, in order to keep watch over the area for a few miles around them in all directions.

Mason took young Steven and a bunch of the scouts up in *The Vulturo's* sister ship, *The Buzzard*, and *The Chickenhawk*, and showed them the lay of the land around the area. It was always good to give scouts an aerial view. Steven and many of them made copious notes on their sketchy maps and in their notebooks.

The cartography teams were more or less having a field day as well. The balloon corps was a huge boon to them. They logged as many hours as they could.

Mason scanned the area around them with his binoculars.

The scouts made use of several field glasses readily available on a such a spotting vessel. There was even a hatch, like an open torus, set in the middle of the blimp's gas bags, with ladders that led up to an oval, aluminum observation deck and railing up top, for about four to five troops.

"What the hell is that!" Steven suddenly shouted. Then he pointed Mason and the others toward shifting shadows among the forest trees. "There's a huge unit of what looks to be enemy mercenaries, sneaking in through the dense woods from the southwest."

Everyone rushed to that side, suddenly tipping the gondola heavily in that direction. The steam magic engines strained.

"Some of you pull back the other way!" Captain Lewis ordered. The vessel recovered, righting itself as they did so.

"Our Khabal friends are preparing a little surprise for us," Mason said, still looking through his field glasses. "Good eyes, Steven. Yep. They have catapults, ballistae, battle mages. I even see a necromancer. They're going to try to take us out even as we get started. Captain Lewis, will your spotters prepare a tactical message?"

Steven finished writing on a notebook, and tore out the page. "Done, sir. Send this."

Mason looked it over. Brief, clear, informative, and precise. Their ground forces would advance to deal with this approaching threat. Early warning would prove to be key.

"I could just toast that entire area," Mason suggested.

"Sir," Steven noted, "with all respect, they're still too close to the tracks, the back of the train, and our supplies. Not only that, with the prevailing winds the resulting forest fire might overtake us as well, or at least delay our actions. I'm sure that the enemy has taken all of those factors into consideration, including the tactical abilities and limits of the Pistoleros and such."

Mason grinned. "I'm sure they have. That's why they always try to sneak in as close as they can before they attack."

"So that you cannot wipe them out from afar with an annihilator round."

"But just keep in mind," Mason said. "For them to win, they need only delay us. We have about three months to reach Indy, and now they know exactly where we are. Trust me. They're going to throw everything at us that they can. Now, do you and the rest of your fellows want to join me in helping attack those oncoming forces?"

Steven snapped to and saluted. "Scouts, prepare for battle!" Steven yelled.

"Captain Lewis," Mason said. "Can you land and put us down near our forces on the right flank?"

The fighting had already started when they joined Rodell and the battle mages with Mason's reloading teams, and the army assault units positioning themselves. The two friends quickly shook hands.

Rodell Kim smiled, dark eyes, short hair, and bronze skin. The medium height, athletic wizard was actually a Tharanorian—a Darshian agent from Mason's hometown of Cleveland-Dorundia, who could pass for being a Korean among Urthers. That was one of his aliases.

"Hey Mace; for a while I thought you were going to sit this one out."

"Rodell, this is Steven Hayward, son of the Haywards I introduced you to."

"Of course. Wellmet, Steven. How are your parents?"

"Just fine, back in South Bend, waiting for the great zombie invasion like everyone else."

No one laughed at that.

Mason and Rodell Spoke with Captain Teasedale on the ground about attacking the enemy. Mason had seen the terrain from the air.

They studied maps and agreed upon a plan of action.

Mason went ahead along the low ridgeline, looking down into the vales and sloughs, with his guards and the scouts with young Steven out in front of them as skirmishers. The army came up behind them in two wings, one high, one low. Rodell covered the rear with two platoons and a dozen mages.

The rest of his battle mages he spread among the front lines to counter enemy mages.

The enemy force of mercenaries and Dark Khabal forces were about five thousand strong, and traveling along a stretch of open highway, where the abandoned vehicles had long ago been shoved aside or into the ditches.

The enemy used those vehicles and the trees for cover, as well as their own wagons and siege weapons still unassembled.

They and the army were taking pot shots at each other.

In reality, the army was holding the enemy in place, waiting for reinforcements to come online.

Mason spotted necromancers and drew iron. If there was anything he despised, it was those filthy, murdering bastards, tossing deadly spells at the Urthers. Necromancers killed anything living, and were cheerfully gleeful about it. The lived to kill and destroy, and Mason had seen their handiwork far too much.

The Pistolero took careful aim and fired three time, gouts of blasting Wild Magic roaring out of his pistols.

And just like that, three necromancers vanished into hot flaming dust, along with their minions around them.

Then the battle was on in earnest. Three thousand and some odd Urthers against five thousand attackers. But the defenders had the high ground in this battle, and they had the additional firepower of Mason's blazing guns, and Rodell and his battle mages.

The remaining enemy battle mages formed a wedge to shield themselves and peppered the Pistoleros position with destructive spells.

The infantry covered up behind the new defensive rune spells on their shields and archery mantlets, that came out of Rob Billing's enchantment labs. They seemed to hold up nicely.

The Pistolero kept up a steady patter of blazing fire, negating several of the enemy spells as he waded in to them.

They were clearly trying to kill him, and his fire canceled out their worst powers.

Ten of the enemy mages gnashed their teeth and shouted curses in determination. Their leader shouted, "This is it, my dark brothers. Death to the Pistolero. In and Kill him!"

Mason rose up tall. "Like hell you will. I'm standing right here you gutless filth! Come ahead and do your worst!"

Finally he stood toe to toe with them and quickly proceeded to shoot their heads and faces off within a stand up range of twenty feet.

His guns were empty, and none of his reloaders could leap up with him in the heat of such action.

A score of slurgs leaped out of hidden pit traps encircling that spot, lunging at Mason with their weapons ready to cut him down.

They had him just like they planned. He could blast some of them, but not all twenty at once.

He kept firing and whirling any way.

Mason heard the slicing of a sword behind him, expecting to feel steel run him through or cut him down.

"I've got your back, Mace!" Steven Hayward shouted. Two slurgs tumbled down the vale in bloody pieces.

Steven leaped one way and took off a slurg's legs and head. He sprang back the other way and cut another slurg in half.

Damn that kid was fast, like a tornado of razor steel.

Mason gunned down four slurgs charging at him from the four corners. He shot the last one right through the mouth.

Steven and the rest of the scouts rammed iron into the nearest slurgs and fell to bitter fighting with the lizard warriors. Army troops charged in to assist.

The enemy's lines crumbled from there, and the Urthers rolled them up on both flanks. The foe had nowhere to run.

Within an hour, the last third of the enemy were put down. As usual, they refused to surrender.

Mason conferred with the officers that night, and kept *corporal* Hayward with him.

"We're going to be fighting the rest of this summer and into the fall to get this track laid, and the train to Indy. What I'm proposing now is an end run. We load the transport station plates on one of these blimps, and race it to Indy. We'll have it set up in a matter of hours, break the siege, and they can start laying track and meet us half way."

Captain Teasedale objected. "That has already been considered, Lieutenant. It's just too risky. With the weight of the plates, there would only be eight people to protect them and crew the dirigible. What if the enemy has a way to down our airships we don't know about? We could lose both the airship, and the crucial plates. And in any case, Indianapolis is already completely surrounded by enemy forces."

Mason smiled. "That's why we're going to fly in, under cover of darkness." He looked at Rodell and Steven. "And I pick the troops going with me."

When all was ready, they set out two hours later.

No lights. As high as they could go. Silent running.

# DAVID

David, the princes, and the entire Vanguard swept down from the north, chasing the Dark Khabal forces who had committed the atrocities on that hill just outside of Battle Creek.

When they had first arrived on scene in the dark, the area stunk to high heaven, and wretched, filthy smoke was everywhere. They encircled the monsters who were bent over, gorging themselves on the vile remains of the Great Dark Ritual, hundreds of sacrificed civilians of all ages.

Skirmishers rushed in to put the monsters to the sword.

The souls of the Urther captives had been offered up to the Dark Ghods. The burnt flesh of the victims was everywhere, mutilated beyond anything imaginable outside of the Nine Hells.

David turned to the princes, drawing his sword and shouting a defiant challenge. "These are our people. Our brothers and sisters that they have done these vile things to, in our lands. I say that this shall not stand. Whatever we do this night, we will overtake these murdering scum, and we shall strike them down. Come. Stiffen your sinews. I summon the Two Hundred once more. You are the finest troops I know. We find these bastards. No mercy.

No quarter. Vengeance upon our foes to the last full measure. We hunt them and hew them down to the last!"

Mighty cheers answered his fierce words. Some were still too busy weeping or being sickened by what little they could see under the starlight.

Thank the heavens that it was not day time.

They set themselves up in a swift pursuit mode with their scouts and skirmishers like a spearhead in front of them, two lines ready to break and maneuver at a moment's notice, infantry on their flanks, and the rear formed up like a moving shield wall.

Minor attacks they ignored. The vanguard continued moving, searching, and hunting. They had the blood scent of their foul quarry and they meant to run them down and encircle them in a deathtrap of steel and spell.

No one spoke. Nearly every eye stayed grim and set. They focused on breathing and marching at the quick step, eating up the ground beneath their feet as they closed the distance with their quarry.

The Khabal forces that had performed the Great Dark Ritual were less than two hours ahead of them now, by all reports.

If they hurried, they might overtake and fall upon the foe as the sun rose in the sky.

The enemy unit turned south somewhat, apparently growing aware that they were being pursued now, by a capable and determined force close to their own size.

From what the scouts said, there was another large enemy host just four hours away. Their quarry sped up, hoping to link up with that larger force and then turn at bay to face their Urther pursuers with greater numbers.

More word reached them. Five hundred Michiana light cavalry, on both horses and mountain bikes raced ahead to cut the enemy off and hold them in place.

When the race brought them within an hour of their targets, David called upon the Blackhawks to put all of their elite training and endurance hardening to the test. For weeks they had run with full gear and packs, for mile after mile, driving themselves to their limits.

Now all of that stamina training was going to pay off.

The Blackhawks lowered their heads and broke into nearly a full run to close the distance with the foe, who were now said to be three thousand strong.

They sent all of their scouts and skirmishers ahead of them, to harass the enemy and slow them down even more.

Finally, the hunters had signs that the enemy was panicking.

The Khabalists slit the throats of their own wounded and dumped them behind.

Then they released their remaining prisoners they kept with them, having no time left to kill them. This was a ploy, giving the captives up, hundreds of mostly attractive young men and women to later be used as slaves or worse.

David and the vanguard ignored even the pleading captives and kept running.

The captives were safe enough. Other troops from 16 would scoop them up as they followed on.

Then word came that Tori Nelson, the Pistolera, was racing up with her reloading teams to assist them.

"We will not hold back until we overtake them!" David shouted at the messenger, his blood and rage beginning to mount. "Tell Tori to join us as able!"

They kept moving through the twilight, eyes fixed and determined.

The vanguard could finally hear the enemy up ahead.

Many of the troops could smell the foe now. Those who conducted the ritual were still drenched in blood, as if they had bathed in it. Perhaps some of them had.

The vanguard crested a lightly wooded hill, poised to fall upon the enemy. They caught sight of the fleeing foe at last. David sent the princes and their mounted forces to envelop the enemy on the left, trample them, and cut them off completely. The outlying cavalry could join in.

The fast infantry from Army 16 closed in from the right. Skirmishers and scouts cut off the enemy at the narrows, dead ahead.

David heard Tori shouting at him as she raced up the hill on Pepper. He would not wait a second, even for her.

"All in," he shouted. "Fall upon them with everything we have. Death to all foes. Leave none alive! Blackhawks, let the Two Hundred Swords stand forth, shield wall and spell swords to the fore. Unleash our volleys upon my command!"

The enemy turned to face them and anchored their forces at three points, bristling with pikes and Dark Mages. Spells shot back and forth with destructive power on both sides as the hosts closed.

David marched at the head of the front line of the Blackhawk vanguard, two hundred enchanted swords and rune shields marching in a 'V,' directing their bright blades at the enemy strong point.

"Cut them down head on. Zara!" David shouted.

Two hundred voices thundered the command word. "Zara!"

Two hundred blinding, blue-white lightning bolts blasted the enemy ranks, crisscrossing between both arms of the 'V.'

The entire enemy front corner shattered and exploded in a hammering wave of blazing thunderbolts. Dark Khabal bodies detonated within their armor. Hundreds of screams were cut off, enemy lines vanished in bright flashes, mowed down and incinerated. Enemy counter-spells withered and vanished in vain flashes amid the waves of destruction.

David did not hold back a second, as the enemy reeled in abject terror and confusion. The Blackhawks marched right up to them in tight formation, trampling what was left of the enemy dead.

"Put fire right in their guts. Kal!"

Blasting fire enveloped the entire enemy left. As it passed, three entire ranks of the foe were reduced to burning charcoal and ash upon the ground. Hundreds more, nearly vaporized as if a furnace suddenly appeared around them.

The Blackhawks flattened out their line, and the Dark Khabal turned to run, barely twenty feet away from the glowing, advancing, avenging swords.

Three necromancers defied the flames and set themselves with their skull staffs to mount a counterattack.

Shots rang out, as Tori pulled up on her horse, firing rapidly from both barrels as her exploding rounds chewed the necromancers to bits and the enemy troops behind them in great swaths of glowing destruction.

The two hundred marched right in at them from behind.

"They will no longer murder our people, old our young. Our women and children. Shi!" David commanded, even as the enemy skull staffs cooked off.

"Shi!" the Two Hundred Swords roared.

Spirit blasts rocked the foe, hurling more bodies in several directions.

David halted, even as Tori and the others rushed in to finish off the remnants. "Spell Swords, stand down. Well done. Hold your positions. Cut down any foes who come our way."

Not one dared to do so. There were none left at hand.

They could not unleash any more blasts without taking the risk of hitting their own people by that time.

David heard many cries from the enemy for surrender and mercy.

All were summarily ignored.

The victims of the Great Dark Ritual were at last avenged. The enemy bodies were left on display where they fell for the enemy to find in Army 16's wake, to be taken as a warning

Tori came rushing up to him on Pepper. "Dave, what the hell was all this about? We've got ten thousand exhausted civilians and counting about to collapse and fall to pieces. Battle Creek was supposed to be a safe place they could rest, but the war zone here is worse than what we left behind at Kalamazoo!"

For once, David snapped at her. "Tori, I can't do shit about any of that. But what we did here had to be done. And while you're at it, we'd better get ready for several thousand more refugees, as bad off as the ones we already have, if not worse."

Tori drew back a bit. "I'm sorry, Dave. What the heck happened? I wasn't trying to blame you for anything. We're just in a bad way and it stinks."

He told her briefly about the Khabal's great ritual site they had discovered. Tori turned a little green.

"Don't tell me any more, Dave," she said stopping him. "I might be sick. You're right. These assholes deserved worse than death. I'm glad we could give it to them." He nodded.

She spat into the smoldering piles of ash with hands and heads and feet sticking out of them. "These pricks won't do that to any of our people ever again."

"Yeah, well this is a drop in the bucket. We've got about fifty thousand more of these jerks to deal with, and maybe more, all the way to Detroit, if we make it there."

"Dave, we can barely keep ourselves alive against such numbers. How are we going to ride herd on twenty-thousand sick, tired, wounded, and helpless civvies? And more are filtering in every minute?"

David swallowed hard. "I don't have an answer for that, Tori."

# JERRIEL

Despite their best efforts to avoid the enemy hunter units, Jerriel, Khia, and Luin could not shake their many pursuers. In fact, the trio was still weakened from their ordeal and their constant flight.

They tried to keep to the forest. A warm rain fell.

The enemy hunters continued to close in at them, and in large numbers, clearly determined to re-capture them all.

Khia took shape, in that of a tiny, green-glowing sprite. Her energy levels were still low, and she mostly traveled with one of her new companions. "Jerriel, Luin. I think our foes have some way of tracking me or my energies."

Jerriel nodded, "There are several spells and magickal crystals, gems, and artifacts that would allow them to detect and trace such energies."

"I want you find a place to leave me behind. I'll go deep into the earth where they cannot reach me."

"No!" Luin said emphatically. "Stay with us, Urth Sister. We will find a way to lose the bad ones. We will not give you up to their evils."

'Yes," Jerriel added. "In your condition Khia, you would expend your powers going into the Urth as you say. That would trap you wherever you ended up. Yet these Dark Mages are very cunning and relentless. They would still be able to sense your presence, and they would use earth magic to tunnel down miles into the Urth, if need be, to capture you. Do not underestimate them. According to my map, there is a ley line less than a league away. Once there, you can re-charge your abilities and find a way to mask your presence from our foes once again. Then we can go where we will."

Luin circled back around carefully while her friends rested, using her innate powers to pass unclad. "There are three large groups of hunters trying to converge on our position," she reported upon returning. "Two are using bright, flickering crystals that seem to flicker faster as they near Khia. The third is using some kind of metal things over his eyes with round panels of green glass that allows them to see where to go. But they did not see me."

"Some kind of goggles of true sight or similar enchantment," Jerriel noted. "They could have seen you with them if you were merely invisible, Luin. Yet not when you are unclad: both invisible and immaterial."

Luin laughed, her broad smile opening her large mouth across her wide, furry face. Despite being a fierce, young Hoonga girl, at only seven feet tall, her long, golden brown fur all over her thick body gave her a beauty that was all her own, and her large, intelligent blue eyes were piercing and intense.

She vanished at will and then re-appeared. Sometimes they only heard her voice.

Khia curled up in the palm of Jerriel's hand, still weak. Jerriel slipped the entity into a soft pocket sewn into her robes, over her heart.

"Hold on, Khia. We're going to reach that ley line."

"Yes, we are," Luin said. She scooped up Jerriel once more and sprinted off at a swift, loping run.

Jerriel could have never run so fast or set such a pace.

Luin sensed her mind and cut her off. "Do not worry, wizard sister. We are close enough. I can smell the ley line now, and I will get us there ahead of the bad ones. Then I will rest while the Urth sister renews her powers."

They ran fast for what seemed a quarter hour or more. Then Luin put Jerriel down back on her feet. They were near a swift stream that was nearly a small rushing river. Luin went to the river's edge to have a long drink.

Khia awoke in Jerriel's mind. "Stop, her, Jerriel. Sometimes among humans, the water in the south is bad."

"Luin, don't drink yet. Let Khia check the water to see if it is safe."

Luin grinned. "Very well, but I can smell if the water is bad or not. Let the Urth sister check it if she wishes."

After a moment Khia said, "this stream is fed mostly by rain water flowing down through the hills, and a few brackish ponds and pools. But Luin can drink from it without harm to her iron like constitution. You would most likely need to boil it first, Jerriel, because of the risk of certain southern water born parasites. Fill your canteens, and I will purify it further for you."

Khia sprang down to the ground out of Jerriel's breast pocket and followed the ley line to the stream's edge, holding out both hands. She swelled up larger and larger with Urth Power as she walked, eventually reaching Jerriel's size. She stretched and sighed in her larger form.

She got down and draped herself over the Urth and the ley line, stretching and sighing as she further renewed herself and her energies.

"You're naked," Jerriel told her flat out. "You should clothe yourself in something when you assume a humanoid form. It is somewhat customary."

"Among humans." Khia laughed. "I shall never be human, and I have no shame for any of my forms, as humans do." But for Jerriel's sake, Khia donned what appeared to be thin robes of green, like the ones she had fashioned before.

They might also run into other humans, and Jerriel was right in a sense. None of them should attract undue attention.

Luin still quenched her thirst from up stream.

Khia went back to stretching out in the long grass, face up above the ley line near the stream, sinking half-way into the ground. "I can sense our pursuers now, and their troops and mages. They are more than two hours behind us. I'm using an ability similar to that of the Hoonga to mask our presence from them, but this is where they last sensed our position with their powers. They will come to this place with all speed. But until they draw closer, we can rest and recover our strength."

"Sisters," Luin said. "I'm sorry, but I am hungry again. The Hoonga feed frequently. It will take precious time to forage. I could run down a deer and kill it for food."

"Ugh," Jerriel said. "Perhaps you enjoy raw venison, but I would need to dress and cook any game we catch. That would take too long."

"I will provide as I did before, from our true mother, our Urth," Khia said. "It is easy to do so, as long as I have access to power such as this. I perceive the both of you and I know what your needs are."

Food took shape up out of the ground in two piles. One for Jerriel, and one larger pile for a much large Luin.

Jerriel had berries, fruit, wild parsnips, lettuce, and spinach. There were also nuts, and a stone bowl filled with a mash of wild brown rice and different kinds of herbs and soft beans, with a touch of honey.

She and Luin both thanked Khia, and then ate their fill.

Jerriel had plenty to spare, tucked the rest away in her pack for later, and then curled up on the cool grass in the shade to catch a short rest.

Luin continued to munch on her melons, squash, and pumpkins, eating even the rinds and seeds. Then she had apples and peaches, nuts, and more fresh water. She too stretched out beneath the light rain and vanished. But Jerriel could still detect the Hoonga's breathing as she slept.

Khia kept watch, sensing everything for miles around them.

Jerriel woke with a slight start about an hour later. The rain had let up, but the air was still humid and misty.

She reached into her bag, and her hand fell upon the enemy secret reports she had taken.

She pulled them out, shuffled them back together by date, and began to read backwards from just a few days ago, on through the last few weeks gone by.

A horrible account it was. Clearly the enemy led a campaign all throughout lower Michigan-Shendor, to eradicate the Urthers and claim the 'Hand,' and the inner seas for their own purposes.

The tally of people killed and prisoners taken was staggering. Now only Anzhalar-Grand Rapids held out in the northwest. All other remaining Urthers had been forced south, captured, or wiped out. To the southeast, only Tornhold-Detroit and the region around it remained undefeated. Large numbers of Urthers around those places held fast against the enemy hordes.

But if they were not able to harvest their crops in the fall, those large numbers would become their own deathtrap that winter, and many would starve.

The enemy also wanted to capture those food stores for their own use, if possible. And indeed, if they could not take down the defenders by sword and spell, they would reduce them by hunger that winter. By the spring the defenders would be sick and famished, and both Tornhold and Kellendra would be ripe for the taking.

Much of this was nothing new, and could very well be guessed at, but some of the details and military plans would be of tactical use to the defenders.

Then Jerriel came across something even more unusual.

Thirty thousand Khabal troops and Dark Mages had been sent north to cross the straights, the top of the inner seas by the big broken Urther bridge between Shendor and the upper land called Shenedar.

Their mission was considered vital to winning the war.

They were apparently after some kind of powerful being or creature, the likes of which the reports said would spell certain defeat for the Urth defenders and cause them to be wiped out with ease, that winter.

Jerriel felt certain that the enemy must have detected or found traces of another Spectral Entity. It had to be. If they captured both Khia and this other entity, they would then have three such beings at their command, making the Dark Khabal virtually unstoppable in the colonies. No Urth or colonial forces could stand against such might.

The bold enemy dared anything, even sending armies of mages and mercenaries up into lands that might be guarded by the Hoonga. The foe would obviously risk much to capture this elusive power in the north, and add it to their arsenal as a new weapon.

Jerriel felt chills shoot through her. The Urth defenders knew nothing of this plan, which might spell their very doom. What other diabolical plans did the Dark Khabal have up and running all over both worlds, plotting to destroy any who resisted them? That was a grim thing to consider.

Yet she saw her duty clearly, and knew what it was that she must do, for the good of all. Even if it took her farther away from David and her friends until the next spring.

She, Khia, and Luin must go north and do all that they could to foil the enemy's foul plans. Even the mighty Hoonga might not know their peril, until it was too late. And Luin had mentioned to them that many of her people took the long sleeps, resting for a month or two at a time as winter ruled the lands.

Jerriel convinced herself that the enemy was after another Spectral Entity. What else could it be?

If only she could send a message to David and Army 16 at Tornhold-Detroit. With Bentar and Huran fallen, that was where David and her friends would end up. She was certain of it. She would speak to Khia and see if there was any way to send such a message.

Khia suddenly flashed in beside her, causing Jerriel to jump slightly.

"Our minds are still linked," Khia said. "So, we go north, across the seas, to see if we can save another entity such as myself? That's your plan, is it not?"

Jerriel nodded, "Indeed. We are the only ones who know about these threats, and who have any power to help. We must go, but I hope the two of you will agree to help me."

"Where are we going now?" Luin ask, popping in on Jerriel's other side.

Jerriel started again, and chuckled. "I wish that I could learn to do that."

"I heard what you said," Luin told them. "I would gladly cross the inner seas to travel up through Shenedar. Then we can rejoin me people and I can return home. How I miss it now. A sudden rock slide and flood in the mountains swept me downstream and I smashed my head on many large rocks before I could go unclad. That's how the bad ones found me, injured and weak, and brought me south in that cage, on a large boat."

Khia stepped forward and placed her hands on Luin's head, growing in size to be able to do so. "I will explain the rest of our plans to Luin through a link. Then I shall transform, and we shall depart."

Jerriel gathered her few things.

In an open meadow, Jerriel and Luin looked on as Khia transformed into a large, green snow goose, nearly the size of an adult dragon.

Jerriel and Luin clambered up, nestling down into the thick, gigantic feathers on Khia's back, holding on out of the way of the enormous wings.

Khia in her spirit-bird form lifted up into the air almost effortlessly, and headed north.

Yet even as she did so, they came under attack so swift and sudden that they could not help but be dismayed.

Four enemy Dark Mages swept down out of the gray, overcast sky, led by a flying necromancer.

All of them wore segmented, machine, and birdlike wings and contraptions strapped to their bodies, giving them the power of flight. They were dressed in some kind of waterproof flight suits: coveralls, boots, gloves, and a face mask complete with goggles.

Jerriel shouted, "The enemy reports mentioned the coming use of air and flying mages, and the new enchanted-mechanical *aerovelocitors*. With them the Dark Mages can attack from the sky as well."

Khia cried out, enduring several powerful magic blasts.

All four attackers circled around quickly like falcons, gaining altitude in order to tuck their wings and dive into another attack.

Khia struggled to evade and get above them, but she was huge—an easy target.

Jerriel called out to Luin. "Hold my ankles!" She stood up into the teeth of the stiff wind and readied her staff to do battle.

She aimed for the necromancer with the black glowing skull staff, but he read her intent and banked away at the last second.

Jerriel corrected and fried the next *aeromage* with a blinding, blue-white lightning bolt. His aerovelocitor burst into flames and streaked down, trailing smoke. He popped an emergency chute, but the flames raced up the cords and ignited the canopy.

He exploded among the trees seconds later.

Khia shrieked, taking two more direct spell hits from a fire strike and a cold blast. They were attacking her wings and tail, trying to bring her down for the approaching capture forces.

The necromancer squared off with Jerriel, locking his eyes upon her. She was the entity's only defense, while Khia continued to try to gain altitude and speed. Another half minute, and she might pull away from the enemy's contraptions.

Yet a lot could take place within twenty or thirty seconds of aerial combat.

Jerriel shielded them from a black ray that would have exploded their bones–a forbidden shadowmagic spell.

She nailed one of the other aeromagi with a gray, paralysis beam.

He froze with his wings outstretched, and spiraled slowly down to the grassy ground.

Now it was only three against one, as the enemy closed with them once more.

Khia surprised them all by suddenly accelerating and passing right through the remaining foes. She banked and smashed right into the trio as they struggled to pull up. Then they toppled out of the air, tumbling and trying to recover their powers of flight.

The entity saw her chance and put on speed, leaving the battle behind.

Luin dragged Jerriel down and stuffed her into the large feathers on the back, but was herself caught by the rushing winds.

Jerriel reached out for her big friend, even as the high winds tore her off Khia's back and swept her behind them into the night. "Luin!"

Luin was gone, just like that, and nothing could be done. Even a Hoonga would not be able to survive such a fall from so high up. Their brave, hairy friend was gone and no doubt slain.

Khia, Luin fell off, Jerriel said telepathically through their link. We must go back for her. She saved me from her fate.

*We cannot turn back. Our foes would be upon us again. I'm sorry. I did not mean for such to happen. But she is gone now. And we must flee further north while I still have the strength.*

Jerriel wept, staring back into the night receding behind them. "Farewell, brave Luin of the Hoonga!" she shouted aloud. "Goodbye, our sister."

163

# SHAEDDOR

Shaeddor jumped down and looked around after he and his team landed at the first destination of their new secret mission for the Dark Khabal. He had traveled swiftly once more, upon the wings of the Tharanorian Spectral Entity of Night, the vast bat creature.

It's speed was amazing, and they brought with them about threescore of Shaeddor's guards and servants, carried aloft in a long, traveling coach-like structure with seats and room for basic supplies. The long pod was made out of metal and wood. His people emerged and formed up behind their master, ready to obey his commands.

The magickal and material components for each transport gateway were supposed to be waiting for them at each stop, according to a schedule.

Shaeddor spoke his commands silently to his Spectral Entity through the key, the priceless onyxian necklace around his throat, on loan from the High Magus. The gigantic bat creature vanished into the night, but the coach pod was left behind on its short stand, for when they needed more from it.

He looked around in the darkness and beheld yet another, once mighty Urther city, sprawled across both sides of the Great River that was the northern tip of the next great inner sea. This was the broad river that divided the northern continent of the colonial wilds east and west. The Urthers, of course, had some silly name for it with far too many consonants.

Rich Sylurrian ships had fought their way up to this place to deliver their cargoes, and hosts of mercenaries had flocked there for high pay.

As for the Urthers in this region, they had indeed suffered loss from the Merge as Urthers did everywhere, but these held out better than most, still maintaining a large bulk of their large population. They banded to together and seemed better supplied than many other Urther cities, unlike Vaejan.

But now those large numbers struggled to raise crops and sustain themselves through the coming winter, and there were still a better part of nearly a million undead roaming around, causing trouble where they could break out.

Shaeddor turned to his aide, Tepperson, a clerkish little wretch of a man. "Tep, what do the Urthers call this place again?"

"The two cities, milord. One is Saint Paul, and the other is Minneapolis; strange names if you ask me."

"What do we call them? Urther names are of no consequence. Under our dominion, that is all that shall matter in the future."

"Milord, we just lump it all in one and call it Zaskakaria."

"Very well. Find out why we are not being met by our contacts. Send messengers. I am a delegate from the High Magus himself. What insult is this?"

"Two messengers have already been sent, milord."

A host of five hundred mercenaries, grun, and Dark Mages marched in minutes later, with their leader on horseback.

Mercenaries. How tedious; always so flamboyant and mouthy, like strutting, crying peacocks—the entire lot of them.

This one rose up in his saddle. "I am Captain Reggario Falkarone Mannestista of the Iron Spears of Khairun. We are your escort back to our fortified areas, close at hand. This area is also under our protection, and was assigned for your safe landing, Great Magioro. Welcome."

The man bowed and was adept enough with the pleasantries.

Shaeddor did not deign to smile. "Thank you, Captain. Would you have our coach brought along? Tepperson, have the wheels cranked down."

"Yes, milord." Tep scurried away to obey.

Captain Mannestista bowed his high, orange-plumed helm once more. "It shall be done as you ask, great lord. If my forces and I can be of further assistance, please let us know. We are at your disposal during your stay with us."

"Excellent, Captain. I am sure that we shall have need of you. Our mission for the High Magus is of paramount importance, and we shall begin our efforts immediately to fulfill his grand design for the colonies."

From the reports that he had read, the Dark Khabal forces only held sway in Zaskakaria over about one fifth of the city on the large side of the river, mostly where the undead were barricaded in by the Urthers, determined to keep them bottled up.

The Khabal forces were waiting for further reinforcements, not wishing to spend themselves needlessly against the determined defenders. Thus the situation was a stalemate.

It was hoped that more of the Urthers would die off that winter, either from starvation, disease, or war, and add to the number of undead by the spring. That and reinforcements would hopefully tip the scales and spell doom for the Urthers.

Shaeddor's mission was meant to assist with some of that. His team would construct the fixed transport gateway that would eventually connect all of the key Dark Khabal cities with each other and make them invincible.

Once the transport network was up and functioning properly, the Dark Khabal could flood massive forces in to city after city, and bring them to ruin like so many ten pins. They would seize the colonial lands of the New World on both sides, and bring them that much closer to becoming part of two new Shadow Worlds, to lay before the feet of the Dark Ghods.

He allowed himself a short, sweet smile.

At least that was the grand plan. Who knew what could possibly go wrong along the way?

Captain Mannestista brought up a horse for Shaeddor to ride, and escorted him with honor to the Dark Khabal stronghold, less than a quarter mile from the landing area. This was the protectorate of the area's virtual ruler, General Chonzen Gordeel, one of the Sixty Dark Lords.

It was near midnight and the general had already retired with his horde of concubines. The captain escorted Shaeddor to his posh quarters, complete with several slaves. He took his ease while servants new and old carried in and unpacked his things.

By then the transport team was already at work. Next, slaves brought him a fine, abundant meal that had been kept waiting just for him.

As the emissary of the High Magus on an important mission, it was his right to inspect the mission log of each protectorate, and any and all reports and communications passing through those areas. In fact, he realized that he was more or less Gorrial's Inspector General.

The Dark Khabal maintained an army of trained handlers of owls, crows, and ravens that they used to send messages, as a functioning back up network.

"Captain. Bring me the general log for the protectorate and all of the reports for the last week. I wish to inspect some of them while I dine, and before I turn in."

The man actually clicked his heels on the marble floor and bowed his head. "You shall have them within the hour, milord."

"Thank you, Captain. You've been most kind. That is all."

"With the compliments of the general," the officer said, motioning with his hand to the doorway to Shaeddor's bedchamber.

Attached to the large iron slave rings on either side, were two pairs of slaves, meant to be used as pleasure slaves.

Shaeddor resisted the urge to roll his eyes in complete disgust. Four half-naked, half-starved Urther slave children, filthy, frightened, and jumpy, with the staring traumatic eyes of the lost.

Who could guess what horrors they had already been through at the hands of the Khabal?

Three girls and one boy. The dark haired boy was the oldest, no more than fifteen. The brown-haired girl with the green eyes was about twelve and looked down at her trembling hands. The last two girls were about nine and seven, if that. One was blond with short hair and blue eyes and the other was very dark-skinned and still had colorful beads in her hair. The pair clung to each other and rocked back and forth.

Pitiful. Again, this was what the Khabal was—vile filth and terror that needed to be wiped out and utterly destroyed.

It could not begin soon enough, but first he needed information, and to secrete himself deep within their counsels and plots.

The Captain sensed Shaeddor hesitating. "Milord, if you wish for something else, please, make your preferences known. We'll drag these vermin away and bring you something else."

Shaeddor thought better of that and sighed. "No, Captain. This will do. I'm already tired in any case."

"Well, then these are your pleasure slaves while you are with us, and they will bathe you and see to your every personal need. Do with them as you will. If you wish to have them beaten, exchanged, or put to death, just let the guards and the other servants know." He handed over a ring of keys to their iron shackles.

"Quite. If you excuse me, Captain. It has been a rather long and tedious day. I'll say goodnight."

"Good night, milord."

Shaeddor turned his back and let the departing servants see the man out.

Finally relatively alone within his private chambers, if he even made a glance at the children, they cringed against the wall and averted their eyes.

Tep arrived with the log and the recent reports and had them organized and ready to peruse. Shaeddor thanked and dismissed him for the night. He quickly became absorbed in what he read as he ate.

Several minutes later he wrinkled his nose at some fresh stench of the human variety.

The two little ones had soiled themselves and still sat together rocking in their own reek.

He went to the outer door quickly. "Guards, have a servant brought to clean up after and watch these children. I shall not be bothered by such things."

"Of course, milord," the larger of the two guards said. "Right away."

In less than ten minutes an older Urther woman in her late thirties was roughly shoved in with a bucket, a mop, and cleaning supplies, as well as fresh clothing for the kids, as needed.

She glared at Shaeddor with total hatred for the barest instant, and then averted her gaze. She did not speak. But he had not missed that look.

As far as this woman knew, he was as bad as the rest of the Dark Khabal.

"Over there," he flatly told her. "Clean them up please, and see that they do not disturb me any further."

The first thing the woman did was to bring the kids one of the chamber pots and then empty it after it was full.

Within a quarter hour, the stench went away, replaced by the aroma of masking cleaners at least.

By then he was done with the protectorate log book and started on the reports. An assessment had been made of the Urther crops and fields, waiting to be harvested that fall. Battle plans were being made to seize or destroy those fields.

Shaeddor used a special enchanted ring with a clear stone, twisted around and inverted on his right hand. As he passed his hand over each document, he barely spoke a spell command aloud, and the ring transferred an image to the pages of the current volume of his own private journal.

His father had invented this magical library device. As well as several spells and enchantments in partnership with Shaeddor's mother to make copies of scrolls and books, and transfer written information. By using small pocket dimension magicks, a wealth of written material could also be carried in secret by any mage who was skilled in such matters. Both of his parents had specialized in such abilities and passed them on to their children.

Another report caught his attention. The new aerovelocitor flying suits had just arrived and were being tested by all of the available air mages.

Shaeddor knew most of the air magicks required to help the suits operate. It would be good to study their secrets and learn to fly one.

One of the children started sobbing, the older girl this time. The cleaning woman was holding her, stroking her hair, and trying to comfort her and keep her quiet.

Soon all four of the kids where straining at their chains, trying to get the woman to hold them all at once.

"What the blazes is it now?" Shaeddor demanded.

The woman shot to her feet and stared at the floor. The children crouched down and cringed against the wall once more at the mere pitch of his voice.

This was getting tiresome.

He went to her and asked plainly. "Talk to me, good woman. I speak Urther and quite fluently. What will it take to keep them quiet?"

She still hesitated a few breaths longer.

"Unchain them, m-m-milord. I'll k-k-keep them out of your way. And...they have not eaten in days. C-c-could you feed them a little?"

The mix of fear and hatred in the woman was so palpable that it nearly came off her in waves of force.

Shaeddor sighed, "Oh, very well."

He retrieved the keys and to the wonder and amazement of them all, he unlocked their shackles. Then he pointed at the copious remains of his fine dinner.

There was still perhaps enough left for several persons, especially one small woman and four children. "You can all clean up the rest of that mess. Just be quiet about it and do not disturb me. That is what I require."

The five Urther slaves stared at him in shock, not knowing what to say.

He simply went back to reading the reports.

The woman and the kids crept around like ghosts, afraid to make a sound as they went to the small, sumptuous table and ate silently, but with obvious hunger.

There were only four ornate wooden chairs at the table, so the smallest child had to sit on the woman's lap to eat.

Shaeddor finished the reports an hour later and felt weary, but he had learned much that would help him.

When he thought about the Urthers again, he looked over at them.

They were all sleeping on the table. Every scrap of food and drink was gone, even the wine and ice water. And the woman and all four kids were fast asleep, the youngest still on the woman's lap.

Shaeddor sighed and tried to wake the woman gently. She looked up at him in terror and opened her mouth to scream. Shaeddor was forced to clamp his hard hand over her mouth to stifle her.

"Madam, I am not going to hurt you. Take up the little one. Let's put them down in my bed."

She glared at him fiercely all of the sudden at the possible evil intent of his words.

Now he did roll his eyes. "Never fear. I'll sleep out here on this spacious divan or the chase. You yourself can stay with them."

Her shocked face stared at him again. Then she managed to nod. She rose up, cradling the smallest in her arms.

With a wave of his hands he cast a simple levitation spell. He floated the other three kids out of their seats and into the air and directed them into his bedchamber. There the woman drew back the covers and tucked the four in, one after the other.

After Shaeddor released his spell completely, he turned to leave.

After another moment, the woman emerged from the darkened room.

"You aren't one of them," she said. "Not really. Are you? You pretend to be. But you don't…you do the things they do."

He looked at her. "I was almost one of them…once," he confessed.

She smiled. "Almost isn't enough. Yet I need to know, if you are a man or one of these devils with human faces. Do you mean to harm those kids in any way?"

Shaeddor shook his head. "No. They have nothing I could possibly need or want. But you must understand, neither am I in a position to save you or them from your fates. In another day or two, I'll be gone. I'm sorry."

"You said you were almost one of them," she said. "Why didn't you join them?"

"Because I found friends and they taught me things that mattered. I met a young woman who meant everything to me, and devils like these thought her worthless, and butchered her without a thought."

"If you did try to help us, they would just catch onto you and murder us all, wouldn't they?"

He nodded. "Yes. Murder is their simple answer to everything."

The woman shrugged. "I guess it doesn't matter. There are plenty of helpless slaves like us now, after the Merge. What do five lives matter compared to the loss of millions, maybe billions worldwide?"

Shaeddor motioned toward the bedchamber. "Go in. Sleep with the children and watch over them. While I am here, your lives will be much easier."

The exhausted woman smiled. "Thank you."

When they were all fast asleep, Shaeddor cast a sleep mist spell over them so that they would not awaken for hours.

Then he readied his own gating spell.

Such magicks would drain him for a day or two in the past, but with the energy crystals embedded in his flesh, not to the mention the mighty energies of his Spectral Key, he could now work them at will.

From his high window he used a large telescope to fix upon a spot outside of the Khabal's control. He opened the gateway first on his side within the large walk in closet, and then on the other other in a dark alley between two abandoned buildings. Then it was merely a matter of levitating the sleeping ones all through as before.

Once on the other side, he left the gate open, but concealed. Nothing could pass through it without his permission, and if he did not return, the spell and the portal would eventually dissolve and fade away completely.

The nights were getting slightly cooler, yet not enough to harm his charges. He floated them upright now, hovering all around him, for ease of travel rather than protection.

Finally, he used a glamour that would disguise his features. No two people looking upon his face or his form would see the same thing, and they would not remember it well. To all he would appear shadowy and out of focus to most untrained eyes.

Next, he located the Urther defensive lines. With the watch late, it was an easy thing with his shadow powers of the Entity of Night to slip past them.

He came to what looked to be some kind of officer's quarters and a garrison of militia set up among an old red brick building. An empty green tent was set up in an open lot, with tables inside, perhaps for training or meetings. It mattered not.

Shaeddor secured the escapees within, and left them sleeping on the tables. He found a clean tarp to pull over them.

Then he went to the nearest guard post, one which happened to have sleeping guards, well behind the lines, fortunately. He awoke one guard, who jumped to his feet and was about to raise the alarm.

Shaeddor wrapped him in bands of shadow and lifted him off the ground, silencing him.

"Be quiet, you slumbering fool. I am not your enemy. I'm a mage agent from your allies, come to make a report. Understand? I'm going to release you, and you are going to quietly awake your equally reposed friend, and then one of you will take me to the officer on duty."

The fellow nodded quite cooperatively, wide-eyed. But when Shaeddor went to release him, he tried to scream once more.

It took some thorough convincing, but finally Shaeddor had the excitable young chap calmed down enough to where he wasn't going to shriek his bloody head off.

After that, it was a few minutes more before Shaeddor came before the officer on duty, a second leftenant, who then awoke the captain of the garrison, Captain Seebold, a stout but short man in his early forties, brown eyes and a head all but shaved bald.

He brought Shaeddor within his office, where they sat in private with the window lightly ajar and cool night air flowing in to the stuffy quarters.

They started speaking while Shaeddor kept an eye on his watch.

Watches were such a fascinating and practical mechanical invention of the cunning Urthers. Mason had given him this one. How he missed his old companion. He even missed their horses.

Back to the present, at first they verbally sparred for a while, until Shaeddor half-convinced the Urther Captain that this was not all part of some elaborate, enemy trick.

Shaeddor pointed out, quite plainly, that with his powers he could have just as easily murdered the people he had rescued, killed the sleeping guards, and most of the garrison itself, had that been his intent.

All of that would have taken as much trouble by half.

Word returned to them that the woman and the four sleeping kids had been located and were now safe and well-cared for.

"Why did you rescue these people? "Captain Seebold asked. "Five strangers you didn't even know?"

"Frankly, I felt sorry for them. The Dark Khabal and its allies treat their slaves very badly, and are quite used to doing so. More than likely, they would have been dead within a matter of days or weeks. And besides, I clearly hoped that an act of kindness would get you to trust me faster, and bloody well listen to what I have to say.

"We are wasting time. I don't have much time to get back before I am missed. So we shouldn't waste so much time on you second guessing whether you can trust me of not. By all means, don't trust me, but at least listen to the information that I am bringing you. If what I say is true, it will confirm itself."

He tossed a plain copy of his own journal in front of the Captain.

"In there you'll find a wealth of concise information about the Merge, the Dark Khabal, and magic–particularly transport, air, and healing magic. There are mechanical plans for transport gates, steam engines and devices of various sizes, balloons and flying machines, parachutes. Next is information on ley lines and the Spectral Keys of both worlds."

By now, Captain Seebold simply stared at him.

"There is also information on Tharanor, the world the where Dark Khabal and their minions came from. I understand, it's a lot to take in. Some of it you might already know. Some of it might come as a shock. You should eventually try to reach out to the other Urther enclaves, such as Michiana, by dirigible if you can build them.

"But definitely avoid Vaejan, or your Chicago, because it is already the Khabal stronghold and a literal dead zone. Oh, and you need to take care. The Khabal intends to steal or destroy all of your crops before the fall and starve you all during the winter. If they can kill you off, they'll turn all of your corpses into more zombies, skeletons, and other undead armies by the spring. You don't want that."

All color had drained from Seebold's face and neck, and by his reaction, he could only stare at the shifting creature sitting across the table from him.

"Where the hell is Michiana?" Seebold croaked. "And why are you just telling and giving us all of this info, out of the blue?"

Shaeddor cocked his head and studied the fellow curiously. "Are you daft, man? I'm trying to help our peoples defeat the Khabal. Can you imagine things if we let them take over our worlds?"

They spoke closely for another few minutes, during which time several messages and messengers passed back and forth between the captain's garrison headquarters and higher ups, it was assumed.

"Well," Shaeddor said, checking his watch once again, "it's time that I must be getting back before the dawn."

Seebold cleared his throat and rested his hand upon the sword at his side. "I'm afraid that is not possible. We have no idea who you are or where you came from. You haven't even given us a name. But my superiors wish to question you at greater length on all of these matters. We cannot let you go. I'm sorry, but you are now our prisoner."

Shaeddor blinked at the man and then burst out laughing.

The lights were suddenly extinguished and a tempest of swirling dark wind upset everything, whipping papers and maps around in the dark as guards waiting outside charged in to fill the small office.

By the time the lamps were most likely re-lit, Shaeddor had swept half way back toward his concealed gateway, cloaked in the shadows and unseen.

Even as the clumsy search for him began among the flabbergasted Urthers, he was already back in his chambers, grabbing a few hours of late sleep in his big comfy bed.

Urthers. By the Powers themselves, how did they expect to win such a war?

Jen came to him, and he took a long while to start to educate her on the dangers she faced as a lost soul or transient spirit. He told her how to practice going unclad, so that she could not be tracked, sensed, or attacked.

Her ghost listed, tossing her head from hand to hand as if it were a ball. But she did take in all that he said, promising to practice the new skills and abilities she would need.

# TORI

Tori spotted the two teens an hour after dawn, lying in the ditch off to the right. Fourteen or fifteen in age, covered with mud, and some blood, very light brown skin, dark brown, straight hair, perhaps of mixed-race. They were clinging to each other and did not move.

They looked enough alike to be twins, or at the very least brother and sister. But Tori felt sorry for them, because she thought they were dead, just two more bodies jammed up under some brush.

All of the bodies they had passed in the ditches had been dead.

Then as she looked back at them, the boy groaned, low and hoarse, and the girl's eyes tried to flutter open.

Tori jumped off Pepper and called troops over to the pair. "They're alive! I heard the boy groan and the girl tried to open her eyes. Medic! Get one of the healers over here, as well."

An army medic and Tori's personal healer, Meaghan Eckhart arrived on scene almost at the same time.

They quickly assessed the stricken pair. The medic reached into a large medical bag and started IVs immediately for both teens.

"Sir," the medic said to Tori, "they're alive, but they're famished and extremely dehydrated. I'm guessing they ran from one of the cities until they dropped, and then they were so weak they couldn't go on. We seen that a lot with refugees. They went, maybe two or three days with little to no water. No one can take that."

"He's right," Meaghan said, "but at least we found these two in time. They're young. In a day or so, they should bounce back okay. I'll help them along with a little healing lifeforce energy, with your permission, sir?"

Tori nodded her assent. Technically, her healer was meant purely for the Pistolera to keep her up and running, but Tori couldn't hold to that when there were so many in need. She kept Meaghan handy as a last resort for everyone. "Put them in one of my reloading wagons, and you two look after them as long as duty permits," Tori told them.

She couldn't put her finger on it, but there was something about these two kids.

As the two started to recover in the wagon, they thrashed around a little, somewhat delirious.

Tori held the girl down and the teen's eyes fluttered open.

Amber eyes, so golden they were nearly orange.

She looked over at her brother. His eyes were the same strange color. How odd.

They were so weak, they couldn't talk, yet they were obviously very afraid.

Tori tried to calm them. It's alright. You're safe, both of you. You're with the army, and we're going to do our best to protect you, and keep you safe. Just get some rest."

"We need to be careful about giving them water and food," the medic told everyone. "We need to give it to them in small amounts when they are feeling better, and see if they can keep it down."

The next day the twins were feeling much better. Tori continued looking in on them, and was around when they came to.

"You're lucky we spotted you two and we didn't just keep going. I'm Tori Nelson, one of the Pistoleros from Michiana. Who are you guys? Tell us your names."

They drank sips of water and ate soft bread and broth.

"I'm Trent," the boy said. "Trent Fillmore, and this is my twin sister Katelyn; we'll be fifteen in October."

"We fled this way from Niles, Michigan when it fell during the Merge. For a while we were safe in Kalamazoo, so we know where Michiana is. Near South Bend, Elkhart, and north and south. Where are we going now?"

Tori looked at them sadly. At least two people had made it out of lost Niles. "This army is headed toward Ann Arbor, if it's still there, and then Detroit and Toledo. We hear that the enemy has forces set up like a gauntlet for us to run all along the way. It's going to be tough punching through, and we have thousands of civilians who are traveling with us now." And slowing them down and putting them at risk.

She didn't want to say the last part aloud, but it was still true.

Army 16 was doing what it could, but it's primary orders were to complete its missions, not protect refugees.

Tori, Meaghan, and others spoke with the pair, hoping to glean some kind of information from kids who had barely survived the spring and summer after the Merge, but their story seem fairly simple.

Yet from their own words, they had covered an immense amount of territory for a pair of kids, especially making it all the way from Niles to Kalamazoo on foot, alone. An according to their reckoning, they had done so very quickly.

When things looked bad for Kalamazoo, they fled again, ending up exhausted and near death a few days later, without enough water to drink.

But how did they travel so far alone?

How had they evaded vast units of monsters and other Dark Khabal forces twenty-four-seven, day after day?

After Trent and Katelyn finished eating a bit more, they drifted off again.

Then there was cause for alarm an hour later.

Katelyn was gone, and Trent was not just asleep, but blacked out, nearly comatose.

Something strange had happened. Meaghan called in some mages. They studied Trent and agreed. Some kind of magic was at work, and it involved the pair directly somehow.

Five hours later, over half of their day into the afternoon, the army stopped for a breather.

Forward scouts found Katelyn Fillmore nearly comatose and sunburned on one side of her body, in the middle of the road.

How did she manage to get ten miles ahead of their most forward advance?

Meaghan, other healers, and several mages examined the twins again.

"They're drained of energy once more," Meaghan said. "Let's try giving them a full healing. At least they're not starving or dehydrated any longer."

After the healers replenished the twins' lifeforce energies, the pair awoke as if from a normal sleep, and asked for more substantial food and drink. It was given to them, in small quantities at first.

Tori explained to the pair what had happened. Katelyn looked worried and felt the side of her face with the sunburn cream on it. She looked at Trent first.

"They saved us," Trent said. "I think we can trust them."

Katelyn nodded. "I think we'd better tell someone." She turned back to Tori and the rest. "It all started after the Merge. My brother and I can see things ahead of us sometimes…in our minds. If we can picture something, or we've seen it before, we can go there, and then the other one can follow. I know it sounds weird. But it's—"

"Omigosh, they're transport mages," Tori exclaimed. "A team of them. Get with David or the General. Have them send a messenger bird back to South Bend and get Rabbi Bergman to pay us a visit, pronto. It's that important. He needs to examine these two. Wow. I wish Jerriel was still here."

Losing Jerriel remained a major setback for all of the defenders of both worlds.

Tori called up a scribe and turned back to the twins. "Tell me about your abilities, and everything that you two are capable of."

They were still working with the twins on the run, three hours later, when Rabbi Bergman and a few of his transport agents popped into the wagon that they were keyed to, the one with the transport station plates.

They quickly took over the examination of the Fillmore twins, and Tori was reduced to being a spectator.

Then David called her away. Whenever Tori looked at him she nearly winced. She could see the worry in him, the pain he endured at not knowing where Jerriel was. It was clearly wearing on him.

They all wanted her back, but she knew that for David, that need must be more like a torment.

Yet he kept going, fulfilling his duties, doing all that he could to assist Army 16 and its growing mass of charges.

The army protected nearly thirty thousand refugees by that time, as humans throughout the area saw the passing army as the last chance for them to get out of that region alive.

They were probably right.

Word spread quickly concerning the bloody fall of Kalamazoo and Battle Creek.

"It's going to get bad tonight," David told her. "We barely have enough troops to defend ourselves, let alone the refugees. If…"

Even someone as brave and dedicated as David hesitated to give voice to the impossible. "If things get bad enough, we may have to fall back to the worst option, and leave the refugees behind, in order to save the army. Our primary mission must get through, at all costs."

Tori just stared at him. All of these poor people at the mercy of enemies who clearly would show them none. The refugees would be completely exposed and helpless, on the wide open roads.

She could tell the very thought of it sickened them both to the core of their guts.

"David," she muttered, "thirty thousands of them…"

He looked away and shuffled nervously. He could no longer look her directly. "We're going to find a defensible area and set up the transport station once more. We'll make a final attempt to get as many of the refugees through, back to Michiana. The youngest first, then the others. After that, I'm not sure what will happen to those who are left behind."

Tori fumed. "I think we know exactly what's going to happen to them, David."

He snapped at her again. They did not always see eye to eye.

"You think I want it this way?"

Tori shook her head. "No, I wasn't saying that. Of course not."

"We…we'll have to hold for as long as we can this evening and into the night. The longer we hold the lines, the more of them can make it out. But eventually, we'll need to execute a fighting retreat, and the remaining refugees won't be able to keep up with us and our movements. The medics and the healers and the mages are already preparing lethal doses…of poisons and sedatives for the sick, the weak, the feeble, and the badly injured. Just in case."

Tori clenched her mouth shut and nervously began checking her guns. It was the only thing she could think of. "Right. That sounds, humane. No need for the helpless to suffer. We'll hold the lines, David. We'll hold them for as long as possible."

They were in the process of hurrying to set up their defenses in the late afternoon when Rabbi Bergman came to them and made a startling announcement.

"I've spoken with General Culpepper and his officers. We might be able to get more of the refugees out of this war zone."

Tori watched David's jaw drop open and felt her own do the same.

Bergman held up a hand and continued speaking.

"Our new young friends, the Fillmore Twins have many strange powers. But the most useful of these, praise God, is the fact that they are a natural, living transport gate. They can open a gateway as wide as a two lane road, and maintain it indefinitely, as long as they remain awake. Each of them acts as an anchor point on the ends, and each can go to the other if they so wish. Yet doing so closes the gateway."

Tori blinked in amazement. "With our transport station, that triples the open access area to the gateways."

"Theoretically," David said, "We can get three times as many people through per minute. Get the damn things set up and race them through!"

Bergman closed his eyes gently and raised both hands palm out. "Already in process. The general wants you two and your forces to help lead the defense of the refugees, and the gates. He will prepare the general retreat and coordinate that with you. He commands that the most able and healthy of the refugees be held back last, and that they be given arms.

"He says that they might not get through the gates this night, but if they run and fight with the army, they might survive to make it out the next day. That is the best offer he can give them. Even with the expanded gateway, there still won't be time to get everyone through. Any who fall behind the army's flight will be on their own."

"Marching with us is still a better chance than certain death."

"Agreed," David noted, "but we still have a night of heavy fighting ahead of us either way."

It turned out to be a tough sell to the refugees, but when they were given that choice or simply face the enemy alone, the practical side of the argument quickly won out. No one liked it, but that was merely the way that things stood.

The enemy seemed to sense something was up, and sent in mercenary units to begin the attacks well before sunset. After dark, as expected, the monster hordes became the lead enemy element, and the shock troops of the foe.

Tori had a vantage point up on a portable tower stand with a few of her loaders going up and down. She fired on the enemy both up close and at a distance, using her various Wild Magic rounds to good effect. She punished the enemy whenever they massed their forces in significant numbers to warrant a long range annihilator round.

Army 16 and the vanguard held firm, bleeding the enemy badly at every turn, but suffering their own losses as well.

Tori glanced behind her. The refugees moved through the two gateways quickly and in good order.

She noted the round observation balloon much higher up in the sky, about three hundred yards away and more or less the same height up in the air, with a crew of four observers.

Blasts of fire suddenly enveloped the balloon and its crew, destroying the balloon and setting most of the plummeting wreckage on fire.

Three of the four crew managed to jump free of the blazing gondola. One crew was clearly on fire, flailing as he or she crashed into a pocket of forest.

The other two opened their rapidly deploying chutes and jerked upwards under the canopies, floating to the ground.

This time, Tori and others spotted several winged objects, machines much like large birds of prey, swooping and diving down.

One parachute exploded in fire, and the person in it fell to his doom. A lightning bolt nailed the other parachutist, slaying that one in mid-air.

Voices shouted that the winged machines were banking, and lining up in the night sky to attack the defenders.

Tori looked at her feet and realized that she and her team were still thirty feet up on their firing platform.

"Get down to the ground. Get out of here!" she yelled at them.

Spotters shouted, "A dozen enemy fliers, two groups of six, attacking from the west and north."

Firebombs began to explode in drop patterns as the enemy swept overhead from the two directions already noted.

Tori did her best to shoot them, but her attacks seemed to fall just behind the enemy flying machines.

Then she recalled something Mason had told her about shooting ducks and other game birds on the wing.

She had to lead her targets a bit, because of their speed.

She raised her guns again and led her target with one gun out wide and the other pistol very wide.

To her amazement, the gun that was very wide blasted the very last machine as it tried to bank away from her blast's area of effect.

That was an ice blast, and covered the flying machine with thick ice. It crashed into the trees and broke apart.

It amazed her just how much she had to lead them.

Then shouts of warning erupted all around her. The next attack from the air was heading straight at her.

She could jump right away, or keep shooting.

Tori clenched her teeth and kept firing at the six machines as they dove down to attack her position at top speed.

She shot two, three, and five, knocking them out of the sky.

A lightning bolt just went by her on the left, missing her by a foot.

Then a fireball erupted at the base of the platform and it buckled almost immediately.

Tori toppled backwards out of the sky, still blazing away at the aerial attackers.

She grunted in pain upon impact with something, and felt all of her wind rush out of her lungs. She gulped and tried to breath, but she more or less just writhed where she crashed and gasped, trying not to black out.

She was in a wagon, one with a canopy that she had collapsed.

Then one of the flying things hovered over her, and she saw that there was a Dark Mage within, operating it.

He was going to finish her off. Tori struggled to raise her pistols, but she knew that was too late.

Several arrows transfixed the flying machine, and the enemy within it. It rose up to get away, and then fell back and crashed.

Tori grunted in pain and rolled out of the wagon onto the grass.

Two of her runners reached her side first, helping her up and checking her for wounds.

She felt battered and in pain, but nothing seemed broken. She staggered over to where the flying machine fell. Other troops examined the machine as well, a marvel of engineering and enchantment.

Tori pointed at four large, strong troops. "You four–pick this thing up. I'm guessing it's going to be lighter than we suspect."

The four of them hoisted it up easily.

"Run to the nearest gateway and take this thing, body and all, back to South Bend for our people to study. Do not fail me. You must make it through."

"Yes, sir," the four said.

Tori stumbled after them, firing and doing her best to cover their retreat.

The fire and chaos that the flying machines brought was massive.

Tori went down on one knee at the transport station after the four ran through.

The several remaining flying machines strafed the area with firebombs and spells; then they broke off.

Tori winged one more, but did not bring it down. Then the aerial attacks stopped as suddenly as they had started. She studied the devastation around them, and then yelled at her runners, "Get me back up to the line, my friends. This long night isn't over yet."

She was right. Tori raced from position to position on Pepper, wherever the fighting was thickest, doing her best to stave off the foe's superior numbers. She was a firefighter, putting out fires wherever they erupted.

Scouts and spotters gave her word as to when and in what direction to fire annihilator rounds.

The clever spotters, forward observers, and army minds had also worked out a roughly mathematical targeting and indirect fire system, based upon their observations of the annihilator round firing trajectories and performance.

Then, as they expected, the sheer weight of the enemy numbers continued to drive Army 16 back after midnight.

They still faced several long hours of night fighting until the first glimmers of dawn.

The defenders held for two hours more.

Then the retreat began.

The army teams took down the transport station as the first enemy arrows began to fall among them.

The twins kept their portal up until the last moment behind rune-shielded archery mantlets. Then Trent slipped through to join his sister in safety.

Eight thousand refugees did not make it through to Michiana, but they had saved the youngest, the oldest, all of the wounded, and the weak. Over twenty thousand refugees would survive that night.

Now the remainder and Army 16 would make a run for it, fighting throughout the night in an attempt to survive to see another day.

Tori was already near the point of exhaustion, and parts of her were still badly bruised from her being blasted out of that firing tower.

Her runners strapped her to her horse as before.

The army formed up and the race was on, with the refugees protecting the core of the center.

Anyone who could not keep up was on their own.

Tori tried to rest for a few minutes on Pepper's neck.

Then she felt hands on her.

"Tori," a familiar voice said, "we've come back. We want to help."

She looked up and saw the Fillmore twins, their faces tired, but eager.

"You idiots! You were safe back in Michiana…relatively. You should have stayed there!"

"We think we have an idea that will buy us all some time. Just hear us out," Katelyn said.

Tori sighed. Teenagers. Even though she herself was just a few weeks past nineteen.

"This better be good," she warned them.

# MASON

The fires of Indianapolis burned up ahead of them, on the outskirts of the city that were still in the hands of the defenders, less that an hour away by air.

But they were up against a stiff headwind out of the southwest, and that had them slowed to almost a crawl.

With it being cloudy, there was no moon or stars, aiding their stealth. Captain Lewis and his team of three: Tillman, Roberts, and Wiesnewski protected the gondola below.

Mason, Rodell, Steven, and Mallory climbed up through the central open torus to the windy catwalk up top with its metal railing. They had their parachutes, but they took up their compass positions and secured their D-ring clips on lifelines.

"Stay sharp and watch for anything coming at us out of the darkness. If they're going to attack us up in the air, it's going to come between here and the city."

As it turned out, they did not have long to wait. Rodell pointed it out first.

They clearly saw three groups of ten winged objects or machines shoot out from the enemy-held areas, straight up into the darkness.

"Damn it," Mason said, "that's a lot of them coming at us. Steven, warn Captain Lewis and the crew below. We're in for one hell of a fight."

As if to make matters worse, a slight rain began to drizzle down; lightning flashed and thunder rumbled on the horizon.

"You won't be able to hit them far away with your crossbows, or your bow, Steven. They'll swoop in too fast. Let them get in close, and then shoot them."

The enemy hit them from three directions, nearly at the same time.

They used fire attacks and lightning, blasting the main air bag of the dirigible several times.

But the Buteo class dirigibles were covered with panels and proofing from the fire trees. Flame and lightning had no effect on them.

Captain Lewis and the crew used the new repeating crossbows, with their magazines of bolts. Their first shots missed.

Steven fired his longbow and shot one flyer through the legs. Rodell used explosive blasts and fireballs as well. He took down two with direct bursts that blew their wings off.

Mason had his guns, and used rounds that had the farthest range and the widest dispersal of blast damage. He caught four of the strange craft and blew them and their flyers to oblivion.

Then the enemy changed tactics.

On their next run they attacked the crew, and the main air bag directly at the same time, two dozen strong.

The enemy swarmed over *The Buzzard*. Now the Pistolero was limited to his dry-fire guns. Up close, his more powerful blasts would bring the dirigible down for certain.

He took careful aim and picked off the enemy flyers with precise bursts of glowing orange power.

Rodell did the same thing with his line of sight fire bolts. Steven was dead on with his longbow.

But that many foes punctured the main air bag in several key places with blade weapons.

Almost immediately, *The Buzzard* began to rapidly lose altitude.

Lightning and fire exploded below them. They heard screams among the crew.

A flyer passed through them and impaled Mallory on a long steel blade, while a sword flashed down and severed her life line as it pulled tight.

She screamed as she was jerked off the top of *The Buzzard*. Her last act was to raise her crossbow. She jammed it right into the flyer's chest and pulled the trigger.

Both of them spiraled into the darkness together.

"We're going down," Mason told Rodell and Steven.

"Let's jump and use our chutes," Steven said.

Rodell looked up at the sky. "We'd never make it to the ground alive. Mace is right. We need to ride the balloon down. It's not going to crash hard at this rate."

"Stay up top and fight them off if they come back," Mason told them. "I'm going down to check on Captain Lewis and the crew."

"We killed at least half of those flyers, if not more," Rodell noted. "But they did their job. Now they'll just hold back and watch us go down. Their friends on the ground will try to finish us off."

Mason nearly jumped down the ladder, sliding down the rails.

At a quick glance, Tillman and Roberts were dead or critically injured. Wiesnewski was banged up and unconscious off to one side, secured to a lifeline.

Captain Lewis was burned and his face was a mask of blood, but he had the wheel tied off, and he struggled with the air valves.

"Mason, help me!"

"Tell me what to do."

"The enemy doesn't know we have a reserve bag. If we can transfer what's left of the helium and empty all of the tanks into it, we might limp our way to the city still. We can still make it!"

Lewis showed him what to do.

Amazingly, they leveled off at about three hundred feet above the ground.

Mason caught Captain Lewis when he fell over from his many wounds. He found a medical bag and bound the man's worst wounds as best he could.

They were still drifting toward Indy.

Lewis came to long enough to clutch at Mason's arm. "Mace, when we land, use your guns. Destroy the steam magic engine and then the transport plates. Don't let the enemy—"

The Captain blacked out again.

"Mason!" Steven shouted down. "Here they come again!"

"You and Rodell fight them off up top. I'll defend the gondola!"

Mason checked his guns. Eleven enemy flyers against three defenders. The attackers would gut the reserve bag for sure and send him and the others down to their deaths. Or the trio could get killed trying to use their chutes.

He could blast the engines and the plates on the way down.

Perhaps he should set off an annihilator round in the gondola. That would do the trick.

He turned and took careful aim at the approaching foes.

Either way, Mason and his friends would go down fighting.

Then an enormous green and gold winged form dove out of the night sky at impossible speed, and ripped right through the eleven enemy flyers as if they were insects.

They fluttered down in pieces.

"Shavalkathar!" Mason shouted.

The big green dragon swept around and kept pace with them on their slow descent toward the front lines outside of Indianapolis.

Mason waved with his hat in his hand. "Thank you, great dragon!"

The vast creature craned its neck toward Mason. "You are the friend of David Pritchard and Jerriel the wizard. I'll go ahead and clear a landing area for you. I wish to speak with you after you land."

With that the dragon banked down and eradicated a vast swath of the foe in a long arc of dragonfire and death.

Shavalkathar gauged it about right. The blimp was going down and would hit just beyond the scorched earth of the dragon's flames. They would need to see to Captain Lewis and the other wounded, if they could be saved.

The blimp, its engines, and the transport plates would need to be carted away to safety. Nothing vital could be allowed to fall into enemy hands.

They dipped down and crashed harder than Mason expected.

He heard Rodell and Steven jump down from up top, and grunt as they hit the ground and rolled. He more or less did the same. The wounded were still held by their lifelines in the gondola.

The deflating main air bag puddled to the ground, stretched out by its lines.

Then more foes, hundreds more, rushed at them out of the darkness, through even the dwindling dragon flames.

They dragged several wagons at the direction of a handful of Dark Mages.

It appeared that the enemy were very well informed, and determined to capture the dirigible and carry it back to their lines.

The Pistolero staggered to his feet, determined to stop them.

He blasted the wagons, and the enemy mages.

But a thousand more foes marched in fast on the left and right flanks.

Shavalkathar was off in the distance, roasting the enemy forces caught out in the open. Rodell covered Mason's left. Steven fired his bow on the right.

Three of them—against thousands.

Roaring voices swelled up behind them.

Rank upon rank of defenders in good order swept from the lines of the city's ramparts and pickets.

It was a question of who would sweep over the balloon and the three first.

In the end, both sides collided, more or less mashing Mason and his friends between them.

Only the Pistolero's blazing guns held the enemy tide back, and just barely at that.

Rodell set off spell after spell. Steven drew his swords and cut down foes on the right in wheeling, slashing, bloody arcs. David was right, the kid could fight.

Yet the monsters were too many and tried to overwhelm him to drag him down to his death.

Defenders charged in to help.

Then a young woman, dressed all in scarlet field plate with a large shield covering her back, leaped in and cast an explosive earth spell directly in front of Steven, hurling the horde back. Then she used her long curved sabre and matching dagger to help hew down the last score or so of the monsters that swarmed around them.

An enormous mor-kahl backhanded Steven and knocked him on his butt, dazed and bloody, even as the foe withdrew.

The fighter mage in scarlet saw her chance and ducked in, driving her dagger into the monster's groin. Then she wheeled around with her sabre and beheaded the roaring creature.

She sprang out from under its bulk as the headless monster toppled forward, its clawed hands still ripping and twitching at the air. She sheathed her dagger and offered Steven her free hand.

Steven took it, staring at the young warrior mage in wonder.

The fighting was over for the time being. The defenders were already dragging out the wounded from the gondola and bringing up carts and wagons for the dirigible engines and the plates.

If possible, they had orders to secure the entire blimp.

Mason pointed out the girl in scarlet to Rodell. "I'm guessing she's another Tharanorian," he said.

"Indeed," Rodell noted. "She appears to be a young battle sorceress from Jattar. We'll need to meet with her."

"Arrows! Arrows!" the warning came.

Rodell threw up a shield of air over them like a dome. It deflected dozens of arrows.

The young lady in scarlet flung herself over Steven and covered up beneath the large shield on her back.

Six arrows bounced off that shield.

"Everyone up," Mason shouted. "Let's get the hell out of here. These people are determined to kill us!"

They leaped up and ran for it, another volley of arrows feathering the ground behind their steps.

The scarlet mage warrior and the defenders led them behind the cover of several buildings, and the ranks of the defenders closed up behind their passing.

Mason figured they ran for another half hour, covering two or more miles.

Finally they stopped for a breather.

They could hear the wagons trundling along from behind, bearing their burdens.

As they entered a clear stretch of highway with little cover nearby, Shavalkathar circled down to land.

The scarlet mage, and some of the defenders lifted their weapons.

"Halt, you fools!" Mason commanded. "That dragon is known to us. He is an ally! Do not harm him."

They looked unsure, but they lowered their weapons and backed away, waiting.

Rodell strode up beside Mason. Steven raced in. The young woman in red hesitated. Then she ran in beside Steven.

"Amazing!" she said, speaking Urther with an exotic accent, unlike even Jerriel's. "You are allied with a dragon? How wonderful!"

Mason smiled at her. She was about Steven's age, no more than fifteen or sixteen, brown haired, pretty almond eyes.

Eyes she could hardly take off of Steven.

That kid seemed to have all the luck, but Mason didn't begrudge him a thing.

"What is a Jattaran battle sorceress doing in Nenarra?" Rodell asked.

She grinned. "The same thing a Darshian wizard agent is doing...trying to stay alive, and work against the Dark Khabal, the great foe of us all!"

"Well said," Mason replied. He held out his right hand to her. "I am Mason Tyler, the Pistolero."

Her eyes widened. "I have heard the many legends about you, not all of them good." She took his hand. "But then, they never are. I am Ishix Zystarida. My parents were both part of a group of explorers, trying to reach this place from Kavendo...your St. Louis. They were slain along the way by the enemy. Out of three thousand of us, barely three hundred made it here."

"We're glad to have you with us, Ishix. Hail and wellmet."

She bowed her head. "I am honored."

Shavalkathar landed an instant later in front of them, splitting the concrete and shaking the ground like an earthquake. Many lost their footing.

# DAVID

Army 16 vanished through the portal that the Fillmore twins set up and proceeded to leap twenty miles ahead of their bewildered enemies. It would be hours before the foe pin-pointed their location once more.

That gave the last eight thousand refugees time to escape through another portal back to Michiana, once the way was opened for them.

After that, the Fillmore twins had done all that they could. They were completely drained.

Troops carried the twins away in honor, and placed them in a wagon for the healers to tend to them.

Without the twins and their powers, the grim day and night could have gone far worse, and many more innocent lives would have been surely lost.

David, Tori, and the princes met with General Culpepper.

"Which do we choose, my friends?" David asked them all, as the leader of the vanguard. "Our troops are exhausted after three days with little rest and constant marching and fighting. Do we press on, and keep going in order to reach Ann Arbor, or do we take some well-needed rest and risk the enemy locating us again, and cutting us off?"

The general thought on those concerns like the rest of them before he finally spoke. "The enemy is spread out all north of us. They will locate us at some point in any case. There are some dense woods nearby where we could hide out for several hours. Our forces cannot keep going forever. I say let's duck down and hide for a bit, while the enemy does not know where we are."

Tori spoke up. "For all they know, we went back to Michiana."

"Unlikely," the general noted. "They know that we are determined to reach Detroit at all costs. They won't think that we've given up completely. But we do have a window here. I say we rest the troops for at least five or six hours. Then we can still march fast enough to reach Ann Arbor by the end of today."

Prince Valandin looked at the maps. "From there it is only a day or so to Tornhold-Detroit."

"Exactly," General Culpepper said. "We should be able to reach our objective within two or three days at the most, even if we must fight all night."

"And once the twins recover," Tori added, "we can pull another vanishing trick on our foes."

David nodded. "I think that's the best we can do. Thank goodness we were able to transport all of those refugees out of the main field of combat."

The general frowned. "I'm afraid we will only encounter more refugees along the way. Jackson, Michigan had already been wiped out, unfortunately. Who knows what we'll find at Ann Arbor? And now we have those enemy flying machines to deal with as well. They can spot us from far away, take out our observation balloons with ease, and bomb and strafe us as much as they care to."

"Our scouts recovered several partial flying machines and the bodies within them," David noted. "Some of those flying suits went back to Michiana for the development teams to examine. Others are still with us. The flying machines appear to be some kind of quasi-enchanted, mechanical suit that allow the wearers to fly. But our people say that the operators must be mages skilled in wind and air magic. As we've witnessed, these machines can soar, dive, hover or float, and cast spells, drop firebombs, or attack with attached blades or hand weapons."

Prince Alendel noted, "They can slow us down, but they are too small and too few to stop us."

"Yet they could attack and destroy our transport gates at a crucial time," Tori said. "We can expect the enemy to use them for precision attacks."

Army 16 ate and then rested for six hours, cold camp, hiding in the forest before sunrise.

They awoke late in the morning close to noon, and marched in good order toward Ann Arbor. With luck, they would reach it by nightfall.

The enemy located and came against them in force at around six that evening. Mercenaries and Dark Khabal forces put up a stiff fight, doing all that they could to harry them and slow them down.

Army 16 kept maneuvering, feinting, fighting, and pushing forward.

At dusk they crested the low rolling hills around Ann Arbor.

The western half of that town was already a blackened ruin. Defenders still held the eastern half and fought for their very lives.

The enemy had pulled back at the rapid advance of 16, and another important factor.

Ann Arbor and the last of its people were surrounded by a river of undead zombies, still pouring up from the south in countless numbers. Everyone in 16 stared at the sheer masses of them.

There were at least a hundred thousand zombies between not only them and Ann Arbor, but also between them and Detroit.

"The foe must have at least one transport gateway that these things are pouring out of, most likely from Chicago-Vaejan." Valandin noted.

"Do you think we could fight our way to those portals and close them?" David suggested.

"Down south where they are the most numerous?" the general said. "Even if we knew where those portals were, and we don't, it would take five to ten armies or more to break through and capture them. Not to mention the rest of the enemy's forces just waiting to descend upon us from the north and fully encircle us."

"Even we might not be able to fight our way out of all of that," Tori said.

Valandin pointed to the northeast and the east where the zombie hordes were the thinnest, perhaps only a few ten thousands, as insane as that sounded. "We could attack at that point up there, where the zombies are hampered by the rivers, streams, and lakes. We can move and maneuver much faster than them."

David saw it as well through his field glasses. "Agreed. We break through to the defenders of the city and carve out an escape route. It will take all night, most likely, but then we can use the transport gates in the morning, and leap closer to Detroit the same way we did today."

General Culpepper also agreed. "That will buy us the time we need to make the final push. But we have to be quick about it. Let's move with a purpose, people."

Army 16 swung north and then to the northeast, fighting its way to their key objectives. They deflected the other enemy attacks until they penetrated the zombie lines.

That was one advantage. The zombies would attack anything living, including the enemy, unless controlled directly in a certain location by a zombie master, or zombie lord.

The rest of the enemy forces could not normally join in to help the undead.

Masses of zombies were difficult to slog through, but a disciplined military force simply focused on cutting them down, smashing their heads open, or chopping them into pieces.

Evil spirits that animated the undead shrieked briefly and rose up from the ruined corpses like puffs of dark vapor, fading on the wind.

The hardest part was that there were so many, and they looked just like dead Urthers, like regular people, now possessed and moved by evil spirits who only wished to kill. They were the bodies of all kinds of Urthers, of all ages.

Those that had rotted down to their animated bones were now blackened skeletons, but most of the creatures seemed to resist decay somehow, perhaps by the sorcerous dark powers that held them together.

During a gap in the fighting, Tori rode along in one of her reloading wagons, and kept Pepper handy. She needed rest when possible, but if the army needed help, the Pistolera had to be ready to rush to the front at a moment's notice.

At least she heard fewer and few complaints about her being the lesser Pistolero.

Finally they made contact with the Ann Arbor defenders, who were stunned and surprised to hear that the forces relieving them had come all the way from Michiana-South Bend.

"We sure are glad to see you, wherever you come from," one of the militia commanders said. "These zombies poured at us out of nowhere yesterday, and we figured it was the end of the world for us. We tried to send riders to reach Detroit and have them send some forces to help us break out. But we've yet to hear anything back. We think those enemy flying things are intercepting our messengers."

David quickly explained that the survivors were going to have to abandon the city, and head for Detroit.

"But how?" the local militia commander said. "We've got kids and old people, and a ton of wounded. They can't fight, and they surely won't get very far."

David smiled. "We've have a way to get them to safety. We'll show you. Start gathering your people together in a safe place at the center of your defenses, the young, the wounded, and the old. We'll help you get them out first, then the rest of your people who can march, are going to need to retreat from the city along with us. We'll help you fight your way out."

The man just stared at him, and then he began to weep. "You can do that? Such a thing is possible?"

David nodded. "I assure you, it is. It's not a perfect system by far, but it's better than being massacred to the last like a lot of towns have been."

Within the hour, they had the transport station set up, and the first kids poured through to Michiana on the other side.

Army 16 and the Pistolera held the bulk of the zombie hordes off to the south. The local defenders held the shorter lines on the west and the north.

But from what David heard, even the annihilator rounds from Tori's most powerful guns wiped out large circles of zombies, only to have them filled in within minutes by more of the countless undead.

Then a great tumult and cries of terror broke out in the north, close by.

David, the princes, and half of their vanguard rode up in haste to meet whatever this new threat was.

They immediately clashed with large zombies that moved fast and wielded weapons: bows, spears, swords, and even shields.

These weren't the regular, shuffling, slow moving variety of undead.

The eyes of these zombies burned with glowing red or greenish hate, and they moved quickly with purpose and cunning.

Hundreds of these new faster zombies fought bitterly with the defenders, killing and wounding many Urthers.

Only the arrival of the vanguard forces stemmed the tide and sealed the breach.

Prince Valandin shouted David's way. "There must be several zombie masters or a zombie lord close by to control this many undead and make them fight in this manner. We need to locate the fiend and destroy him. Doing so will not be easy!"

David quickly sent word to the general, and summoned Tori to join them at their position.

From the looks of things, they were going to need the Pistolera's firepower and all the help they could get to crush this new threat.

"Hundreds more of these monsters are racing this way!" someone on the line warned.

# JERRIEL

Jerriel and Khia watched a large flotilla of ships that the enemy had cobbled together in sight of the immense, but damaged Mackinac Bridge of the Urthers. The Khabal had even somehow managed to commandeer what looked to be a very old Urther steamship, probably a coal or ore hauler, and were preparing to load their main forces into it.

The enemy reports that Jerriel had read made several mentions about the secret mission being sent north across the lakes, or what the enemy called the Inner Seas, to track down and capture some elusive creature.

Perhaps even another Urth or Tharanorian Spectral Entity.

Either way, it was some powerful force that the enemy meant to enslave to its will, and Jerriel and Khia were the only ones who knew about it and could hope to do anything concerning the situation.

Both of them felt compelled to do so.

Yet, sadly, they had already lost Luin, their young Hoonga friend, and numerous other foes were still sweeping their way, searching for them.

At least now, Khia was able to suppress and mask her energies and abilities and keep the hunters from detecting and tracking her.

In their haste, Jerriel and Khia had also met several individuals, or small bands of Urther survivors, scavenging for food or trying to get by. They had suffered greatly since the Merge, and did not know what to do with so many of the enemy around.

Khia created amounts of food and fresh water for them, and healed their injuries.

Jerriel told them to flee south, either to Grand Rapids, or Detroit, whichever they thought they might reach first. She warned them about the masses of enemies near the southern Michigan border, and the hunting parties that were nearby.

To lure the enemy away from the refugees, Khia and Jerriel would simply travel in an opposite direction and let some of the entity's powers slip out for a bit. Then they would flee from that place as well.

But bunched up near the broken bridge, all of the enemies in the region were converging on that spot, which made it rather difficult to hide.

"We need to locate a boat of some kind," Jerriel said. "It's only five or six miles across the straights from here, and the winds and the waters seem calm. If we had to, we could row across. People have done it before. But the best thing would be a small sailboat with oars. I know how to sail such small boats. I did so as a young girl."

"I could simply fly us across," Khia said.

"Yes, we'll keep that as a last resort. But then they'll detect you, and I don't want to be attacked by those aerovelocitors over open water. Come with me. There are numerous Urther cottages and lake houses along the shore lines. David told me about them. With it being summer, I think we'll locate what we need on a dock somewhere or in a boathouse along the way."

Three hours passed. It was getting close to dusk for that day, when they located the perfect small vessel. Close to shore, tied up to a dock was a small, twelve foot sloop that one or two people could easily sail in calm waters, and it had oars as well.

There were large pieces of huge driftwood trees washed up on the beach. Some of them were pretty amazing.

Jerriel first went up to the main house to see if the owners were home. There were no lights inside and no footprints, trash, or any sign that anyone had been there for months.

Jerriel left a quick note on a page torn from one of her notebooks, explaining that the boat had only been borrowed, not stolen. She would bring it back if she was able, but they were in danger.

She placed the note in the back door. Then she looked around for anything that might help them. But when she took the cover off the boat, it appeared to be ready for duty.

She quickly made the small vessel ready to launch and sail, to tack against the mild, late summer winds up from the southwest and allow them to reach the other side.

Then in her mind, she had a warning from Khia.

*Alas, the enemy is upon us. One of the hunting teams has tracked us down.*

Jerriel turned upon the dock, her staff ready.

She saw a necromancer, holding his black glowing skull staff, two more Dark Mages behind him, and hunting forces with nets and vicious looking mancatchers and fierce gulluk hounds filling in along the beach, about three score in all.

An Urther male with his hands bound painfully behind him was shoved up in front of the necromancer, who only smiled in triumph.

The Urther had been badly beaten and cringed. He looked up sadly at Jerriel. She recognized him as one of the Urthers she and Khia had assisted.

"I'm sorry," the poor man said, nearly weeping. "I had to tell them what direction I'd seen you go. They said they'd kill my wife and my little girl if I didn't help them find you."

The poor man looked up at the necromancer. "There, I've done what you forced me to do. Cut me loose. Let me go back to my family and we'll be on our way."

The necromancer chortled, "Yes, fool. Join them now—in death!" He stabbed the man in the neck and tore out his throat.

"My men slew your wife and daughter as soon as you were out of earshot." He tossed the dying man into the lake, just off the side of the dock.

Jerriel fired a lightning bolt straight at the necromancer, who lifted his skull staff casually and absorbed the energy. "Surrender, you Sylurrian bitch. Your powers are no match for mine. There's nowhere for you to run, and the Sprectral Entity within you is too weak; she cannot save you."

Khia joined with Jerriel, unmasking her powers.

"Come. Let us show them how weak we are!"

The face of the necromancer twisted, but he held his ground. The other Dark Mages channeled their forces into him.

Out of nowhere, a huge driftwood trunk, weighing tons, smashed into the enemy and rolled right over them, crushing many.

To the right, Luin of the Hoonga appeared, raised her mighty fists, and beat the air, unleashing a bloodthirsty, terrifying howl that seemed to shatter the very sky.

When the stupefied necromancer struggled to rise, Jerriel-Khia blasted the entire end of the dock and incinerated all within that space of the beach into a glowing green crater of fused glass at the core.

Any of the enemy who survived whimpered in terror and tried to crawl away.

Luin ran around the crater, and mashed them in to the bloody sand with her great fists and stamping feet. Then she sprang onto the dock, nearly smashing it, and rejoined her friends.

Jerriel and Khia leaped into the Hoonga girl's arms and wept for joy.

Luin held them like small pets and rubbed her furry cheeks against their faces.

"How did you possibly survive?" Jerriel said. "We thought you were dead for certain. You fell from so high up."

Luin put them back down and shrugged. "I simply went unclad before I hit the ground and thus took no harm. Like our enemies, I've been tracking you ever since, but the distance was very great."

Jerriel pointed to the sailboat. "Luin, get in the boat, near the center, and watch out for the boom of the sail. You might have to duck or even lie down on your side."

The Hoonga looked completely confused. "The what?"

"I'll show you. We must hurry. That little battle will attract the others, I'm certain. Perhaps we can get out of sight or even all the way across before they reach this spot."

Luin followed Jerriel's lead, climbed in with her and sat down, but she was so huge. She looked rather silly, a big hairy thing just sitting upright in a small sailboat and looking around.

Jerriel secured her staff and scurried around, casting off and putting them out into the open water.

As soon as Jerriel got the sail up, they began to move forward.

Luin sniffed the air and made her happy keening sound. "At last, I return to the lands of my kind. We shall be safer there."

"The enemy is coming over in a great many ships," Jerriel warned. "They are both powerful and in great numbers. They seek something important. I do not think that they will leave without it."

Luin smiled fiercely. "The Hoonga shall hear of their coming. We have dealt with invaders before, long ago."

Jerriel wasn't so sure. The enemy had to know of the Hoonga, and must possess some way to counter or deal with them and their powers by now. The Dark Khabal planned for all things and was very powerful.

She focused on sailing the small boat and getting them safely to the Upper Peninsula of Shendor, now called Shenedar.

# SHAEDDOR

Shaeddor left the Khabal library for the final time and prepared to depart from Zaskakaria. He had completed almost all of his research on both ghosts and the lost souls of the dead, and the realms of the spirits.

The transport portal was up and running. By that hour, Tep would have everything packed up and ready. Time to move on to his next destination.

He stood before General Chonzen Gordeel before he departed. The corpulent fool looked to be in a sour mood.

"Agent Shaeddor, even if you be the Dark Magus himself, and not merely his servant, you must answer for your actions while you are under the authority of my protectorate. Please explain yourself and the reported irregularities that you have committed."

Shaeddor raised an eyebrow. "Of what irregularities do you refer to, General? I have done all that my master commanded me in his orders. Your transport portal here is operating perfectly. We must be going; our overall mission is urgent and has the highest clearance."

The general scowled even more. "Yes, yes, of course. But what of the four pleasure slaves and the cleaning wench I allowed you? Word has it that for some inexplicable reason, you actually returned them to the Urthers and set them free. Why would you do such an idiotic thing?"

"Oh, that. I assure you, general. I had my reasons for doing so. Just a little personal experiment of mine. It might even work to your advantage in the long run. Only time will tell."

The oaf just stared at him. "I'm afraid that you will need to explain things further than that, Agent Shaeddor. I must know why you did what you did?"

"Certainly. If you must know, I infected the slaves in question with several of our known diseases, and then returned them to their population as part of an experiment, to see if our diseases would spread among the Urthers, and how lethal they might be."

"And you did not think to clear these matters with me? What if these diseases affect our people as well?"

Shaeddor shrugged. "Hardly a danger for us. We already have resistances built up against these common illnesses. But the Urthers might not. You know how us mages like to tinker with things? It's just a little experiment of mine. And it might only cost us a few worthless Urthers to spread one or more epidemics this winter."

General Gordeel laughed. "I might have known the Black Prince would have darker, ulterior motives. Very well. We shall wait and watch to see what sicknesses affect the Urthers. May these illnesses kill them all off. I didn't think it made any sense for you to be freeing a handful of slaves for no apparent reason."

"By the Powers," Shaeddor said, yawning, "you delay my primary mission for such frivolities? Might I ask you just how many captured Urther slaves you presently have at your disposal?"

"Tens of thousands," Gordeel admitted. "We slay dozens out of hand each day as examples, if they do not obey. They are a stiff-necked people and defiant. Most of them make poor slaves unless we break them first."

"Indeed. So, why are we even discussing the loss of a few more?" He did his best to sound incredibly indignant.

"Quite right. I'm sorry I even questioned your actions, Agent Shaeddor. Oh, this message came through the portal as soon as it was tested. It is from the High Magus. He commands that you proceed to Gundi and assist one of the Six Dark Champions with an urgent matter there and set up another gateway."

Shaeddor shook himself. "Where in the bloody hell is Gundi? I thought I was going to Ducallasto?"

The general waved him over to a map table. "They are close to each other. The High Magus has decided to place the Ducallasto transport gate at nearby Gundi for greater security."

Shaeddor read the open order. It was all there, clear for any with access to the secured intelligence pouch to read. Very well. One destination was as good as another, and he was currently in the business of gathering intelligence.

"Which of the Six will be at Gundi?" he asked.

"Temuen the Miser, the exchequer of the Khabal. He has chosen far off Gundi for his primary base of operations in the colonies, once it is linked to the rest of the Khabal cities."

Shaeddor said his farewells to the general and summoned the vast bat Entity of Night. He gathered up his team, launched up into the darkness, and quickly gained speed.

The trip only took a matter of hours to reach the former, major national landmark that the Urthers referred to as Mount Rushmore. The tiny Urther hamlet of Keystone had been easily wiped out by the Khabal subjugation forces. Now the entire region belonged to the Dark Mages, and the only threat was Ducallasto, the place the Urthers called Rapid City.

The current problem was negotiating a treaty with the local, wild centaur populations who roamed the plains of the New World and held their territory against any invaders, including the monster hordes from east of the Inner Seas.

There were four main tribes of the centaur creatures. The Keth-thon were half horse and half humanoid. The Tan-thon were half buffalo and half humanoid. Next came the Ban-thon, who were half pronghorn and half humanoid. And finally there were the Seth-thon, who also lived in the northern tundra of far northern Khanada. They were half reindeer and half humanoid.

These four tribes of centaurs currently controlled the northern plains for thousands of miles from the Inner Seas to the great Western Ocean, and they were a force to be reckoned with, in great numbers. When put to it, they could be incredibly warlike and did not take kindly to invaders of any variety.

They reserved a special hatred for the spawn of the Dark Ones, the monsters who only came out at night. Great wars had been fought in the Dream Time, the ancient days, and the centaurs eradicated all of the Darkspawn from their lands with their magicks, and by force of arms.

They called both Urthers and Tharanorians *ta-sae*, or 'two legs,' and according to their tribal lore, two legs could never be trusted.

That made negotiating treaties with them extremely difficult.

Not that the Khabal meant to keep such treaties in any case, once they were negotiated. Such pieces of paper would only last long enough for the Dark Mages to flood superior numbers in the region to beat down all resistance.

Then it would be seen who would be eradicated.

Shaeddor marveled at the gargantuan, ancient mountain heads of the Darkspawn, mixed up quite comically with the mountain heads of the Urthers.

The Merge took some hilarious turns at times.

Shaeddor did not really know who the Urther mountain heads represented. Perhaps great kings or mages from Urther history.

The darkspawn monster heads had been carved out of the rocks by millions of the creatures, directed by the first Dark Shaman who worshipped the Dark Ghods.

The four misshapen, grotesque monster heads were originally, in order from left to right: Gorgush the gozog demigod, Kukloth the demigod of the mor-kahls, Thrak the demigod of the ka-torgs, and Nuzz, the torg demigod.

Yet after the Merge, the mountain heads were now mixed up. On this side, it was: unknown Urther, Kukloth, unknown Urther, and Nuzz.

That meant that on the other side, the mountain heads were: Gorgush, unknown Urther, Thrak, and the final unknown Urther.

The mix up made Shaeddor chuckle just staring up at them. He guessed that Urthers would not find the Cosmic jest so hilarious. Mason had been very fond of the Urther historical period, and the geographical area he referred to as the West. His Urther friend would most likely be appalled and deeply offended.

Yet it was still funny.

Now that they had landed near the mountain heads, they made initial contact with the Khabal forces protecting the new stronghold. The position looked incredibly defensible, nearly impregnable, and they clearly had good access to fresh water. Even a small, determined force could hold the area against many armies.

The construction team was shown where to start putting up the transport portal. Tepperson saw that they went to work immediately.

Shaeddor went up to meet with Temuen the Miser, another one of the Six.

The Miser had chosen an excellent spot for his new stronghold.

But Shaeddor quickly balked at the long climb. He told his guides that he would fly ahead, up above. Using the powers of the bat entity, that was but a short flight up to the top of the compound.

Within minutes of arriving, Khabal guards brought him before the throne room, meeting hall, and counting room of the Khabal's chief financier.

The entire, immense hall had been wall-papered in the Urthers' strange paper money, of various denominations. Even in some cases, big, uncut sheets of certain bills. Quite fitting for the Khabal, who wanted to conquer this strange world with its equally strange peoples and various defunct monies.

There were tables where various forms of gathered wealth were being counted, weighed, measured, and tabulated by counting clerks with guards watching over them. Numerous tables and desks had been brought in by slaves and workers. Bright oil lanterns burned over the tables to provide islands of light.

Most of this wealth had been collected from dead Urthers.

There were tables heaped with every type of gold fashioned in any way imaginable, from coins, to bullion, nuggets, dust, and a myriad of jewelry. Other tables stood heaped with silver in any form. He saw one table of platinum.

More tables had convenient Urther 'plastic' tubs heaped with diamonds, rubies, emeralds, sapphires and other precious and semi-precious stones. Scales and scopes stood at had for enslaved jewelers to examine and appraise the stones.

Guards watched over each station, other guards on a catwalk up above them watched the guards. Other areas had comfortable chairs, sofas, beds, and cots set up for the counters to rest in when they were not on duty.

Everywhere he looked there were guards stationed.

The Miser's golden throne was actually empty at this time. An aide brought Shaeddor into a rather small office close at hand where Temuen sat at a regular desk, going over a pile of ledgers and expense reports. He examined them very closely. The small room was littered with scrap paper crumpled up and tossed all about.

A small tub of various pens was on the Miser's desk, along with stacks of scrap paper from other notebooks and ledgers lined up on a bookcase beside him and his creaky old, padded wooden chair where he sat, hunched over his work.

Temuen was a Sylurrian also, at least in his late forties, if not older. Grayish and balding, he had pale, sallow skin, steel blue keen, sunken eyes, behind thick spectacles that he would push back with a finger every now and then. He wore somber black robes like those of a Sylurrian banker or magistrate.

This was the Greedmaster of the Dark Khabal. He and his team of servants hoarded, tracked, and spent the Khabal's vast systems of wealth, graft, organized theft, black markets, corruption, and usury across two worlds.

And this place would become one of their main hoards and distribution points, once the transport gate network was fully up and running.

Then the Khabal could go anywhere in both worlds at a moment's notice, spread their disease of greed, and work the Khabal's dark will.

The room and the halls without had tough looking necromancer and warrior guards protecting and watching everything, as usual.

Temuen did not even bother looking up from his books and numbers. "So, the High Magus sends one of his chief little toadies, the traitorous Black Prince of Holleth to set up our transport network. How long will you be with us, Betrayer?"

"A day or so, Grand Master Temuen. Then we'll be moving on."

"Very well. As you can see, you will be watched quite closely whilst you are within my domain. I shall brook no experiments or liberties as you took with that fool, General Gordeel. Do you understand?"

"Perfectly. I see that you are well-informed, Grand Master."

"I keep my spies everywhere. Everyone is a potential traitor; it is only a matter of time and opportunity. We all betray one another, in small ways or large, if we think we can get away with it. It is in our blood, it is in our very nature. We are all born to betray each other at some point, so it is only to be expected and discouraged where possible."

"An interesting philosophy, Grand Master."

Temuen snorted. "The only truth there is, besides Death itself. No other truth in life is as certain. Mark my words. You shall see it. What other actions do you plan to take within the expanse of my widening realm?"

"I have sent for one of the new aerovelocitor suits, made to my specifications. I will practice with it."

"Interesting. You are an air mage? My sources did not tell me this."

"I am a sorcerer, as you know well, Grand Master. I can approximate all of the necessary air and wind spells with my powers and abilities."

"Yes, sorcerers are so versatile. Yet why bother?" Temuen asked. "Why waste your time with such toys? You already have the Spectral Entity of Night. With such powers of flight and surpassing speed, the performance of the aerovelocitor suits is by far inferior. Why waste your time?"

"Because it is mine to waste, and I delight in such machines and devices. They fascinate me. And so I dabble in new things and advancements."

Temuen laugh slightly. "Toys and curiosities; mere vanity and waste. Just stay away from the centaurs, as you well know. They will pluck your mechanical wings and roast you alive in their fires, one piece of you at a time, starting with your feet and hands, until they finally reach your head. They say the entire process takes days, and they keep healing and feeding you just enough to keep you strong and screaming all that time."

"What a lark," Shaeddor noted. "Their skill seems to rival even those of our own practices."

"Just so. Do not underestimate them, Betrayer. But once the gateways are open and working, we will eventually find a way to deceive those ignorant, tribal fools, murder them and all their savage spawn, and seize their lands and all of the wealth they hold. Just as we hope to do everywhere."

"Grand Master Temuen. Is there any humble service that I might perform for you while I am here?"

Temuen shook his head. "None that I can think of. None that I would trust to one such as you. Do what you have come to do, play with your silly toys, and stay out of my way. Do not give me any reason to have you slain in some creative fashion. You shall wear out your usefulness to the Khabal one day, Betrayer. And on that day your life shall be forfeit."

Temuen waved him away with one skeletal, claw-like hand.

"If you need food or drink or slaves to screw, ask my servants about such matters. And you need not bother to come to me again when you and your people depart. Just go forth, and do not waste any more of my time. There. You are dismissed. That is all...Betrayer. Remember this. I shall always have eyes on you, whenever and wherever possible. I watch everyone."

Shaeddor bowed and left without further word.

He flew out that night and went many miles into the dark hills and mountains exploring. With some effort he located a cave that pulsed with ancient magicks.

Shaeddor brought a medical kit and under bright lamp light in that cave, he opened a deep wound in his right forearm. He recalled his anatomy lessons on corpses and avoided major arteries, veins, and ligaments. Then he inserted another Istyxian power crystal, aligning it with the ones in his right breast and upper right arm.

Then he called upon the Spectral Entity to heal his wound, and fix the energy crystal within him fast.

He would continue to install each of the crystals throughout his body, one a time. This was one way to greater power. The crystals became one with him and could not be detected. In time, his entire body would become a powerful energy collector of any type or power he encountered.

The process was always painful and taxing, but what of that? Shaeddor ate rations and drank fluids to help sustain and heal himself. He stretched out on his padded bedroll. A night in the mountain airs might do him good.

Jennifer's ghost came to him in that ancient cave, drawn to both him and his spilled blood. She found that she could lie beside him in that place, without passing through him, yet they still could not touch.

She still wore the bright red, wide silken band around her slender neck, under her glowing hair.

Shaeddor sensed that she was more frightened than usual. "What is it?" he asked her.

"I was exploring the Void and saw a Dark Gatherer drag down one of the souls of the damned to the Nine Hells," she said. "It was the soul of a dead woman, older, but not unlike myself. It was a terrible, fearful thing to witness. The Dark Gatherer came for her soon after she left her body.

"She had not gone very far when the Black Gate opened around her. The Gatherer encircled her in his burning shackles that whipped around her like snakes. Then the flaming hooks built into those chains cut and bit into her seared flesh. She screamed and continued to scream, as she was dragged down to one of the Black Gates, far below. The gate closed up and vanished. Her screams were cut off. I feared a Gatherer would come for me next." Jen dropped her face into her hands.

Shaeddor sat up next to her. "You are not one of the damned," he told her.

"How do you know?" she asked, gasping. She almost flickered out of sight.

"This cave is steeped in ancient power. It is a place where we can talk openly, and you can maintain your ghostly form with ease. You are a classic lost soul, my love. A wandering shade, stranded between the light and the darkness in Limbo. Had you been one of the damned, you are correct. One of the Dark Gatherers probably would have come for you by now. That is just fact."

The two of them were silent for a time.

"I know that I am dead," she said. "I just don't understand what's going to happen to me, and I feel afraid all of the time. I have seen horrible things that I did not see while I was living. Some of your instructions and warnings frighten me even more."

"That is Limbo," Shaeddor told her. "A waypoint. A place of the lost, of many who are trapped there and can go no further, because something or things still bind them to a place, or the material world in general. Yet the Merge has made reality among Urth and Tharanor even more unstable than before. For example: you may not have tried this, but in theory, you should be able to pass between both sides of the Merge at will. You only need to focus upon doing so."

"Why am I so afraid, unless I am near you?" she asked. "I don't want to be afraid all of the time."

"Through our love that we shared, I am one of the things keeping you drawn back to the Prime Material Plane. I ground you here."

"And when I am away from you?"

"Limbo is a place of uncertainty and fear, my heart. And as the no man's land between the Dark and the Light, fearful things from both sides can pass through such a place, on their way to whatever other place, for whatever reason. Many types of spirits and other things can lurk there. As

I have explained, you must be careful. There are many things that could still do you harm in your current state of existence."

"I was from Urth," Jen said. "All that we knew of such things were like fairy tales to us—myths, legends, and superstitions. How do your people know of these things?"

"Mages from Tharanor have known about the various planes of existence and their perils for eons. Countless mages have explored them, and many a mage has never returned. The High Mages of Tharanor banned all travel to and through the known planes, for the safety of all. They set up potent, magickal barriers on Tharanor to prevent such travels. Too many mages were being lost. But the Merge shattered the power of the High Mages, and the barrier is no more. Those with the skill and knowledge can travel to the planes of Limbo and beyond once again."

Jen shook her head and hugged her knees to herself. "I'm not a mage like you, Shae. I don't understand all of that. But you have said that there are many dangers for me to look out for. Continue to instruct me. What should I beware of?"

Shaeddor sighed heavily. "As a lost soul, a shade or ghost, you cannot on your own ascend or go into the light. The light must open a gateway for you of its own accord, or some power of the light must bring you there. Even that is not sure, for once there, the Powers of Light shall judge you and decide your eternal fate."

"What of the Darkness?" she whispered.

Shaeddor snorted. "Alas, the way to the Darkness always yawns open and wide before you and others at any time. Much of the Darkness is just that—dark. But eventually the realms of darkness descend deeper into the dark and to the gates of the Nine Hells, at the very bottom of the Void and then the Abyss. As you descend into the Shadow Realms, the dangers increase, and the forces of Darkness, Shadow, and Hell grow stronger. The trick then becomes not getting in, but getting back out."

"What if I explored those regions?" Jen asked.

"If I had the time, I might try to explore the Nine Hells and find the lost souls of my dead parents. After my mother and father were slain by the Khabal, that was not enough. The necromancers captured their souls and sent them into the Hells to be trapped and tormented there. Neither of them had deserved such. What happened to them both was wrong."

"I'm sorry, my love," Jen said. "Is there anything I might do to find them?"

He looked her in the eyes. "Had they taken your spirit there, I would have come for you, Jennifer, if such were possible. But you would have many advantages as a ghost, if you learned how to use them. But it would still be perilous for anyone."

"Oh, Shaeddor. I wish I were strong like you are. I don't know if I could say that I would do the same for you. The knowledge and powers you have are beyond me."

"It's all right, Jen. I just want you to be careful. You are essentially a spirit now. You have a spirit form. You are neither good nor evil, neither of the darkness or the light. Somewhat neutral I would say. But any spirit or being greater than yourself could pursue you, attack you, and do you great harm. Even destroy or devour you, in order to add your spirit strength to their own, if nothing else."

He could tell just by looking at her that Jen was both curious and fearful.

"Yet as a spirit, you are not without powers or defenses. You can turn invisible, you can dematerialize at will. You can learn to walk unclad. You can hide yourself in almost anything. What you should fear is the classic Magic Jar, the classic magic or spell to capture spirits of all kinds. It can take various forms."

"I don't know what that is?"

He shook his head. "Whether great or small, most spirits can be trapped within an enchanted, sealed container, if it can be closed around them, or if they can be forced or tricked into it. You must never allow yourself to be so taken, my beloved."

She looked at him. "I shall try to avoid it."

"There are creatures, monsters, and beings who feast upon and eat souls and spirit energy like food. You must learn to sense their hunger and their intent. Practice doing so; it will be palpable to you.

"Other fell things of the Shadow, like the Dark Gatherers will attempt to ensnare you in various ways, and drag you captive into the Nine Hells, in order to torment you or feed your spirit energy to various beings who hunger for it. You shall be the hunted, and as their quarry, you must learn to sense them and avoid the hunters. I have some descriptions and sketches of these threats. We will go over them."

"Where am I safest, my love? Is there any safe place for me?"

Shaeddor nearly broke down. This was all his fault. Her love for him brought her to this grim fate. "Nothing is sure for the lost. Limbo means uncertainty. Yet the closer you are to the Prime Material Plane, the safer you are. And the farther away, the more your peril mounts."

"Then as I have already done," she told him, "I will strive to stay close to you, because that is when my fear and pain are at their least. But I will also do what I must to learn how to defend and protect myself. I will need to explore my world to learn its perils."

"My heart. My Jen. If there is a way to release you from this torment and these threats, I shall find it."

207

She smiled. "We shall find it together."

"Stay with me this night in this ancient place," he told her. "Please. In places of power such as these, we can nearly touch. Haunt me all night if you must, but stay near to me."

"No power that exists shall take my ghost from your side this night."

For the first time in many weeks, Shaeddor mourned for her loss as he should have all along. Together, the two of them finally found some peace together.

# 

The new transport gateway was up and working shortly after noon the next day. They still had various tests to make, so they would stay another night.

Shaeddor slept most of that day, and woke in the afternoon to break his fast.

His personal aerovelocitor suit arrived with one of the first shipments that came through, made to his exact specifications. Shaeddor smiled. It was all shiny, blue-violet-black like the feathers of a giant raven.

Because they were up so high, it would be easy to test the suit, and he always had a built-in reserve chute and the entity as well to back him up if something went wrong.

He spent hours before and after dinner testing the suit's working parts and enchantments that helped it function, float, and fly. Even he had to marvel at its clever mecho-magical construction.

His dinner had been passable, but somewhat bland. Temuen the Miser was not known for his love of rich food or fine wine. He did not have a reputation for being the best host or entertainer of guests.

In the vernacular of the Urthers, the Miser did not party very much. That was not in his nature.

Shaeddor made his first aerovelocitor flight in the darkness after sunset. His efforts were at first clumsy, awkward, and inefficient, like most fledging birds attempting to soar. He quickly exhausted himself and had to rest in between then and his next attempt.

On his third attempt after midnight, he finally figured things out and did very well after that point. He learned to find thermals and updrafts and ride them as he should, and streamline his need to use further magic to assist the enchantments of the suit itself.

Now if he wished, he could stay up in the sky for as long as he wanted and keep flying for as long as he could remain awake.

In his fledgling travels he had located several encampments of the tribal centaurs. With the aid of the bat entity, he could see as well in the darkest night as if it were bright twilight around him.

He hovered over a large Ban-thon village and called down to its leaders. "Ho-tah to the Ban-thon and their chiefs. I am a night spirit, come to bring warning of what is to come. Will you hear my dread words?"

He also used telepathy to sense their emotions and read their thoughts selectively.

Many of the Ban-thon grew afraid of his voice and took shelter in their large square and triangular tents, strung up on their poles and lines. While warriors grabbed their spears and bows, looking up into the dark night for something to shoot at.

Three chiefs and three shaman emerged and came together with their feathered headdresses, one pair old, one in their prime, and one pair very young. None of them carried weapons, for weapons were no proof against spirits, but they did wear their ghost shirts, which should protect them against spells.

They stood bravely while their mightiest warriors stood ready all around their leaders.

All three of the shaman began chanting, most likely protective spells.

"Ho-tah, night spirit," the old chief said. "Come down that we might see you and hear your words. So that we might know that you are indeed a spirit, and not some demon come to deceive us and do us harm with false words."

Shaeddor cloaked his face and form in shadows from the entity of night, like the shape of a great black owl.

Several of the Ban-thon shrieked in terror at the very sight of him.

"Aaiee. A demon!"

They launched their weapons at him in fear.

Shaeddor deflected them with a simple air shield and rose up out of sight and range.

He sent a black lightning bolt down into one of the village's large, dying bonfires. The blast scattered ash, dust, and embers everywhere.

"I come to bring you warning, and your people attack me? Speak great chiefs. Why should I not unleash my spirit powers and lay waste to your entire village and all within it?"

The old chief lifted both hands in the sign of peace. "Stay your powers, night spirit. The people are frightened by your fierce face and your mighty powers. I beg of you. Spare us, and give to us your warning. Tell us what doom you bring? I promise you safety among us. None shall dare attack you."

Shaeddor used levitation to wrap his wings around his form and float in place above where the lightning struck.

"Know that all the peoples of the plains face a great threat. New ta-sae have come with the strange shifting of the lands, and the return of the Dark Ones."

Many Ban-thon wailed and wept to hear these grim words.

The youngest chief roared back, "Then we shall gather all the tribes, and sweep across the lands, to kill all of the two-legs!"

"Such cannot be done. The ta-sae have brought their war here from other worlds, and it shall be a war of great magicks between them, the likes of which the centaurs have never seen. The only way for the centaurs to survive and keep their lives and their lands, is to ally themselves with the ta-sae of light, against the ta-sae of darkness, who always bring evil. You will know them by what they do.

"Those of the evil ones will always lie and kill. Those of the light will try to live in peace with you and speak strange tongues, given a chance. Yet like all creatures, they will defend themselves if you attack them without cause."

"All two legs are liars," the chief in his prime noted. "How can we make alliance with these ta-sae?"

"They come from two worlds. The Dark Ones bring only death, like those who now hold the mountain heads. They will try to kill the ta-sae in Ducallasto, just as they slew all of the few ta-sae in Gundi. Did they not hang the Gundi dead by their feet without their heads, and let their blood stain the mountain heads with black evil?

"They will lie to you and offer you many things to get you to help them kill the ta-sae in Ducallasto. Then when the ta-sae of light are all dead, the evil ones will turn on the centaurs and bring back the Darkspawn in great numbers to murder you all."

The old chief spoke once more. "How do we know your words are true?"

"You will know the truth by what you see and what your hearts tell you. You cannot win this war without an alliance with the ta-sae of light. And the Dark Ones will always try to trick you or force you into doing what they wish. They will put you at the head of the battle to spend your lives, while they stay safe behind you like cowards. The ta-sae of light will offer to fight at your side as brothers and sisters, not at your back. That is how you will know what side to choose."

"Thank you, night spirit. Thank you for this warning. We shall think quickly upon the weight of these things that we have heard, and spread your warning to the other tribes. Go, with the blessings of the true peoples and the Great Mystery."

"I have spoken the warning. My task is done. It is up to you and the true peoples to decide what it is you will do. Choose wisely."

Shaeddor flew off and soared over the plains in the night.

He took out a sliver of soulstone and studied the ley lines of power in that region.

Then the crystal flashed toward the north.

He was weary now, and could not investigate, but he felt certain that either another power nexus or another Urth Spectral Entity was hiding somewhere in the vast mountains of the northwest.

Shaeddor returned to the mountain heads. He took off his aerovelocitor suit and tucked it away in an enchanted, magic fold. Now he could summon it upon himself at his need, like any change of clothing.

The night had proven very profitable once more. Everywhere he went, he learned more about the enemy, their plans, and how he might in the end, take them apart like a machine and finally bring them down.

His own mind worked on that possibility, even while he slept.

He rose with the dawn the next day and took his leave, almost without speaking another word. His business with the Miser was complete, for the moment. On to Pelantis, what the Urthers called Boise, Idaho.

# TORI

The Pistolera rode to the northern front of Ann Arbor, just as David commanded, her reloaders racing behind her. She could not believe her eyes.

Fast moving zombies and skeletons with weapons and shields—even bows—were punching through the thin lines of defenders at several key points, attacking at will with cunning, speed, and precision.

A living army could not have done worse.

Some of the undead even attacked horrified civilians behind the lines.

She drew her pistols and blasted zombie heads off at will, some at close range.

Tori fought her way up to the front.

She switched guns and got up on top of a three story building with her runners, where she had a vantage point above the seething battle.

Guards with rune shields protected her all around, but she still had to expose herself to direct and indirect fire.

Down below, she saw David and the princes and their forces, punching and hacking their way through the zombie hordes, putting them down. They continued to spread out and attempt to seal off the various breaches.

Tori saw her chance and fired off an annihilator round at the packed ranks of undead out beyond them.

This was going to be a close one.

David and the others saw it arc off into the distance and began counting down the seconds.

After the blast dome rose up, they timed it right and dropped down just as the thermal waves and blast effects shredded and flattened the foes still standing.

Then David and the defenders were right back up, surging forward, spearing and splitting zombie heads like machines, stomping on and hewing the undead into the ground.

A spotter pointed out an enemy leader to Tori as the dust from the blast cleared. "Pistolera, look! On that far hilltop. That must be a Zombie Master!"

She snatched the field glasses held out to her and tried to focus, estimating the range.

Damn it, he was too far away, even for her guns.

The Zombie Master looked like some kind of strange witch doctor, with a terrifying mask made from dried human and humanoid faces stitched together, armor made of various skulls, and strange symbols tattooed on his body. His staff was topped by some kind of moaning, evil spirit in the form of a small, burning infant, writhing in dark flames of red and black.

As the battle ebbed for the time being, Tori shouted down at David and the princes. "David, we've spotted the Zombie Master, about a half mile or more away, due north on the top of the next hill. Do we want to try to reach him and take him out?"

David quickly conferred with the princes. "Yes!" David shouted. "Get down here and ride with us on your horse. We'll take the vanguard out on a sortie and destroy that bastard!"

She quickly climbed down a tall ladder that had been set up against the building from down below, for a quick escape.

In no time Tori was riding full tilt, trying to catch up to her friends.

The vanguard charged behind the full weight of the knights of Marrandor, their lances leveled, and their heavy, armored war horses thundering across the vale. Behind them came ranks of infantry and archers, with pike and spear on the flanks, and the rest of the Blackhawks protecting their rear as they passed through the hosts of the undead.

They flowed together up the low bank, pounding straight at the Zombie Master.

Their foe seemed unphased by the force rushing straight at him.

Tori could not get into a position where she had a clear shot.

The Zombie Master cast some kind of Dark Magic, and summoned several gigantic, glowing humanoid skeletons right up out of the ground. And behind them, an entire herd of large, undead animals crested the hill and careened down into the vale, fully intending to trample the vanguard's sortie.

Tori saw animated corpses of charging cattle, horses, bears, even an elephant and a giraffe, most likely taken from some Urther zoo. There were moose, elk, and deer—all of their eyes glowing red with the murderous hate of the fell spirits driving them forward to kill.

She finally pulled up and snapped off shots, cutting down the zombie elephant and all of the large undead that she could blast into dust and fading chunks of glowing bone.

David and the princes surged through the openings she created and led the knights right up against the Zombie Master.

They fought with an enemy bodyguard of undead in full armor, and wielding their weapons with great speed and skill.

Damn it. If her friends weren't engaged up there, she could blast the entire hilltop and roast the Zombie Master for sure. But that time was past.

Now she had to pick her shots carefully and fight her way up there with them.

Tori urged Pepper on, trying to gun down any undead that came at them. But she couldn't get them all. There were too many.

A rampaging dead moose smashed into one of her reloading wagons and tipped it over to one side, the horses screaming as it toppled.

Several undead creatures tried to trample them. They fought them off with massed pikes set for charge and the Pistolera's blazing guns.

Finally they reach the top of the hill off to one side.

David and the princes hewed their way through the Zombie Master's blood guard.

Yet their quarry leaped up into the saddle of what looked to be a dead horse, and prepared to slip away.

"Oh, no you don't!" Tori yelled, trying to close for a clear shot without blasting her friends. "Archers, cut that bastard down!"

The archers fired every arrow they had, but the shafts feathered the undead and had little effect.

The bolts meant for the Zombie Master seemed to hit, and then fall away. He was under some kind of protective spell.

He gave a command, and several zombies began to swell up and glow from within. When they hit Tori's defensive lines in front of her, the monsters exploded with great destructive force, hurling the defenders back.

Tori shot several of the suicide zombies who came at them at a dead run, blowing them up before they could hit the lines.

She drew up even with the Zombie Master, as he prepared another spell. Jagged blades and shards of glowing bone rose up all around the mage, ready to shoot at Tori and her people.

"You picked the wrong people to mess with!" she yelled.

She took a steady bead on the Zombie Master's repulsive mask and shot out both of his eyes.

Her next devastator rounds followed fast, overlapping and obliterating the body as it fell, and the foes bunching to either side.

Cheers went up from the defenders for the Pistolera.

Then they turned about and fought their way back to their own lines as the normal, slower, shuffling undead closed upon them again in endless numbers.

But with the Zombie Master dead, the defenders didn't see any more fast undead for the rest of that night.

They succeeded in holding off the foe until most of the helpless refugees and non-combatants made it through the gateways to Michiana.

Then the massive press of the zombie numbers forced them to pull up stakes, secure the transport station, and make a fighting retreat out of Ann Arbor with tens of thousands of ambulatory refugees. The latter were lightly armed and could fight if they were put to it, but they most likely would not last very long in a pitched battle against such enemy numbers.

By eleven in the morning, they were set up to pull off another vanishing, act courtesy of the fully rested Fillmore twins. This leap would take them twenty miles down their road, and only a half a day's march to the front lines of the defenders of Detroit-Tornhold.

With a forced march they could still reach their primary destination by nightfall, but all of them would definitely be exhausted and worn out.

Getting the mass of undisciplined refugees through took an hour longer than expected, and Army 16 took a pounding at the rear, as the undead mounted in numbers and nearly overwhelmed them on the open road.

The rear guard and Trent Fillmore raced into the portal and barely got it closed off behind them.

Even so, a few dozen zombies came through after them and had to be put down. Some of them had been cut in half by the portal closing as they pushed in.

Trent seemed to take great note of that effect and stood pondering the ramification of that fact.

Tori went up to the youth and put a hand on his shoulder. "I see the wheels turning, Trent. What are you plotting now."

He grinned viciously. "I think we might have a way to use the portals as weapons. I'll need to discuss it with Katelyn and the other mages."

215

Then word reached them. Captain David Pritchard and many others had collapsed with high fevers and were taken ill. The healers said that it was either some kind of stomach virus or possibly food poisoning.

But the sickness was spreading, and the wagons were already filled with the stricken and the wounded from the most recent fighting.

It was imperative that they reached the Detroit lines now.

By dawn, if things kept up, over a third of their forces might be incapacitated by sickness. The refugees did not seem to be affected yet, so the bug must be something the army had encountered within the last week to ten days or so.

If it was food poisoning, all of their supplies needed to be double-checked for spoilage and contamination, while they continued to march.

Then Prince Valandin took sick, and his twin brother helped tend to him. Tori waited to see if she felt ill, but thankfully, nothing happened.

She tried to check on David, but he was wracked by vomiting and diarrhea. No fun for anyone involved.

When word came that General Culpepper and Prince Alendel were the next to succumb, all eyes turned to the Pistolera to help lead them to safety.

She met briefly with the officers who were unaffected, and they kept the hosts together.

When they were just a few miles out, a thousand enemy mercenaries rushed to block the road.

Tori did not hesitate. They could not be delayed while more foes raced up to cut them off. Then the Khabal would simply withdraw and let the undead sweep over them.

The Pistolera led the remainder of the vanguard forward to blast their way through the enemy roadblock, put the merc survivors to flight, and keep marching on.

Everyone was slowing down, however. They had to keep going. Falling short in their condition would mean death. They were in no shape to fight all day and night again.

Less than an hour after sunset, they found the lines of Detroit-Tornhold.

A large trench or canal had been dug, apparently assisted by Urth magic spells, most likely a fairly large number of earth mages. The trench was filled with only a few feet of swampy, brackish water, and there were also pickets of wood and jagged metal rebar set in the moat as well.

Up the steep sandy earth, and mixed gray clay sides, the berm had been raised up thirty feet or more at a steep incline, with more pickets and coils of razor wire stuck out above.

Tori had the buglers announce their arrival.

"Defenders of Detroit-Tornhold," Tori shouted. "Army 16 from Michiana comes to you with refugees from Ann Arbor. Please, direct us through your defensive lines. The enemy is fast upon our heels in great numbers."

A voice called down, an Urther voice, although when she looked up, she spotted Thulls and Urthers standing together in mixed ranks.

"Army 16. Proceed a quarter mile north, skirting the moat and the defensive wall. "You'll come to a a drawbridge gate, and once we confirm your identity with the messengers you sent up ahead, we'll lower the bridge and start letting you cross over. Send the refugees over first."

The full process took longer than Tori wished.

By the end, she and the Blackhawks helped the remaining rear guard retreat across the bridge, even as undead began to sweep into the area.

The drawbridge had to be raised with a score of undead still swarming over it and tumbling down. Tori and her fighters finished the vermin off.

Heavy fighting erupted all along that section of moat.

Tori and Army 16 had to spread out and help defend the battlements.

When dawn came the undead stopped attacking for some reason, perhaps because their attacks had no affect.

She slumped down against the wall and immediately tried to go to sleep.

The next thing she knew, she was hoisted into the air by gigantic hands and closed within a breath-robbing bear hug.

"Hail and wellmet, mighty Pistolera! We are proud to fight beside you, and we have heard of your many brave deeds. You bring a host of heroes with you!"

Yep. Definitely a Thul. Her feet dangled far up off the ground.

She stared into a big, jovial face up close. A winged helmet over thick dark hair in gilded braids, a big bushy beard and moustache, also decorated. One bright gray eye on the right, a deep old white scar and an eye patch on the left, made of some kind of strange, padded monster hide.

His breath over his many white teeth already smelled of mead.

"I'm General Thul-Tokk of the Royal Thull Army of Tornhold. Are you ready to meet Death with us this fine day, my brave lass?"

Tori blinked. "I'd rather have some sleep before doing so," she noted.

Thul-Tokk laughed heartily, kissed her on both cheeks and mashed her to him again.

"Gaah! My spine!" she cried out, trying to pull away. "Please, no killing or crushing for the time being, General."

He roared with laughter once again. "Well said, my valiant lass. Let's get you and your folk a mouthful of cram, a nip of grog, and a few minutes rest. Death can go screw himself for a while, and wait for our souls a bit longer."

He continued to carry her off in his mighty arms as if she were a small child.

Thulls. God love them.

# MASON

The Pistolero stared face to face with the great green dragon Shavalkathar, it's slitted, glowing eyes as big as round shields when they opened wide. Mason bowed low in deep respect.

David had warned him how much courtesy and manners meant to all but the most evil of dragons.

"Greetings, and many thanks be unto you, our good and mighty friend, Shavalkathar, greatest of dragons. I am Mason Tyler, the Pistolero."

The dragon's voice boomed, rumbling out like an earthquake itself. "You are the Wild Magic sorcerer, you and your female, who fire Wild Magic itself out of your strange metal devices. How very odd. And you are the friends of my great friends. I was glad to help save you, in your strange floating bag of gas. You Urthers are a strange folk indeed. How cunning and foolish you are, all at once."

"We owe you our lives, great dragon. Will you stay with us for a time? Your aid would be invaluable in the defense of this city. We would do our best to feed you well."

The dragon actually grinned. "No doubt, yet alas, I have urgent matters of my own that must be attended to in my own time. I seek our friends,

David Pritchard and the Princess Jerriel, the enchantress. I require their assistance. I was hoping that they might be with you or in this city."

Mason lifted the front of his hat and scratched his head. "Many apologies, mighty Shavalkathar. But David and Jerriel went with Army 16 to Detroit-Tornhold, the city of the Urthers and the Thulls, on the far eastern lower banks of the Hand of Shendor. With any luck they should be there soon."

The dragon craned his neck northeast. "Very well. If that is where they have gone, I must seek them there. Ugh! Thulls."

"Is there anything that we can do to help?" Mason asked.

"I accept your kind offer," the dragon said, "but no. I must take my leave. I will burn the enemy in my path as I depart. Good luck to you and your battles here, Pistolero. Of course, you are aware of the incredible numbers of undead that are heading this way down from Vaejan, correct?"

"Unfortunately, we are," Mason said. "We'll find a way to defeat them."

"Too bad you do not have more of your flying gas bags. You could burn the undead and reduce their numbers from the safety of the sky."

"Perhaps one day soon," Mason said. "Good fortune to you, great dragon. Success on your mission and give good tidings to our friends, David and Jerriel and all of the rest."

"This has been a a fair meeting, Mason Tyler. I will not forget it. Good fortune to us all. Fight well." With that the dragon shot into the sky like a rocket, winging its way northeast. Seconds later, dragon fire scorched the ranks of the Dark Khabal.

Hundreds of screams went up from the foe.

Mason went on to speak with the commander of that part of Indy's defenses. The transport station was set up immediately, and messengers went back and forth between Indy and Michiana.

After a quick meal, Mason helped check on their wounded. Then he and his friends tried to grab some sleep.

A short while later that night, the distinctive sounds of intense fighting increased to Mason's sensitive ears. He, Rodell, and Steven had been dozing for a while in a barracks close to the front, one that wasn't being used.

But outside it sounded as if the front was coming straight at them.

Minutes later, Ishix and several panicked Indy militia rushed in to request their assistance at the rapidly collapsing front lines.

Mason, Rodell, and Steven came running.

Then the floodgates seemed to open. Michiana troops poured out from near the transport station and formed their ranks. Then they came up behind Mason and his friends, marching toward the front lines.

He noted troops from three separate armies, one each from South Bend, Mishawaka, and Elkhart.

The High Command of Michiana was sending thirty thousand hardened troops to help raise the siege of Indianapolis.

At the front, Mason picked his shots, using the correct loads to drive the enemy back, right before they were about to breach the city and pour in. Rodell used spells, while Steven covered them all with his bow.

Never in their dreams did the enemy expect three new hand-picked armies to appear out of the mists—out of nowhere—and begin to roll over them.

After two hours of doing little more than fighting an off balance retreat, the enemy quickly attacked with their battle wizards to break off, a standard enemy ploy, and then they withdrew in a near rout.

The three armies did not stop there. They pushed on and overtook the enemy camps.

For now, the siege of Indianapolis-Nenarra was effectively broken, but that was going to shift again within the next two weeks, as the hordes of undead continued to arrive.

It became a race to see if the armies of Indy could now link up with the Army train and complete the tracks establishing rail service between them and Michiana. The countless zombies would more than likely ignore the tracks. They might even ignore the train itself as it whizzed by. And the enemy could not approach the tracks without being attacked by their own undead.

Word came from General Blackwood in South Bend. All available workers and earth mages were being called up to dig a steep walled ditch on the western side of the tracks. Another train was even being sent from Elkhart in all haste, with steam shovels to assist in the great task.

Concrete and rubble were going to be torn up from the broken patch of highway nearby to make a low defensive wall where garrisoned troops could defend the rail line. Eventually, the plans were to have a series of forts and defensive hard points lining the entire way between Michiana and Indy, and protecting the rich farm lands between them as well.

Another rail line would be added in the spring, so that they could have trains coming and going at the same time.

But first they had to fight off the enemy and the undead that fall, and somehow make it possible for the rich, vitally needed crops to be brought in to feed everyone throughout the coming harsh winter.

There was certainly going to be a lot of 'ifs,' and plenty else that needed to get done.

Mason noted that young, handsome Steven and pretty Ishi had taken a shine to one another. They spent all of their time together when they could, and the Jattaran battle mage was a great addition to their little band.

He smiled watching them hold hands and stare into each other's eyes.

Let the young lovers have their fun.

There was already far too much death, sorrow, and bad luck to go around as it was. These days, people needed to take happiness where they could find it, and hang on for dear life with both hands.

No one knew to what end anything or anyone might come to in such times.

Let the lovers of both stricken worlds know their joy while they still could. Any of them could be dead the next minute.

Mason knew very well that he missed his sweet Tori every second that they were apart. He prayed daily for her safety, but he knew that she could handle herself. That was the best any of them could do.

There was plenty of fighting in the days that followed. The enemy tried something new every day, and lives were lost in bloody piles and large numbers on both sides.

Word finally reached them that Tori was safe in Detroit-Tornhold, but alas, Jerriel had been taken by the enemy—by Blondie—her own brother, of all things. Everyone, even Dave, said that Blondie was back working with the enemy and his old master once more. He had gone back to the enemy.

But Mason still couldn't believe it. In his heart, he still hoped that his old buddy was staying true to the threats he made, to play all sides against the middle. Then one day, Blondie would orchestrate his revenge against the Dark Khabal to repay them all a thousandfold for his sweet Jen's murder at the Khabal's bloodstained hands.

But if Blondie had turned bad again, Mason felt that it might be his duty one day to put his old friend down at some point, much like a mad dog on the rampage.

He secretly prayed that things would not come to that.

And still he wondered what that damn dragon was up to.

Both sides fought, and the Urthers laid track each day. Squadrons of dirigible gunships patrolled Michiana. Some even dared to reach Detroit-Tornhold.

It wasn't until the end of September and they went into the Indian summer days of October that the rail link was finally completed.

Trains went back and forth each day after that, under heavy guard, sometimes two and three trains back to back. Armored blimps and dirigible gunships routinely escorted the trains, strafed and firebombed the undead, and patrolled the skies above the Urther cities.

The construction teams would continue working on the defensive ditch and the hard points and forts throughout the winter, whenever possible.

In the end, it took sixteen armies to guard the tracks all along the way, and the fighting never seemed to let up. The countless undead were hurled back each day, but they kept on coming.

More transport stations were set up, and by now they also had gateways linked up with the other side in their sister dimension of the Merge.

Track service would be established on the other side the following year. For now, the transport stations would have to serve.

There was even talk among the research and development teams from Robert Billings about making transport gates large enough that even a train or a blimp could past through between both sides.

But first they had to survive the winter.

With armies on the line, entire populations nearly went out into the fields, almost everyone going out to help bring the various crops in as fast as possible, under guard. The Allied cities tried to help each other.

A bottling and canning factory in South Bend was converted to steam power and ran full on, day and night, preserving food in cans, and even jars, both plastic and glass.

Similar plants were modified in Michiana and Indy.

Factory farms were now stepping up their production of eggs, chickens, pigs, sheep, cattle, and even horses.

In every neighborhood people now had local bakers and butchers. Every family was allotted food by the rationing board, and nothing was allowed to go to waste. Excess milk was made into cheese that could be stored, or reduced to powdered milk that could be reconstituted at any time.

Each family or person was later allotted a month of survival rations.

Corn and soybeans were processed into food goods, including corn sugars and sweeteners. Wheat was ground into flour. Rice and beans were dried and preserved, along with spices. Fruits and vegetables were canned and stored. So was meat when it could be processed in large quantities at slaughterhouses. Concerted effort was made to keep food stores safe and reliable.

Construction already ramped up for an explosion of hundreds of ice houses to help keep frozen foods cold and provide ice, all throughout the next year, and for years to come.

Hell, by next summer, there might even be ice cream shops.

As things began to look better, more marriages took place, and more babies would come. If the Urthers lived long enough, their populations would finally begin to increase, and stop decreasing from the wars.

They just needed to survive long enough to turn the tide.

The Allies brought in the harvest, but just barely.

Fighting kept all troops busy at their posts. Mason watched the first snow flakes of winter fall during the last week of October. The battles and the fighting finally slacked off with colder weather on the way.

No doubt there would be plenty more fighting come spring. If possible, they wouldn't just wait to be hit.

They wanted to go on the offensive.

# DAVID

David Pritchard recovered from his stomach sickness during the next week.

He quickly learned three important things about Detroit-Tornhold.

First, the millions who remained free there were in desperate circumstances. Too many mouths to feed and not enough food. They were still a month of more away from harvesting their first main crops from their fields that year.

And they were almost completely out of food and more or less beginning to starve, despite excellent efforts at rationing.

Next, the Urthers actually worked very well with the Thulls. Thulls were very much into freedom–almost like hippies in that regard–very big, violent hippies with lots of weapons. But Thulls strongly did not believe in subjugating others. They managed their own affairs, and allowed the Urthers to manage theirs, and they were all at risk of dying and getting killed in any case.

Many Urthers also thought the Thull bathing rituals to be quite entertaining, and gladly joined in as onlookers to the amusing spectacle.

All of this was very conducive to working together against countless determined enemies in order to keep breathing.

Third and finally, Thulls were, of course, undeniably batcrap crazy.

Even while facing starvation and death that winter, the giddy, loopy bastards sang like lunatics and laughed in the face of it all, especially with them liking to eat so much, so much so that starvation was particularly painful for them.

Yet they faced privation and hardship with what appeared to be something akin to sheer joy. They seemed to thrive upon adversity and peril.

And they literally looked forward to a glorious death in battle the way Urther children used to look forward to going to Disney World.

Thulkara and Thul-Kazar were received in triumph, and when that pair of loons announced their engagement, the Thulls went wild.

The only hope was for everyone in Detroit-Tornhold to tighten their belts and make it through that winter, was to protect their fields, and tough it out until harvest time. At least their fields would ripen that fall, and they should be bountiful.

Everyone had taken steps to boost food production, but those efforts still took months and weeks to pay off. There was no changing that.

But with the transport station up and running, it did provide certain options.

The crops in the south around Michiana and Indy were going to come in weeks ahead those up north around Detroit.

Field hands and workers from the north went south first through the gateways on both sides, and helped bring in the crops and livestock into the canning and processing plants.

Or they helped protect the fields and the workers from the enemy during that same time period.

Urther dirigibles grew to become an air force to be reckoned with, while the enemy aerovelocitor forces diminished, shot from the skies and too dependent on the lengthy time it took to train air mages.

David had joined in on one such air battle protecting the harvest, with over two score armored and rune-shielded dirigibles of various sizes. They were now armed to the teeth with the latest steam cannons and steam guns, as well as defended by mages and the occasional Champion.

The enemy sent over one hundred aerovelocitors to fire bomb the Urther crops they could not seize through combat.

David fought beside his old friend, Lieutenant Pete Steiner atop *The War Eagle*, spearheading the Urther defenses in the sky.

The brief encounter was nonetheless furious and bloody.

The enemy air forces hit the dirigibles with everything they had: firebombs, spells, and weapons.

One medium class airship was swarmed on and lost. Two other blimps endured serious damage.

Pete directed deadly volleys of steam canon and steam gun fire from the parapets atop his warship with his cutlass. The cannons were firing canister shells like big shotguns, shredding the elusive enemy when they did strike. There were also bolo round and rounds of expanding, weighted nets to ensnare the foe.

The enemy's only defense was speed and maneuverability, but forty airships soon filled the sky with steam gun fire.

David tried his hand at the new steam guns, but kept his longsword in hand, prepared against boarders and direct attacks.

A dozen foes with drawn weapons dropped down on the battlement and folded their wings, intent on close combat.

But this time, they focused their energies on cutting and slashing the vulnerable steam hoses leading to the cannons and guns.

David led Pete and several crew straight into them with swords and pikes.

The Dark Mages tried to blast them with several spells.

With his Null magic, David leaped right in and took the brunt of the spells upon himself with little negative effect, except for having to grit his teeth and grunt against some of the residual shock and pain.

They cut the attackers down or chased them off after a brief but fierce skirmish.

Pete hoisted one of the enemy flyers up that he had simply dazed with the bell of his cutlass to the face a few times. He dragged the fellow over to the edge of the fighting platform's railing.

Other crew made sure the enemy mage didn't have any hidden weapons one him along the way.

The Khabalist blinked in stunned rage as Pete shook him and pointed out at the battle with his bloody cutlass. An engagement that was all but over.

Only a handful of the enemy fliers limped away.

"Can you fly?" Pete asked the man.

The Khabalist looked himself over and then nodded.

"Good. Remember what you've seen here today. Go back and warn your friends. Warn your leaders. You invaders have continually underestimate us Urthers. You think us stupid and weak. We are neither. You thought that if you crippled our world and took the magic of our technology away from us, that we'd be pushovers. That you could just walk in, wipe us out, or enslave us.

"Well let me tell you bastards a thing or two. When put to it, we are the most vicious, the most cunning and destructive, warlike species our world has ever seen fit to produce. And you've gone and pissed us off by killing a bunch of our people and acting as if you could take us down so easy! Well get ready, because every day we grow stronger and smarter and more powerful. One day soon, we'll be coming for all of you assholes, to gut you and burn you out of every shithole you try to crawl into. And we won't stop until we've blasted all of you to dust. Go now. Take that message back to your bloody leaders!"

The enemy flyer launched in speechless terror, panic-stricken to tear away and escape.

David clapped Pete on the back. "Well said, brother!"

Pete grinned. "It ought to be. I wrote all that down and I've been rehearsing it in front of a mirror for weeks, just in the hopes of having the occasion to try it out!"

"Well you did good," David said with a laugh. "There's a story to tell your kids one day."

David helped the crew raise a cheer for their lieutenant's bravado, and the fighters joined in.

# 

There were a handful of such battles to protect the fields that fall, and one that was even fought at night. The airships took casualties and damage, but in every encounter, the blimps won out and drove the attackers from the skies.

It took a matter of mere weeks to construct and launch a dirigible, and load it with deadly weapons and a decently trained crew with no magickal ability whatsoever.

On the other hand, it took years to groom and train an air mage, and then even more time for that mage to learn to fly an aerovelocitor suit.

Just doing the math demonstrated why the Urthers soon dominated the skies.

Some fields were lost. Each field could not be protected perfectly. But once the crops in the south on both sides were mostly in, Detroit received similar help from Michiana and Indy protecting and bringing in their harvests.

The new transport station network was a huge boon. Yet even with sharing supplies and food back and forth, both sides were more or less in the same predicament as far as food went.

Everyone barely had enough food to feed their populations through the winter and into the coming year.

Everyone's stores had already been running thin or out by harvest time, and there was little to share and spread around, but they all did what they could. Michiana and Indy had surplus of corn and soy beans for example.

For some odd reason, thanks to some stranded trains, Detroit was sitting on a bunch of sugar and vegetable oil from the time of the Merge. Everyone did their best to share what they had.

As fall took the turn toward winter, the Urthers in Detroit continued to combine the technology and magic progress of Michiana with their own ideas. They strove not only to survive the winter they had been preparing for, but the expanded wars in the coming spring.

All of the Urther Allied cities had similar development programs running. Steam trains and steam magic dirigibles of various designs were the future for now. Detroit had lots of big empty factories that had been sitting idle for decades.

Now they fired up and made many different kinds of steam machines, tractors to aid food production, and blimps.

From the several enemy aerovelocitor suits captured, both whole and in pieces, the Allied cities learned that they could duplicate the suits and their enchantments.

Yet unlike Sylurria and the Dark Khabal, they did not currently possess a sufficient population of mages to draw upon to find or train enough competent air mage specialists to make producing more of the flying suits practical for their purposes.

But wheels were turning, and designers and engineers experimented, practiced, and planned how to apply and exploit the new possibilities of the powerful, hybrid steam magic engines.

War production had also increased greatly, and various weapons and types of armor were mass produced, including siege weapons. Fortification projects continued to expand in and around all of the human enclaves.

Detroit-Tornhold became a very well-armed, if hungry city.

Competent mages were still in high demand. The mages among the Thulls had a robust training program for Urther mages, but the former were known to be a bit heavy handed and not the best of teachers. On top of everything else, they were somewhat lacking in tomes and books of magic instruction, spellcraft, enchantment, and the general use of magic.

Such education materials in magic had to be mass produced, and that also took precious time.

The wizards with the princes did their best to help out, but they chafed to return home and help their people lift the siege there. They also had a full reference library in Kellendra–including a complete section on magic–that could be copied and distributed to the growing list of Allied cities.

As if to dramatize the pressing need to link up with their friends in the south and other places, more portable transport stations came through, this time earmarked for both sides of Toledo-Kellendra.

Overland, to go there now they would need to fight their way through hundreds of thousands of zombies, not to mention tens of thousands of other foes bent on cutting them off and destroying them.

But there was still another option. There were several Great Lakes freighters and other ships being converted to steam engine power. Two such ships stood ready to sail, but their original orders were to go out to fish the inner seas for badly needed foodstocks before the Great Lakes froze over.

It was decided that the vanguard and the princes could take one steam ship down to Toledo and the Marrandorians. Who, it was last reported, still controlled most of the ports and access points to the Inner Seas, and even had several sailing vessels and warships of their own.

The vanguard on the steamship could reach Toledo before the harvest ended, and before winter fully set in. Four dirigible gunships would escort them there.

Another active plan was to send a squadron of ten military blimps to take transport stations to Grand Rapids-Anzhalar, and possibly from there on to St. Paul/Minneapolis-Zaskakaria. Unlike going to Kellendra-Toledo, the heavily armed airships could circle far to the north, well beyond the enemy's current reach.

Long Range Scouts reported that a large enemy force had gone up far north, and perhaps even crossed over into the Upper Peninsula and Canada.

But the rest of Michigan was fairly clear, and the airships could easily make a run for it before winter.

It was also believed that after several air engagements, the enemy had very few of the aerovelocitor forces left on hand, probably due to the limited availability of air mages.

David knew the opinions of Tori and the princes; they wanted to push on to Toledo. That would open the way to Cleveland-Dorundia, and on to the east coast of the New World colonies.

He went to speak with Thul-Kazar and Thulkara that morning. Both of them were busy helping train a bunch of eager young Thulls who did not mind getting the crap stomped out of them by two of their champions.

Like all good Thulls, they actually seemed to enjoy a sound thrashing and think it all great fun, the loons.

When David proposed going to Kellendra, at first neither of the barbarian pair were very interested in leaving their people while Tornhold was still in danger, and before the harvest finished up, and before their approaching nuptials.

Then David explained that it was vital to set up the transport station in Kellendra, and possibly in Anzhalar and Dorundia before winter. Doing so might save hundreds of thousands, if not millions of lives.

The Thulls finally gave in and agreed to help lead a Thull battle group on one of the steam ships, if they could come back through the transport station as soon as conditions allowed.

But above all else, David still worried constantly about Jerriel. Where was she? Was she still alive? No word came to them, and that only made him fear the worst.

While waiting for the steamship to load up, he pored over the scouting reports and other records the Thulls and the Urthers of Detroit-Tornhold kept, to see if anyone had sighted anything concerning Jerriel, however small.

Nothing. He was beside himself and didn't know what else to do.

Then he read some scouting reports from the outer defenses.

Something stopped him cold.

Back while he had been sick and bedridden, a green dragon had approached the front lines each day at dawn, flying in circles, hovering, dipping its wings, even landing.

The dragon behaved almost as if it was trying to signal the Thulls somehow or parlay with them.

Of course the barbarians dismissed it out of hand. The dragon had to be crazy. Thulls and dragons had always been bitter enemies. Why this one did not simply attack them was beyond their comprehension. The fact that it was trying to reason with them was beyond the Thull realm of possibility.

Of course David knew instantly that the green dragon was most likely Shavalkathar, and if he came back day after day in an attempt to try to make contact with them, he must have a very good reason for doing so.

But the dragon wasn't stupid, either. He wasn't going to get close enough to let the fool barbarians shoot him down and kill him.

David rushed out to the front lines up in one of the sleek new dirigible gunships on patrol as quick as he was able, bringing a young, female signal mage with him.

It was well past the hour the dragon usually appeared to the defenders, but the scouts on the walls reported that they had seen the dragon earlier, just as before.

David ordered the mage to cut loose with a skyfire display, all in green fire, as high up as she could send it up. The bright display went on for almost fifteen minutes, most likely visible for dozens of miles or more in all directions.

They waited as long as they could and were just about to give up.

The signal mage was exhausted by that time, and their blimp circled around back toward the city.

The armies below fended off the teeming hordes of zombies as they always did these days, with the help of flame sprayers, steam cannons, and steam guns.

Then the spotters on the blimp called out something glowing bright green upon the northern horizon.

David saw it in his binoculars. It was Shavalkathar, returning at top speed to speak with him. He knew it.

He ordered the blimp to speed to the coastline, to a section of beach that was within the city's defenses.

The signal mage had enough juice left to target the beach with her last strike. There they landed nearby, and army forces guarding the beaches helped them moor the airship to the trees.

The troops looked nervous, especially when David informed them that a dragon was coming.

He tried to tell them that the dragon was an ally, and not to be afraid, but they still looked scared.

"Everyone back away three hundred yards and leave me to speak with the dragon alone."

The Thulls present did not like the sound of that at all, just in case something went wrong. David assured them that it would not.

Some of the Thulls were hungry, and thought the dragon would make a fine meal. They went away in disgust and disappointment.

The others ran for cover even as the dragon circled in.

David waited with his hands outstretched in welcome.

Shavalkathar made the ground shake as he always did. Then he snorted a bit of flame and smoke. "Greetings to you, David Pritchard. You had to pick a city half-full of blockheaded Thulls, did you not? I've been trying for days to get you or Jerriel to notice my presence. At least the hunting is good in the hand, and the Inner Seas. I have feasted well."

David bowed. "It is most excellent to see you, Mighty Shavalkathar. Forgive me; I was taken ill a while back." But secretly, his heart remained heavy, because the dragon already mentioned her name as if he thought she were still at Tornhold-Detroit. That much was clear.

"I'm sorry that you were sick," Shavalkathar said, "but I have some urgent matters to discuss with you and your mate Jerriel."

He flung down a mashed up and broken, gold and copper belt or collar, and what appeared to be several large, steel ballista bolts with strange heads. The heads were unusual in the fashion that they did not seem to be designed to kill, but rather like large collapsible darts, designed to inject either poison...or perhaps even drugs into very large creatures.

"Where did you get these things?" David asked.

"Weeks ago, I was out hunting in the wilds nearer to Vaejan and was attacked by a common brown wyvern wearing this odd collar. He still had one of these darts stuck in him. It was all very strange."

"Why strange?" David asked.

"Wyverns are half the size of grown dragons, and though they have a stinger in their tail which can incapacitate their normal prey, they are no real threat to dragonkind. We prey upon them, not the other way around. So you see, for such a creature to attack me was completely insane."

"So, you freed him of these items and let him go on his way?"

"Or course not. I was hungry that hour and thus I slew and ate the mad fool, and crapped out his bones the very next day. Yet while munching on him, I removed the collar and the dart, which clearly were not edible. But the collar reeks of Dark Khabal magicks, and the dart smelled as if it had contained a powerful sleep potion or some kind of paralyzing narcotic."

David saw the plot immediately. "My dragon friend, I think the Khabal is capturing these and other creatures somehow, putting these collars on them and forcing them to fight for them. Perhaps they are even being used to guard certain places or areas."

Shavalkathar nodded his rather large, spikey head. "I would not put it past them. On another hunting trip in the hand, I found a cold drake riddled with these same darts. It had somehow managed to escape by falling down a ravine, into a river, and was swept away. But the drugs in the darts did their work too well. The creature had passed out and drowned, washed up on a riverbank where it provided another fine meal for myself."

David stopped himself from asking what did not provide the dragon with a fine meal, but of course he knew that the answer to that—not much.

"I thought that you and Jerriel should know about such things," Shavalkathar said, although it was very clear that he was still holding back something else.

David tried to guess. "So, you're afraid the Khabal might try to take control of more dragons?" he said.

The green dragon paused. "Horrors. I had not considered that. If they did, they would soon have all of dragonkind actively marshalled against them. Dragons do not take their liberty lightly, David Pritchard. Any who attempt to enslave us earn our wroth to the highest degree."

"You want something or help with something," David said right off. "Just come out and tell me. I will help you if I can. I owe you. You have helped us when we sorely needed you."

Shavalkathar the Mighty lowered his head to the sand, rolled over on his side and actually heaved forth a great dragon sigh. "David, it saddens me to admit that many young dragons such as myself do not know everything. I am truly melancholy. I am a strong, young male dragon in his prime in every way. Every instinct, every fiber of my being is screaming for me to soar forth and court a mate. I…I was hoping that you and Jerriel might come with me and assist me in doing so."

David did not know what to say. He was stunned. What could he say?

"Great Shavalkathar. It pains me immensely to see you suffering. If there is any way that I can be of service," he said, "I will gladly do so. Tell me what I can do to help."

The dragon closed his eyes and sighed even deeper. "Well, that's just the thing. I don't quite know what it is I am supposed to do, say, or feel. I have no surviving parents as it turns out, and no friendly dragons to speak with in the wilds. I don't really know what our courtship is supposed to be like. I need a friend and ally to speak with. I need lore about such things. Tharanorian mages keep such lore.

"Not knowing what to do. All of this. It's…it's rather humiliating to be sure, but I can no longer resist these powerful urges. I have heard rumors that there are several fine young, female dragons to the west and south, and especially to the north. The north is supposedly teeming with dragons of all kinds, because of the excellent hunting up that way."

"I'm sorry to inform you," David said, "but Jerriel was captured by the enemy a while back, and now we have no knowledge of where she is. We fear that she has been transported back to Vaejan. I fear for her very life."

The dragon shook his head. "I am very sorry to hear all of that David. I like the princess immensely, and I know how much she means to you. Let me make you this bargain, therefore. Come with me to the north lands. Help me find my mate, and as soon as that is done, I shall help you locate and retrieve yours. You have my word."

"The word of a dragon is a noble thing," David said. "And I do want to help you."

"The Dark Khabal will see Jerriel as a valuable prisoner, David. As a princess of the royal line, she could still be ransomed. They will keep her safe, question her, even try to seduce her to their cause if they can, the way they did her brother. And the brother might find a way to protect her as well."

Now it was David's turn to shake his head in disbelief. "Not from what I saw. He seems to be part of the Khabal in a big way. It was her older brother who went very far to take her from us. His powers are very great."

"That still does not mean he seeks her death. If he had her helpless, he could have killed her easily, if that was his primary goal."

Having a dragon's help would be infinitely better than simply sitting on his hands all autumn and winter. Dragons could hunt and track like no other creature, Jerriel had told him once. And they could literally smell magicks of all kinds and parse them out, she said.

David clapped his hands together. "I accept your kind and noble offer, Shavalkathar. I give you my word. I will go with you into the north, even through this coming winter if need be, and we shall locate a fine mate for you, if one can be found. I will speak to the other wizards about dragon courtships and learn what I can. And once that is done, we shall find and free Jerriel. Then we shall all know happiness once more."

"Thank you," Shavalkathar said, his voice very low. "Thank you from my heart, David Pritchard...my noble friend. I will linger upon this shore and hunt until we set out. Can you talk the Thulls into not attacking me here? I would hate to be forced to kill some of them. You need those warlike idiots so badly as fighters.

"By the way, did you know that, at least to dragons, Thulls taste absolutely terrible? Something nasty in their growth glands. Ugh! My stomach churns just thinking about it. Thulls are one of the few things that we prefer *not* to eat, unless we are utterly famished. How disgusting; and yet, Thulls think dragons to be a great delicacy. The fools mistakenly believe that if thy eat us they will somehow gain our strength. What rubbish and nonsense."

"Shavalkathar, I depart in haste to seek the lore we need, and provisions and gear for myself. I will return as able."

The dragon called after him. "Bring warm clothing for flight and harsh weather in the north. I suppose I must tolerate some kind of harness and saddle, made out of strong materials. We can't have you falling off me to your doom. Thunderbolts! The things I do for dragon love. Alas."

David ran back to the waiting blimp.

He was going to have fun explaining all of this.

# JERRIEL

Snows came early to Shenedar, what Urthers called the Upper Peninsula of Michigan. It was mostly harvest time down south in October, but up in the north, with the short growing seasons there, the harvests had already come and gone.

She and her friends explored the area, waiting for the coming of the enemy to make landfall, but for some reason the enemy delayed and did not cross right away.

Jerriel and Khia had tried to warn the people across the Inner Seas that a great enemy was coming to attack them, but for some reason, perhaps because of the protection of the Hoonga in the north lands, the Urthers and Tharanorians there had not yet suffered any attacks after the Merge.

That did not mean that they never would.

They had not endured the monster hordes at night, and the Dark Khabal had not come against them yet. Thus the people of Shenedar—who called their new realm Superiorland—thought themselves somehow invulnerable.

They listened to Jerriel and Khia very little and paid no heed to their dire warnings, especially when the big enemy attack did not strike or land right away, as was first claimed.

Some even assumed that it never would come, and that any supernatural forces were protecting their lands would somehow protect them still.

As November approached, the snow showers came regularly and increased during the last days of October. Winter came a few days early in the north

Luin stayed with them or in range nearby, but she normally went unclad, so as not to cause attention or dismay around the gan, or Urthers.

From studying Jerriel so closely and being joined with her, Khia took a Tharanorian female form very similar to Jerriel's in order to pass among the humans. But she was so much like Jerriel in face and shape, that at first others could barely tell them apart. Many they met thought them twins.

Jerriel suggested that they would attract less attention, and that it might be better if they were seen merely as mage sisters. Thus Khia changed herself slightly to be a few inches shorter, a bit curvier, and with light brown hair and green eyes.

While they waited to follow the invaders toward whatever quarry the enemy sought in the north, Jerriel and her friend's lives were not without peril.

The fame of their great beauty had spread.

A gang of roving Urther thugs, a dozen in all, took it upon themselves to attempt to visit the two strange, but no doubt beautiful sisters one night, with the intent to molest them in a drunken rampage.

They drew knives in the dark as they surrounded and crept up on the cottage Jerriel and Khia slept in during that time. The attackers brought rope with them and boasted and bragged in the cold night air about all of the vile things they were going to do to the two, helpless young women.

They could not have made a worse miscalculation.

After that night, those dozen thugs were never seen again. At least not alive.

Many breathed a sigh of relief and thought that a good thing, hoping that the vicious looking wretches had moved on.

But some who lived closer by to the cabin of the two sisters had heard strange, blood thirsty, inhuman cries that night, and seen bright flashes of strange lights from that direction, almost like blue lightning and bright green explosions.

Days thereafter along the river nearby, it was said that there was a place where the birds and the scavenger animals picked at twelve male heads staked out along the shore within a few miles of the sisters' cabin, and below them, their long knives had been thrusted into the ground in front of each pole.

While the skulls still had flesh on them, it was said that those twelve dead faces had all looked very startled indeed.

But with the coming of winter, Jerriel and Khia could wait no longer, whether the enemy came across or not.

Luin suggested that perhaps the enemy was waiting for the Hoonga to take one of their long winter sleeps, of which there were usually two or three, depending upon the severity and length of the winter.

Khia felt certain that there was another nexus up north, in what was now called the White Mountains, that formed a partial border between Shenedar and Khanada.

She and Jerriel feared that another Spectral Entity might be found there and that now they should try to reach it before the enemy might.

Luin needed no preparation. Weather was as nothing to her, with her fur coat. Khia was also nature spirit, and thus immune.

But as their weak link, Jerriel needed to bundle up and use protective spells to keep from succumbing to the harsh elements. Khia assisted her when and where possible, boosting her abilities with Urth Power.

They left the Urthers of Superiorland along the southern shore of the Inner Seas with their final warnings and headed north, tracking the ley lines.

When the going became too tough, Khia floated them above the trees, or Luin simply carried them effortlessly on the run with her great strength.

They made steady progress each day, and Khia provided for them in snow and ice caves that they fashioned. Jerriel learned much about the animals of the north and how they survived the winter.

Then Khia's face grew grave one day.

"The enemy has landed in Shenedar, and in great numbers," she warned. "They have spilled much Urther blood, and are now marching this way, laying waste to all things in their path."

Jerriel clutched her face with both hands, just imagining the hapless Urthers who had not believed them, and thought themselves so safe.

Khia continued, her eyes closed, sensing and seeing things through the Urth itself. "The land groans beneath the enemy's feet…and they have brought Darkspawn, and other monsters with them to work their evils."

A red glow near them suddenly caught their attention, and when they looked up, they both started and pulled away.

Luin's eyes glowed bright red with wrath and hatred, and her normally kind face was a mask of violence and what could only presage death.

"The Hoonga shall not stand for this. It has been eons, since the first battles of the Light and the Shadow covered our world in the ancient days, when the curse of the first Darkspawn set foot upon the lands of north."

"They move rapidly and with great purpose," Khia said. "I think they mean to seize their prize, whatever it is, and get away with it before any defense or attack can be raised. Tell me Luin; am I right in assuming that most of the Hoonga are now unaware, and down for the first long sleep?"

Luin nodded. "And worse yet, my people sometimes travel this far south because they like the blueberries here, but never during the winter. Shenedar is not considered to be a true part of the north. Too many gan live here."

Jerriel shook her staff. "The Khabal could do their worst and be gone before the Hoonga are even made aware that the enemy is so near."

"Yes, that is all possible," Luin said.

Jerriel clenched her free fist. "Then it remains up to us. We must stop the Khabal!"

# SHAEDDOR

Pelantis-Boise was initially going to be a quick layover. Not much going on there. Shaeddor had his people set up the transport gate. The fledgling Khabal forces in that region were busy fighting both the scattered, sporadic centaurs and the Urthers at the same time, so there wasn't much to do but move on.

Jen's ghost kept herself busy exploring the upper realms of Darkness and Shadow that lay above the Abyss and the Void, before the dark descended into the depths of the Nine Hells.

She did so under his tutelage, to the extent of his knowledge, but they both discovered many things not in the known lore. Jen grew more confident and less fearful as she gained proficiency in how to protect and conceal herself properly.

She explored deeper and deeper into the darkness.

As for the Merge Wars, the story was very different at the west coast cities of Chaetel and Shodis when they pressed on. Or at what the Urthers called Portland and Seattle. This key region was a definite hot zone, as his old friend Mace would have called it.

Shodis was doubly at war, surrounded by a sea of undead millions from the Merge, and the resulting war with Sylurria, which was still strong in that area and even had ships coming in from the Old World still.

There was yet another war with the Urthers who retreated around Chaetel and now held it and its outlying farms and fields in an attempt to survive the coming winter.

Even the westernmost centaurs were also involved who, given the chance, fought against all two legs.

Perhaps the latter required a visit from the night spirit to get them off the backs of the Urthers, as well as Shaeddor's own people.

Things were going to work out much better in the end if there was less confusion and everyone fought together against the Khabal.

Shaeddor explored the streets of the Dark Khabal-controlled city of Shodis. Khabal forces and mercenaries had turned their part of the city into one huge cesspool of drunkenness, debauchery, gambling, and blood sports.

He marveled.

Wherever there were people there were always opportunities for them to corrupt and destroy themselves. The Khabal only encouraged vice, black markets, illicit deals, thievery, violence—and allowed them to thrive under their control.

Shaeddor was very surprised when the blowgun darts struck him minutes later, in Khabal controlled territory, as he just finished crossing a dark street.

When he came to, he was trussed up and gagged expertly, tossed in a small, dusty room on a bed that did not smell very well. If he struggled, the wet cords and leather straps would only bind him tighter.

He relaxed and kept his breathing even.

The gag consisted of an equally nasty-tasting ball of rag stuffed in his mouth, with a strip of the same vile cloth tied tight between his lips and teeth behind the back of his neck, forcing him to breathe through his nose.

He worked the spit-soaked ball of rag around the tied part and expelled it finally, allowing him to breathe and think better. Most captors did not think to plug a captive's ears.

Next, he chewed through the gag, listening intensely all the while.

Subdued voices were discussing something in the next room over. Unfortunately, he could not hear enough of what they were saying, so he switched to using telepathy.

Bounty hunters.

The three men were opportunistic, Tharanorian bounty hunters: Skets the Darshian, Trilby the Jattarran, and the big leader, Mennesh the

Sylurrian. They always used blowguns at night to take their prey down alive. They were experts in that much at least.

The fast acting sleep and paralyzing poisons they used took their targets down and did not kill them. Five or six darts took even the largest opponent down fast.

Shaeddor could see from their petty, avaricious minds that there were many such groups at work now, what with the war on. These three competed with that breed, and they all infiltrated many areas.

They got paid either way. There were lots of bounties posted by all sides. Any Khabalists they caught got sold to the Sylurrians or the Urthers. Urthers were sold to the Sylurrians or the Khabalists, and so on—whoever paid the most. Scum such as these weren't above ransoming a captive to the highest bidder, and were more than happy to conduct running auctions.

This made them hated by all factions, and if a team of such bounty hunters became too successful, assassins and kill teams were sent to make them disappear. They might show up hanged in some dark alley by their necks or feet, dead, a warning to others who became too ambitious.

Yet all sides used them from time to time, so a certain level of their existence was tolerated.

Shaeddor made a point of not carrying any identifying papers of any kind on his person, in case he was found by anyone. Of course they had stripped him of the weapons they could find, but they had not been able to remove the Spectral Key from around his neck.

This pained Mennesh the leader, because he wanted those valuable onyxian jewels. But Skets had tried to pinch it first, and was nearly shocked to death, and came to an hour later.

None of them wanted to touch it now.

Trilby, in his infinite wisdom, was all for getting a big, heavy beheading axe and quickly chopping the captive's head clean off. Then it would be easy to take the necklace and simply clean it off.

Mennesh still wasn't so sure.

They didn't quite know what to do. To their knowledge, their captive was clearly a Sylurrian, but he might or might not be a Khabalist. He was definitely not a necromancer. Logic then dictated that they therefore sell him to the Urthers, but that lot always tried to lowball bounty hunters, especially unknowns who had no papers posted on them.

Shaeddor had a problem with their plans, because they all apparently ended in the three cutthroats murdering him at any rate, once they had their pay.

The bastards even planned on selling his long golden hair and fine clothing. Nothing would go to waste.

While waiting for the oafs to decide on a course of action, he cast a whirling blade spell, in its lesser form, directing some small, spinning blades of magical ice to slice through his bonds. He had to endure a few nicks and cuts, but that was well worth it.

The entity healed his small wounds almost instantly in any case, just as it neutralized the residual blowgun poison much faster than the thugs expected, estimating that he would be out for hours.

Now that he was free, he considered simply slaying the three fools outright for accosting and delaying him. But perhaps he could make good use of them.

First he made certain that the Spectral Entity formulated an antidote for their blowgun poison, and put it actively into his blood. Then he cast an air shield spell that should deflect the darts, and anything further up to a heavy crossbow bolt.

There were limits to such protective spells. This one would not save him from a heavy spear or lance strike, a ballista bolt, or other artillery.

Shaeddor turned immaterial and passed right through the wall and came at the men, wreathed in dark vapors swirling around him for an eerie effect.

The three startled cowards tumbled back out of their seats and over each other, trying to get away.

Yet two of them did manage to get off blowgun hits.

One needle went through him, and the other bounced off of his shield a split second later as Shaeddor reformed.

Gray blasts of painful energy transfixed the three. They froze in place or toppled over. The spell paralyzed them, but they were quite conscious, and could still hear everything he said.

"Let me make this clear," Shaeddor told them. "You work for me now. And if you ever attack me again, you die, plain and simple. Got it?"

In their minds, the three terrified men understood that fact very well.

While they all waited for the spell to wear off, Shaeddor busied himself with retrieving his belongings and unleashing more magic.

Why the devil didn't he think about this before? He should have done so at his other stops as well. He could have his own agents everywhere.

But now that the transport gates were up, he could always go back and fix things to his liking.

He could have his own spy network.

He explained the situation to his new servants. "You three are going to go about your business more or less as you normally do, without raising too much suspicion. But from now on, you three are my eyes and ears in this area. You can slip in and out of anywhere. You don't go after anyone or take anyone without my permission."

They all whimpered in their minds and wondered how they would get paid.

Shaeddor sighed and reached into his robes, dipping into his own secret reserves, provided to him by the Dark Khabal.

He tossed a heavy bag of gold coins into each of their frozen faces, one after the other. They mentally grunted in pain.

That should keep them all living well for a year or two.

"I have cast familis magic. A servant creature that I have bound to me will arrive shortly, and I will also bind it to the three of you. Care for the creature and feed it. If it perishes or you kill it, I will know of it, and I shall track you down and make you sorry for doing so. I will be able to hear and see all that I wish through the familis, and through any of you, while it is in contact with you. If I so choose, I can convey thoughts and directions to the familis, and through it to your minds."

And, being able to see where they are, he could also cast the teleportation magic through them at any time in order to join them. How convenient.

"I want you to stay in this area and be my agents. Stay abreast of what is going on in the cities and the various wars. Keep track of anyone or anything new that comes around. Keep a written journal, day by day, of what is happening. If you are lazy and do not attend to these things, or simply lie and make something up, again, I will know and you will regret your actions."

He gave them all a jolt of agonizing pain for a brief instant to stick his point home.

Excellent, a night raven familis flew in the open window and landed on the back of a chair the next moment. It hopped around with its quickness and cocked its cunning head to take in all. It was useful day or night, but its excellent night vision would be a great help.

Shaeddor bound the familis to the three men. "These are my terms. Do my will and otherwise, you are free to do yours. A most generous bargain I say. The ample gold should last you a year or two. If you lose or waste it all, do not come begging for more."

He gave them little choice really. It was either serve him or die. As if these murderous wretches had something better to do with their time.

Shaeddor had retrieved his other possessions from them by then. He transformed into mist and shadow and swept out the window.

A tribe of Keth-thon being visited by a tribe of Tan-Thon on the plains were about to have a visit from a certain night spirit. The wasteful fighting going on between all sides needed to stop.

Their real enemies were the Dark Khabal and the masses of undead.

Then Jen came to him in her ghost form, floating beside him in the dark veils of night.

He was glad to see her shade. "I have not seen you for a while my heart. I was starting to get worried. Have you been practicing to safely move in the shadows?"

She grinned "As safe as I can be. I have been experimenting and exploring, making good use of all of the information you gave me. I have briefly entered the Abyss, and even the first of the Nine Hells."

He gasped. "You risked going there? I expressly told you to avoid those places for the time being, until you are stronger. You disobeyed me!"

"I'm tired of obeying you! Tired of you protecting me. I wish to be of help to you, Shaeddor. I'm growing much stronger and more cunning every day. And I'm getting sick of merely hiding and slinking about, just because you tell me to!"

"That's…that's crazy, Jen. What are you trying to prove?"

Jen folded her arms in front of herself defiantly. "That I can be more useful, if you let me. I want to locate the souls of your lost parents where they are being held in torment and help you rescue them. I'm willing to accept the risks involved. And that is my decision, whether you like it or not!"

# TORI

The Pistolera became a big hit among the Thulls from day one on.

Most of the others, especially with David being ill, and the princes, the Thulls laughed at or ignored them.

But Tori managed to capture their madcap fancy. She, her colorful garb, and her talents and skills with her strange weapons were in high demand as entertainment, and a daily distraction from them all starving, even as the harvests were being made.

New fish stocks from the Inner Seas had helped somewhat, but not enough.

Therefore, that first week while David recovered, Tori put on daily shooting exhibitions for big crowds as if she were some kind of a Post-Merge Annie Oakley, using only her dry fire pistols which shot out blasts of harmless blue energy, when she made it so by concentration.

She dazzled her audiences; she and her teams thought up new tricks every day.

The Thulls in turn always felt the need to snatch her up from the ground like some pet and hug her until she could not breathe.

Then one day, a Thull who was too eager for a hug jumped in and caught a stray blast while she was finishing a routine. Just what she had feared all along.

Everyone gasped at first when the big Thull seized up and dropped, with a stupid look of amazement frozen on his goofy mug.

Tori waved at the crowd in the mid-sized arena, most likely for some old high school or college. "It's all right folks," she announced. "Those bolts of blue energy are not lethal in any way. He will wake up in an hour or so."

Some of the Thulls actually looked a little disappointed at that.

"I repeat, all of these blasts do is knock a person out for about an hour. This guy will wake up after that time and wonder what the heck happened to him!"

To her great surprise, several Thulls volunteered to get shot in the same way. Tori was flabbergasted.

"Apeshit crazy Thull nutballs!" She muttered.

"Do me!"

"No me!

"I want to get shot!"

"Back off, ass wiper. I was here first. Pistolera, please shoot me. Me!"

The way they came jumping out of the stands and running at her from all directions like bloated football linebackers, she might just have to gun some of them down, simply to avoid being trampled.

"Let's make a game out of it!" One whacked out Thull bastard shrieked with joy, like a little girl at a tea party.

"First one to touch the pistol girl wins this round!" a Thull woman shouted. "Yo, ho!"

"Yay! Let's go!"

"Hey everyone, we're playing 'Shoot the Thull!'"

The crowd began chanting. "Shoot the Thull. Shoot the Thull. Shoot the Thull!"

In no time at all, Tori was surrounded by a ring of stunned Thulls as she whirled and fire rapidly to hold off the growing crowd.

It was terrifying, like being in a cattle stampede heading straight at her from all directions.

More Thulls climbed over the top of their zapped comrades or blasted their way through at a dead run.

Tori had to work this carefully. If she didn't let someone touch her, the round would never end. If she let too many of them charge in at her, they'd trample and pulverize every bone in her body.

She spiraled around, letting them get closer and closer, gunning down some even as they sprang at her and she had to dodge.

In the end Tori basically let a teen Thull girl with long red braids sneak in behind some of the bigger adults. The Pistolera pretended not to see her coming.

Tori zapped everyone else and was about to turn and fire on the teen when the redheaded girl, who was only about six foot four, grabbed Tori by her slender waist and lifted her yelling and kicking into the air.

"I win!"

"Yo-ho!" Everyone cheered.

And so ended the first and last round of Shoot the Thull. Tori was exhausted anyway, and said that she would never play again unless the Thulls worked out some kind of actual rules for the game.

They all blinked and stared at her as if to say, 'Rules? What the heck do we need rules for?'

But some people actually did start to work on codifying the game in some way from that point on. They promised they'd get back to her.

Tori told them to do just that.

The Thulls collected their people from the field, carrying them off, or just left them there to wake up later. The show was over for that day.

Tori learned from David after his recovery that more converted or refurbished steamships were being made ready each day. The leaders of Detroit-Tornhold had agreed completely to allow one of the ships to take a new transport station to Toledo-Kellendra, along with a dirigible escort, sporting some of the latest defenses and weapons.

She was all for completing the last leg of their mission. If they could lift the siege and stabilize things in Toledo, she could then return to South Bend and spend the winter keeping warm with her sweetheart Mace.

She missed him something terrible as it was. But by now she knew that the Pistolero, her counterpart in so many ways, was actually helping defend Indy-Nenarra and the rail line established between there and Michiana.

Either way, she would go wherever he was as soon as she had the chance. Perhaps her missing family members were in Indy as well. If things calmed down that winter, she might have time to search and ask around for them.

Another surprise came when David announced that he had made further contact with the green dragon, Shavalkathar. The dragon who had aided them before in Elkhart.

Tori knew that dragons were a touchy subject with Thulls, except as a dinner option. Thulls had a deep-seated hatred of all things dragon. It was nearly a knee-jerk reaction that the only good dragon, was a dead dragon to the stubborn Thull mind. Yeesh!

David acted somewhat secretive , and that was strange. He spent a day or two confirming some kind of library research with the wizards, then he actually came to her and said his goodbyes.

"Goodbye?" she said. "You mean that you aren't going with us to lead your own troops in the battle for Toledo?"

"I'm sorry, Tori. Tell Dirk and Mace and everyone else that this is something I must do. Shavalkathar has personally asked for my help on...a private matter. He's already helped us so much; I couldn't say no. And with any luck, we might be able to locate Jerriel as well."

So that's what it was about. If he helped the dragon with whatever, the dragon was going to help him try to get Jerriel back. But it wasn't like David to run off like this on his own. Mason, certainly, but not David.

"What about your troops, David? This is all happening too fast. What about the battle for Toledo?"

"Tori, with winter starting up, even if you go to Toledo, odds are that there won't be much more fighting now until the spring comes. It's simply getting too late in the year for war making by anyone's standards. So go there, set up the transport stations, and help out where you can. Once you're done, go back and find Mace, wherever he is by that time, and be with him. I know that's what you both want. With any luck, Jerriel and I will join you sometime later this winter."

"David. Wait. This is crazy. You're rushing off without thinking. Jerriel would never forgive us if we let you go off on your own and something happened to you. Think about it. Take one of your healers at the very least. And how about this? Take one of the twins, like Trent. He's itching to go on some kind of adventure. Then if you find Jerriel, he can use his gating powers to bring you home right away. And if you get stuck where you need help, he can summon help right to you—even an army if you need it."

David just stared at her. "Tori, those are all excellent ideas. I was so wrapped up in what I was doing, I didn't even think about any of that. Let's get one of the healers to volunteer from the Blackhawks, and like you say, I'm sure Trent would want to go on an adventure. He and his sister are so grateful to us for saving them."

Therefore it was three persons who brought their specially designed dragon saddles and harnesses, along with their winter gear to the beach to wait for Shavalkathar's arrival on the fifth day. David, his healer Stacy Keller, and Trent Fillmore, the young transport mage.

It took several minutes to square it all with the green dragon, who wasn't that keen about one human on his back, let along three.

Not because of the weight, which was negligible to the dragon, but because of his pride. But finally David assured Shavalkathar that they now possessed the lore they required, and the dragon gave in.

The odd team of four said their farewells to all present, and launched into a low gray sky. They disappeared into the distance up north.

When Thulls came to her with the newly minted rules for Shoot the Thull, Tori begged off, saying that she had to plan battle strategy with the princes for their upcoming attack on Toledo.

Their ship steamed out of harbor the following morning.

Tori promised to look the rules over in their printed form and play a game first thing, the next time she was in town.

# MASON

Things settled down around Indy and the train line in November, especially with the coming of winter. As the first snows fell that second week, it looked like another harsh, midwestern winter.

He made one major observation.

The zombies pulled back and either buried themselves in the ground, in piles of leaves, in caves, or were simply covered up by snow on the ground. Some of them leaned or sat back against trees. Many of them even remained standing out in open fields and meadows.

But Zombies froze in the winter time.

That made them helpless.

The High Command ordered army units rotated along the railroad line for winter combat training. Supplies were brought up and train loads of firewood were distributed to help keep the bundled up troops warmer than they would be.

Each day that they were able, army units went out in at least company strength and destroyed frozen zombies wherever they could be located. They did so systematically, and when one sector was eradicated, they moved on to the next in the grid.

They were determined to face far fewer zombies in the spring.

And as a bonus, with that many troops at hand, the track teams were brought back in and would work as able to construct as much of the second southern line that winter as conditions allowed.

Many had questioned the work stoppage in the first place. This simply made good sense, as long as sufficient troops were going to be around to protect and assist the workers in any case. Military and railroad shanty towns sprang up all along the stops to provide food and shelter for the soldiers and workers.

Back in South Bend, Mason needed to hop back through the transport station to help charge a new load of shooting supplies with wild magic that was attuned to both him and Tori. What worked for one, worked for another.

They had learned how to make the process repeatable. The rectangular pool of Wild Magic in Elkhart was now contained in a newly erected greenhouse with steam magic heaters.

Extended lightning rods helped activate the Wild Magic when there was a thunderstorm, like the ones expected that morning and afternoon. The last warm winds came up and swept through suddenly from the south, clashing with the colder air.

When Mason arrived, there were winches set up to quickly draw the line of shooting supply wagons through the charged water. That way no one but Mason or Tori had to brave the Wild Magic, which for others was unpredictable and potentially deadly.

Yet despite that danger, three volunteers stood at hand with General Bill Avery, wearing cowboy gear, pistols in holsters, and even black powder rifles slung on their backs.

It was warm inside the greenhouse, so the trio took off their outer clothes, revealing bathing suits underneath.

They came prepared to get wet. Aides handed them all colorful snorkels and diving masks. Another such set was handed to Mason as he stripped down behind a screen and threw on some swim trunks.

Among the three new recruits to the program was a guy in his late forties, who still seemed in good shape. The next was a woman, in her early thirties, and the last was a kid about seventeen or eighteen.

Mason looked at their grim faces and figured it all out.

"These three are goin in?" he asked. "They understand what the risks are?"

As the storms swept in on the outside, the skies darkened and the first thunderbolt struck one of the lightning rods leading into the water.

The water began to glow as the thunder roared.

"They understand," Bill said. "They're willing to risk death to become like you and Tori and help our people. All of them fit the bill. They just started to show the beginnings of becoming sorcerers, so their powers are not focused or set."

"That doesn't mean they won't die, Bill. The transformation nearly killed Tori."

"But she lived. This is their choice, Mace. They're walking into that water of their own free will. We'll have lines on them if something goes wrong."

"By the time you pull them out, Bill, it could be too late. I'm just saying."

Another bolt hit.

"Time to get wet," General Bill announced.

Mason shook his head and turned to the three newbs. "Hope you folks have all said your prayers. Let's do this. But I still don't like it."

"No one's asking you to like it," the older galoot said.

The winches started pulling the wagons down into the water. The water was only five or six feet deep at the ends of the pool, and only seven feet deep in the center, like a wide 'U.'

Mason went in first.

The three others went in with him. They gasped as the glowing waters closed over their heads, despite the snorkels they all wore in order to help with breathing.

They were beyond Mason's help now. He secretly prayed that they'd be all right.

He checked on the supplies, a long train of powder, shot, primers, and lead for load making being pulled through the charged water down a short wooden ramp.

The Wild Magic pulsed and flowed through everything. Mason had made his peace with these strange energies long ago, and they never seemed to harm or affect him any further.

At times he did feel a bit re-charged and invigorated by immersing himself back into the glowing waters, but that was just him.

When he came up out of the waters with the second supply wagon, he already heard voices screaming.

Mason's heart sank as he tore off his snorkel mask and spluttered, wiping the water out of his eyes.

At a glance, the older guy was clearly dead.

They had pulled him out, but all that was left was a glowing, pulsing skeleton. All of his flesh had dissolved. Mason hoped it happened fast, and that the poor bastard didn't suffer.

It was a different story with the woman in her thirties.

Mason suddenly felt ashamed that he hadn't asked them their names, but there hadn't been time.

The woman kept screaming for someone to help her as parts of her body expanded with glowing energy and then burst, going flaccid like punctured balloons. First her legs, then her arms and abdomen, and finally her shoulders, upper torso, and her head.

Someone flung a blanket over her before her top parts burst.

It wasn't exactly messy. Once the glowing energy faded, there was no blood or gore–just flaps of skin. Not even any bones left behind.

The teenager stumbled up out of the water, choking and gasping. He looked a bit weak, but whole.

His team dried him off and doctors and healers checked him over, wheeling him away on a medical cart.

Mason went up to the general. "Bill, you're my brother and my friend, but damn it, don't you do this to me or Tori ever again. We won't be a part of this!"

"We need you and Tori, Mace. The truth is, we need a thousand just like you. But you're probably right. Your kind are too rare, and it's clearly too risky to try to make more of you."

"We won't be a part of letting these people kill themselves. I don't care if they are willing to risk it. We will not be part of their deaths!"

Bill nodded. "I understand. Don't worry, Mace. I'm the one who is going to have to explain it all to their families and friends after this disaster. Not you. So don't tell me I don't understand the costs."

The teen's name was Luke Baldridge. After he caught his breath and got back into his clean, dry clothes, the introductions were made.

Mason and General Avery brought Luke out to the shooting range nearby.

First he tried one of his dry pistols.

A thin red streak punched into the outer edge of the target in front of him.

Another shootist was born.

They agreed to call Luke: the Gunslinger, to tell him apart from the Pistolero, and Pistolera. He liked the code name.

Then he tried his loaded pistol, with the new magnetized, charged rounds.

A bolt of thin purple lightning shot out of the barrel, expanding and forking as it went forth.

It blew the target to bits.

Everyone cheered. Luke tried several different weapons and various loads, all except the annihilator rounds.

Mason noticed that Luke still needed to improve his marksmanship. He wasn't that accurate, but without working firearms, he could only learn so much.

They set him up to practice every day for so many hours, and with Mason when the Pistolero would be available. If Tori ever made it back, she could help Luke out as well. He'd be up on par with them in a matter of months.

Despite the terrible losses they had suffered, Mason did feel a little better, knowing that those sacrifices at least had not been in vain. If he and Tori were away on other missions, there would still be a shootist on hand to help defend Michiana.

He suddenly felt his heart ache. He missed his sweet Tori now more than ever. But she was already on a steamship, heading toward Toledo. Even if he wanted to join her, which he could not because of his own current duties and obligations, there wasn't a way to reach her.

Mason said farewell to Luke and told him to go celebrate. The young man's life was going to change drastically. As a Champion, he'd become an elite part of the army and have his own guards and runners, and people around him constantly. They'd become his new comrades—his new family.

Let the kid bask in the light of this new glory.

Mason found Rodell, and they wandered back to Bill's office, where they found Bill going over some progress reports from Rob Billings.

Mason and Bill were still in a grim mood, so the good general ordered dinner to be brought in for them all, and some stiff drinks.

Bill went by the book normally, but he kept mighty fine whiskey, scotch, and even mead and wine on hand.

A general never knew when he would need to entertain guests.

Rodell and Rob attempted to toast the rise of a new shootist. Mason and Bill waved them off. In the end, they agreed to toast young Luke's health, and wish the lad well. They did need his help something fierce.

"Mace, as you know, we call your kind Champions now. You and Tori, David and Jerriel, the Shooting Stars, Rabbi Bergman, the Fillmore twins…Luke. A Champion is anyone with special powers that we can use to help defend our peoples and our allies. Some wizards like Rodell are very close to being Champions. Rob, as our chief enchanter and magickal researcher, you are a Champion in your own right."

Rob waved his hands. "I don't care about any of that. I'm fascinated by this work, and I want to help out, in every way that I can. I can't wait until we can get access to those Tharanorian magic libraries in Detroit and Toledo. Jerriel just hinted at the secrets we can find there. New spells to learn and apply. Our mages will be able to specialize even further. We will have new weapons and artifacts to enchant."

Mason laughed. Rob looked as if he were about to drool or something.

They all felt bad about Jerriel being missing still and worried about Dave.

"Has there been any word on Jerriel?" Rodell asked.

Bill shook his head. "Nothing. She's probably in Vaejan, if she's still alive."

Rob looked down. "That would be an incredible loss to us. She's a magical genius."

Mason sighed. "Poor Dave. He must be going nuts. I know I would be." At least Tori had armies and brave comrades to protect her. What if poor Jerriel was alone in some dungeon somewhere, being tortured by the enemy?

"Getting back to Champions," Bill said. "We are discovering new ones all the time, but they still seem very rare. Elkhart has sixteen year old girl who fell into a glowing pool. Sound familiar? At first she could only form blobs of Wild Magic energy in her hands and fling them at things, causing them to freeze, burst into flames, or explode.

She has since refined the technique and can now hurl javelins and spears formed out of that same energy, even lightning in one form. She chose her own code name, and said she wants to be known as the Spearmaiden. We gave her a suit polished golden field plate made just for her, and we're in luck. She can throw her bolts with both hands."

"So, there are others?" Rob asked, sounding as curious as the rest of them now.

"Indeed. A young blind man from Indy in his mid-twenties did not step into a pool, but was out in the open and struck by lightning one day. Not only did his vision return in a unique way, but he can shoot what can only be described as laser beams out of his eyes that can cut through several inches of cold steel armor. His code name is Blaster.

"And that's not all. The Indy scientists and mages have made special lens-changing goggles, fitted into a protective helmet. It has lenses made of or coated with different light-diffracting gems and crystals that cause his beams to do different things: stun, cold, lightning. He can even produce fog and smoke screens in the air with his beams."

Bill stopped to take a breath. "We have a crossbowman in Detroit who can fire magic bolts similar to the arrows of the Shooting Stars. Codename: the Marksman. Then there are the Fillmore twins from lost Niles, natural transport mages with innate abilities to teleport themselves to each other, or to places they know or can envision in their minds. Each of them is one end of a natural transport gateway, which they can control at will."

The general picked up a new report from the other side that he had not read yet. "And listen to this, just as we were mentioning it. Captain Pritchard has joined up with the green dragon Shavalkathar to assist the dragon in some fashion. David is only taking a healer and one of the Fillmore twins with them, in case they end up in any trouble."

"Where are they going with the dragon in the winter time?" Mason asked.

"That is not known," Bill noted. "All the report says is that they will be going north up through Michigan and probably into Canada. There's also a mention that they hope to search for Jerriel at some point."

"It all sounds crazy," Mason said, "but I'll have to trust Dave. If he's doing it, it must be important."

Mason didn't say a word, but he was glad they hadn't had any further reports of Blondie working with the enemy. In fact, he seemed to have disappeared. At least the Pistolero wasn't being forced to deal with that unpleasant prospect.

The four of them ate, got a bit tipsy on great booze, and spoke long into the night about other various important prospects and developments for the expanding Alliance of the free cities.

Mason couldn't wait for the transport stations to be set up in Toledo and beyond.

Then he might get Tori to come back to him, or else he'd get permission to go help her and the others out.

# DAVID

Even as they flew north on the green dragon's neck and back, they spotted the handiwork of the enemy below them. It was a path of ruin, devastation, and death, clearly visible and trackable from the air. The dark trail, now being covered by snow, led all the way up toward the ruined Mackinac Bridge.

Shavalkathar used telepathy to speak to them while flying.

*A great enemy host has passed this way recently, destroying anything or anyone they found, but they were also in much haste. I would estimate a very large force, at least the size of one or two of your armies.*

Dragons were extremely intelligent in many ways, but they normally did not speak in terms of actual places or numbers. They could do math if forced to it, but who would wish to be the ones to attempt something so foolish as that?

They came to the coast of the Inner Seas-the Great Lakes. The ruined Mackinac Bridge was now little more than a monument to the Urther past, before the Merge. The enemy's passing ended at the water's edge, close to a port and a large marina.

All that was left was an assortment of damaged and ruined boats and vessels there, some of them partially dismantled and cannibalized for working parts.

"I'm guessing the enemy found enough boats to get their forces over to the other side," he said. "It's only several miles across. Not very far."

Shavalkathar was only too happy to be shed of them and their riding gear, which he still saw as a great concession on his part, and an even greater imposition on theirs.

"We shall pass over into the north after sunset," the dragon said. Until then, see to your own needs. I'm going hunting." He flew off.

Had the dragon seemed nervous?

It saddened David, and perhaps the others. At least he could remember all of the great vacation trips that his deceased parents had taken with the family up into the Upper Peninsula, or Shenedar.

Now, after the enemy had passed through, the place was more or less a ghost town. Any surviving humans had wisely fled the area, most likely finding a place somewhere else to winter.

Anyone with half a brain would know that if the enemy passed through that way, they would most likely come back on the return leg at some point.

David still wondered what they were after. Perhaps Jerriel had been right, and the Khabal had hunting armies like this out on both sides, looking for more of the scattered Spectral Keys and entities of either world.

Together with Stacy and Trent, they pitched their pop up tent in a hidden area that was not easily reached. After a quick meal over their camp stove, they nestled down into their tent and slept.

Sleep did not come easily while zooming along in the icy winds on a dragon's back. It could be quite bracing to say the least, putting all of their cold weather gear to the ultimate test.

They heard no sounds of foes moving around or left stationed on this side, but they did not like taking chances either. Normally, the enemy kept all of their forces with them and simply pushed on. David hoped such practices continued.

There was yet another major task coming up shortly for the small group.

David went over in his mind the lore he had read and copied over about dragon courtships and mating. They would be in the Upper Peninsula and then on into Canada proper very shortly, which was said to now contain a significant population of young dragons of mating age.

Dragons were extremely complex and dangerous creatures. And supposedly, each one was different in personality, temperament, and demeanor. The pressure to mate could ever lead them act very odd or strange it was said, even for dragons.

When he stopped to ponder the entire situation, it was rather funny, him being a wingman for a dragon who was now desperate to find a mate. So desperate that he was willing to let humans ride him, when such thoughts would have been impossible to entertain before.

But David was so tired at that moment that his thoughts merely carried him on into sleep.

Sunset was long gone and it was well into the night when Shavalkathar finally woke them up briefly to let them know he had finished feeding. The dragon smelled of the lakes but he seemed well-sated and in an excellent mood, almost giddy, if such could be said.

"Good news. The winds from the north are just ripe with the far off scents of unmated female dragonkind…of many types. I can't wait to pursue them. I'll be able to take my pick!"

They knew the dragon's pattern by now. After a quick nap of a few more hours, the great beast would relieve himself, hopefully somewhere down wind, and then they would be off.

Dragon turds were among some of the worst reeking odors in the universe, in David's opinion.

They would now depart closer to midnight of thereafter, but the three Urthers could use some more rest as well. They needed to sleep when and where they could. They were living on dragon time, which did not hold schedules of any kind. When Shavalkathar said they stopped, they stopped. When he said they went, they went.

They ended up flying off at two in the morning by the Urthers' mechanical watches.

By then the starry sky and air were incredibly crisp, and biting cold. There was what appeared to be halo of ice crystals in the sky around the moon.

Fresh inches of snow covered the land below, twisted and changed by the Merge, parts of Tharanor now blended with parts of Urth under the same mantle of white. Plus, there was the addition of the broken White Mountains to the north of the Upper Peninsula.

And that was exactly where the enemy seemed to be heading, at a steady pace. They were probably only a few days away from reaching their objective up in those mountains.

David told the green dragon, through their mental link, let's give the foe a wide berth. As much as I would like to know what they are doing, we're still only four of us, even if one is a dragon. That might even the odds somewhat, but there still what looks to be twenty to thirty thousand of them, from the size of their camp when viewed from up in the air.

*I quite agree. Our business is not with the Dark Khabal at this time. In the future, that might change. On to our business then. I have already caught the distant fragrance of three, unmated female dragons within a three hundred mile radius, David. We shall begin pursuing them tomorrow.*

Already? That was fast.

*My heart aches to be mated. I do not believe in wasting time.*

David looked northeast of them toward the White Mountains and then back at the enemy camp, wondering if they were doing the right thing. What if this group of foes had Jerriel with them, but then, why would they? It was crazy to think that.

He had given his word to his dragon friend and ally to pursue their current venture. He needed to see that mission through.

A little ego stroking would not hurt. His dragon friend could use some through their link.

Shavalkathar, you're a magnificent young dragon in the prime of life. I don't think we'll have much trouble finding a mate for you.

As it turned out, finding a mate for a dragon proved much harder than expected.

The very next day, they spotted a plump, bright red fire dragon only slightly smaller than Shavalkathar himself.

He immediately dipped down into the snowy forests so as not to be detected.

*What a beauty. She's absolutely magnificent! I can't wait to meet her. So tell me, what in blazes do I do to attract her attention?*

David studied his notes, while Stacy and Trent set up their human camp.

"Okay, it says here that the male dragon circles the female a few times, keeping his distance, showing off for her and demonstrating his great speed, stamina, and strength. Then he flies high above and parallel to her, spouting flame in another display of virility, which also lets her know that he is not trying to hunt or eat her as food."

*Yes, I think that not trying to kill and devour her would lend very much to a better romantic ambience. But what if she tries to make a meal of me?*

"If the female of the species is in a voracious hunting mood, the male flies off, and can try her another day when she is less famished, and perhaps more open to mating advances. Unmated female dragons are also usually stricken with an intense desire to mate, lay eggs, and produce offspring. Some loremasters said that such drives are even greater in females than in males and leads to radical mood swings and bizarre behaviors. Only deep hunger or starvation can get in the way of these strong drives for the dragons to mate."

Shavalkathar the Mighty actually licked his chops. *Did you see the sensuous tail on that little scarlet vixen? Oooh…how I could wrap myself around her and make love to her all day long until we both passed out!*

David had no idea what to say back to that.

Those were way too many visual's for David's imagination, and he was still struggling with a massive, lethal red dragon being described as, "a little vixen." Humping dragons passing out from strenuous sex was simply beyond the pale.

*So, when do I get to meet her? When can I introduce myself?*

"Don't get ahead of yourself, my vast and enormous friend. It says that the female of the species will remain aloof and ignore the male completely, pretending to not notice him. All the while, she is taking in information very closely, calculating for herself in her mind, what kind of mate the male dragon would make. Of course, much of her information will be based upon the male's display of virility, strength, and prowess. The other facts about him she will deduce from his traces of dragon scent on the winds."

*Enough! When do I announce myself to her and we launch our sinewy bodies into the sky to hump each others' scales for days upon end. Ahhh…I can't wait until our passions are sated and fulfilled!*

David put his notes down and frowned, still going back and forth with telepathy. Listen, big guy, before any passions even begin to get sated or filled, you'll spend an entire day hunting, finding her delicacies and laying them out for her to come and feast upon. Got me? Then you wait nearby, casually, for the female to land and begin her delicate feasting while she keeps an eye on you.

*Then, when she is weighed down by the meal I have so richly provided, I introduce myself, we talk as the passions between us build. Then, when neither of us can stand to wait a second longer, I pounce upon her and our necks twine together in lusty dragon love rubbing. Then I stare into her eyes and we rise up from the ground and at last I twist my tail around hers, draw our heaving bodies close, open my genital pouch, and insert my—*

David was forced to roll his eyes and fling the notebook in some bushes nearby. Look, do you want help with this or not? There's still no twining or twisting of dragon bodies. No…opening of pouches or inserting of anything, just yet.

As terrifying as all of that sounded.

There's no heated mating flights or dragon boogie-woogie, understand? Get me? He retrieved his notebooks. Now focus. Stay on task you lovesick fool!

The mighty Shavalkathar rubbed his paw sheepishly with the other. *My apologies, David. I don't know what came over me. I can smell her and it is driving me mad. I simply lost all control for a moment. I admit it.*

Keep it together, dragon. You are losing it. You are a majestic dragon, the ruler of the skies, not some twitter pated, thirteen-year-old human boy who just splooged himself because a cute girl bent over nearby.

*I have no idea what that means, but I will endeavor to control my erupting emotions and desires.*

Okay. No erupting anything until the deal is sealed. That much is clear. It says here, that the male knows when his advances to mate have been accepted, when the female bends her head around his, and they coo and caress each other with their necks.

*See, I told you their was neck twining.*

I stand corrected. You still need to bloody well wait until the female accepts you. If you pounce upon her, she might take it as an attack. Once she has demonstrated her acceptance, then the two of you will fly up and consummate your union high in the sky, parting at the last instant before you crash into the ground. Which of course could cause injury or death.

*That sounds sensible. Do we always have sex in the sky?*

No, not always, but the first joining is usually up in the air, unless there is some kind of danger to avoid.

*Okay, got it. What if another male happens along?*

Look, you didn't ask me to research that. I was in a hurry. I imagine you would need to attack him, drive him off, or attempt to kill him. He might do the same to you. I don't know for certain.

*At least that much sounds fun. Very well, wish me luck. I'm off to circle her and make my displays. Then I'll hunt all night for her if I have to. I haven't been able to catch any of those fresh water whales I've spotted yet. And there are mammoths and other gigantic creatures in the wilds of the north. Some of them will do. Oh my scarlet beauty! How I long for you!*

The big gooney bird swept away.

David and his two friends ate brunch as the day went on. played some cards, portable backgammon and chess. They talked and joked around for a long while, had a fine meal of freeze-dried foods and assorted snacks at dusk.

Then they went to bed once more to enjoy a good night's sleep.

Shavalkathar awoke David before dawn, and asked him to join him and keep watch at the feast sight to observe.

But first, David had to agree to coat himself in dragon urine to cover his scent.

When it became clear just how foul that was going to be, David balked, and said that he would only agree to soak his poncho in the nasty liquid, and only don that once it was dry.

The dragon said that would suffice.

Even that was putrid enough, once David put the damn thing over his head. He could barely stand the stench. The wretched odor would cover up anything else it was put up against.

David's eyes watered and he thought he might pass out at several points.

They had a new chemical weapon to use against the enemy. To hell with dragon fire; just have the big lizards drink their fill and then piss all over the enemy troops. They'd drop in their tracks and gag, or run screaming for the hills, tearing their armor and clothing off.

He only wondered if the military use of dragon pee was too inhumane to contemplate.

Yet the female red dragon did eventually come down and land at the feast site just after sunrise, as expected.

The green dragon used his telepathy to maintain a link with David so that he could listen in, and masked the human's mind from the other dragon, who might decide he was part of the menu.

As for the feast itself, Shavalkathar had certainly outdone himself as a hunter.

He proved that he could provide, and how.

All that was spread out for dragon breakfast astonished David. There was indeed some kind of species of Tharanorian whale, perhaps evolved for both fresh and salt water, as some sharks and dolphins were. It did not look like a baleen whale. More like a somewhat smaller relative of the sperm whale, with a larger, blunter, bulbous head and enormous eyes that now looked both dead and rather sad. The hide was dark blue with gray-blue stripes and wrinkles.

Next came a big hairy mammoth, slightly smaller than the whale in mass. A gigantic sloth of some kind was after that, three moose, and dozens of white tailed deer, slightly roasted and in a pile like appetizers or candy. And finally, several domesticated hogs, that looked to have escaped and gone back to being feral, getting by in the winter somehow.

Or at least up until death from above in the form of a green dragon ended their lives. Dragons loved pigs like confections, and ate them the same way humans relished fine pastries, decadent desserts, or candies.

The red female stared at Shavalkathar for a bit after she landed.

The green dragon smiled and looked away casually, saying nothing. Waiting patiently to see what she would do.

The red female turned to the feast before her and began gobbling, roasting whatever with her fire when it suited her.

In the end, it was all too much even for her. She ate one quarter of the whale, half of the mammoth, half of the sloth, two moose, half of the deer pile, and all of the hogs.

But once she was done, the scarlet dragoness showed absolutely no other interest and made to fly away, with great effort, but not so much as a word of thanks to her host.

Shavalkathar was stunned, and broke his composure. "Won't you at least speak with me a while?" he inquired.

She halted, laughed out loud, and then fell back on telepathy. *You know, I don't really care where you hot to blow young drakes come from, or why you do all of this stupid stuff. I don't need to know. But if you males want to keep bringing me food that I don't have to hunt for, then go right ahead. I'm sure not going to stop any of you. You aren't the first and I'm guessing you won't be the last. But thanks any way. Keep up the good work.*

*Lovely red dragon, I do not know your name, but I will gladly tell you mine.*

*Don't bother, greenie.*

*The other males and I are trying to court with you. We want you to choose one of us to mate with for life and raise a family.*

She laughed again, even harder. *You don't say? Is that what all this nonsense is about? Well look, greenie, don't you know that some dragons only mate with their own kind...their own color?*

*I understand that some few do so, but we are of such a variety of colors that that is not the normal rule among our kind.*

*Well, it is with me. So you can give it up, greenie. I'm waiting for another hot young red like me to come along. And I'm not saying you're not cute enough on your own. We can be friends. I wouldn't hunt or eat other dragons, unless I had to. I'm no cannibal. But as far as you and me mating—it would never work out in any case. Me a red, and you a green? Blazes, our kids would be browns for sure. Tell you what, greenie. Why don't you go check out that big blue hunk of love east of here? She'll gab your wings off. If you two manage to have dragonets, they might even be turquoise, or sea foam, or some such.*

Shavalkathar was almost at a complete loss for words. *Uh, thanks.*

*Don't mention it, greenie. And hey, thanks for the great chow, again. I'll be set for a couple of days still, with all of this. I gotta say, you're going to make some female very happy one day, with all of this impressive providing. It's a shame you're not red. Oh, well. So long.*

Shavalkathar was so humiliated he unceremoniously snatched up David and shot away from that place.

Their next encounter with the blue female to the east went rather differently.

Not much better—just plain weird.

As soon as the green dragon began his circling and showing off, the big blue female lumbered up into the sky and came straight at him. She was nearly half again as big as Shavalkathar, and that alone was scary.

*Hey, pretty greenboy!* she shouted telepathically. *Don't worry, I'm not trying to eat you, as if you aren't delicious. I just want to save you all that time and effort. Save all of that pent up energy for better things. I don't go for all of that old fashioned mating crap! What a load, you know?*

She soared right over the top of Shavalkathar and began to descend, more or less forcing him down toward a clear swath of snow field with her massive bulk.

He managed to come down near where David, Stacy, and Trent were.

*If you wanna talk, let's talk a while and get to know each other. I already think you're a real cutie. And if you and I decide to take the big tumble. My name's Zuvramathrodal, but lover drakes like you can just call me Zuvi.*

*You see, I have my own ideas about all of this mating stuff. You got me? I'm not like all of those other stupid dragon cows. And I'm sure not like that crazy ass red bitch to the west, am I right? You're green, so don't even bother with her, am I right? She's missing out on a totally massive amount of sexy dragon fun by limiting herself to one stupid color of male. Or to just one male, to my mind.*

Shavalkathar tried to get a word in edgewise, but to no effect.

Zuvi kept rambling right over the top of him. *Here's the really great part. Thunderbolts, I never really wanted hatchlings anyway. What a relief! All of that getting fat, and laying eggs, keeping them safe, then they hatch and its baby dragon mess everywhere, then teaching them not to eat the neighbors or get eaten by them, it's a flaming nightmare, that's what it is. Who wants all of the dung when we can just have the fun part, you know what I mean?"*

She grinned like only a dragon could and raised her eyebrows suggestively.

Shavalkathar could only stammer. *I…uh…I…*

The forward blue had him off guard and off balance.

Zuvi actually bent right over in front of him, hiked her massive dragon bootie in the air, and began twirling her tail around even more suggestively. *Come on, my pretty little greenboy. How about it? You wanna have sex, don't you? Let's have some hot, steamy, dragon love right now. What do you say to that? I'd be glad to lift my tail for you. And here's the best part! We hump each others' brains out for a few hours, days, or months, and then you can even move on. Just take off whenever you like. I don't care. It doesn't matter to me. It's not like I'm going to lay eggs for you or something.*

Shavalkathar was terrified by this time. He backed away and tripped over some trees, falling back into them.

David was pretty much stunned as well. Who knew that dragons could be so freaky?

Zuvi turn around and grabbed his long green and gold tail, putting it over her shoulder and hauling him back into the open.

*I can see…you're a little shy…that's okay. Look, we don't even have to hunt much. Let's eat first. I've been in this place for years. I know where the whales are, and we can scoop them up easy. And the tundra is just filled with herds of mastodon and mammoth. I love roasted mammoth! Then I can show you the tricks I can do. Of course, with me being a blue dragon, I can shoot lightning out of my maw instead of fire. But did you know, that with our digestive tract and our inner magic energy source which is innate to us, we can train ourselves to make it work both ways?*

Shavalkathar finally clawed his way free and shot up into the air, hovering over her. *Zuvi, I'm sorry, but this just isn't going to work out between us, I'm afraid.*

She gazed up at him, looking somewhat disappointed. *Why not? Oh, fireballs! And we were doing so well.*

*I'm quite sorry about that. I guess I'm...I'm...a lot more...traditional than you. I'm not the free spirit that you are.*

*Well, it's your loss, greendrake. If you wanna limit your experiences to all of that old fashioned crap, be my guest. I could have tied that tail of yours into knots and curled you horns for you. That's just how good I am in the dragon love pit.*

*I will take your word for that, Zuvi. I must be going now. Let us part friends at least.*

*Sure,* she said, with a ready smile. *Why not? You know where the good stuff is, if you want it. Just change you dumbass mind, greendrake. So long.*

Shavalkathar stopped long enough to pick up his human comrades and they went back south a ways for a breather. They were back near the western edge of the broken White Mountains.

Thus far, their efforts had not gone very well at all.

*My friends,* the dragon noted, *I don't know how much more of this I can take. Every one of these females is...so different. They all seem quite insane. Is this what I really want? Is this what dragon mating is really like? It's madness.*

David snorted. Dating. Who knew. It was just as crazy for dragons as it seemed to be for other sentient creatures, including humans. "Well, you've only made two attempts, my friend. Don't judge all females by those two. They did seem a bit...odd. You should have seen me trying to get a date back in junior high, I was pitiful.

*I don't know what any of that means, but I shall try to take comfort in your intent, at least.*

Without warning, over to the east of the White Mountains, massive green, white, and blue explosions of magickal energy erupted, visible for many miles around.

All of them were startled.

"What in the holy hell is happening over there?" David asked.

Shavalkathar looked out with his farseeing dragon sight. *The enemy armies make war upon something over that way,* he said. *Strange. The ley lines form a nexus in that place; I wonder why that has attracted them. What could they possibly be after in the dead of winter?*

David was already running for his saddle and his gear, shouting for the others to join him.

"Shavalkathar," he yelled back, "I'll explain along the way, but if this is what I think it is, we need to get over there as fast as we can."

There was even a slight chance—however slim—that it might be Jerriel and Khia, somehow.

# JERRIEL

When they reached the enemy camp, Khia flew off immediately with Luin, to take her to locate her people and try to raise the alarm that the Darkspawn had invaded the north once again.

Khia promised to return quickly.

Jerriel remained behind to spy upon the enemy and try to figure out what they were up to.

She still could not walk unclad yet, as Luin and Khia could at will, but she could use her arts to remain relatively invisible, and unseen, blending in with the shadows and the darkness.

Jerriel also called upon three of her seven enchanted tattoo guardians on her back, Mubo the winged mouse, Nakal the black wolf, and Osna the shadow owl. With her increased energies from bonding with Khia, she could now remain conscious and send forth her spies and protectors as needed.

Through their eyes and enchanted senses, she could see and detect much that she could not on her own.

She learned to detect the enchantments of the Dark Mages posted as spotters, who wore the glowing green goggles that allowed them to spot magical, ethereal, invisible, and other hidden things in the material spectrum. Only moving unclad defeated such devices.

But once she could detect the posted watchers, she could avoid and move around them to a large degree.

Residual magic was practically everywhere on hand, and the ley lines coming together under the mountain to form a nexus wasn't helping. But that would also help conceal her as well.

Still, there had been a major battle nearby involving magic, just within the last few days. Now the enemy seemed to be busy with some kind of construction or mining project. They were using earth mages and even blasting spells to excavate or work their way into, or *back* into the mountain.

Some kind of earthquake, massive landslide, or cave in had occurred around that part of the mountain at some point.

Off to the sides she saw war machines, shielded ballista like gigantic crossbows, that fired some kind of odd-shaped, metal tipped dart.

Several of the siege weapons looked ruined or partially melted. Those that could be repaired had crews swarming antlike over them. Others that were ruined were being used for parts.

There were nets made of metal links, as if to capture something very large and mechanical arms to advance the nets forward on wheels.

She saw pumper carts, not for spraying water, but liquid fire.

Then there were the wagons filled with golden hoops of various sizes that simply radiated strong magic on their own. Some of them were gigantic.

Then she spotted those same type of hoops around the necks of two huge, wingless firedrakes, posted as guardians on either sides of the excavation. And similar collars on mammoths being used with big iron carts to drag the rubble away. Both types of creatures had slack-jawed looks on their faces, even when their masters whipped them and jolted them with magic to urge them on.

The golden hoops were clearly some kind of magickal control collar, allowing the Khabal to manipulate these beasts against their will.

There was no limit to Khabal's evils.

Jerriel crept around quickly with her pets watching out for her. She quietly circled back to one of the wagons and stole a small golden collar for later study.

Then she heard a buzzing sound of a transport gate opening nearby. She went over in that direction to investigate, and saw a full platoon of grun goatmen march through, and then another platoon of reptilian slurgs. Next came a large horde of regular Darkspawn.

The enemy had designed some kind of portable transport gate of their own, based upon the enchanted copper pillars set in iron bases. They needed to be aligned and calibrated just so in order to be activated, but it looked as if they could be assembled within the space of a half hour.

The gateway that formed between the pillars was a flat sheet or screen of what appeared to be flickering, silver-gray particles suspended in the air.

Once the reinforcements came through, Khabal wounded and dead troops were taken back, getting them out of the way. Jerriel could not hear where they were being taken, whether to Vaejan, Kellendra, or some such.

Yet one thing was clear. This was a very important operation, and whatever it was that the enemy was after, they were determined to get it.

For many weeks, Jerriel had been merged with an Urth Spirit, a powerful Spectral Entity of great might and wisdom. And though she could not walk unclad, Jerriel had boosted her own powers, and otherwise learned many powerful Urth spells and spell-like abilities.

Jerriel called her tattoo servants back to her, and used an enhanced form of stonemeld to pass through the mountain itself, on a vector well away from the enemy camp. She phased through the stone, until she came to the large caves within, sections of which had not been collapsed yet.

The inhabitants of these caves who fought the enemy must have caused the cave ins, and retreated back further within in order to save themselves.

But in doing so, such a desperate act had now trapped them as well.

Now it was only a matter of time, mere hours or days, before the enemy cleared the way, and came at them once more.

Jerriel finally detected a faint light up ahead, and went forward to explore, uncertain of what she would find. Again, with the nexus present in the mountain, magickal energy was everywhere, washing out any attempt at detection or identification.

When she emerged on a low shelf overlooking a breathtaking, cavernous expanse, she saw where the light came from.

It was, in fact, not another Spectral Entity. It was an enormous white dragon—a young queen or a princess of dragons. For among dragons, female queens were always white, just as male kings were always black. None knew whence they came, and the odd thing was that they could be born at random from any mated pair of any combination of colors. This was said to be a random kind of fate among dragons, and there was no rhyme or reason or predicting of such rare births.

Yet only a mated dragon prince and princess could produce Celestial offspring, or spirit dragons: copper, silver, or golden dragons, who usually lived within the Celestial Planes of Light.

Yet alas, this white princess appeared dead already, slain by many violent and critical wounds all across her sleek body. What a battle she

271

must have put up, and then brought the cave in down in a last ditch attempt to save herself. Only to perish from her many injuries.

It was incredibly sad. The enemy had clearly been trying to weaken and then capture her. Jerriel remembered the golden control collars, some of them large enough to fit a dragon. Most dragonkind, like many people, would rather fight to the death than be turned into a witless slave against their will.

Jerriel used levitation to take herself down to the poor thing.

When she came to the great head of the dragon, both it and the neck lay twisted upside down, with the great red tongue flopped into the dirt like a stricken serpent in its own right. The eyes were closed from what Jerriel could tell.

Then a breeze stirred the dirt and dust.

Not a breeze. This air was hot.

The white dragon was near to death, but not yet dead. It still barely breathed. But where there was life, there was still hope.

Jerriel was a powerful wizard, an amazing enchantress, yet her healing skills were small and quite limited.

She summoned several light globes and anchored them to the nexus, illuminating the cavern better. She took off her small pack, rolled up her sleeves, and went to work.

Starting at the head, she tended to whatever wounds she could reach. The white dragon had endured many wounds and spells. On top of that, she bled from dozens of those barbed darts with the wings that allowed them to just penetrate the surface.

It took Jerriel all her strength to jerk just one of the weird darts out with both hands. She fell back and sat down hard. Then she smelled something sickeningly sweet.

The barbed darts had liquid in them—some kind of poison she guessed that the darts injected. Of course, the Khabal was trying to capture the dragon and use her as a weapon, just like the firedrakes.

Immediately she went around and pulled out all of of the injection darts.

Within minutes, the dragon started breathing better, stronger and more even.

Jerriel went back to dressing wounds as best she could, one by one. She cleaned them, put healing salve on them, and bound them. She used a large steel needle meant for sewing canvas sails, and a ball of thick cotton cord drenched in alcohol.

When each wound was closed and bound, she gave it a small dose of healing energy to advance the process further. She hoped the effect would be cumulative. But it would most likely be many days before this dragon could fight, let alone fly away.

Jerriel heard rumblings and put her ears to the stone.

The enemy excavating progress continued unabated. It was hard to know when they might break through and where.

Jerriel could only continue doing what she could. She stitched and bound the holes in the damaged wing that was exposed, lying limp. Neither wing appeared broken, but they had been battered, torn, punctured, and scraped up in the course of heavy fighting.

The dragon stirred a couple of times, but did not regain consciousness.

Jerriel was exhausted by then, and slept for an hour on her own. She started when she awoke, and went to check on the cave in. If only the white dragon would wake up and eat something to help regain her strength. But there was nothing to eat, and no way for the dragon to get out and hunt in her condition.

Yet around the edge of the cave in site, Jerriel found five enemy bodies that had penetrated that far: two Khabalists, and three mercenaries, all dead from dragon claws and some kind of lightning or flame.

Jerriel stripped the bodies to make them lighter, tied rope around their ankles, and dragged them back right under the dragon's nose. It was all disgusting, but she had to arouse the dragon somehow.

If food would not, nothing else would.

After another short rest, Jerriel took some food and water herself to keep up her own strength.

While she ate and drank, she suddenly noticed that the dragon clutched something in her claws, something the dragon had protected with her own body.

The white dragon had shifted slightly at some point without her noticing, perhaps while Jerriel had closed her eyes and passed out from being spent.

As it was, Jerriel had to worm her way into the darkness to see what the dragon was clutching and protecting.

If the dragon shifted and rolled back over, it could crush her like an egg.

The white dragon's exposed forearm was clearly riddled with numerous, broken off arrow and spear hafts. Jerriel sighed. She would need to remove and tend to those injuries as well.

The she gasped.

The dragon had been clearly protecting two smaller dragons, or dragonets, very young dragons—extremely rare celestial dragons.

As the white dragon breathed, even and strong, the dragonets slipped through her clawed hands where she had clutched and protected them.

Both of them were battered and injured as well, slick with their own glowing blood.

The first was a golden female dragon about the size of a small horse with wings, although one wing was clearly broken. From her size, the gold could be anywhere from ten to twenty years old–a toddler among dragonkind. The third and smallest was a silver male dragon about Jerriel's own size, a hatchling barely five to seven years of age. His wings were still too small to allow him to fly.

Clearly the white dragon had protected these younglings with her very life. But the dragonets had also been wounded during the fighting as well. Each had been shot with the barbed drug darts. Jerriel removed them immediately. The younglings had also endured spell damage, and they were also stuck with broken off arrows in their arms and legs.

Jerriel stumbled in her weariness, but she put ropes on the dragonets, and dragged them free of the stricken princess, just for the sake of safety. Then she bent to the task of dressing the dragonets' wounds. When she was done, and she stumbled away to rest once more, she noticed that something had changed. She had used up all of her medical kit and healing abilities.

The five bodies were also gone.

The dragon princess still slumbered, but with a toothy grin on her long dragon face, and a thin trail of smoke circled out from her graceful nostrils. For a dragon, Jerriel guessed that she was quite lovely.

But she still found a place away from them to sleep.

She did not want to become a dragon snack while she rested. Dragons were, after all, quite voracious and unpredictable.

Despite her efforts at concealment, the gold and the silver dragonets stared down at her when she woke up. They cocked their heads at her.

"Where did you come from, wizard?" the gold said.

"Were you the one who healed us?' the silver asked.

She smiled up at them, happy that they did not immediately see her as food. At least not yet. "From the south, and yes. I did what I could to heal both of you two, and the–"

"Our older sister?" the gold said. "I am called Glauriel. This is my baby brother, Talorian."

"I am not a baby!"

"Then stop acting like one, hatchling."

"Listen you two," Jerriel said. "I was hoping that we could wake up your…older sister, and that she might be strong enough to dig us out an escape route. The enemy is still outside of the cave in, and making their way inside. I don't see how else we are going to escape."

Jerriel did not mention that she could escape at any time, but that meant abandoning the trio to the enemy.

Glauriel frowned. "We were all badly injured during the last battle. Vajja did her best to protect us, but there were too many. After the Merge, the citadel of our parents on the border with the dimensions of light and dark was attacked, and only we three escaped. The other adults all stayed behind to fight, but we fear that they were bested, because the Shadowlords brought to bear two avatars of the Dark Ghods against our outpost there. We fear that our citadel was destroyed, and all slain, before any of the Guardians of Light could respond."

Talorian sobbed. "I don't like to think about that time, sister. Are you sure that all of our family and friends were killed? I still can't believe it."

"I'm sorry, little brother. But we need to face facts. No others have escaped and given any sign that they search for us, as we know they would, if they were able. The only ones who have come after us are these minions of the Shadow Ghods, trying to take us captive on this strange world."

The hatchling began to actually weep. "Just thinking about it all makes me sad, and angry."

"I am sorry for all of that," Jerriel told the two immature dragons, "but if we don't find a way out of here, we're all going to be dead, or worse. The enemy intends to capture all of us and force us to serve their will in some capacity. They have mind-control collars for every size of creature, even dragons. If they can't make us their slaves, they will kill us."

The white dragon suddenly reared up and shook herself, still weak but defiant. "I am Vajjanthokrix, the Fury. I will not allow such a thing to happen. They will not take us alive. I will destroy us all before I allow that to take place. Explain yourself, Sylurrian mage. How and why have you come to us? Why have you helped us?"

"Your foes, are my foes, princess" Jerriel said. "I am Jerriel Andelora Holleth of both Sylurria and Marrandor. The Dark Khabal slew my parents."

The white dragon's sapphire eyes burned suddenly as she bowed her head. "Then we have something in common, wizard Jerriel, princess of the House of Holleth. We thank you for your assistance, but alas, I am far too weak yet to dig our way out of the mountain. Can any of your magicks help us?"

"I have spent much of my own energies tending to the many wounds of you and the young ones. I don't know if I could even escape on my own at this time. Nor do I know how much longer we have before the foe bursts in on us once more. They seem very determined to capture you three. And why not? One dragon princess and two celestial dragons all at once for them to control? What a prize for the Dark Khabal."

The white dragon hung her head wearily. "Indeed. I did all that I could to get away from them, but still they tracked us down and trapped us in this place that I hoped would be safe."

Jerriel brought out her iron pliers, clacking them together. "I do not think anywhere in the two worlds is entirely safe from our foes at this time. Let me see your arm, you still have several smaller wounds, and I should check your other side for injuries also. I have seen how fast dragons can heal if they are tended to properly."

"You two need to talk and make plans." Glauriel took Talorian in tow. "We go to check on the enemy's progress," she said. "Talorian, stay close beside me."

"But I do not wish to go. Why can't we hear what they say?"

"You're coming with me, hatchling, and that is final. Someone needs to go, and we must stay useful."

She nearly had to drag him along with her.

At last Jerriel and the white dragon could talk openly. Both of them knew very well that their situation remained dire.

"Princess Jerriel, have you had the opportunity to heal many dragonkind?" the white dragon asked.

Jerriel shrugged and smiled. "Just one, but that is enough, Great Vajjanthokrix. I am not much of a healer, I'm afraid. And please, just call me Jerriel; I normally dispense with titles."

She began yanking broken arrows and spearheads out of the dragon's forearm with the set of iron tongs from her bag.

The white dragon winced as Jerriel continued plucking out weapon heads and casting them aside. "Then call me Vajja, just as my kin and friends do likewise, Jerriel. We shall face these foes together. But after the beating we endured, I must also admit, I do not feel so great or mighty, and our foes seem powerful and endless."

"They are not endless, Vajja, but we are only four, and they are indeed many, and powerful. The stronger we can make you, the better off we shall be."

Vajja staggered, leaning over to the other side, and bowing her head. "In truth, I can barely stand, I am so weak. They kept shooting me with those darts that made me feel either poisoned or drugged. I grew so sleepy, and it takes quite a lot to bring a dragon down that way."

Vajja's wounds did not bleed much, whether that was a good sign or not.

Jerriel switched around to Vajja's other side and was forced to remove several more broken off darts and weapon heads from the dragon's flesh. Then Jerriel brought out her big needle and cord again.

"I'm sorry. I can seal up some of these wounds with stitches, but I'm out of healing salve and bandages. And my poor healing energies are already taxed beyond my limits."

Vajja stretched out on her mended side, clearly trying to conserve her strength. "We appreciate you giving us what help you have, Jerriel. We would probably still be unconscious if not for you. But I still fear greatly, that once the enemy breaks through, we will not be able to endure their onset for very long."

"What about bringing down more of these caverns to hold them off?"

Vajja snorted in the dust. "That would not buy us much more time, even if I had the strength to do so, but I suppose we could attempt that as a last resort. Yet we will only make things tighter in here and perhaps cut off our air. That is yet another concern. Until I regain my strength more, we will not be able to tunnel out."

Khia suddenly appeared right beside Jerriel. "Greetings, all. Perhaps I might be of assistance?"

Jerriel felt so surprised and relieved, she shrieked with joy and hugged her spirit friend. "Khia! How did you find us, sister?"

Khia grinned. "I told you I would. With you wearing the keys, and the two of us merged together as one, I could come to you anywhere on either of our two worlds, Tharanor or Urth. And remember, I see and know what your mind sees and knows."

"How is this possible?" Vajja exclaimed. "You are merged with one of this planet's Spectral Entities? You are full of surprises, wizard Jerriel."

Khia grinned and filled herself with Urth Power from the nearby nexus, enveloping herself in the green glowing lifeforce of the world.

"Hold still, Vajjanthokrix; you are a living creature of our world. Feel the might of the Great Mother as her will flows through me, and begins to heal your many hurts. First I shall purge the enemy's poison from your veins, and then begin to renew your energies!"

Vajja lifted her head and gasped. "It will take many hours to heal me. We still do not have enough time to escape."

Khia had just begun to heal Vajja, when the younger dragons rushed back in a panic. Jerriel could tell something was very wrong.

"The enemy!" Glauriel shouted, nearly breathless.

"They've broken through!" Talorian yelled, shaking with fear. "They're coming for us. Are we going to die?"

"We remain fairly trapped in here," Vajja exclaimed.

Khia broke off her healing for the moment and actually laughed. "I am part of our Great Mother, and her mighty songs sing through me. I am one with the Urth and all things that live. I can pass through rock, Urth, and stone as if they were air, and leave no trace of our passing to confound our enemies. Behold, go forth by my hand!"

The cavern seemed to race past them at great speed, and for an instant all that they could see was the entity's flashing green energy.

In that flash, they emerged out onto the other side of the mountain, down into a snowy vale nearby with few trees for a space.

The two young dragons were still weak as well. Khia sensed that and took a moment to heal them, and also to refresh Jerriel's waning energies. They would all need to fight for their lives.

Then she went back to trying to heal Vajja, a much greater task.

"Look!" Glauriel cried out, rising up on her wings, a dozen feet off the ground.

The enemy was still camped about the mountain in a wide arc. They spotted the white dragon, and Khia in her growing Urthpower form, and immediately moved forces to attack them.

Arrows and drug darts fell short, but they would come closer.

Jerriel went out before her friends and held her ground, staff at the ready. Each second that Khia could heal and regenerate Vajja, the more likely it would be that they could make good their escape. Once the white dragon regained enough of her strength, they could fly away.

Jerriel cast shields of air over Khia and the younglings. Vajja was simply too big to protect her completely.

Then Jerriel took advantage of their conditions and began using ice blasts and magickal ice attacks. Ice waves held off the lesser foes.

But the necromancers with their burning skull staffs advanced with wedges and formations of dark mages behind them.

Then for some reason, the enemy halted.

The big wingless firedrakes flanked the enemy on either side of the draw, up on the ridge lines, poised to race down and attack with flame, teeth, claws, and armored tail spikes.

"There isn't enough time," Khia herself admitted, as she kept going. "Your injuries are still many and grave. I need more time that we do not have, and you still cannot fly."

Vajja glanced up at the armies of foes waiting to sweep over them. Then she turned back to her comrades without hesitation. "Go, all of you can get away. I shall give them what fight I can."

"No!" Talorian screamed. "We lost mother and father. We lost everyone else. I will not lose you as well, sister!"

"We will die with you," Glauriel said. "If that is what must be. We shall not leave you!"

"They will not slay you," Jerriel said. "Look at those firedrakes, the mastodons. The Khabal shall beat you down, make you their slaves with those magickal control collars, and use you as weapons to kill many others, perhaps even more of your own kind."

Jerriel renewed her defenses, as more missiles deflected and bounced off of her ice and air shields.

Then she sensed something. Khia felt it as well.

Khia glanced back up at their foes, especially the Dark Mages. "It cannot be, the fools! They draw the power from the nexus of the living world, only to defile and corrupt it. They seek to summon something greater than all of us, to serve as their champion in this battle and beyond, to crush their foes beneath its accursed feet!

An earthquake rattled and shook the mountains themselves and the earth itself split open, forming an open wound in the planet. Jerriel could partially sense what it was that Khia feared.

The enemy had two transport gates set up. They intentionally overloaded one of them, drew energy from the nexus, and tore open a gateway to one of domains of darkness itself. The Third Hell of the Nine now yawned open and exposed.

Something massive grasped the gateway to either side and wrenched it open still further, in order to lurch and clamber out, and rise up to tower against the cold night stars and blot them out.

It was vaguely humanoid, but like a gigantic, twisted scarecrow or other lanky form, sixty feet high. It's overlong legs and arms ended thicker than they began, in powerful clawed hands and taloned feet.

Upon the great abomination's thick neck, was a single lidless, roving black eye that pulsed and steamed with unlight, and darkest Hellfire itself.

A thick beam punched out from that eye and blasted off the next mountain top across the way, causing avalanche and great ruin that way, cutting off any retreat on foot to the rear.

"A Balor, an abomination," Khia muttered, "an infernal gargantuan of the Evil Eye, a champion of the Third Circle of Hell. What a great and terrible power have they summoned against us."

They watched in horror as lesser hellspawn poured out around it from the hell-breach, like a dark spreading blight. A horde of lesser evil eye creatures, bi-pedal, long hunching arms with claws that dragged upon the ground.

They also had one large eye set in their faces, from which lesser beams of hellish energy shot forth, doing damage to all before them.

Soon the entire vale on that side was being reduced to ash.

The Khabalists stayed well behind the hellspawn.

Jerriel trembled with fear. "How can we face such a thing, and such a host of foes as these?"

Vajja bowed her head and sighed. "We cannot. Now, the time has come. You four must flee in the face of such hellish might. Go, leave me to my death. I will not let them capture me alive and use me against you. Do not fear."

"No!" Khia shouted. "We still have our world and this nexus to defend. We are not powerless. These foes, however great, must be opposed, and the songs of the Creator still burn with bright flame in our Mother's heart!"

Before their eyes, she swelled with glowing green Urthpower and rocketed fifty feet in the sky, her feet astride the ground. Khia sang aloud, a tempest of energy whirled around her. She brought her fists together and blasted the Balor, even as it bent its gaze upon her and its great eye glowed with the fires of unlight.

Khia struck first, and she struck hard and true.

The verdant blast slammed into the gargantuan full in the chest and knocked the Hellthing back, shrieking in a thundering fell voice that caused many present to cover their splitting ears in agony at the vile sound.

The Balor toppled back in a great tumult, rolling end over and away from the hellish gateway, as the enemy cried out in despair.

The necromancers gave the order for their other forces to commence an all out, immediate attack.

# SHAEDDOR

A fierce war was already being waged between the western coastal Urth cities of Bellaeron-San Francisco, and Xancekthal-Los Angeles.

The latter was an ocean of undead from the fallen populations who perished directly after the Merge. Half of the Dark Khabal's Zombie Lords and Masters, and undead Ghool Lords and Masters were in Xancekthal directing and controlling the vast armies of undead at their command.

And with the powers of the undead masters at hand, bending their dark will, anyone among the defenders who perished, rose up in seconds, possessed by fell spirits who merely waited for a host body, and began to fight for the Shadows.

Shaeddor had heard rumors that there were even more undead in that place than around Naugredoth, or New York, on the Urther east coast.

Only the former Urther nations of China and India boasted much larger swaths of undead in those grim realms, as the lost became the armies of Darkness serving the Dark Ghods of the Nine Hells. They were bent upon transforming both Tharanor and Urth into Shadow Worlds.

Yet the light always rallied against the tainted darkness, and rose up to shine bright and fierce once more, faced with little choice but survival or death.

Two worlds fought to survive, even though all of the momentum was still with the Shadow Mages.

The Allied forces of Tharanorian colonists and Urth survivors still had large populations, and enormous armies to defend themselves with. And they did so, with cunning and courage, protecting their vast fields of crops desperately, since that was all that was keeping them alive.

Thus the defenders held firm. They had also managed to ally themselves with various factions in the colonial wild lands: centaurs, kavoks, shagga, lo-shang, the mystarian unicorns, korro, and durthor.

It was a hodge-podge of peoples and species out west, trying to save their world from descending into the Shadows.

Shaeddor set his construction crew to work, as always, and then went to be received by another of the Six Dark Champions.

Kuregoth the Slug always appeared indolent and lazy, a great corpulent sack of a woman, with rolls of flab spilling out all over her enormous girth, dressed in the latest slinky Sylurrian fashions from the continent. They made her all the more loathsome and obscene.

Shaeddor felt a deep revulsion as they were introduced, and he bent to kiss her balloon-like fingers at the end of her bloated forearm. And despite being bathed in perfume, the fat murderous hag stunk like a cargo net full of mashed up dead, rotting skunks.

"Great Lady Kuregoth; greetings. I am the Prince of the House of Holleth, sent to you by our great master, the High Magus. I have come here, according to his word and my will, to install the transport gate that will link all of our cities and forces and help bring us victory over the two worlds. I am humbled by your presence."

She chortled from among the nest of her many chin and cheek rolls, "As well you should be. Yet they did not tell me that the notorious Black Prince was such a pretty boy. I love pretty boys who love to give me pleasure and make be quiver with delight."

The fact that she was nearly naked and her suggestive words and stench made him feel as if he might vomit right then and there.

Shaeddor choked back his own sick. Thank goodness he had not eaten much.

"Ahhh…" she said. "But I can see from your eyes that you are a creature of the deep mind, just as I am. They said you were a crafty plotter. We shall share our thoughts on many things, later."

She was carried everywhere by an increasing number of burly slaves wearing the new golden control collars, which seemed to be working quite nicely.

He was forced to listen as Kuregoth droned on, usually about herself.

She bragged about how much she currently weighed, nearly eight hundred pounds by now. She kept healers on hand to keep her healthy, keep her turned properly, and treat any bed sores, skin infections, boils, or lesions. She boasted of the carriages she broke, and the new, stronger custom palanquins and sedans she had to have built.

Yet Shaeddor knew from discussions with his master, the High Magus, that Kuregoth was by far the Khabal's most brilliant strategist. She was constantly thinking up plots and tactics to inflict upon their foes. She was an exceptional long range thinker.

It was said that the mastermind focused on staying many steps ahead of the Khabal's opponents all over both worlds.

And one of the best defenses of all was secrecy.

She and Gorrial were also the only ones in direct contact with the Dark Ghods concerning their super secret plot to somehow attack and destroy the Celestial Guardians of Light. If such an impossible thing could be accomplished, the universe as they knew it would become all but defenseless, and the untold legions of the Shadow Worlds and the Nine Hells could break out in earnest, and attack and lay waste to countless new worlds that had long been considered safe.

Shaeddor knew from hints that his master had let slip that Kuregoth was close to unleashing one of the very first, preliminary stages of that plan. The results of which, would possibly even destroy much of the western coast of Urth, including the cities of Bellaeron, and Xancekthal. Yet even that would be a small price to pay if ultimate victory could be theirs in the end.

What were the lives of so many millions? The Khabal had risked destroying both worlds outright at the Merge, from the very beginning. What did they care if any lived or died?

After dinner that night, Kuregoth and Shaeddor were hoisted extremely high up onto the precipice of one of the Urth Skyscrapers, that looked out across the western ocean and it's coastlands for many miles before sunset.

Kuregoth cackled and boasted, "I am departing tonight for a place of safety from which to view the disaster that we shall soon inflict along these shores. You have the Spectral Entity of Night to protect you sweet boy. Gorrial and I want you to stay here and observe from the safety of the air, and report back to us what you see take place. It should be quite a show. But there is always the chance of... Celestial interference."

He bowed. "I shall do so, but can you even give me a hint as to what I should expect? What should I be looking for? What is going to take place?"

Kuregoth laughed. "You are about to witness one of most ambitious plans, one that we have been concocting for years. The Dark Ghods have blessed us with their destroying powers. Ever since the Merge, for months we have been using power orbs to pump highly volatile and explosive Hellfire into the major fault line areas of this entire western coastal region on Urth, on this one side.

"Thus far, our mighty ghods have kept these volatile pockets stable, isolated, and contained, but only until tomorrow night. At the Dark Hour, those protections shall be removed all at once, and those pockets of volatile Hellfire shall be detonated, all at one time. Over seventy such pockets, all told. These already deeply fractured lands shall break asunder and collapse. Massive waves of chaos and destruction shall be unleashed on land and sea.

"As a result, the entire coastline shall be devastated, and trigger tidal waves that will further inundate the costal cities, causing greater death and destruction on a near continental scale.

"Truly inspired," Shaeddor said, in mock awe.

Would there even be a way for him to warn the defenders, and get them to try to evacuate their cities, without exposing himself? Surely there was nothing that he could do to prevent such a grand plot from taking place in one mere day.

The scale was simply too large for any one person to deal with.

Kuregoth chortled, "Gorrial even said that there was a small chance that the entire west coast might break off, and slip into the great ocean, taking untold millions with it. We can only hope for that. Of course, all of our important persons will be evacuated by tomorrow. Our common troops, allies, and slaves will be considered a small price to pay for such a mighty victory. I envy you being able to watch it first hand, sweet boy."

What could he possibly do within twenty-four hours? His hands were all but tied. The Khabal was on the brink of another major, world changing victory.

And there was nothing he could do to prevent it.

"I must be going, sweet boy. See my leftenant, Marrid Laighul, for the details of the best vantage point to watch the fun.

"He and his air mages will also be overseeing the disaster, in their aerovelocitors, at the direction of the Dark Ones. Then they can help direct the invading hordes."

Shaeddor shook his head. "I don't understand. What invading hordes?"

The Slug grinned rapaciously, from ear to ear, and her jowls shook with glee. "Didn't I tell you? As an added bonus, the Dark Ghods will be channeling the massive energy spikes from the explosions to open *permanent* gateways between Urth, to the Nine Hells. Their dark armies shall march forth, from each of the Hells and the Shadow Worlds. They shall triumph amid the chaos and despair. Our time is at hand, and both of these Merged worlds shall at last fall to the Darkness!"

Shaeddor did not like this Marrid Laighul in the least. They were old adversaries, from many years back, before Marrid made the move to become a necromancer, and eventually one of the Sixty Dark Lords of the Dark Khabal.

Back then, there was one prime opportunity open for one mage to become the top apprentice of the High Mage of Sylurria. Shaeddor and Marrid squared off in a mage duel to decide who that lucky mage would be.

In the end, Marrid defeated Shaeddor. Then Shaeddor revealed that Marrid had his younger brother, Eridus, concealed beneath the arena, feeding him extra magickal power and helping deflect Shaeddor's attacks.

Marrid and his brother were dismissed in disgrace, and Shaeddor took the coveted position for his own.

Now word had it that poor little brother Eridus became Marrid's Great Sacrifice in order to become a necromancer. The person Marrid supposedly cared about more than anyone else.

But Shaeddor guessed the real secret.

Assknobs like Marrid never loved anything but power, and only power for themselves. Now he was leading the disaster observation team. There was some worry that the Celestials or the Guardians of Light might attempt to interfere.

Shaeddor went out in secret that night. His team would go on to Allestan-Phoenix for him, once their work was done.

He did his best to try to convince the defenders in that area that a major earthquake-supernatural disaster event was going to take place the next day. Not only that, but it would also open up numerous gateways to the Nine Hells and the Shadow Worlds that would pour out even more enemy armies to deal with.

Most Urthers and Tharanorians dismissed, distrusted him, or simply laughed him off.

Some went out afterwards on their own to actually check along some of the fault lines. They ran afoul of undead armies protecting each of the seventy locations.

Fools. By the time they confirmed anything, it would all be too late.

They were all out of time.

Then he noticed one good thing. At least people were starting to move away from the coasts to higher ground, as a precaution against a predicted earthquake-induced tidal wave. The Urthers had a strange word for tidal waves that Shaeddor couldn't recall, try as he might, not being an Urther.

At least those people wouldn't be among the first to die.

Shaeddor reluctantly reported to necromancer Marrid who led the observation teams, three hours before dawn.

Marrid grinned and even offered him his hand. Shaeddor found a clever way to dodge taking it.

"So, this is where we get to watch the beginning of the end for the Urthers," Shaeddor said.

The first great explosion began, timed along with all of the others, within the space of an instant. And Urth itself groaned and split asunder.

Shaeddor instinctively covered himself in a shield of darkness, as an attack from Marrid and the other observers struck him. "Have you gone mad again?" he called out.

"Betrayer! I followed you last night. Why would a faithful Khabalist spend hours trying to warn our enemies?"

"Simple. I knew they wouldn't believe me. But I wanted to cause panic and see them all scurry like so many little bugs about to be mashed. Think about it. Even with a warning, there is no time to escape. Now we can listen to them all scream and perish."

"Liar! This is more of your sickness, Holleth. You delight in playing everyone against everyone else. No one ever knows what side you are on. You enjoy it that way. You do it on purpose. I know you, you sick bastard!"

Shaeddor shrugged, as they circled each other up in th air. "Easy enough to figure out. Like yourself, I'm always on my side. And I was not born out of wedlock, by the way. What is your parentage?"

The Khabal aerovelocitors circled around Shaeddor in the sky like swarming vultures.

"Do shut up, Holleth! After I expose you to our masters, it won't matter. You'll already be dead, by my hand!"

"You've miscalculated once more, Marrid. I wield the might of the Spectral Entity."

Several powerful negation rays struck him all at once from the other Dark Mages.

Shaeddor plummeted down through the dark sky, the Spectral Key no longer responding to his will.

Marrid dove down out of the air beside him, gloating and shouting, "You don't think I planned for all of this? All of your magicks will be out for a few minutes, asshole. Just long enough for you to go splat, Holleth. You die. I win!"

He extended his wings and shot back skyward.

Shaeddor allowed himself to drop out of sight into the darkness, trying to slow his descent.

Then he summoned his own private aerovelocitor suit.

He knew that it would come in handy one day. And its shielded magicks were not negated, nor were his own innate abilities.

Negation spells could never take those away from him.

But Marrid and his goons did spot him soar up as he recovered, and dove down to attack, six against one.

Shaeddor led them right into the explosions blasting out from the shattering earth.

He took out half of them in one gigantic flare of Hellfire.

Marrid and the other two closed in for the kill.

Then the sky went blinding white, and the late morning firmament was filled with a radiant shower of falling stars.

These glowing objects penetrated the exposed, blazing fault lines even as the fissures fractured, split open, and somehow warred with the Hellfire energies deep within, effectively cancelling most of them out.

Some supernatural power was actually working against the Khabal for once, snuffing out its powers. Even Shaeddor was amazed.

Two aerovelocitors crashed into him from separate directions, nearly winding him.

Shaeddor and the pair tumbled out of the sky once more, heading down into the blazing crevasse. He cast a lightning spike spell and impaled the attackers, wounding them both.

Yet Marrid followed them down, nailing them all with spells with vicious indifference.

Marrid would gladly slay all three of them in order to take Shaeddor down.

Shaeddor, in turn, had no compunction about using the two wounded foes as his own human shields to absorb Marrid's spells.

Then as quick as they arrived, the bright falling stars shot back up out of the blazing, exploding fault lines. Their work effectively neutralizing the exploding Hellfire was all but finished.

Shaeddor spotted an open gateway to one of the Nine Hells directly beneath them, right as it exploded and caught them all up in a massive explosion from the conflicting positive and negative energies at war with each other.

He rocketed up on the updraft, pulling free of the two shrieking foes as they were incinerated. Only the Spectral Key protections kicking back in saved him from a similar fate, at least right away.

Marrid dove straight down at him in hatred, wreathed in flames, a blazing red skull staff firing disintegration spells at him.

Shaeddor deflected four such attacks.

He no longer had the strength to survive another.

A blinding, dazzling humanoid form crashed into them both. They all three fought and tumbled together. Actual powerful wings smashed into Shaeddor, nearly knocking him out. They battered him that hard, like hammers pounding on him.

Even in his dazed state, the next thing he saw was Marrid's face, teeth clenched, a mask of hate, as he drew back and brought his burning skull staff back with both hands.

"I will slay you, Holleth. No matter what else happens!" When Marrid brought the staff down toward Shaeddor's face, the glowing wings enveloped the latter.

Right as shining white hands shot out to intercept the necromancer's burning skull staff.

The resulting detonation sent them all streaking to the earth in smoking ruin and flames.

Shaeddor struggled to call upon the Spectral Entity's powers to shield both himself and the entity of light that had saved him. They cratered into the ground.

When he came to, Marrid was splattered in broken, bloody pieces like some kind of nasty, sticky puzzle. Shaeddor himself had two crushed legs, internal damage, and a concussion. The celestial being they had crashed into crawled upon her battered hands and knees, her hands and forearms scorched and blackened up to her elbows.

She actually had two pairs of feathered wings, some of them damaged and scorched in places. She moaned and reached up desperately at the other fallen stars, as they shot back up into the sky, receding through a ring of light that closed about them.

"No, no!" she wailed. "Now I am world bound, damaged and trapped–cut off from the Realms of Light!"

She curled up beneath her wings and wept, shuddering in terror and obvious pain.

The ground trembled, and the aftershocks of the earth splitting open rumbled and thundered. Lava and geysers of destructive energies ripped skyward and fell ruinous for miles all about them.

The Spectral Entity healed him enough so that he could move, yet not without intense distress.

"Whoever, whatever you are," Shaeddor said, clenching his teeth. "We must get away before we are destroyed!"

The Celestial creature toppled over, completely spent; her radiance had even winked out. He tried to drag her away.

"Bloody hell!" Shaeddor shouted in pain, close to blacking out himself.

# TORI

The waters of the Great Lakes in the later parts of fall were much rougher than Tori ever expected. The steam freighter eventually made it to Toledo with their airship escort intact, but it took much longer than anyone thought it would, fighting the rough seas and winds.

Even some of the brave Thulls and other troops learned firsthand what seasickness was, as the rolling ship was tossed about.

But at last they made it to port safely, in a snow storm, and were received with great cheer by the Urth and Tharanor defenders of Kellendra-Toledo.

The first order of business was to set up the transport station right away, and bring much needed relief to the besieged city. Vital supplies and medical assistance poured in. Wounded who could be moved were spread out across the known, Allied cities where care could be spread out under less stressful conditions.

The returning princes were a huge boost to the morale of the Marrandorians, and they immediately went to their family, to check on the health of their wounded parents. Tori had never specifically heard how the king and queen had both been wounded, in the early days of the invasion, and why they had not fully recovered by now.

The coming winter weather had frozen the battle lines. And there were tens of thousands if not more undead frozen like statues out in the cold air.

Immediately, the new arrivals took counsel with the defenders of Kellendra and began to go over all of the intelligence they had.

Tori finally learned what had happened to the king and queen.

A female assassin—at least they thought the creature had been female, because as it turned out, she was a shapeshifter of some kind—had disguised herself to look exactly like the queen.

So adept was her performance that she fooled even their closest friends and servants, and managed to get close to the king in private and alone.

The killer stabbed the king thrice with a poisoned blade as they struggled together. Only the real queen coming in saved him from certain death.

The real queen raised the alarm and attacked the assassin, wrestling the knife from her, but was also cut by it in the process.

When the guards rushed in, the killer smiled and vanished in a bright flash and a large cloud of dense smoke. They searched the entire royal palace, but the killer clearly being an expert mage, made good her escape.

The queen was also an accomplished healer, saved the king once more by neutralizing the poison and closing the wounds before she herself succumbed. Others did the same for her.

But the poison was virulent, and even many weeks later, the recovery of the royal couple remained a slow process, and required more healing at every step along the way.

The remaining leaders guided the people and their Urth Allies through the tense and terrible days of the invasion. The enemy had clearly hoped to slay at least the king, if not both the king and queen.

The royal mages now took further precautions to attempt to detect other such shapeshifters and invisible attackers.

Next, Tori, the princes, and the Thulls took a few days to fully support and secure the safety of the people of Toledo-Kellendra.

Then after careful planning, the defenders chose to go on the offensive one final time that fall, damn the weather.

Tori helped spearhead the sweeping advance. Her blazing guns cut through enemy strong points.

The Pistolera, backed by the strike force of Thulls, led by Champions Thulkara and Thul-Kazar, blasted through the surprised enemy front lines. The princes and their forces anchored the right flank. The Urth forces and their mages guarded the left flank, with reserves at the rear.

The dirigible gunships covered the attack from the air to ward off any aerovelocitors, and firebombed the foe on the ground in close support.

They enveloped entire sections of the enemy lines with such tactics and devoured them.

Together the Allies reclaimed almost one quarter of the city that had been lost in a matter of three days. That gave them room to break out of the city more, both west and north, and bust up thousands of zombies each day thereafter into little more than ice cubes.

The Dark Khabal forces retreated, and reset their lines behind positions that could be held much better during the winter. But they had lost valuable ground and mercenary forces they had thought secure.

Not only that, but the attacking forces also captured many siege weapons and ammunition, a few valuable enemy leaders, and much enemy intelligence that was left behind.

Another force of five heavily armed dirigibles from Detroit-Tornhold made a trip in all on their own, a week later.

When the enemy attempted to launch an aerovelocitor attack to bring them down, the enemy air mages were nearly shot out of the air by steam guns and steam cannons and other weapons mounted on the blimps.

Rumors abounded that the Khabal was rushing to develop its own airships, but thus far, none had been seen.

At last the situations among the Allied cities stabilized to the point that winter where Tori thought she could go home, home to wherever Mason was.

By that time she missed him so much that it hurt inside. She could not wait to be reunited, and requested permission from Generals Blackwood and Avery to rejoin the Pistolero wherever he was stationed.

Mason was back in Indy by then, helping oversee the increased work on the city's defenses, and continuing to help train the new Gunslinger.

She looked forward to meeting and working with the new Wild Magic shootist, but even that would have to take a back seat to a ten day leave approved for her and Mace.

Damn it, they had earned it. Tori could not wait, shivering and getting teary in anticipation. She could not wait to see his face, take it in her hands and feel his touch.

She packed her things and prepared to go to Indy.

Rodell met her and hugged her when she arrived. He helped her carry her things and escort her to where Mace was waiting.

Young Steven and his hot Jattaran girlfriend Ishi paled and looked confused as they came down the stairs in the hotel the other way.

"What's wrong?" Rodell asked.

Steven stammered, "W...we just took Tori up to Mace."

Ishi grew suspicious. "How did you change your clothes and get down here again so fast?"

Tori felt her blood go cold.

"Oh, no! Out of my way. Raise the alarm!" She dropped her gear and drew her pistols, racing up the stairs, taking them two at a time. Their friends followed close behind, calling for the guards.

She raced down the hall until she saw the door with the "Welcome Tori!" sign on it.

She assumed the door was locked and blasted her way within.

The first thing she saw was a room service cart tipped over, with spilled food and a broken champagne bottle spread across the wet carpeting.

Sounds of a struggle further in caught her ears.

She charged in, only to see Mace struggling with a woman in a slinky red dress.

The shapeshifter looked exactly just like her, in both face and form. But she held a strange, twisted dagger that she was trying to stab the Pistolero with. And she seemed stronger or at the very least more determined than the average person to punch holes into him.

Mason struggled hard to fend her off and not be wounded by that knife.

Just before Tori fired, the struggle yanked Mason's larger form in front, blocking out the shapeshifter. Tori couldn't get a clean shot.

She drew her pistol back just in time.

The assassin was clearly an expert fighter. She kicked Mace in the face and head twice, very fast. Then she blasted him with magic, knocking him across the room to smash into Tori.

Both of them fell backwards, and Mace was out cold, his dead weight nearly crushing Tori and pinning her partially to the ground.

Tori had no idea whether he was dead or alive at the point.

The killer sprang at them with her dagger clutched in both hands to stab down with great force. Tori saw no sign of blood on it.

She snapped off a hurried shot that should have winged the attacker.

But even as her shot hurled it back, warped energies around the shapeshifter deflected most of the damage away. The creature was shielded and relatively unharmed, even as it slammed into the wall and window, shattering the glass.

Those crucial seconds gave Tori a chance to pull herself free and blaze away at the assassin with both barrels.

The creature moved incredibly fast and managed to stay just ahead of the Pistolera's blasts as shots blew out the outer wall of the hotel.

The wind whipped in, there was a bright flash and blinding smoke, and the attacker escaped through the window, despite how high up they were.

Tori looked out the gaping hole, scanning the area and tracking with her guns, but she saw nothing but guards and troops still pouring into the hotel from down below.

The Khabal assassin had escaped yet again.

The Pistolera holstered her guns and went to check on Mace. She didn't find any stab marks, puncture wounds, or cuts. He appeared to have been knocked out by the heavy kicks and the magic blasting him into the wall.

Tori recalled that the Queen of Kellendra had been sickened for weeks, just from a few minor cuts. The king had been stabbed three times, and he was still bedridden.

She checked Mace again to be sure.

They had the dagger this time. The killer dropped it when Tori blasted her.

Tori carefully picked the dagger up by the handle and wrapped it up in a clear plastic bag from the closet that the hotel kept handy. Now they could analyze the poison and perhaps find a proper antidote, or let the healers discover a way to fully neutralize it with healing magic.

Guards poured in with Steven, Ishi, and Rodell the next instant, giving her plenty of help getting Mace up onto the bed.

Once they were certain he was all right, they moved him to an adjacent room that did not have a big drafty hole in the wall. Troops brought up plywood and supplies to block off the breach and brick it up quickly.

A doctor and a healer came up to the room. The Pistolero had been stunned by magic. He should wake up in an hour or less, and perhaps be a bit sore.

Guards and more guards were posted nearly everywhere after that.

Rodell offered to make the reports. Tori thanked him and all of the others.

Then she kicked them all out without hesitation.

Assassin or no assassin, she was going to be there when Mace came to. And she was going to take care of him and see to his needs, dammit. All of them.

# MASON

The last thing Mason remembered was Tori kicking him in the head and then zapping him with a spell somehow.

When he woke up and saw Tori's pretty face across from him with her eyes closed, he started, and fell off the side of the bed onto the floor.

Tori's big brown eyes snapped open. One of her hands under her pillow clutched a pistol.

He gasped.

"Mace, it's all right. It's me. The real me."

He shook his head. It still felt dizzy and somehow fuzzy inside. "The real you?" he muttered.

"The enemy has a shapeshifter, honey. It made itself look just like me in order to get close to you and try to kill you. I came in just in time. It stunned you and I chased it off. It escaped out the window; it can use magic. I wish I could have killed the damn thing."

"Where'd we go on our first real date?"

She frowned. "Oh, so you're testing me, now? After we've been sleeping side by side? A little late, don't you think? I could have offed you at any time, bucko!"

"You still haven't answered my question."

She huffed. "Fiddler's Hearth. I had the steak salad. You had the fish and chips. It's me, you idiot!"

He nearly sprang at her and locked his arms around her. He didn't want to let her go.

For a long time, they merely held each other and calmed down.

They stayed together on their bed, still in their travel clothes, gear, and boots. As if they were waiting for another attack.

Mason told her all about what he had been doing since they parted.

When he was finished, she told her story to him.

Then Mason took her shining face in his hands and kissed her.

After that, it was getting dark outside. For a long while there wasn't much reason to say anything more. At least not with words.

Mason and Tori had two whole days together before another urgent summons came from the army, demanding their presence.

They suited up and went running to the transport station. A military aide briefed them along the way.

"We've received word from Captain David Pritchard via the transport mage, Trent Fillmore. Some kind of terrible battle is taking place in the north, near upper Michigan and Canada. There are mountains up there now, and the Dark Khabal has opened up a gateway to one of the Nine Hells. Monsters, demons, and something far more horrible has emerged out of the gateway thus far to assist our foes. Pritchard says that this new Hellthing is over sixty feet high and nothing can bring it down.

"Several armies are being dispatched up that way immediately, in order to take the Khabal out, destroy this new monstrosity, and close the hellish portal before even worse things emerge from it."

Mason grinned and shook his head, turning to Tori. "Looks like we've got our marching orders. Let's go save Dave's butt."

"I'm locked an loaded," Tori said. "Did they transfer our loaders to sleds, and get snowshoes for our runners?"

Mason nodded. "I oversaw all of that a few days ago."

From what they observed near the gateway, at least one army in winter gear stood ready to march through and join the fight.

The Pistoleros strode through the station, walking their horses.

They emerged on the lee side of a windswept winter vale, out of sight from where the ground shook and the battle was already taking place on the other side of a mountain.

Both of them got out their binoculars and struggled to reach the crest and assess the situation on the other side and below.

They did not need field glasses. The battle was right there for anyone to see.

The Hellthing was a large, flat black, relatively stick-like monstrosity that defied all reason. It's overly long arms and massive feet and hands were like claws and talons, and it somewhat moved, bent over like an ape. Yet there all comparison ended. The insane thing had a black, lidless eyeball for a head, glowing with unlight. Lesser man-sized freaks just like the big one charged and loped out of the yawning maw of the Hellgate, laying waste to all before them with the dark energy beams from their eyes.

Whether the giant Hellthing sensed them or not, it suddenly turned its baleful eye in their general direction.

Without warning, a black beam of hellish might speared out from the eye, and bored through the earth itself. The same beam exited the other side of the rocky ridge and up into the sky, leaving a red glowing tunnel behind through hundreds of feet of solid rock.

A green dragon swooped down from the darkness, roaring at top speed.

"Shavalkathar!" Tori cheered. More cheers came from down below, somewhere in the trees. There was a rider on his back, wearing armor.

"That must be Dave!" Mason shouted.

The dragon circled in close and engulfed the Hellthing in blazing green dragon flames from head to foot.

The thing covered up and protected its head with its oversized forearms. The dragon flames seemed to do little damage to the giant, but the heat incinerated dozens of the lesser demonspawn on the ground.

Shavalkathar whipped it in the back with his spiked tail, nearly sending the gargantua flying.

The Hellthing lowered its arms in response, twisted its head, and fired another darkfire blast into the sky, just missing the dragon and rider as they banked away behind the cover of the ridge.

Mason and Tori turned as the green dragon came in for a landing and buried them in a wave of snow. They had to dig their way out, spluttering.

Dave was off the dragon and quickly removed the saddle as they emerged. Troops were marching out of the transport station by that time and taking up positions nearby, staying out of the dragon's way. Trent Fillmore suddenly popped in to join them all.

David grabbed him by both arms and nearly shook the kid's teeth loose. "Was that Jerriel with the Urth entity and the white dragon?"

Trent tried to pull away. "Yes, she's all right, for now. She told me to tell you to coordinate all attacks with her group once they hit the Balor monster with everything they have. Aim for the head, its only weak spot. The body is almost invulnerable in this state. I'm going to open up another gateway further back in the forest for more of our armies to pour through and maneuver."

David clapped him on the back. "Excellent. Get going, Trent. Good work, lad!"

"Wait," the youth said. "There's more, I nearly forgot." He glanced up at the green dragon. "She wants the green dragon to blast the Balor with as much flame as he can, once the white dragon covers it in ice. She was very insistent on that point."

Shavalkathar himself laughed. "Ice and fire to help take down a Balor. Very clever. I understand. It shall be done." He shot up into the sky, just barely dodging a massive blast that would have surely brought him down.

Tori suddenly ran after Trent. "Take me with you, Trent!"

"What are you doing?" Mason said.

"I can hit the thing from that distance with an annihilator round. Let's see how the bastard eats that! You guys all duck down when you see it arcing in. Then, if it's still up, we'll catch it in a crossfire when everyone else lights it up."

"Good plan. Be careful. Trent, if things go bad, take Tori and get the hell out of Dodge. You got me?"

Trent saluted. "I will, sir. You can count on me." They both vanished into the dense trees a second later.

A few minutes later, a white star rocketed up into the sky from the far off trees and descended toward the creature.

The Hellthing somehow sensed the devastation that hurtled its way and turned its back, crouching down and curling up into a protective ball.

"Down!" Mason shouted. "This is going to be a close one. Everyone get down and take cover!"

The blast turned day into night.

When the blast waves passed, another nearly equal explosion rocked the region.

After several earth-shuddering moments, the dust and smoke cleared, and two glowing craters now pocked the earth. Many of the advancing enemy monsters had been obliterated.

At least the Hellgate was destroyed, completely taken out.

But the humongous Balor demon rose up out of the devastation, its body glowing from within like coals and cinders. Then it seemed to go mad. It charged forward, smashing through the tall trees of the mountain forest at the tree line, setting them ablaze in its passing.

Without warning its swiveled its eye and nailed the area around the transport gate, even as troops were trying to rush through. Hundreds nearby perished. Mason and David only had time to dive into a snow-filed crevice and cover their heads

The transport station detonated like a bomb, causing even further casualties.

Not enough troops had made it through.

David and Mason crawled out of their cover. "All troops, anyone left alive, draw your weapons and follow us!" They raced down into the trees.

Down in the vale the rampaging Balor was nearly unstoppable, charging straight toward its targets.

Spells shot out and struck its feet and legs.

They did not even slow it down.

Mason and Dave led a few hundred troops down the vale. He was almost clear of the trees enough to start shooting.

Then a tremendous ice blast erupted, almost completely encasing the head and upper torso of the Hellthing in a solid block of thick, crystalline magickal ice, wedged in among the thick trees.

Yet the ice already began to melt and crack under the intense heat within.

Shavalkathar hovered over the monster, dousing it with wave after wave of immolating dragonfire.

Glowing cracks began to appear all over the main eye's surface from deep within the ice.

A dark blast still shot out from the eye, piercing the magickal ice and finally slamming into the green dragon. The strike hurled him back, spiraling down to crash among the trees.

Exploding devastator rounds and other blasts from the Pistoleros peppered the damaged head like machine gun fire as the shootists fanned their pistols up at the horror, emptying gun after gun into the eye.

The Balor broke free, dropped to its hands and knees, shielding itself with its thick hands and arms. It struggled to rise again.

Khia raced forward, glowing green with Urth Power.

She took a blast from the Balor full on, and was hurled back. She rose up and charged at it once more until she became of blur of green Urth Force.

With little thought to herself, Khia streaked forward like a missile and pierced the Hellthing's great eye dead center with a spear of green energy, just as Shavalkathar landed.

Like Mason, he saw exactly what was about to happen and flung himself and his wings over Jerriel, and Vajja who was spent, in order to protect them.

The detonation of the Balor demon took out hundreds of feet forest in all directions.

Shavalkathar cried out, and rolled in the ashes, as Hellfire scorched his body, and threatened to burn through the membranes of his great wings. His left forearm was shattered.

Jerriel cast water and ice spells upon him to quench the Hellfire. Then she bade him go roll in the great troughs of snow up in the mountains, until all the burning in his flesh ceased.

"Wait," Vajja called out to him. She sealed his broken arm in ice to hold it in place.

Shavalkathar turned to her and bowed his head. "My thanks. Rest now, princess. The evil thing is no more. All of us will heal. We could not have taken the Balor down without that ice strike of yours."

"Stay," Vajja told him. "Stay at my side, for all the danger has not passed as yet. I can heal your burns with with my enchanted ice breath. Stand still and lift your wings."

She breathed soothing ice crystals over all of Shavalkathar's wounds, and he lifted his mighty head and wings, sighing in great relief from the Hellfire's agony, which seemed to keep burning.

Mason pointed at the dragons. "Dave, is something funny going on with those two big lizards?"

David chuckled. "I think we're witnessing some alternate version of dragon courtship, Mace. They picked one hell of time, but let them go at it. I think we'll have more to do in just a bit."

"I don't doubt that," Mason said, checking his guns.

"Khia? Khia!" Jerriel cried out for the entity in despair, but no answer came back.

All wondered if the Spectral Entity had also been destroyed by the clash of opposing forces and energies. Speculation abounded.

Could Khia reform or regenerate after such destruction, or was she gone forever?

"Brave Khia! There's no time to mourn for my brave sister, now." Jerriel added. "Our foes still have two great hosts, coming straight at us from the other sides of this mountain. They will overwhelm us!"

"Then we shall fight them until they are dust." Shavalkathar said.

Vajja shook her head. "Alas, they are many, my champion. And they want to take us alive, and put enchanted collars around our necks to make us their slaves and their weapons. I am still too weak and injured, I cannot fly or escape. You must help the survivors get away. We have destroyed the Hellgate. We took out the Balor. We have done far more than we ever thought we could. Please, leave me now."

"That I will never do," Shavalkathar told her. "You have my word, princess. I shall not abandon you. I will fight for you, and none shall harm you while we yet last. And if we are to die, then we shall die just as we have always lived–free as dragonkind are meant to be!"

David checked his snowshoes as he strapped them on. "I'm going back to see Trent," he said. "If we can get enough of our armies through his gateway in time, and maybe another transport station or two, we can make this a proper fight by morning! We just have to hold them off."

Tori came up from that exact direction in great haste with the survivors from that direction.

Trent Fillmore was wounded and on a stretcher between two troops, unconscious and clearly unable to do much of anything.

"They attacked us by surprise and in large numbers," Tori said. "The gateway went down when Trent was wounded. We barely broke off, but I think they were driving us this way."

"They were," David said. Jerriel finally drew close enough to fly into his embrace and wrap her arms around him.

Things were about to turn interesting.

They still had less than seven hundred able troops against two entire enemy armies, two firedrakes, Dark Mages, and who knew what else. And no transport gates to escape through or bring in more of their forces.

Mason saw it all. This was it.

"Dig trenches, everyone. Tori, loaders," Mason commanded, "get all of our guns set and ready. Things are going to get hot here."

# DAVID

There was little time to prepare only three arcs of entrenched defenses up the side of the wooded vale. That still left them vulnerable in more ways than David could count.

There wasn't any time to do anything else.

Hell, if the enemy was smart, they'd simply have the firedrakes set the woods ablaze and roast them to death in the updrafts or at the very least smoke them out.

Shavalkathar took Princess Vajja onto his back, and half-flew, half carried her to the top of the crest of the foothill, up behind the trenches. That way they could survey the battle from up there and provide what help they could.

The dragons could also conserve their energies, hurl stones and trees at the attackers when they came, and use their precious breath weapons sparingly.

Shavalkathar remained strong and hale. If the battle permitted, he could swoop over the enemy repeatedly and attack their massed formations at will.

But would there be time?

The green dragon knew about the drugged ballista darts, and would do his best to avoid them.

David shook his head, his heart pounding. He kissed Jerriel again.

Who were they kidding?

They weren't going to last half an hour against a force of this size.

The big firedrakes marched forward, melting the snow and ice around them with their very presence.

Then they parted to either side and a wedge of Dark Mages came up behind thirteen Necromancers with their blazing skull staffs, both red and black.

Enemy monsters on the left. Khabal forces in the center. And mercenaries and siege weapons on the right.

They could hear the entire second enemy army flanking them upon the extreme right and circling around wide to cut off their rear.

The chief necromancer called out to them in the darkness, for dawn was still an hour or two away at least. "Let us call a truce, and speak of terms for your immediate surrender, Urthers. I assure your safety while the truce lasts. Come, let your leaders step forward. We are not uncivilized."

David led the way, with Jerriel on his right, Mason on her right, and Tori on his left. The four of them walked about half the distance and stopped.

At least they could perhaps buy some time by negotiating and stalling, if nothing else. The enemy was exceptional at gloating and acting superior.

One of the other necromancers came forward, with two Dark Mages and several mercenaries with loaded crossbows at their sides.

"I am Captain David Pritchard—"

The necromancer waved his hand to cut him off. "Names are meaningless, Urthers. Give yourselves up, fools. That is your only chance. Take it. You can still live out this war. We shall conquer these worlds shortly. But you and these others need not die this hour. As you Urthers say, you shall become prisoners of war."

No reason not to at least attempt a bluff. "We have several armies converging on this area while we speak," David said. "They will arrive in a matter of minutes, and then all of you will be surrounded."

The necromancer chuckled. "You Urthers. Such poor liars. You seem to know nothing of the art. Come. We shall not waste time. No help is coming for you. I must have your answer."

David grinned. "And if we do not capitulate?"

The necromancer shrugged, grinning eagerly at Jerriel and Tori. "Then we kill you, and spend the rest of the night and part of the morning gang raping your women, be they alive or dead. When we grow tired that, we will slash open their throats and bellies, and add their heads to the pile with yours to set the proper example."

Mason caught the necromancer's eyes. "Why, that doesn't sound very neighborly at all."

"Don't try anything, fool. Truce or no, one false move and those firedrakes will coat you all with fire, and I will gladly piss on your melting faces as you thrash on the ground and scream. Now come with me, and surrender yourselves and your weapons. Your hands shall be bound. Notify your paltry numbers to come in, a score at a time to be searched and disarmed. They too shall be bound. Any who resist shall be slain on the spot."

Dave let out a breath. Like hell.

Suddenly, Mason lifted his hands in the air. "Well, damn me all to hell. I guess we'd better do like the man says. They've got us. Dave, tell the troops to start coming down." Dave caught Mace's wink.

"I thought this was a truce," David persisted. "Your leader guaranteed our safety while the truce lasted."

The necromancer grinned. "Dull-headed Urther. We never promised we'd let you return to your forces." He snapped his fingers. "And lo, now the truce is over, just like that."

"In that case," Mason said. He drew so fast and fired so quickly up close that the blasts hollowed out the necromancer as he jerked with his mouth hanging open.

Mace spat in the open body cavity for good measure. "Eat shit with a spoon, you dead, dumb bastard!"

Tori gunned down several of the guards the next instant, as they backed away fast.

Jerriel shielded them under a dome of magic energy as they continued to fall back toward their thin lines.

The firedrakes vomited gluts of flame at them.

The small knot of defenders kept fighting, as the attackers hit them from all sides.

Mason and Tori launched as many annihilator round as they could, but after that they were kept busy up close, fending off the onrushing hordes to either side.

Time seemed to flash by as the heat of battle roared around them.

They held the enemy off for fifteen long minutes, then twenty.

But at last the enemy dislodged them and drove them up toward the flat top of a mountain foothill where the two dragons were.

The small band was minutes, perhaps seconds away from being dragged down and wiped out.

Suddenly a mighty gale swept down from the north, bringing with it sudden waves of snow and stinging cold that blinded both friend and foe. The enemy were hurled back by an avalanche.

Just as instantly, the winds stopped, and a million eerie screams ripped across the sky and the mountains, causing more heavy avalanches all throughout the extended range.

The very bedrock of the Urth seemed to shudder at those terrifying cries.

In the darkness, what seemed like millions of pairs of red glowing eyes repeatedly appeared in the frosty gloom and faded away in waves. The enemy fired every weapon and spell at them in order to hold those hateful eyes back, but they would simply vanish and then show up even closer to one side or the other, with the passing of each second.

Closer and closer the unseen horror advanced.

The ground continued to shake as if millions of gigantic feet stomped the entire area, almost causing another earthquake.

Jerriel shouted to all of their friends and allies. "Hold your fire. Do not attack, whatever you see or hear. Our deliverance is coming. If only Khia could be here to see it!"

David still wondered. Had Khia truly been destroyed, taking out the Balor?

The head necromancer cried out, his voice amplified by magic. "Spirits of the north. Let us call a truce. We have what we came for. There is no reason for further conflict. We are already returning to the south!"

Jerriel gasped, her gauntlets suddenly flared bright green.

Khia actually appeared once again, about thirty feet tall, directly across from the enemy leader.

"Servants of the Great Shadow. These worlds and these lands shall never be yours. Our Great Mothers yet live, they are strong, and the eternal flame of the Great Mystery still sings with love in their hearts. There can be only one answer, as it was in the Dream Times. The disease of your poison must be destroyed, and you shall know oblivion!"

She sheared the collars off the firedrakes and the mastodons with whirling slashes of green Urth Power.

The creatures broke free and rampaged through the enemy to get away.

A gigantic Hoonga female, twelve feet tall, her fur all white, appeared next to Khia. She shrieked the terrifying war cry of the mighty Hoonga, and time itself seemed to stand still.

It was the most bone-chilling cry David had ever heard, even more frightening than all the others leading up to it. Countless Hoonga voiced that cry in answer, appeared, and closed in on the enemy with their mighty thews, and their tearing hands and stomping feet.

Jerriel spoke in awe. "Behold, we witness a thing that has not happened since the Age of Legends back on Tharanor!"

Each Hoonga was ten to twelve feet tall and incredibly broad and covered with thick hair, ranging from dark to light. They moved with unbelievable speed and power that crushed and shattered any foe, and they could also vanish and reappear at will.

After voicing their war cry, the Hoonga killed swiftly and silently. All that could be heard were the screams and shrieks of the enemy as they attempted to run, and were torn apart, or mashed into the earth by the trampling feet of the invincible Hoonga.

Two entire enemy reinforced armies. Thirty-thousand troops and additional monsters.

All completely wiped out in less than half and hour.

David and his friends watched it all take place before their eyes.

Still they could not believe it. The snowy mountain ran red with blood, and none could look upon the site without trembling and fear.

Thereafter, that peak would be known as Red Mountain.

It was the most crushing defeat David had ever witnessed by any army of any kind.

At the foot of the mountain, Khia had the Hoonga gather the bodies of the necromancers and Dark Mages—a few of them still somewhat alive—and impaled them on cold iron spikes she drew up from the mountain rock.

Then she made an example of them by immolating them with Urth Fire, green flames fed by the nexus that she said would keep burning for many years to come as a sign and a warning.

Let the Dark Mages beware the power of the north.

Everyone finally moved away from that grim place, but Mason stayed behind a bit longer.

David called back. "You coming, Mace?"

"I'll be along directly, Dave. Gotta milk a rattler." The Pistolero stared at the burning necromancers and grinned.

When they all returned to camp up above, a smaller Hoonga, smaller in being only seven feet tall or more, appeared out of nowhere and hugged Jerriel, scooping her off the ground.

David wrinkled his nose. Hoonga did not smell very good up close. They stunk worse than bears, and that was pretty bad.

Khia appeared, and soon the three of them were embracing like old friends. Neither of them seemed to mind the smell.

Jerriel introduced her Hoonga friend. "David, Mason. This is our dear friend, young Luin. She summoned her people here to save us. They have a deep and abiding history and hatred with the Darkspawn."

"Do tell," Mason said, walking back in. "I never would have guessed that."

"You can all thank her now. We can all thank her and her people for saving us all."

After the proper gratitude was shown, David spoke to Jerriel in earnest. "Please, please tell me these creatures are going to be our allies."

Mason joined in, his face pale and drained of blood. "By the Powers, they are the most terrifying force that I have seen on either of the two worlds!"

Jerriel laughed. "They are indeed our friends, and our allies to be sure. But you must understand…"

Khia stepped in to explain. "Good to see you again, David Pritchard. Know that the Hoonga are guardian Urth spirits, bound to their lands. Here they reign supreme and they are indeed a terrible force to be reckoned with. Yet their domain has never extended to the south where the gan and other peoples rule. I do not know if their powers would fail them at some point or not if they left their lands. I do not know if they could be convinced to do so in any case."

"Well," David said, "We're still grateful for the major rescue they pulled off tonight. We owe them our lives and more."

David sat down, putting his head in both hands. Jerriel crouched down with and snuggled up to him in the crunchy snow. He was done in from everything they had faced that night. "I need a stiff drink."

Mason and Tori took their flasks from their lips and handed them at him. They both enjoyed good Irish whiskey.

All of the survivors were still pretty much locked in stunned, horrified amazement and shock. They had all faced death, and a frightening supernatural force had rescued them at the last second. It was a lot to deal with.

# JERRIEL

The long, cold bloody night was over at last. The dawn finally came, no less cold, but at least all of the fighting was over.

The main body of the Hoonga were already unclad and heading home, their work done. Their great leader, Luin, and several of her family came to their new allies, nearly hugged the human leaders to death, and then said their farewells.

Khia told the Hoonga that she would be among them again shortly.

The mighty Hoonga vanished, continuing on their way home to a well-deserved long rest.

Fresh snow fell, covering the great red stain upon the Urth that had once been the Khabal's forces.

Jerriel remarked repeatedly that she thought it very advantageous to have a Spectral Entity of Urth allied with them.

Not just an ally, but to Jerriel, a sister.

Khia had indeed come in very handy, an only continued to do so.

She fashioned caves in the mountainside nearby for the survivors to camp and stay warm within. It looked as if they might be there for a few days, until Trent Fillmore felt better and he could open a gateway between him and his sister Katelyn.

David informed the military, through the twins, that the Dark Khabal forces had been fully defeated, their evil plots utterly and completely ruined in an astonishing outcome.

Khia even created a larger lair and cave network on the backside of the mountains for the dragons. She also helped Jerriel and the healers with the wounded.

Then she focused all of her abilities to finally finish healing Princess Vajja. That took many hours, almost an entire day. Then she healed Shavalkathar's broken arm.

Yet there were things that even a Spectral Entity could not heal.

Over the days that passed, Shavalkathar took over bringing the princess the choicest prey for her to feast upon and gain her strength back. He sliced her food up for her with his razor sharp claws, and toasted the bits she liked best, roasted to perfection with his flames.

When Jerriel and David checked in on the dragon pair from time to time, they saw Vajja warming up to her new partner and protector each day.

Soon the two dragons could be seen entwining their necks against each other, and crooning a strange sound not unlike that of doves, but amplified by dragon windpipes. That was scary.

David laughed. "I guess Shavalkathar didn't need my help much after all."

"Oh yes he did," Jerriel insisted. "Without your efforts and guidance, he wouldn't have found us."

"It was a mutual thing, at best," David said.

"Look how happy they are. Dragons cannot be all bad, can they? Not if they can love each other so."

"It is not their capacity for love that is the concern. It is their appetites and who and what they choose to dine upon that causes most of the problems."

"Yet they are sentient beings, David. We can try to reason with them. These two are our friends now. And we still have those dragon eggs back home to hatch at some point."

"Don't remind me," David told her. "Even Shavalkathar agrees with me. They and their children will probably be better off up here in the north. There's plenty of game, and the Khabal won't dare come up here now."

"That's for sure," Jerriel said. "Will we ever see our dragon friends again, David?"

"Sure we will. After their courtship, and Vajja can fly unhindered by her injuries, I asked them to come south to Detroit and make a non-aggression pact between them and our allies. And to include all dragons they meet who would be willing to do the same."

"They're going to warn all dragonkind about the Khabal control collars, right?"

David nodded. "Of course. They said they would, and that dragonkind would be very angry with the Khabal. Vajja's word carries great weight as that of a dragon queen."

Now it was Jerriel who laughed. "Shavalkathar never imagined he would become a dragon queen's consort, I would guess. They could still give birth to other royal dragons by chance."

"But not celestial dragons like Glauriel and Talorian?"

"That's correct, David. Only a pair of royal dragons have a chance of producing offspring that are Celestial, who can live in the Celestial Planes."

She suddenly took David by the hand. "All right, we've done our duty. Now come with me, Captain."

He chuckled. "Where are we going to go, around here, in the middle of nowhere?"

"We still have a day or two before Trent is well enough to gate us out with Katelyn. Until then we're stuck, so why do we not make the most of it?"

"I'm all in agreement with you, my delightful little minx. But how? Do you have an igloo or a private snow cave somewhere that I don't know about?"

"Better. I asked Khia to make a couple of private caves for you and I, and Tori and Mace. She even created fresh food and drink for us, and for all of the troops. Much better than dry rations, right?"

He looked around them. "So, let's go. Where are Mace and Tori?

She smiled. "Those two didn't waste any time, as soon as I told them. As a matter of fact, why should we?"

"Lead on, sweetie. I am in solid agreement."

"Jerriel, what's going to happen between you and Khia once we leave?"

"She wants to stay with the Hoonga. I say that is a perfect idea." Jerriel pulled away for a moment and held up her gauntlets, the Spectral Keys. "But don't worry about us. We're sisters now; we'll stay in touch."

# SHAEDDOR

Another big tremor from the nearby fault lines shook Shaeddor awake. He had struggled greatly to drag both himself and the Celestial being away from the deadly, deep cracks in the earth. They were still tangled together, and for him at least, it was very uncomfortable.

He recalled how a blast of superheated air had flung them hundreds of feet away, only to slip into this smaller crack. The Spectral Entity had protected him and slowly healed him while he was unconscious.

The Celestial messenger had to regenerate on her own. He referred to her as female because her outward form was at least shaped like a humanoid female. Spirit lore said that the Celestials were practically made entirely out of energy, whatever their outer veil or form was. Some did not have a physical sex. But other legends said that certain Celestials had favored the daughters of mortal men and women, and even mated and bred with them on many of the mortal worlds.

Therefore, there had to be some among the Celestials who were male and female in the same sense as mortals—if it was possible for them to mate and breed offspring. Celestials were powerful spirit beings and relatively immortal, not bound to any world the way nature spirits were. Yet as proved in the ancient wars between the Darkness and the Light, they could still be destroyed and thus slain.

And they certainly had mass and weight. This one was heavy, nearly pinning him down, despite her slender shape. Celestials seemed more dense than mere human flesh. He struggled to disentangle himself and get out from under her. He finally had to augment his strength from his Spectral Entity to be able to do so.

Once he extracted himself, he drew her out with levitation magic.

A first look at her face made Shaeddor gasp. This was a being born of the light.

She was undeniably, extremely beautiful, stretched out on her back, all four of her big wings extended. The wings were much bigger and longer than one thought, and he struggled not to trod upon them. She wore some kind of ancient style, one piece sleeveless tunic of fine silk or linen that went down to her knees, and belted at the waist with a golden belt. She had high pale boots of the softest material possible, that came to just below her knees.

She wore a golden band across her forehead, concealed by hair so blazing white, plus it had a faint pink, rosy hue to it. Her slightly parted lips were glimmering, coral pink. She did have teeth, a small nose, and matching sculpted ears. Her neck was very slender, like the rest of her.

The Celestial's veil of flesh was so white, she could have been fashioned from the purest snows themselves.

She was regenerating, right before Shaeddor's eyes. The scorched parts on her arms had originally been all the way up to her elbows. Now the blackened parts had receded down to her wrists.

He checked her for other injuries, and found several deep gashes and open wounds in her body—hurts that would have proven mortal to normal humans. She even had a small, deep wound on the back of her head.

All of these injuries did not bleed. Celestials did not seem to have blood inside their flesh. She had some kind of semi-liquid energy or matter, or a combination of the two that slowly filled back in and regenerated such wounds and sealed them off without any sign of a scar.

Shaeddor attempted to use the entity to apply healing energies to the deep head wound. It worked. As soon as the wound closed, the celestial being flickered her eyes open.

He gasped once again. They were bright, glittering pink eyes flecked with gold. He had never seen such eyes before. They were quite breathtaking, not unlike liquid jewels.

It was said that each of the celestials was unique and beautiful beyond all hope. This was the first such being he had observed up close, but thus far, all of the legends seemed to hold true.

In an instant she drew herself up to her feet, with the assistance of her wings, and suddenly glared at him in confusion.

"Why did you attack me, mortal? How dare you interfere with a Celestial Messenger! Do you realize what you have done?"

Shaeddor smiled, swept his broad-brimmed hat from his golden head, and bowed low. "I did not attack you, Celestial one. I was locked in mortal combat with a necromancer trying to slay me. You, in fact, slammed into the both of us, and became tangled up in our fight. I had no desire to interfere with you or your mission. I was too busy fighting to survive on my own, and the both of us just came to here, right now. Other than that, I have no idea what you are referring to."

She nearly sobbed, bowing her head and clenching her fists. "I'm stranded here. Don't you understand? All of the others fulfilled their missions and made it out. I was supposed to do the same. Now I'm trapped here!"

"Then continuing to yell at me and blame me will not solve anything. Perhaps I can find a way to help you. Here, on these broken worlds, I am a powerful sorcerer."

She stared at him and then burst out laughing, finally covering her face in her hands and crying. "I'm sure that you are considered mighty on your mortal worlds. And I have not asked why you were fighting that necromancer. But what do you know of us Celestials? I have no way back now to the dimensions of Celestial Light. Can you send me back?"

He had no answer for her yet. Any such attempt could be deadly. "I have at least heard of such things. Perhaps a way can be found. If you came here, why can you not return the same way? Why then did you come to this place?"

She held up her hands in apparent loss and frustration. "I came because I was sent, and I am still obedient. The Guardians cannot be everywhere at once, and mortal worlds are too fragile for them to bring their full powers to bear. They might destroy the very worlds they are trying to help against the Shadows. Thus they have taken to sending us lesser spirits and messengers, charged with just enough Celestial power to negate or counteract that of the Shadows. Then we return through the brief gateways formed in the heavens."

"What happens to those spirits who, like yourself, are left behind?" he inquired.

She collapsed to the ground and hung her head down. "Those who are not captured or destroyed outright can only linger, and hide, hoping not to be noticed, or to have a gateway to the light opened for them once more."

"You cannot create your own?"

"I would not be here still if I could! I told you. I know nothing of such things. Those are not my gifts. I did as I was told to do, and now I am stuck here, trapped in a world that is under siege by the Shadows. Soon they will sense my presence and hunt me down at every turn, just to torment and drain me of my Celestial energies."

"What was your purpose before, spirit?"

She laughed slightly, and then her voice became laden with sorrow and sadness as if it were a great enchantment. "Long ago, before the Great Fall of so many of my kind, I was mighty among the *Anfalar Ellathiel.*"

"I do not know what that means," he told her.

"Of course you do not, mortal." She shook her head. "I was a special spirit of inspiration. I was a spirit of Love and Peace, if you could believe such things possible.

Shaeddor most definitely could. "Yet, you did not fall, clearly."

"No, I remained faithful, even though I was still diminished in many ways. Even though my choice cost me dearly. For what need is there now in such ages as these for Love and Peace, when they know them so little?"

"Perhaps the need is greater than ever before on such worlds, more than you may know," Shaeddor said. With that he touched her hand with his, and the last vestige of the black scorching faded, and her hand shined from within with a brilliant radiance that spread throughout all of her form.

She gasped and drew her hand away, studying it for a moment, and then him.

"You have indeed known love and its great loss and sorrow. You cannot hide such from me. The life you have led has been dark and difficult. You have not always followed the correct path, but at least you have known the truth of love, and that has given you a strength and a force of will beyond all of your mortal limits."

He smiled. "You can tell all of that, from a mere touch of my hand?"

She transfixed him with her eyes.

He could not pull away this time.

"You speak to one who was once an *Anfalar Ellathiel.* I *was* Love! The soul of love, and even more. Then I lost all, and became one of the least of messengers, a pale remnant of my former self."

"What happened to you?" Shaeddor asked.

"Even among all the orders of my kind, there was a time when it was still not known if it was right for one of us to love another, and take a mate, as other beings do. I, a spirit of Love and Peace, lost myself, heart and soul to one who stood great among the Guardians, the most fair leftenant of the shining hosts of the Protectors, Naerel the Steadfast. Oh, mortal. If you could have seen him as he once was. How could I not have loved him? Yet time and fate were against us, alas."

She wept. She placed her shining face into her glowing hands, and she wept.

Shaeddor's own heart could not help but break for her.

"What happened?" he begged to know.

"We made a petition, even to the Most High, openly declaring our love and our wish to be together to the Great Mystery which is the Creator. But we meant no disrespect nor disobedience. We only asked of our Creator who loved us, and whom we adored with all of our hearts, to bestow upon us a way for us to be happy and content, and we promised that we would abide by that decision.

We offered to take any form, be it mortal, spirit, elf, or even among the beasts, so long as we could know life and love and peace together. All else we would gladly surrender—even our immortality.

"The Divine Spirit of the Flame Eternal spoke to us in response, saying that this was a great matter, with enormous ramifications for all of the Celestials and other beings in Creation. A verdict would be sent down in three days time. Thus we waited.

"As the third day waned, the Great Rebellion unfolded, and being impatient, Naerel made the mistake of hearkening to the words, as many did, of the chief rebel, Great Shining Lusinitar himself. Naerel took no part in any fighting, but he did stand with rebels, and he was counted among them, even as he went before the shining throne to demand an answer to his petition that he had made with myself.

"Thus he too was struck down in the Great Fall with the entire one third of the Guardians, who awakened the next instant, stunned and forever transformed in the depths of the Abyss. They found themselves cut off from the Realms of Light, and the love of the Creator most of all. Lusinitar was transformed into Shaihalatan, the chief of the Dark Ghods. And with great regret, Naerel became the Demonlord Zhoggorroth, and like many, forever lamented his foolish choice.

"And I too was stricken at the loss of my love. And the verdict came down to me in the last moments of the third day, even as the Fallen were being stunned, blasted, and swept away:

*Lyssiel of the Anfalar Ellathiel and Naerel of the Guardians, remain as you are or choose whatever form and path you wish, and it shall be done as you choose. The freedom of these choices are yours, but once chosen, they can never be changed and shall be fixed. If it still be possible after all things have unfolded, love one another and know peace as is your want, for as long as you shall exist.*

"Yet in that instant, my heart was broken, and I was forever stricken. A greater conflagration trumped our little affairs and brought us both to ruin. Because my Naerel was no more, forever estranged from me and broken, twisted, and reshaped beyond recognition into a thing of abject horror. We could never be together after that, and both of us mourned our deep losses.

That is how I lost myself and all my powers, until I became merely a shade of my former self. I faded into becoming the least of messengers, Lyssiel of the Shattered Heart.

"And now," she said, "I have lost even the little I had left and I am even forsaken by my kindred."

Shaeddor could not speak. Were the Celestial any more beautiful, no mortal heart could bear to look upon her, and yet live.

He rose up. "Lyssiel of the *Anfalar Ellathiel*. I am Shaeddor, known as the Black Prince of the House of Holleth. Rise up and take my hands. Allow me to link with your mind. Show me where it is that you reside in the Realms of Light, so that I might know them as you envision them."

She held his eye. "I will do so. What is it that you intend to do?"

Lyssiel put her hands in his, and he felt himself tremble. Who could endure such loveliness?

She shook her head. "I see now what a fearful path you have chosen, Shaeddor. You dare that which is beyond all mortals to accomplish. You must have loved her very much. Yet even if you succeed, there is little chance that you shall survive."

"Still I dare," he said, "with little thought to whatever happens to myself."

He joined with her mind and was nearly stunned. He saw the fabled Planes of Celestial Light, their radiance, and the greater lights beyond them.

"But for now, with every ounce of power I possess at my disposal, I am a Traveler. I am going to send you home."

It did take every mote of his power, his energy crystals, the Spectral Entity, even much of his own life force—but he opened the portal for Lyssiel to escape through.

It felt as if he were tearing his own rib cage open with his bare hands.

She stared in wonder. "You are but a mortal. How can this be?"

"Quickly," he said, still straining. "Get you hence, fair Lyssiel. Yet do me this boon: go to the Guardians. Tell them what took place here, and let them know of me. I am the secret foe of the Dark Ghods. I will find a way to come to the Guardians and stand before their might. I will have words with them, concerning the Dark Khabal's plots on these two worlds of the Merge, and even of plots against them directly."

She took both of his hands, kissed them, and placed a spirit crystal in his palm. "We are now friends, sorcerer. Hold this lightstone and call upon my name, and I will hear thee. I shall bear your message to the Guardians of Light. What good it will do I cannot say. Yet I shall do as you ask. Thank you, my friend."

He released her, she passed within, and the portal vanished.

315

Shaeddor lay spent upon the barren ground once more, waiting for the Spectral Entity to heal him yet again. Sending the Celestial back had taken everything he had. In truth, the act of doing so had come close to slaying him outright.

He still was not strong enough, and had to continue to find ways to make himself even more powerful.

He inserted another energy crystal into his upper left arm.

Then Shaeddor allowed the entity to finish healing him.

When he awoke again, Jennifer's shade lay beside him, semi-transparent, looking into his eyes. Always so close, and yet never touching. How he missed her each time she left him; he nearly wept again.

Her ghost smiled, and spoke to him through their link.

*I have done as I promised I would. After much searching through the first three of the Nine Hells, and many trials, I have found them. I have found the lost souls of your parents, where they are being held, and tormented in bondage. When you have regained your full strength, I can take you there.*

He smiled at her, aching to be able to touch her, yet that was impossible. "You have done well, my love, and at great risk to yourself. Very well indeed, thank you. Curse the day the enemy took you from me. Yet I will see the souls of my Father and Mother set free from eternal torment. Neither of them deserved such."

He laughed aloud and then muttered. "And if the ways to Heaven are barred against us, then at least let me take myself into the Nine Hells when the time is right, to see what can be done."

# TORI

The two happily mated dragons came to Tornhold-Detroit in late January, and they brought Khia and even Luin and her father Murn with them. If the Hoonga and a Spectral Entity weren't amazing enough, the young dragon queen and her doting green consort were a complete surprise and utter shock to the system of even the Thulls.

As the winter held, food issues were still a great concern for all of the Allied cities.

Khia made short work of that, at least for a time. She commanded the Urth itself. She created food at will and in great variety, plenty, and abundance. For a short while, there was enough and to spare. Enough to send on to the other cities to help end the rationing that winter.

Squadrons of the latest airships, armed to the teeth, made it to Anzhalar-Grand Rapids and back regularly now, on top of the established transport stations on both sides of the Merge. A similar force made it to Cleveland-Dorundia, but there was a major problem on both sides. There the Urthers fought not only with the Khabal, but also with the Old World Dorundians from Darshia as well.

On one side the Urthers were in command, on the other side, the Tharanorians, primarily led by the Darshians, Rodell's people.

Many stated that such a conflict was bound to happen somewhere. Mason and Rodell both agonized over the situation, but the other Tharanorians promised that they would help begin a process, and negotiate a full truce in the spring, and bring both sides into the Alliance fold.

After much discussion and urging, Thul-Kazar and Thulkara helped convince the Thulls into declaring a formal truce and non-aggression pact with Queen Vajjanthokrix, her consort Shavalkathar, and any dragonkind who wished to join in the agreement and live in peace together. Allowances were made for dragons to hunt within reason in the region, as long as they did not attack humans, or seriously deplete food sources in any given area.

When livestock reached certain levels, they could even be herded into accepted hunting areas for the dragons.

To celebrate the new members of the Alliance, Khia made it possible to hold so great a midwinter feast in early February, that even the Thulls were completely bloated, and sang songs of such a pig out session thereafter.

Amazing to all, Luin's father Murn was twelve feet tall, somewhat stoic, and yet jovial at the same time. He liked to eat deer and elk raw, but Hoonga were not used to being around so many gan.

The Thulls were like astonished children before the mighty Hoonga, and rejoiced at the tale of them wiping out the Dark Khabal's army in the north, within mere minutes.

The silly Thulls wished to test their strength against the Hoonga Urth spirits, but quickly learned that they had met their match.

The Hoonga were strong and powerful beyond belief. Even Thul-Kazar was no match for Murn, who did not even exert himself, not wishing to harm his new friends. Both Murn and Luin were incredibly gentle with all natural living things, and demanded that others be the same way as well.

It was not wise at all to mistreat or abuse an animal near a Hoonga. While out for a stroll in the city one night with Tori, Mason, David, Jerriel, and Khia, a drunken Urther man was heard beating a small dog nearby, and the creature yelped.

Murn and Luin flashed in on the drunk so fast, towering over him with their eyes blazing red. The poor bastard screamed, shit himself, and then fainted.

Luin brought the poor little, mistreated dog back with her and insisted that it be healed and given to a better home.

Khia later explained to the Thulls and others that the Hoonga were the mighty spirit guardians of the natural world. The strength of the Urth itself was their might. They could not be considered purely flesh and blood.

When the dragons departed back to the north, they took Khia and the Hoonga with them. The dragons promised to return in the summer, after a sufficient time of dragon mating.

Vajja said that she could help the humans with their many ice houses. Her magickal crystal ice, properly insulated, was more resistant to heat and could last for years.

Yet once Khia and the dragons were gone, the defenders shared a flurry of information and intelligence back and forth, and began to prepare for the coming spring. The wars they would face together would be greater than ever. The Dark Khabal fully meant to conquer both worlds, and continued to marshall their forces in order to do so.

Jerriel shared the reports, papers, and maps that she had stolen from the enemy camp when she rescued Luin, but many of these were now months old. Still, they revealed the enemy mind, and the names of some of the players.

One thing was clear to Tori and everyone else. The enemy was going to do everything it could think of to take them down. They needed to be ready, and they only had a handful of weeks in which to prepare.

This year, everywhere in the New World and the Old World, both sides would be up for grabs, and fully engulfed by the Khabal's wars of subjugation and enslavement.

That's what was coming their way.

A war blazing across two entire worlds.

# THE END

## Please Post A Book Review Right Now

Please post a review of this book if you enjoyed it. Twenty little words are all that is required. Twenty words that say what you liked about this book while it is still fresh in your heart, mind, and soul. Please do so now before something else makes you forget.

Here is the link for *Mergeworld, Book Three* if you purchased it on Amazon:

http://amzn.to/1OOFNXo

Please click on the link and post your review now.
Done? The authors would personally like to thank you very much.

In this busy world, everyone is pressed for time. Our time is so important, no doubt.

In the publish or perish work of competitive fiction, book reviews from readers are golden.

Many in the business even consider book reviews as important, or even more important than book sales in some ways. As crazy as that sounds.

So therefore, trust us in this. If you have authors whom you adore, and you want to read more of their books in the future, please post as many reviews for them as you can in all of the forms of social media that you use.

Doing so will help your favorite authors in numerous ways that you cannot even possibly imagine. Never forget that fact. Book reviews matter a great deal.

Amazon Kindle Review Link for *Mergeworld, Book Three*:

http://amzn.to/1OOFNXo

Barnes & Noble Review Link


Smashwords Review Link


Please post one or more reviews for Mason & Garan and each of their books, everywhere that you can.

Cheers and many thanks,

Mason Elliott & Garan R. R. Faraday

# SF Author Mason Elliott's Contact Information

Please Join Mason Elliott's New Releases Email List

Use either of these. If one is broken, try the other:

Mailchimp Readers List. Sign up Bitly link:
http://bit.ly/1L2QpUL

Reader's List Back Up Link:
http://eepurl.com/FgQzv

Be among the first to learn about my writing projects and new releases. I promise that I will not share your info or spam you. I will use the list only to inform you about matters directly connected to my writing projects, and any free stuff.

About the Author

Mason Elliott grew up loving Science Fiction and Fantasy in all of their myriad forms. That love has transferred into his dedicated writing. Like most writers, he lives a spartan lifestyle and yearns to devote his life even more to his writing, and someday retire on the Pacific Coast. So be a fan, buy his stuff, and enjoy!

Like, friend, and follow Mason on Facebook, where he does most of his blogging at:

https://www.facebook.com/masonelliott731

or use the shorter link:

http://on.fb.me/1mQkv0B

Mason's full link for friending him on FB:

https://www.facebook.com/?ref=tn_tnmn#!/mason.e.elliott.9

Mason's shorter link for friending him on FB:

http://on.fb.me/1E466TV

And on Twitter at
*http://bit.ly/1nsqOSs*

Visit Mason Elliott's website at
www.masonelliott.authorcontacts.com

And for even more information on Mason Elliott and his works, visit
High Mark Publishing online at

www.HighMarkPublishing.com

# Fantasy Author Garan R. R. Faraday's Contact Information

<u>Please Join Garan's Publishing Update e-List</u>

Garan's Reader's List:

http://eepurl.com/YHOS5

I promise you that I will only send you emails connected to my writing projects and new releases. I do not spam. Watch for occasional FREE stuff!

<u>About the Author</u>

Garan Reginald Remington Faraday was fortunate to be the child of loving parents who adored all things Fantasy, and passed that love onto their son. It has been said by some that with such a name, he was born to become a Fantasy writer. Garan, or "Reg" to his closest friends, has written Fantasy stories since the Seventh grade, and completed his first Fantasy novel at the age of sixteen. If you enjoy anything Fantasy, you most likely have something in common with Garan. His lifelong dream has always been to publish as many Fantasy novels and stories as he possibly can.

Garan's Facebook fan page link:
https://www.facebook.com/pages/Fantasy-Author-Garan-R-R-Faraday
Garan's FB friends page link:
https://www.facebook.com/GaranRRFaraday
Garan's Twitter link:

https://twitter.com/GaranRRFaraday

Garan's website and blog link:

http://garanfaraday.authorcontacts.com/

And for even more information on Garan R. R. Faraday and his works, visit High Mark Publishing online at:

www.HighMarkPublishing.com

## Mason's Acknowledgements

I love this series and these characters, and I can't say enough about collaborating on this amazing Fantasy series with my best friend Reg. Thanks to High Mark Publishing and the crew there, for making this series possible. Thanks to my beta readers, and to all of our fans. There's more where this came from. Just wait!

# Garan's Acknowledgements

This book is just another dream come true. My co-author M is my best of friends, and this series has put me on a path to publish more and more. I may not be the fastest writer, but I love Fantasy. I can't wait to get more books out and one day quit my day job. I was born to be a Fantasy writer. Soon I hope to do all this full time. Thanks to High Mark Publishing and all of my family and friends who have supported me and my writing efforts.

# NAERO'S RUN

*http://amzn.to/1eRKCOb*

*Book 1 in the Spacer Clans Adventure Series, Cycle 1*

# NAERO'S WAR: THE ANNEXATION WAR

*http://amzn.to/1gmxGQk*

Book 1 in the Citation Series, Cycle 1

# NAERO'S
# GAMBIT

*http://amzn.to/1lx5Tyy*

*Book 2 in the Spacer Clans Adventure Series, Cycle 1*

# NAERO'S
# WAR:

# THE
# HIGH
# CRUSADE

http://amzn.to/1DbFD5F

Book 2 in the Citation Series, Cycle 1

# NAERO'S
# FURY

Amazon Link to Naero's Fury: http://amzn.to/1hLrPpO

*Book 3 in the Spacer Clans Adventure Series, Cycle 1*

## NAERO'S
## WAR:

# NAERO'S
# TRIAL

http://amzn.to/1oaMNE3

Book 3 in the Citation Series, Cycle 1

# Mergeworld

## Book One

http://amzn.to/1uboBDC

## by Mason Elliott & Garan R. R. Faraday

# MERGEWORLD

## Book Two

http://amzn.to/1neuq0x

## by Mason Elliott and Garan R. R Faraday

### Book Two

Edition Notes
If you do not see this edition note here in this spot on the copyright
page and on the very last page of your ebook or print version of this title,
then you are not getting the final, polished version of this novel that the
publisher, editors, and author intended for you to receive. Please contact
either the publisher or the author via their emails if you do not see the
following update code:

High Mark Publishing Update Code C4832A

Become a fan of my books.
Please join my Readers List:

http://bit.ly/1L2QpUL

www.ingramcontent.com/pod-product-compliance
Lightning Source LLC
Chambersburg PA
CBHW020214260626
47156CB00002B/378

* 9 7 8 1 9 3 0 4 5 1 2 0 9 *